SKYCASTLE

ALSO BY STEVE KRANTZ:
Laurel Canyon

Steve Krantz

Macmillan Publishing Co., Inc. NEW YORK

Collier Macmillan Publishers LONDON

Macmillan Publishing Co., Inc.
866 Third Avenue, New York, N.Y. 10022
Collier Macmillan Canada, Inc.

Library of Congress Cataloging in Publication Data
Krantz, Steve, 1923-
    Skycastle.
    I. Title.
PS3561.R267S5   813'.54   81-19283
ISBN 0-02-566690-8   AACR2

10 9 8 7 6 5 4 3 2 1

Designed by Jack Meserole

Printed in the United States of America

For Judy, once more with feeling.

ACKNOWLEDGMENTS

Thanks to the people of Houston who assisted me in my research, and to many others in Texas who enlarged my passion for their remarkable state.

To those friends and others, please note that as this is a work of fiction, I have changed some geography, dates, and events in order to entertain.

SKYCASTLE

1

DEVLIN hurried into her father's study to answer the ringing telephone. She sat astride a corner of his ancient desk, tossed off her Stetson, rested her boots on the back of a wooden chair and picked up the instrument.

A thought occurred to her. It might be God on the line with an offer to lend her the five hundred million dollars she desperately needed. The earpiece was full of static. It was not the Almighty. He would never put up with that kind of service.

"Hello Houston, I have Rome on the line. Please hold for Rome. Is this Houston?"

"Hello Rome, this is Houston. I have your party."

"Pronto. Houston, I have a call for a Miss Devlin Younger."

Devlin was frustrated. It was ten in the morning and she had a million things to do. As she waited with the phone crooked between her shoulder and ear, she turned to the *Wall Street Journal*. Her green eyes grew cold. The front page article was about her. Any one of her hundreds of enemies could have given the newspaper the intimate details of the disaster she faced. If only it had been full of lies. Unfortunately, the *Journal* had the facts, all of them.

"Hello, Devlin," the voice on the phone crackled through. She recognized it as belonging to Gino Pratesi, a handsome Italian who called himself Count Pratesi. Gino had married and divorced three Houston heiresses, each time earning himself a generous settlement from their fathers. His charm, good looks, and spending habits made him a prospect for a fourth go-round.

"Gino, yes, it's me." Devlin's eyes scanned the story as she disinterestedly listened to the conversation.

"*Cara,* listen to me. I know that it's sudden notice, but I thought it would be fun to charter a yacht and sail around the Greek Islands. There would be three couples. You and me, and some charming English

1

people you will adore." There was a pause. "Is this a new telephone number for you Devlin, *cara*? Have you moved from your beautiful home in River Oaks?"

Devlin tossed her ginger-colored curls in a defiant shake as she shifted the telephone. "Gino, I know it won't make any difference to you. But my place in River Oaks has been taken over by an army of accountants. They have been making a list—an inventory of everything I own. They say it belongs to them."

"To them? Tell them to go away."

"Gino, don't you read the papers?"

"No, I do not have the time, Devlin. Besides, they bore me."

"Gino, I think that I can end this phone call quickly. In a nutshell, I am almost broke. My company Younger Oil owes more money than the government of Italy. I'm not even sure if I can pay for the gas in my car. I'm living at my father's house, and he's dying. Somebody else might cry at my story, Gino, but if it doesn't make you throw-up, I don't know you very well."

She waited.

"Devlin, my other phone is ringing. I will call you back."

The international line clicked off.

At twenty-eight, Devlin Younger was certainly the youngest and the most unusual oil wildcatter in Texas. In seven years, completely on her own, she had built a huge fortune, fighting and winning fierce battles against the Big Seven oil companies, and against other entrenched interests in the Texas business world. They thought her too young, too pretty, and too much a woman to challenge them in their own backyard, and get away with it.

Just yesterday, Devlin left her producing wells in West Texas and drove through the night. She ignored all the speed limits in order to get to Houston in the hope of warding off disaster. The telephone call from Gino came through just as Devlin arrived at her father's house. It was a faded mansion in Houston's Montrose section that retained the last vestige of elegance in a neighborhood that had once been Houston's most fashionable. Today, Montrose was dotted with gas stations, boutiques, sex shops, and souvenir vendors.

Now, dusty and parched, Devlin swept through the hall in her faded jeans and work shirt. Her boots made a staccato sound on the hardwood floor. Devlin's tall five foot ten frame, her tiny high-perched rear and her long legs in pipe stem jeans, made her look like an unsteady filly, full of youthful anticipation, instead of a young woman on the verge of financial disaster.

She swung into the large old-fashioned kitchen, greeted the Mexican maid, pulled open a closet door and grabbed a bottle of Coke. In a practiced movement, Devlin removed the cap on a nail that had performed that function for her whole lifetime.

2

Swigging the warm Coke, Devlin rummaged through a bread box for a doughnut. She grabbed it and walked out the kitchen and up the stairs to finish her strange breakfast, shower, dress, and get to her appointment.

At the top of the wide stairway was the room which had been hers from birth. It was full of momentos of childhood. Devlin tossed her shoulder bag on the bed, and began to undress. She would have to be at her best today for her appointment. Looking at her watch, she understood it would be close.

Undressed, Devlin stood tall and statuesque. Her lines resembled those of a showgirl in the Folies Bergère—long legs, narrow waist, a full bosom and a childlike face. She was the same young woman who had spent hours, days and weeks along with hard driving men in the oil fields, covered with mud and grime, finally hitting it big. But that was another day.

Stepping into the bathroom, she turned on the shower and luxuriated in the soothing warm spray and caressing lather.

Reluctantly she turned the water off, and reached for a towel. Emerging from the shower, she began to towel herself dry, when the telephone rang once more. Still dripping, Devlin ran into her bedroom to pick up the phone.

"Darling . . . you certainly are hard to reach. I didn't know you were staying with your father."

"Imogene, I really can't talk."

"Oh Devlin, perhaps I shouldn't burden you in the midst of your tiresome problems. I hope you get it all behind you, darling. You've been touched by too many bad things in your life, and you're such a wonderful, giving person. It seems such a shame . . ."

"Imogene, thanks for your concern. I've got to be going."

"Devlin, I hate to ask you for something like this at such a time, but I wonder if you could give me the Palm Springs telephone number of David Hampton?"

Devlin broke into laughter. "My David Hampton?" He was a world famous movie star, and part of Devlin's colorful past—a vain and selfish man whom Devlin had nearly married. The breakup had been violent, angry and headline making.

"Yes, Devlin. I haven't the right to ask this I know, but you see, I had this brunch planned in honor of Dustin Hoffman, and he had a car accident—at least that's what his manager said. Well, I phoned around, so I'd have a celebrity. People like them so. I tried Robert Redford, but he's in Utah. I tried John Travolta, but he's filming a movie in Europe or Africa or someplace. Of course Henry will send our Gulfstream for anyone we get. Now, I know that your relationship with David was a little, how would you say, stormy, but you wouldn't have to *come* to the brunch if you didn't want to. *I'd* understand."

3

Imogene's voice trailed off.

Slowly and with incredible self control, Devlin gently pushed down the disconnect. Imogene would be faced with dial tone. She *might* think that Devlin hung up on her, but more likely, she would have Henry telephone Southwestern Bell and give them a piece of his mind for the terrible telephone service poor Imogene had to put up with.

Now, high in the sky above Houston, helicopters are reporting traffic to hundreds of thousands of moving vehicles on the freeways below. Drivers, with their windows tightly closed to avoid the hot humidity, are cheerfully exchanging the outdoors for the arctic blasts of their car air conditioning, without which no native of Houston can exist during a typical day.

From above, Devlin's vintage red Eldorado convertible, with the top down, snakes in and out of traffic, with a sureness and ease that mystifies the pilots of the choppers overhead, and appears to infuriate the drivers of the cars below.

Devlin's hand hangs over the side of the car displaying a priceless four-inch-wide Bulgari bracelet on her wrist. It is a spectacular display of rubies, diamonds and sapphires. She wears custom-made suede pants and cowboy boots, both the color of palest mocha. Her silk shirt, turquoise in color, is three buttons open. The whipping wind slashes it open further to reveal her lovely rounded breasts.

Devlin drives as if she hadn't a care in the world.

Devlin is an oil wildcatter in the killer game that once had no room for a woman. Now she is in the biggest trouble of her life, the longest gamble of her short but meteoric career. She crosses lanes with a practiced skill. The Bulgari bracelet acts like a million-dollar turn indicator.

The Eldorado slows and exits down an offramp. Devlin guides it past Navigation Boulevard to the edge of the harbor. The Houston Ship Channel before her is alive with boat traffic. This second biggest port in North America is fifty miles from the sea. It was constructed out of Buffalo Bayou and the San Jacinto River—the bayou of the bison and the river of St. Hyacinth. They both are the main reasons for Houston's existence and for the city's site.

Devlin is heading toward the explosive conclusion of a story that has been splashed across the pages of newspapers in Texas for months.

As she approaches the channel, facing her is a huge paint-peeled sign that proclaims SKYCASTLE. Another huge sign trumpets the marvels to come—a 100-story business complex; five hotels; separate condominiums; shopping arcades. There is to be a gigantic sports arena, movie making studios, an outdoor rodeo, an indoor aquacade.

Skycastle is to be Houston size—the biggest in the world.

Nothing stirs.

Devlin stops the Eldorado, and gets out. She walks slowly in the direction of the cavernous hole that covers more than ten city blocks. A guard approaches and smiles. "Soon?" he asks hopefully.

Devlin returns the smile, "Don't give up, Ralph."

"Don't you either, Miss Younger."

Devlin's soft Texas voice is warm and melodic, surrounding words musically. It goes with her face and figure—remarkably female and incredibly seductive.

She walks along the gravel road and peers down into the huge abyss that Texas papers laughingly call "Houston's Grand Canyon." Devlin stares at the immense open space, hearing only the deadly quiet from within, ignoring the sounds of the waterfront. She drinks in her vision of Skycastle, the project she began just a year ago—the project which will be her ruin.

A wildcatter to the core, Devlin has bet all her chips on the outcome of this crazy gamble. Everything she has, her home, her business, the bracelet she wears and the car she drives, is mortgaged in her struggle to keep Skycastle.

Devlin stares in the distance at the gleaming spires of downtown Houston. Its extraordinary beauty and majesty prove once again that nothing is too good, nothing too miraculous for this magic city of the twenty-first century, a city of such energy and excitement that it seems as if each day were planned for a celebration.

Devlin wanders closer to the excavation, picks up a stone and tosses it into the depths. She hears a distant sound in the watery bottom. The ground she stands on and the harbor beyond are the work of one man, her father, L.C. Younger. The development of the Port of Houston from little more than a fantasy into this gateway between the riches of Texas and the world is an astonishing feat of a few determined men. L.C. was one of the most determined.

In these few thoughtful moments, Devlin reflects back to the time she was a child, living in the same house on Montrose that is her refuge today. Perched on her father's knee, L.C. smilingly repeated a refrain that he delighted in. "The first Devlin Younger, darlin', your granddaddy, was a murderer. Yep, that's right." Then he laughed. "Your daddy is a millionaire, and guess what you are?"

The adorable ginger-haired child snuggled close to this man who was her life and asked happily, playing the familiar game, "What am I?"

L.C. hugged her to him. "You're my princess, honey—my very own princess. That's what you were put on earth to be. And I was put on earth to be your daddy—someone for you to love and to be proud of."

Skycastle was to be a testament to her father. Here on the ground that had once been the headquarters for the Black Diamond Harbor

Company, from which he controlled the entire Port of Houston, it was to have been homage to L.C. Younger, now near death. He had finally been humbled by the men he had once ruled.

The *Wall Street Journal* printed the ghastly truth this morning. For the past week dozens of dark-suited, faceless men had quietly invaded every portion of her empire. Into the late night, they poured over pages and pages of ledgers to find and inventory every single piece of equipment, every barrel of oil, every lease and contract that contained an asset, which had been pledged against the monstrous loans Devlin had made to keep Skycastle afloat.

That was not all. Another plague of soft spoken and endlessly polite locusts had gone through every one of her personal possessions, hunted through her closets, demanded access to her safe, listed and valued her jewelry, cars, furniture, drapes, silver, paintings and even the contents of her wine cellar. Devlin bit her lip through the ordeal, staring resolutely ahead, while the employees of Younger Oil suffered the indignities of the endless questioning, tabulating and note taking. The servants at her mansion in River Oaks looked to her in desperation while they waited patiently, feeling her shame.

Devlin sets her jaw and turns away from the vision before her. She returns to her convertible, starts it and throws it into gear. She heads back to the freeway to travel downtown to her destination.

The last page of this last chapter will be written today. As the car picks up speed, Devlin rehearses for this final confrontation that could rescue her dream and her fortune.

The Eldorado is back on the freeway. It pulls out of the pack at eighty. Devlin's ginger curls are buffeted in the whipping wind that hits the open convertible. Now, the car is at 100, her green eyes fixed and determined.

Devlin Younger, like all the Youngers, has always travelled as fast as she had to, to get where she wanted to go.

IN October 1933, L.C. Younger walked into the Texas National Bank Building on Fanin. Black Diamond, the harbor and towing company which he had founded fourteen years earlier, had been a customer of Texas National from the very first.

Black Diamond's growth had been spectacular. It now consisted of one hundred and fifty barges, eighteen tugs, and wharf and stevedoring facilities employing over three hundred men. Nevertheless, business in the port had fallen off considerably because of the Great Depression.

Grain elevators, into which L.C. had placed a substantial amount of Black Diamond's money, were empty. The port of Houston had more than it needed. Even the flow of oil from the refineries alongside the ship channel had slowed. Worldwide, there was an overabundance of petroleum, and L.C. was in serious financial trouble.

The Texas National Bank in Houston had easily survived the bank holiday that took place after Roosevelt was elected. It had ridden through the boom of the '20s and the bust of 1929, and today in 1933, it stood strong, a testament to the wisdom and conservatism of its founder and president, John Jurdam.

Jurdam was Mr. Houston. His great wealth and influence extended to every corner of life in the city, and his advice and assistance were constantly sought by elected officials, even presidents. A great source of John Jurdam's influence, in addition to his owning the bank and huge stretches of real estate in downtown Houston, was his ownership of the *Houston Journal,* the most important daily in the city.

The bank building, occupying half a city block, was Houston's pride. It was an impressive fifteen-story structure, marble-fronted and heavily ornate. On the wall of the two-story ground floor was a twenty-foot standing portrait of John Jurdam, painted in 1915, the year the bank building was completed. The building's wrought-iron fixtures, open-

7

wire elevators, and original furniture were reminiscent of the early days of Houston. It was John Jurdam's creed to leave things just as they were. Walking into the Texas National was like walking into the past.

In the changing and dangerous world of banks going belly up, one a week across the country, it was nice to know that old John Jurdam still ran the bank the way it should be run. Depositors' money was as safe as John Jurdam, and that was as safe as Texas.

Seated in the waiting area of the bank, with its hardbacked wooden benches, L.C. stared at the customers walking to and from the tellers' cages. He noted that each of them knew every customer by name. From his austere perch, Texas National's patron saint John Jurdam looked down beneficently. The founder was placed by the artist against a version of the future Houston skyline. Towering skyscrapers were placed in the background along with futuristic aircraft and autogyros. Tear-drop shaped autos were pictured driving on elevated skyways in a dreamlike pink and blue cloudland. Even that early, it was a permissible fantasy to imagine Houston would grow to giant size.

L.C. leaned back comfortably in his carefully tailored cowboy clothes. It wasn't unusual to find ranchers wearing cowboy boots, narrow-legged pants, ranch-style jackets, and Stetsons, but Houston in 1933 still suffered from the belief that New York and Chicago were their models. Most of the businessmen in Houston wore Eastern suits, white shirts, and starched collars along with conservative vests and ties.

L.C. pulled a thin Cuban cigar from his pocket and lit it. He was in a pretty serious predicament now, and he needed a fair chunk of money, but that was what banks were for. A million dollars would tide him through this bad time.

L.C. smoked his first puff contentedly. He was in the middle of a tough time, but he had been through much worse. He had come a long way for an orphan boy, born the night of the big hurricane in Galveston that destroyed half the city. He always felt that it was a mark of his fate to have survived that fateful night in 1900. It was a mark of his luck, he was certain, to grow up next to the waterway that was the foundation of his fortune.

As a youngster growing up in Harrisburg, Texas, L.C. was fascinated watching the thin march of water traffic that meandered through the serpentine route from Galveston through Buffalo Bayou to Houston.

When he was only five, the blue-eyed, tow-headed boy spent hour after hour during the hot, steamy afternoons, wading through the shallow waters of the bayou, marveling at its wonders. The sky was filled with whooping cranes traveling to the gulf from their summer homes in Canada. Inland, wild hogs, known as Javelina, could be seen grazing the groves of live oaks, along with beaver, muskrat, and whitetailed deer.

River boats and old shallow draft paddle wheelers chugged manfully

8

where the bayou narrowed, through the leafy overhang covered by vines and near jungle growth.

It was a time when animal life abounded. Only men were scarce.

After heavy rains, silt poured into the bayou, and sawmill operators alongside it dumped their wastes into the stream, making the water route impassable without constant dredging. A rash of epidemics frightened away new settlers, and a visitor to Houston, just twenty miles to the north, labeled it "the greatest sink of dissipation and vice that modern times have known."

Even the modest amount of water traffic on the bayou was controlled by the Four Families of Galveston. Under the leadership of a hard-bitten man named John Dowie, the families ran the shipping, wharfing, repairing, and provisioning of everything that sailed in from the gulf. It was rumored that John Dowie controlled the price of the whores who frequented Galveston's Post Office Street.

Sometimes passengers on the river steamers amused themselves by shooting alligators that settled into the waters from the cypress knees and logs. Then, after a modest beginning in 1903, serious dredging began, with the dream still unrealized of making a navigable channel all the way to Houston.

On the seventh day of September in 1914, at precisely 11:15 in the morning, an all-clear whistle was blown. L.C. stood in the huge crowd at the foot of Main Street in Houston when President Woodrow Wilson in Washington pressed the button to signal the completion of the ship channel.

Over the next five years, the young man became a fixture on the Houston Ship Channel. Alongside its banks, storage tanks were being built to accept the flood of oil that was being piped from the Spindletop field near Beaumont in East Texas. There, the single richest strike of oil took place in 1901, the year after L.C. was born. The Port of Houston was the single most important depot for shipping the liquid gold which seemed to flow without limit from underneath Texas.

By the time he was nineteen, L.C. was a strapping six foot three, weighing 190 very hard-packed pounds. He was handsome, with bright blue eyes and straight blonde hair that tumbled down over his forehead. He seldom smiled, except when he beat you at something. Then, a quiet half grin was his mark of a done deal, and he could relax his eternal vigilance for an instant, and savor his win. One thing was certain, he knew every niche of the channel and everything about it.

Then, two years before his majority, he was aboard the lumber ship *Washington* on his way to Panama. The ship carried a cargo of Texas pine for delivery to the Canal Zone. L.C. had been able to hitch a ride with a grateful first mate, whom he had saved from a beating in a Galveston whorehouse. L.C. had a very special reason for going to Panama. In Galveston, he heard that several tugs that had been used in the building

9

of the canal were to be auctioned. This ride figured to get him there in time.

He had one thousand two hundred dollars pinned inside his pocket from poker winnings. He had won most of it in Galveston, and some of it aboard the *Washington*, most particularly from the first mate, who was both a willing gambler and an inevitable victim.

The small city of Colón, at the tip of the peninsula which fronts into Manzanillo and Limón bays, was the port city for Panama that allowed you to avoid entry into the canal system, through Gatun lock into the Gatun Lake. A town of fewer than seven thousand people, it had swollen to twenty thousand during the time of the building of the canal, which had been finished four years earlier.

Colón was a mass of pockets of refuse and garbage, sniffing dogs, occasional automobile traffic of ancient model As, and barely useful trucks. Naked children played in the muddy streets and on the wooden boardwalks.

L.C. searched out Rupert Loftus, the man in charge of the auction for the Penrose Towing Company. He confronted a fat, sweating, and foul smelling man who did his best to ignore him. "What time is the auction tomorrow?" he asked.

The man replied disdainfully. "You're too late. The auction was today. In any event, it was for business people. Those tugs are not toys, young man."

"I know all about those tugs, Mr. Loftus. The Galveston papers said that the auction was tomorrow. I came all the way to bid on them tugs."

"With what, young man?"

"Dammit, Mr. Loftus, with money. I got money, and the auction is supposed to be tomorrow."

Loftus removed his hat, pulled a colored kerchief from his pocket, and wiped his brow. It didn't help. Instantly, rivulets regained their place on his forehead, and he returned his hat. "I don't have time to talk to you."

With that, Loftus turned away. L.C. retreated to the road and cursed loudly. Standing in the center of the road, he nursed the cud in his jaw, and spat mightily against the side of a building. Then he retrieved his duffle and headed for a cantina he had passed earlier. Now it was open. He walked inside through the knotted strings that separated the interior from the street and sat down at one of the three tables. A small wizened man came over to him and perched his head on the side.

"Cerveza," L.C. ordered, and when the bottle was served, he swigged it back, once, and emptied it. He pointed to the bottle for a refill.

It was five in the afternoon, and he had drunk a dozen beers. He made his way to the back of the cantina, relieved himself against the wall in the yard, returned, picked up his duffle, and left.

The sun was setting, and some of the heat had dissipated. An idea suddenly formed in his mind. He knew the direction of the wharf. Throwing the duffle over his shoulder, he walked the quarter of a mile to the water's edge. It was quiet alongside the bay. In the distance, L.C. could make out a group of small boats tied up. A half mile further, among the fishing boats, he spied the three tugs that he had traveled two thousand miles to buy.

On inspection, he saw that one was a side-wheeler named *Colfax* that L.C. recognized as the kind used in logging on Puget Sound. It had a floating donkey engine that even from a distance appeared barely able to function. A single cabin served as its pilot house and lodging. The second and third were screw-driven tugs. Each had crew's quarters and coal-fired boilers. L.C. had seen many like them and frequently had been pilot on similar tugs. They were ancient but appeared seaworthy.

There was no one about as he stepped aboard the *Colfax*. He had always liked side-wheelers. How he desperately wanted to own this one and the other two. He sighed at his bad luck, then he sat down on the deck and pondered.

Moments later, he crossed the deck and uncovered the seacock on the *Colfax* and twisted it open. He heard the satisfying sound of inrushing water. He jumped onto the second and the third, found each of the seacocks, opened them, and listened for the water rushing in. Satisfied, he climbed onto the dock and walked on shore. The sun had almost set when L.C. lay down on the ground and fell asleep with his head resting against his duffle.

When he awoke the sun was up, and it was seven A.M. He was hungry, but he decided to still his hunger. He would remain where he was. He looked to the bay, and he saw the three tugs submerged in the water. The *Colfax* was in the worst shape; it barely had its pilot house above water. Yes, L.C. decided that what he had done was right. Now he would wait.

At ten in the morning, a white-suited Panamanian emerged from a taxi on the road above and gingerly walked down the sloping bank in L.C.'s direction. As he approached, he saw the three submerged tugs and looked at them in horror.

The Panamanian, a dark, middle-aged man with a carefully waxed mustache, slapped his face. "They are sunk!"

L.C. nodded. "Couldn't have been worth much. Probably not worthwhile to even raise them."

"Who are you, señor?"

"Oh, I'm from Galveston. Came down here to bid on the tugs, but damn lucky I didn't get them. Owner will probably have to spend good money to break 'em up. Not even worth it for the firewood."

The Panamanian stood speechless. At that moment, a car arrived on the road behind the taxi, and Loftus emerged. He was dressed in his stained white suit of yesterday. Even this early he was perspiring heavily as he negotiated the incline to where L.C. and the Panamanian were standing. Then he saw the tugs and nearly fainted.

The Panamanian breathed fire. "Señor Loftus, I promised you a bribe in exchange for these boats, but you must be taking me for a fool."

Still unbelieving, Loftus looked at the Panamanian.

L.C. nodded at the sight ahead of him. "You supposed to be bidding on them today, right?"

The Panamanian looked at the young man, no longer interested in the deception. "This man Loftus was cheating me. He promised me that I could buy the tugs if I gave him five hundred dollars for himself. He told everybody else that the auction already took place."

L.C. smiled. "That's what I figured when I saw the boats just sitting in the water, without anybody minding them. I figured that if some private person bought 'em, he wouldn't chance leaving 'em unguarded. Meaning no offense, señor, but if you owned them, you wouldn't leave three of your tugs unguarded, even as mangy and unseaworthy as those three."

L.C. smiled at Loftus. "Figured that out myself, Mr. Loftus, figured that for a big company like Penrose, it wouldn't make no difference, but if a private person paid good money, he wouldn't 'a left 'em be unwatched."

The Panamanian had already disappeared, clambering up the bank, leaving L.C. standing with the sweaty Loftus.

"Okay, Mister Loftus. I guess you can start the auction now." L.C. smiled a wide-faced grin, which marked the conclusion of a gamble he had just won handsomely.

By the end of the afternoon, with the help of fifteen young teen-age boys, led by an enthusiastic fourteen-year-old named Hector, L.C. had closed the seacocks on all three of the tugs and had pumped enough air into the *Colfax* to get its deck raised to the level of the water. L.C. went aboard to examine the engine and began to dismantle it, preparatory to drying and cleaning it for its trip back to the gulf. He proceeded to do the same with the rest of his miniature fleet.

L.C. figured that it would take him ten days or more to put things right with the tugs. All he needed now were two men to ride the second and third in line, to bail if necessary. He was prepared to captain the *Colfax* and tow the other two. If his luck held out, and there weren't too many serious pieces of weather on the way back, he might be able to be in Galveston in a month, and Houston, days later.

The three-tug caravan that left Colón two weeks later was the strangest sea armada ever seen leaving Panama. His passengers consisted of Hector, his mother and father, his grandmother, and two of Hector's brothers, the youngest of whom was only three weeks old and still feeding at his mother's breast.

L.C. figured that the trip to Galveston would take four weeks. It took

12

even longer, since not only did the tugs have to keep within sight of land the entire time, but he had to deal with the sickness of the three-week-old infant, who suddenly refused to drink his mother's milk. Then, there was the death of Hector's grandmother.

Hector's mother screamed passionately at L.C.'s suggestion that the woman be buried at sea. The armada headed for shore to allow for a burial service in the small town of La Ceiba in Honduras.

Other stops had to be made to replenish food, to repair the *Colfax*'s engine, and because of Hector's mother, who threatened to cut the last tug adrift unless she was allowed to go to church on Palm Sunday. L.C. marveled at how the woman was able to keep track of the days and her religious obligations. L.C. succumbed to her threats and put into Veracruz just in time for the holiday.

Hector had taken to the voyage. He was learning English from L.C. and managed to serve as a mediator between his mother and the *Capitano*. Hector managed to solve one of the problems on board by stealing a goat from shore to provide fresh milk for his baby brother. It was miraculous how the now-satisfied infant influenced the remainder of the voyage. The baby's mother was happy at last that she was able to feed her infant and as far as L.C. was concerned, after the arrival of the goat, the remainder of the trip was a vacation.

As L.C. remembered in years to come, the voyage north from Veracruz was one of the happiest times of his life. He had gone on a mission to set himself up in business, on the seemingly impossible prospect of securing three tugs. And he had come back with them. He had no money, only a strange cargo of passengers, with whom he now felt a curious bond. The world was ahead of him, but his first challenge had been met, and bested.

By his reckoning there was another week to go before they reached Galveston and then the real work would begin. He had to make the tugs shipshape so he could get towing work. He had to find someone to give him credit for the repairs that had to be made, find men to hire, and to secure towing jobs against the competition of the companies in Galveston. He was only nineteen, and he was certain that he could accomplish all of those things, and more.

L.C. stood at the helm of the *Colfax*, wishing that he had some chewing tobacco, but he had run out weeks before. He stuck an empty pipe in his mouth, bit down on the stem, and leaned over the wheel as he looked out on the limitless horizon of the gulf.

Things weren't going too damn bad, after all.

•

L.C.'s reverie vanished. He was once more waiting in the Texas National Bank, and his present troubles flooded back.

Now, at the bottom of the depression, competition from the Families

13

in Galveston was the thing that was really killing him. With a last contented puff of smoke, L.C. was comfortably prepared to see his patron, John Jurdam. First he would arrange to borrow the money he needed, and then he would finally deal with the Families and particularly with John Dowie. L.C.'s thinking was broken by a cold, cutting voice behind him.

"I'm Melvin Jurdam," a tall, heavy-set, young man of L.C.'s age said. "My father is in Washington, but I'm familiar with your file. Please follow me."

The dark-suited man led L.C. to a small desk among the twenty that held bank executives. Young Jurdam sat and motioned L.C. to a wooden chair. He put on a pair of rimless glasses, and opened a folder.

"Let me check on a few things."

L.C. nodded. He stubbed out his thin cigar and waited.

"You are the only shareholder of Black Diamond Towing, Black Diamond Harbor, and Black Diamond Grain Storage."

L.C. nodded. "Yes, and Black Diamond Stevedoring and Equipment."

"What are they?"

L.C. was visibly annoyed. "Your daddy knows all about that."

Jurdam stared, then said peevishly, "You'll have to tell me. My father is in Washington, and you are looking for a substantial loan. *I* need to know."

L.C. pulled another cigar out of his pocket. He lit it with the swipe of a wooden match on the side of the young man's desk. Young Jurdam was visibly annoyed.

"What do you want to know?"

"What is Black Diamond Stevedoring and Equipment?"

"Just like it says. We do the stevedoring for pretty much all the loading and unloading in the ship channel."

"Why do you need another company?"

"I don't get your drift."

"Why did you go to the trouble of organizing another company? You made yourself more vulnerable to certain taxes which are presently being discussed in Washington . . . but I suppose you have competent advice."

"What advice is that?"

"Do you have business advisers?"

"No." L.C. frowned.

Jurdam sat quietly. "You live on Montrose and Alabama?"

"Yes . . . that's what it says."

"Is that the new house on the corner, the white brick? I pass it every day."

"That's the one."

"How much did that cost you?"

14

"I don't rightly know. It don't make any difference. I can afford it. I need a fit home for my wife."

"I am given to understand that it cost almost two hundred and fifty thousand dollars . . . and that you imported marble from Italy, and stained glass windows from Germany, in addition to hand-carved mantles and very expensive chandeliers."

L.C. was confused. He threw one long leg over the other, bit the end of a fresh cigar, and leaned back precipitously in his chair. There was nothing behind him should the chair tip, but it gave L.C. something to do while he was deciding how much longer to sit and listen to this son-of-a-bitch.

"Listen, Jurdam . . . what damn business is it of yours what I have in my house? I'm here talking to you instead of your daddy because your daddy is in Washington. I'd walk right out of here like a shot if I didn't respect Big John. Stop your pestering questions, and show me where to sign, and put the money into my account."

Young Jurdam smiled. "I think you have the wrong idea about banks, at least the way this bank is being run, *now*. My father is about to take over one of the president's major cabinet posts, and it may come as an unpleasant surprise to you, but I happen to be the man in charge of this bank, and the one who can approve or disapprove your request for a loan."

L.C. glowered. Jurdam smiled in an oily and self-satisfied way.

"Shall I continue? Our records indicate that Black Diamond has almost eight hundred thousand dollars invested in grain elevators, which, I understand, have been lying empty for over a year."

L.C. spit out his words, "The Depression won't last forever."

"No, of course not, but you want the money today."

L.C. said nothing.

"You owe almost two million dollars on equipment which you purchased over the last five years, tugs, barges and the like, which you acquired, I believe, in anticipation of continuous boom times." Jurdam stared at L.C. and said unctuously, "You are not the first to learn that we always have to pay the piper."

"Let me ask you, Jurdam. Are you gonna give me the money, or am I wasting your time, and my own?"

"I don't know. I just have not yet made up my mind. Tell me, what use do you intend to make of this money? I need to put it in my report, and of course, monitor its disbursements to ensure that it goes to the places you tell me."

L.C. fell forward, slamming the chair on the marble floor. "Are you telling me that you're gonna insist on looking over my shoulder to see how I spend the money?"

"Of course. It's sound banking."

L.C. stood up. "Listen sonny, I don't want your damn money, but if I

15

had it, I would roll it up in a nice little ball, and shove it piece by piece down your mouth, and then I would make you swallow every damn dollar, and I would wait around until you shit every one of 'em, because I'm telling you, sonny, the only control of my money you're gonna have is out your ass."

With that, L.C. turned and walked across the marble floor, and out the bank, his cowboy heels clicking as he proudly made his exit.

For some time, L.C. had maintained a suite of rooms at the Rice Hotel on the corner of Texas and Main. As he walked the few blocks to the Rice, he returned the greetings of storekeepers he knew. L.C. was pleased to notice that they knew who he was, and knew his reputation. That was another thing. The house he built on Montrose was a hell of a good investment. It was the fanciest street, in one of the fanciest neighborhoods in town, and he had built the finest house in the section. He certainly wasn't going to admit to that no good bastard that he had no idea of what the house cost him. The banker said a quarter of a million. Maybe, and maybe not, but it was worth every penny, and hell, he had *made* the money, and what else was money good for?

As he turned into the lobby, the desk clerk nodded politely, as did the bell captain. L.C. paused to talk to him.

"Send up some bourbon, Henry."

"Yes sir . . . right away. Pretty soon, it's gonna be legal. All they need is two more states to repeal Prohibition."

"That's not gonna do anything for Texas. We'll make up our own damn minds. Send up some ice, too."

L.C. turned and walked into the elevator. The operator let him off at the accustomed floor. He turned and walked down the carpeted hallway to the end, took a key from his pocket and opened the door. From the other side of the lock, he heard the familiar voice of a woman.

"That you L.C.?"

"Yeah . . . who did you think it was?"

Mingled with the sound of a running shower were the sounds of a soap opera. Without a pause, he went to the console radio in the living room and switched it off.

From the bathroom he heard, "Oh Christ, L.C., now I'll never know what Helen Trent is going to do."

"The hell with Helen Trent. I'll tell you what you're going to do—you're gonna get your ass out of that shower, and dry it, and put it on top of that bed, and you're gonna be ready to receive your man, 'cause all the way over here, I've been thinking about only one thing that I'm gonna do with you, and for that we don't need no radio."

There was a knock on the door. L.C. opened it for the bell captain, and as he put the bottle on the table with the ice, he received a five-dollar bill and saluted.

"Bourbon?" she asked from the shower.

"Yeah . . . haven't the vaguest idea where it all goes."

16

"I douche with it, L.C."

"Don't talk like that."

"Like what?"

"You heard me. I don't like that kind of rough talk from a lady."

At that moment, a resplendent blonde, in a towel that barely covered her, entered the living room. Her full figure overlapped the covering. She smiled at the sight of L.C.

"They keep calling from New York."

"Tell them you're busy," he replied gruffly.

"L.C., my agent says that he can get me a part in a new movie."

"Tell him no."

"But L.C., how long can this go on?"

"As long as I want to, honey. Do you have any complaints?"

"Christ, no, L.C., if all there was to living was fucking, then I'd be in seventh heaven."

"Don't say those words. You know I don't like to hear them from a woman."

She pouted prettily. "You don't care what you do to me, time after time . . . that's what they call it. You like it well enough to use the word when you're doing it to me."

"That's different."

"Okay, okay . . . but can I tell my agent I'll go to Hollywood at the end of the week?"

"Look, Cherry, I'll tell you when. Just pour us a drink, and let's move on into the bedroom. I want to stop thinking about it, and talking about it, and just do it."

"Yeah," she said drily, "I forgot, you're from Texas."

L.C.'s control over women was even greater than his control over men. It had nothing to do with understanding the little things about them, the appreciation of their wants or needs, only the rawest kind of sexual energy that never ceased to bewilder and surprise even the most experienced of them. His capacity for lovemaking was remarkable. As it was today, L.C. made love four times in less than an hour, and he still wasn't satisfied. As he sipped his bourbon, he looked at his watch and finally roused himself from bed. Nude, with his penis enlarged from lovemaking, he looked awesome as he padded into the living room and sat himself in a corner of the couch. He picked up the telephone extension and gave the operator instructions. Cherry, languid and surfeited, came out of the bedroom and sat alongside him. The feel of her body next to his began to excite him once again.

"My God, don't you ever stop?" she gasped.

He shook his head no, as he picked up the ringing telephone. Cherry giggled as she bent her head to encircle his penis with her mouth. Undisturbed, L.C. began to talk.

"Mr. Jurdam? Yep, it's L.C. calling from Houston. You're probably busy in Washington with the president, like your little boy said this morning, but I've got to tell you that I sure pulled a turkey this morning when I talked to him. Now, I tell you this for sure, John, he may be a chip off your block, but he's got a different kind of wood between his ears than you got in yours."

L.C. laughed and listened. Cherry's head was contentedly bobbing around his huge erection.

"Okay, but that's not the deal," he continued. "I need a million dollars to tide me over. Things have got a little rough, and some of the things I counted on didn't happen the way they should. Some of the people in Galveston—John Dowie and his tribe—have been playing a little rough on us boys in Houston. I got some plans of my own to deal with them, but I figure if I do things the right way, and if you give me the million, in about two or three weeks things should be looking real good."

L.C. listened. Cherry stopped for a moment, tilted her head, and smiled at him. Annoyed, L.C. forced her head down once again to continue its assigned work.

"Sure, I said weeks, not months. Now, I'll need the money longer than that, but you'll be able to see the Galveston Families ease off a bit and give us folks in Houston a square shot at the business before too long."

L.C. listened to Jurdam's reply.

"Okay, then you'll call him and tell him it's okay. John, look, do me a favor and keep him out of my sight. I can talk easy to you, John, but I'm liable to squash him sooner than say hello."

L.C. smiled as he replaced the phone. Cherry lifted her head inquisitively.

"Don't stop now, honey. It'll be just a little while more. One more phone call." He picked up the phone again and gave the operator a number to call. "Cherry, why don't you just forget that business of you being a movie star?"

L.C. was connected with Black Diamond and listened as one of his employees said, "L.C., we've got a problem. John Dowie's boys just ripped into the hold of the *Texas Queen* and poured tar all over the tools and machinery. Cost us a bundle, and we'll lose the account for sure. Gonna make some of our other shippers a little nervous, too. One of their men said that he thought we was getting too big for ourselves."

"Look—I'm busy now, but you get about a dozen of the boys together, and we'll settle this John Dowie thing for good."

"What are you meaning to do, L.C.?"

"I'm gonna eliminate that son-of-a-bitch."

L.C. hung up and guided Cherry's head into a satisfying rhythm. "That's nice darling," he said, contentedly. "You're doin' real nice. I'm just gonna lean back and enjoy your fine work."

18

3

ONE WEEK later, on a Saturday night, the *Colfax II* sailed quietly down the Houston Ship Channel, and just as quietly pulled into the darkness of John Dowie's Galveston pier. There was no activity along the entire waterfront. A half dozen freighters were tied up alongside, but the unloading had stopped. Except for a few work lights, the port was dark and deathly quiet.

On shore, the huge sheds that held thousands of bales of cotton, tools, hardware, and hundreds of thousands of dollars of merchandise were unguarded, and unmarked save for a few solitary lights, which identified the entrances. The huge galvanized metal sheds lay silent and inviting.

Aboard the *Colfax II* were L.C., his chief lieutenant, Royce Richards, and twelve handpicked men. The men were Houston toughs whom Royce had recruited for the night's action. They consisted of ex-convicts, drifters, and vagrants, each of whom would receive $100 for his efforts. L.C. had used them before when there had been threats of union organizing. They had done their jobs well, dealt with the troublemakers, and, most importantly, had kept their mouths shut.

At twenty-eight, Royce Richards was five years younger than L.C. He had worked at Black Diamond since his discharge from the Army. Royce had been a hero in the war, having survived a gas attack in the Argonne and having been awarded a Bronze Star for heroism. He was L.C.'s perfect second in command. Devotion and total loyalty were precisely what L.C. demanded and exactly what Royce gave him.

In the darkness, the deck hands on the *Colfax II* tied up to the pilings. The men stood ready.

"Royce . . . are you set?"

"L.C., I'm gonna try just one more time to convince you to forget your part of it. It just isn't necessary. The rest of it should do the trick."

L.C. turned quickly to face him. In the light from the wheelhouse, L.C. was seen to have a pistol in his belt. "Royce, I'm not asking for your advice. I'm telling you what we're gonna do, and if you don't like it, you can get yourself another job of work. Maybe you'd like to get associated with your friends here in Galveston? Maybe John Dowie? He'd like you fine."

"L.C.," Royce said angrily, "I don't have no objections to destroying his sheds, and doing what we have to do to get in and out. That's in the game, but torching a man's home is another thing."

L.C. shook his head violently. "Royce, there's nobody home. That's the reason I picked tonight. We lost a couple of our good men. I was the one to explain it to their wives—remember? I'm in this for keeps."

"Three men."

"Yeah, well, two or three, don't make any difference. We lost cargoes, one tug was set fire to, and a lot of business lost. I made a promise to old John Jurdam that the situation with the Families would be straightened away before long. I'll bet he's home waiting for word from me that I kept my promise."

Royce shook his head in disbelief.

"Jurdam doesn't want you killing anyone to keep a promise."

L.C. slapped his pistol. "He don't maybe want it—but it may come to him like a bonus, like 'interest' on a loan. Shit, Royce, you're a damn hero of the damn war, and now you're chickening out on me. What was it like over there, with them Germans shooting at you, and throwing poison gas at you? Was that any more a test of you than this here tonight? Royce, I'm talking about holding my head high—and you too. Are we in charge of our own lives? Are we gonna have to kiss ass every time we see that son-of-a-bitch Dowie, and pay him ransom for breathin'?"

"But if someone in the house dies . . . ?"

"Shit, Royce . . . dyin' is the price you pay for living. Some bastard can put a stop to that anytime he wants to."

Royce shook his head in wonder.

"People will know that I won't stop at nothing if I'm stirred up. Won't stop at nothin' to see that justice is done." L.C. smiled. "Now, are you with me, are you against me?" L.C. didn't wait for an answer. Royce turned away and motioned to his group of men. L.C. laughed to himself, pointed to the three he had selected to join him, and began to mount the ladder alongside the pier.

L.C. was at home again. He was fighting for what he wanted. He was prepared to live or die on the turn of a card. He didn't give a damn. He was going to give it his best, and nobody was gonna make him eat dirt. What he hadn't been able to figure out for himself was what had taken him so long. John Dowie and the Families *had* made him suffer for years. They had had their way in the gulf. Black Diamond and all the other companies in the Houston Channel had taken the leavings. As the men climbed up the ladder to the pier behind him, L.C. figured out what had been different. It had been that son-of-a-bitch Melvin Jurdam who had made the difference. L.C. had gone over Melvin's head and appealed to his father. Then he found himself saying to John Jurdam over the phone that he, L.C., was going to settle things once and for all, in favor of Houston. He was bragging in front of the old man. Shit, that's what did it, he realized. Bragging. Well, it *was* about time.

He motioned to the men to follow him. Each of them carried two 5-gallon tins of gasoline. They headed for a small pickup truck parked at the end of the road. L.C. had arranged for it. It had cost him two hundred to have it left at the end of the pier, with the keys inside. Whose truck it was, L.C. didn't know and didn't care. It would get to John Dowie's house and back, and then he would push it into the bay. That's whose pickup it would be—the damn city of Galveston's.

The four men walked purposefully toward the end of the pier. The pickup was there. L.C. reached inside and found the keys on the floor where they had been promised. He motioned to the men behind him, and they climbed into the rear. The splashing of the liquid in the tins and the hollow metal sound on the floor was comforting. All his men had pistols. L.C. hoped they wouldn't have to use them. What he was about to do would put things out of control for a little while, and then he had to put the lid on, fast.

L.C. started the pickup and threw it into gear. The truck lurched off, and as it moved into each gear, it picked up speed and joined the roadway in the direction of the handsome Victorian homes that made up the Families' holy enclave.

A huge, white confection of a hotel, the Galvez, on 21st and Beach Boulevard, had long been the favored location for big parties and balls in the city of Galveston. That Saturday night, Lucinda Shearman was being honored by her mother and father Lloyd and Natalie, at Lucinda's marriage to Donovan Bedloe, the son of David and Clarissa Bedloe. Since the couple were both children of the four Families, the event was more important than usual. If anything, it bound the Families to each other still more closely. A prince and princess of friendly nations were sealing the alliance.

In the Crystal Room of the Galvez, Morty Gunther and his Society Orchestra were playing the bride's favorite song, "Did You Ever See a Dream Walking?". A crowd of two hundred guests, the finest and most important people in Galveston, even including some of the bride's family from as far away as Tulsa and Kansas City, crowded the room on this very warm night.

Lucinda, dark-haired, spirited, and happier than she had ever been, danced with her father.

"Daddy, this wedding was the most wonderful thing that ever happened to me. You made me the happiest girl in Texas."

"I'm glad darlin'. Your mother and I want nothing more than your happiness. You have made *us* very proud. I don't have to tell you that a lot of girls don't think that they have a responsibility to behave properly any more, and we're glad, your mother and I, that you aren't one of them."

The music continued. Now the orchestra segued into "Easter Parade," another of Lucinda's favorites.

"I'm glad I didn't go away to college, daddy. I think that getting married was a better idea. I'm . . . I mean, we," Lucinda blushed, "are going to have a dozen kids, and the first one will be named after you, daddy . . . Lloyd Shearman Bedloe. Would you like that, daddy?"

Lucinda's father swept his sixteen-year-old daughter up in his arms and whirled her around to the music of the Irving Berlin tune. All the world could be going to hell, and Roosevelt might be taking the country down with him, but he had the best little girl in Texas, and the white satin gown she wore had been the same gown that his own wife Natalie wore the night of *her* wedding, and if tradition remained, then maybe it would fit his daughter's daughter. The youthful vision in satin and lace, her dark hair flying, whirled round and round as Lloyd got into the spirit of the fox-trot. The dance floor cleared to allow the bride and her father to dance in the center of an admiring crowd.

Agatha and John Dowie sat at a table by themselves. He was hot and uncomfortable. His wife was sick, from the food and her uncertain digestion of her fourth month of pregnancy. John Dowie had been a bachelor until a year ago, when he finally married Agatha Turner, a remarkably plain and terribly shy schoolteacher. This first pregnancy had not gone well, and on top of her repeated difficulties, Agatha now imagined that she had been poisoned by the seafood cocktail she ate not an hour ago. She had taken sick twice in the last fifteen minutes, and she wanted to go home.

People wondered why John Dowie married, when he kept himself occupied with the madam of a whorehouse on Post Office Street that he secretly owned. He had no use for Agatha. He had nothing but contempt for the other members of the Families, but he wanted a son. In spite of Dowie's ability to organize them and to keep their monopoly alive and prosperous, each of the other Families feared and loathed this man who was a Northerner and a stranger to their polite ways.

"John . . . I don't like to interfere with your good time."

"You look sick."

"Well, yes . . . I've got to go home, John, but I can ask someone to get a taxicab. Don't disturb yourself, John . . . and make my apologies. I know it's wrong to leave before the bride and groom."

"Agatha, I'll take you home. This damn thing is just a waste of good money."

Dowie grabbed his wife under the arm and commandingly led her out the entrance and across the ornamental carpet in the lobby. He was glad of any excuse to be out of there. They disgusted him with their fancy ways. He'd be better off with a bottle of decent rye.

It had been a lot easier than Royce had imagined. There had only been one watchman for the entire group of sheds that contained the bulk of the merchandise ready for loading. Royce split up his men. He himself would attend to the watchman. He spied him a hundred yards away barely awake, sitting against a post.

Keeping in the shadows, Royce came up behind the man and laid him out with a single swipe of the butt end of his revolver. He dragged the watchman's body out of the light and out of the way of harm. That done, he moved swiftly to the first of the loading docks, where the smell of gasoline was already noticeable. His men raced down the far aisles, leaving a trail of liquid. The entire building would be a pyre at the touch of a match. Royce waited till his men returned. He dispatched two of them to the other buildings, and waited for their signal. Minutes later it came. A long low whistle indicated that everything was ready.

Royce whistled back. He lit a match at the doorway of the first shed, and tossed it on the pool of gasoline. He watched the flame speed down the aisle and spread. Then he quickly walked outside. From inside, he heard first one, and then repeated small muffled explosions as the fire began to catch onto flammable stuffs. Against the black sky, Royce saw tongues of fire appear from the other sheds, and then flickering orange lights appeared through the windows. In the near distance he heard the low rumble of the flames inside the metal buildings.

The men from his group gathered around him. They walked quickly in the direction of the pier to return to the *Colfax II*. Royce looked at his watch.

"You men get back on deck. I'm gonna check on what's happening to L.C. If I'm not back in fifteen minutes, I want you to get the *Colfax II* back to Houston and disappear."

They listened, uncertain.

Royce took charge. "Damn it, do what I tell you to."

As John Dowie drove his car along Beach Boulevard, he heard the sound of fire engines in the distance. He stopped the car momentarily and stared. Far away, the sky was alight. Agatha moaned in pain, stretched out on the cushions in the back seat of his Packard.

"John, please get me home."

Dowie cursed his luck. "Okay, hold yourself together."

He put the car back in gear, and pressed down on the gas pedal, divided between his intense desire to get down to the docks, and his obligation to his wife. A quarter of a mile away from his home, he was panicked still further. Over the trees, he saw flames shooting skyward. He knew they came from his home. He pressed harder on the accelerator, and the car careened as Dowie perilously took the last turns. He narrowly missed a dark pickup truck as it appeared on the road heading directly at his car. Dowie swerved, and the two vehicles narrowly avoided a head-on crash. Dowie took note of the grinning face of the driver, and the men in the back.

From a hundred yards away, Dowie saw his handsome Victorian mansion, the single most impressive building in this stand of stately homes, ablaze from every window. Fire was consuming every shingle, pilaster, and board on the porch. In the distance, he heard the sound of an approaching siren. As he stopped the car opposite the flaming wreck of his house, a group of servants from homes nearby, and the two of his own, stood in front of the building.

The sound of the fire engine died as the lone pumper pulled in front of his house. The firemen hopped off to connect their hoses. The building was a mass of flames. Dowie knew that nothing would be left, as he turned away to head back to the car.

One of the firemen nodded to him as he passed. "Would 'a been here sooner, Mister Dowie, but most of the engines are down at the docks. One heck of a fire down there."

John Dowie knew very well what docks were in flames.

At three in the morning, two lone figures sat in L.C.'s office in Houston. L.C. was grinning broadly, as he took a swig from a bottle of bourbon and passed it across the desk to Royce. A single gooosenecked lamp illuminated their faces.

"Mighty proud of tonight, Royce . . . mighty proud."

Royce took a drink from the bottle and nodded. "Yeah, it went off like it was supposed to."

L.C. picked up the phone on his desk. "It's about time I put a period on this little episode." Speaking to the operator, he gave her a number in Galveston, and waited on the line as he was being connected. The number rang. A man's voice came on the line.

"Who is this?" the voice inquired sleepily.

"Hell, Mr. Shearman . . . I wanted to congratulate you and your little lady on the marriage of your daughter tonight."

"Who the hell is this?" the voice demanded.

"Don't make no difference, Shearman—just the fellow who knows about those fires, that's who I am. If I guess right, the one on the docks is still burning."

The voice was cold. "The cops will get you."

"No, that's what I called about, Shearman. I want you and the others to put a stop to that, and a couple of other things I want to have stopped—doing damage to the shipping headed for Houston, or interfering in any way with our legitimate competition. Us here in Houston have a right to live . . . or if we don't, *you* don't, Shearman."

There was silence.

"Now, you got yourself a new son-in-law and lovely wife and kids, and the same with the McCoveneys and the Bedloes. I don't give a damn what happens to John Dowie, and if I was you and the rest, I wouldn't pay him no mind about the police, or revenge, or any of that tired shit that he preaches."

"What are you telling me?"

"Just that Dowie got a sample of what's in store for any one of you unless you leave us in Houston to grow the way we have a right to . . . and unless you tell your police chief and your mayor to forget about tonight. Shit, Shearman, put it down as John Dowie's present to the bride and groom. If it hadn't been for him, it would 'a happened to *you*. Do I make myself clear?"

For a moment there was quiet, and then Shearman answered. "I can talk for myself and the other two, but John Dowie may have some other ideas."

L.C. laughed, "Just you talk for the three Families. It don't do me no mind at all who Dowie talks to, or what he says . . . or even what he *does*."

L.C. put the phone back on the receiver, smiled broadly at Royce and grabbed the bourbon from his hand, and downed a very healthy pull.

"Goddamn," he shouted. "This was one hell of a night." He smiled wryly. "Wish I could 'a been at the wedding. Love to dance with pretty gals, Royce . . . sure do. Say, why don't we quit this place. You can drop me off at the Rice—there's a little gal I can wake up. She'll help me celebrate."

In one stroke, L.C. had destroyed John Dowie and immobilized the three other Families in Galveston. It was a bloody triumph, and L.C. gloated in its success.

Unknown to him, a number of Houston's business leaders were appalled at the act, which put L.C. Younger above the law. Houston was a frontier city, but what L.C. had done was criminal, and he had gotten away with it. Melvin Jurdam, son of the unquestioned leader in Houston's civic community, was more than outraged. He had been bested in his first encounter with L.C., when L.C. had gone over his head to appeal to his father. Now, although he was powerless to do anything legally against this man, there was one way, through the newspaper owned by the Jurdam family—the *Houston Journal*.

During his father's absence in Washington, Melvin Jurdam set reporters to work to get something on L.C., and do him as much damage as possible.

Three weeks later, Melvin Jurdam signed an editorial in the *Journal* calling for an end to L.C. and his nightriders. The editorial called attention to a news story which he placed on the front page about L.C.'s father, Devlin Younger, outlining parts of his life that the *Journal* had researched and documented. The editorial was titled "Like Father, Like Son."

L.C. went into seclusion for three days. He disappeared from the house on Montrose, from the offices of Black Diamond, and couldn't even be reached at his apartment at the Rice Hotel.

One day later, a full-page advertisement appeared in every major newspaper throughout the state of Texas.

A BASTARD HAS FOUND HIS DADDY!

> **For a lot of years, I have been trying to get information about my real daddy. The folks at a scandal sheet in Houston have done it for me.**
>
> **For those of you who didn't see it, I want you to know my real daddy was Devlin Younger and he escaped from Galveston during the hurricane in 1900.**
>
> **The state of Florida hung him by the neck in 1912 for killing a man. They say my daddy had a hand in other killings and less serious deals.**
>
> **All well and good, but he was my daddy, and that makes me his son. That's the name I go by. Don't you forget it.**
>
> **L.C. Younger**

L.C. never forgave the *Houston Journal* for its attack, nor the *Journal's* powerful owner, Melvin Jurdam. On the other hand, Melvin Jurdam discovered that his thrust against L.C. had been blunted by L.C.'s audacious ad.

The two were now the bitterest of enemies, and leaders in the city of Houston had discovered another reason to hate L.C. Younger.

For a period of time, there was peace in the Houston Ship Channel. In 1938, a sustained strike by longshoremen and seafarers caused an eruption of violence once again at Black Diamond. Armed men were aboard each of L.C.'s vessels, and at his warehouse facilities. It was the last gasp by one lone individual, L.C. Younger, to fight off the inevitability of the union. In the final analysis, L.C.'s way of doing business had to die. He was forced to accommodate the hated forces of labor. Surprisingly enough, Black Diamond continued to prosper as Houston became the hub in the Southwest for cotton, grain, oil, and even armaments that were beginning to be needed by the countries allied against Nazi Germany.

In Galveston, the Families put a stop to their battle with the port of Houston. The example of what had happened to John Dowie was more telling than the occasional natural disasters, the hurricanes and floods that plagued the island port. John Dowie never recovered from the destruction of that night in 1933. Over the next years he had no influence with the Families. He became a bitter man, barely managing to maintain himself as a shipping agent.

When war broke out in Europe in September of 1939, the flood tide of commerce in Houston trebled the importance of the ship channel overnight. Over a million and a half men at Army and Air Force installations were stationed in the Houston area, and Black Diamond became pivotal to the war effort.

At that peak moment in L.C.'s importance, an event took place which shook him thoroughly. On a night in April of 1945, the *Colfax II* pulled into a pier in Galveston. The tug, together with eight other Black Diamond vessels, had been requisitioned to tow barges full of defective ammunition into the gulf, to be sunk. The night before the rendezvous, an unexplained fire and explosion took place aboard the *Colfax II*, killing Royce Richards and three other men. A military court of inquiry was called upon to investigate the incident, but several days later, it became clear to L.C. just what had happened.

The body of John Dowie was found covered in oil slick and badly burned. It was discovered under a pier close to where the *Colfax II* had been berthed. L.C. was certain that finally John Dowie had sought revenge and Royce had paid the price.

L.C. broke the news to Royce's widow. He promised her that whatever happened, she and her young son Methune, now only a year old, could count on him for anything. Nadine Richards cried at the stonyfaced man who had demanded so much of her husband. She raced from the room in tears.

L.C. was drawn to the playpen in the center of the living room, where a handsome, wide-eyed, blond-haired youngster stood holding onto the railing, staring at him. L.C. bent to pick up the child. He held him at arm's length and the baby smiled.

Methune "Tune" Richards looked just like his father. L.C. tossed the baby high in the air and caught him handily.

Tune Richards laughed.

THE MARRIAGE of L.C. Younger to Vonnie Moore, the daughter of J.T. Moore, was not marked with any pleasure by her family. Despite the fact that Vonnie was incredibly shy, she defied her father's wrath and eloped with the handsome and reckless L.C. Younger, about whom few people had anything good to say.

As far as L.C. was concerned, Vonnie represented respectability in a community that grudgingly accepted him when it had to, but soundly scorned him for his violent and hardheaded ways.

When Vonnie informed L.C. that she was pregnant, there was no way to measure his happiness. Nobody could have understood how much L.C. had been yearning for a child. Perhaps if he had thought about it, L.C. might have understood that his own failure to know his own natural parents made him very ready to start his own dynasty. The house on Montrose rang with his joyous laughter and high spirits.

Vonnie, on the other hand, was in despair. At the age of 32, the prospect of becoming a mother should not have been surprising. But it was. In her deepest heart she resented the intrusion into her body of something over which she had no control. The morning sickness, the new things that were happening to her, were unpleasant for her to contemplate. From waking to sleeping, Vonnie moved around the house in her long flowing dressing gown as if she were a convalescent, waiting for some dire news that would mean a fatal reoccurrence of a dread disease. Finally L.C. forced her to select an obstetrician, and the two of them began what seemed like an endless search for someone Vonnie would accept.

L.C. proposed the most important and best-known doctors in Houston and dutifully escorted her to each of their offices. He waited patiently while Vonnie was examined, and sat reassuringly with her for an interview with each in turn. After two days, Vonnie walked away from the last doctor in tears.

"Vonnie, come on now. You're going to have a baby. It's the best present a man and a woman could ever have."

Vonnie came into L.C.'s arms. He was welcoming and tender as they stood out on the street. He paid no attention to the inquiring eyes of people passing.

"L.C. I don't want to have a baby. I'm not ready to have a baby. There are other things that I want from life."

L.C. was perplexed. "There's nothing to it, Vonnie. You're a grown woman. I've been trying for years and now it's happened. Every day ten billion women spread their legs and pop out a kid. It's as easy as pie, and it don't hurt none, at least, only a little. If it was such a problem, you think they would have thought of another way, by this time."

She smiled through her tears. "You're laughing at me."

L.C. took her chin in his hand, "Hell no, I ain't laughing. I know that it's no joke. The thing that a man does takes less than a minute, and you ladies have the problem. But I want this baby so bad, Von, that whatever makes you happy, will make me happy, and whatever it takes to give your mind peace . . . that's what I'll do."

"Do you mean that?"

"Of course I do."

"About the doctor . . . "

"What about him, Von? If the ones we saw ain't good enough, or don't suit you, then we'll go see five more, and if they don't suit you, because their hands are cold, or they smile the wrong way, we'll find ten more."

"I know the doctor I want."

"Just tell me, and I'll get him for you—even if he's that hairy doctor who takes care of the savages of Africa."

"You mean Dr. Schweitzer. I want Doctor McCauley. He was the man who delivered me, and I was a healthy baby and my mamma never complained, and I have confidence in him."

"Hell, is that all? We'll get McCauley on the phone, and make an appointment. That's easy."

"I think he's retired, L.C."

"Von, we'll unretire him. There's nothing that I won't do . . ."

"L.C.?"

"Yes?"

"I don't want to go to a hospital. I want to have the baby right here in the house on Montrose."

"But it's safer in the hospital, Von, you know that."

"I don't want them to change the baby. There are stories of mothers going home with the wrong baby. I don't *want* any other baby. I want *my* baby, and I'm not going to have it in some hospital where some nurse is

29

going to mix up babies, and you and I will come home with someone else's."

L.C. shook his head in wonderment. He put his arm around Vonnie and led her to the parked car. "Von, I promise you McCauley is going to deliver our baby, and we'll turn the house into a hospital, and put armed guards right out in front, so no one will *dare* attack us and try to exchange our baby for some lesser kid." He smiled at the thought.

Vonnie grinned through her tears. Then she stifled an embarrassed laugh. "You're laughing at me, L.C., but remember you promised."

The period of Vonnie's pregnancy was trying for the entire household. L.C. was almost as good as his word. He managed to convince Dr. McCauley to come out of retirement, and he also convinced him to deliver the baby in the house on Montrose. But as strongly and as resolutely as he promised not to let Vonnie out of his sight, L.C. eventually succumbed to the lust of his own flesh. It was during that time that L.C. kept his suite at the Rice occupied with a progression of women. He had never been so active. Never had his sexual appetite been greater. It was simply a matter of joyous celebration at becoming a father. At forty-five, L.C. was incredibly vigorous. He had never once thought that Vonnie's inability to conceive had anything to do with him, but that it finally happened called forth a celebration of sexuality that surprised even him.

Vonnie was cared for, pampered, and treated as if she were made of fine porcelain. If the servants failed to perform a simple task, or something was forgotten that she considered important, L.C. would step in. He spent countless hours dealing with the real or imagined problems that Vonnie regaled him with. Vonnie's pains and aches were well beyond anything that L.C. had imagined. Doctor McCauley himself began to lose patience, but curiously L.C. never did.

Nurses were brought into the house during the last month, in preparation for the delivery. They fluttered around, vying with each other to protect Vonnie against chills, mix rich milk and egg drinks, and fluff up pillows behind her at each and every occasion. Vonnie was late, and the waiting was painful for L.C. Matters of importance at Black Diamond were left hanging—L.C. hardly ever left the house. Even his sexual appetite was stilled during the final wait.

Vonnie was petrified when she went into labor. No matter what her doctor and the nurses said to prepare her for the event, it struck her as totally unexpected. It was as if she had anticipated the state of pregnancy would go on forever, and having accomplished that, she would have no need of any other event to take place. Even though the doctor was not needed, Vonnie insisted that he remain at her side for the entire eighteen-hour vigil. L.C. sat next to the bed attempting to reassure her.

Finally Vonnie gave birth to a son. When she first saw the infant, she appeared convinced that no other woman in the world before had ever achieved what she had accomplished. No woman had ever consecrated her body the way she had. That sacrifice, that part of her body, lay in her arms. Whatever might happen to the world, no one would take that infant away from her. How right she had been to have had the child at home. Even the brief moments during which the baby was removed from her sight filled her with extraordinary panic. What if someone were to drop the baby? What if the baby cried and she were not on hand to comfort it, or feed it?

The child was named John Travis by his mother, in honor of her own father. The matter had never been discussed before, but L.C. was so pleased to have a son that he willingly acceded. Unfortunately, he failed to recognize that from the very first moment he was entering a struggle for the possession of their son. It was a struggle that weak, frail, prone-to-sickness Vonnie Younger would not lose. Whatever it cost, Vonnie swore that she would continue the sacrifice that she had initiated with John Travis's birth.

As the days progressed, Vonnie never left her child's side. If the air was suspiciously hot or cold, his mother virtually breathed *for* him to test it. Vonnie tasted every spoonful of food before she gave it to him to eat. The consistency and flavor of the second or third spoonful might be injurious to her son. In addition, the danger of the temperature's changing from start to finish was always a grave peril. His food was in constant need of reheating or cooling, and only Vonnie could do it properly. Vonnie Younger was lost in a world of her first-born son. She considered that his fate was exclusively in her hands, and she was terrified that this miracle, produced from her body, might be taken from her. For if that happened, she would surely perish.

From the moment of their son's birth, Vonnie became remote and inaccessible to her husband. She extended her breast feeding weeks beyond the time that her doctor recommended. The child remained at all times in her room. L.C. found himself frozen out of contact with his son, and his wife.

It is hard to say when L.C. recognized that John Travis would never be *his* child. It was not only that for the first time in his life he lost the battle for possession of something he desperately wanted, but also, from the very first, it was evident that there was nothing of L.C. in the boy.

When John Travis was almost five, L.C. came home late at night drunk and angry. He found Vonnie in John Travis's room sitting in the near dark, watching his son sleep. L.C. was infuriated. In his anger, he seized her and dragged her screaming into her bedroom. Out of his frustration, L.C. seized and raped his wife. Vonnie became pregnant. Months of anger followed, but in every way, L.C. declared to himself that no matter what, the child to be born would finally be his.

Christmas Day 1951, a robust little girl was born to Vonnie Younger in Hermann Hospital. After the birth, Vonnie returned to her palatial suite, and from that moment, there was not a moment's wavering in L.C.'s love for his daughter. He wasn't even disappointed about her not being a boy. The tiny wisps of moist red hair that curled on the infant's forehead and in the folds of her tiny neck, the spirited cries and the happy look of the deliciously big baby, found L.C. overjoyed. This time he named the child. He chose the name Devlin. It was his father's name, but it seemed strangely appropriate.

From that moment, life in the house on Montrose focused on Devlin. L.C. made it his business to be home each night. It was he, and only he, who put Devlin to bed, spending hours telling her stories, reading her poetry, and devising an entire world of fairy tales that were the delight of the child's life. L.C. didn't know *how* he came to invent the stories. When he saw Devlin's adorable face, and felt her delectable peachlike skin, heard her lusty laughter, he was sure that somehow he had been blessed with a princess. And so, his stories were about Devlin, *his* princess.

There was no corner of the household, no staircase or ladder, window or chair, that Devlin did not venture on. She terrified the household with her daredevil antics. When L.C. heard the cook Alma speak of them, he laughed.

"She's still alive, isn't she?"

"*Si, señor* . . . but she is only three years old."

"She'll get worse when she gets older," L.C. remarked wisely.

Vonnie accepted the division in the household without comment. She was consumed with her son. At eight, John Travis was a hulking lad. He was secretive and full of guile. When he was alone with Devlin, he found ways to torment her. Devlin, open, loving and adoring, saw only good in her brother and was confused at his rejection and hostility. After a time, Devlin drew away, still uncertain whether her brother's reaction was a result of something she had done, and was too young to understand.

Matters changed with the entry of Tune Richards into her life. All Devlin knew was that this young boy was full of fun, braver than anyone she had ever seen, the leader at every game that was played in the backyard or the park, and most important of all, he liked her. Devlin, longing to join him, dutifully watched and waited while the older boys played. Little by little she was drawn into their games. First, it was Tune who permitted her in. Later, it was because Devlin was as good as many of the boys at everything they did.

There was no challenge that Devlin refused. Hardly a day went by when she failed to return home covered with bruises, or with her hair matted and clothing torn. In the beginning, Alma brought the child to Vonnie, who was too horrified to deal with Devlin. As time went on, the cook began to deal with Devlin as if *she* were her mother. Whenever Devlin was reminded she was a girl, and should avail herself of the company of girls, and do the things they did, she gritted her teeth. The girls at school didn't like her, and she didn't like them. They were stupid and childish. She would *not* be reduced to that.

Vonnie's overwhelming attention to John Travis finally met with the only opposition that counted—her son's. Deserved or not, John Travis discovered that he could treat his mother as a virtual slave. His anger against the world was vented in his abuse of her. He shamed her in front of the servants and in private. Only in the presence of his father was he at least civil. Vonnie tragically bewailed her son's treatment, but nothing could deny her abject need of him, even with its humiliating consequences. L.C. couldn't, had he even been willing to join the contest at this point, provide either Vonnie or John Travis with an ally; he had totally committed himself to Devlin. No one else existed for him. Everything he had hoped for had come true in the enchantress—his red-haired, green-eyed daughter, Devlin.

By the time Devlin was eight, her idol Tune, nearing fifteen, had begun to have wider interests. There were the sports activities at San Jacinto High, the pretty girls who admired him, and his schoolmates and friends in high school who fell into line behind his leadership. The afternoons he spent in the house on Montrose were less frequent. On one occasion, Devlin trapped him in a hidden recess of the basement of the house that she used as her hideout. She sat Tune on an old stool, while Devlin squatted on the old piece of carpeting with which she had furnished her tiny lair.

"Tunafish," she pleaded, "tell me what I did wrong."

"Devlin . . . how many times do I have to tell you not to call me that. My name is Tune, and I want you to call me that."

Devlin smiled coquettishly. "You can call me any name *you* want. I don't care. That just proves that I'm a better person than you are, in case you had any *dumb* ideas."

"Devlin, why did you bring me down here?"

"Tunafish—oops, excuse me—Tune, I want to know why you don't come around any more."

"Devlin . . . you know that I have football practice . . . and there's a whole new gang of guys at school that I hang around with. I just don't have the time. Look, you're a girl. Why don't you find some girls your own age and play with them. I never see you ever with anybody."

"You know why?"

"Why?"

"Girls are stupid. I hate them."

"Yeah?"

Devlin stared at him cooly. "Do you have a girl at high school?"

"No, I don't, and if I did, what business is it of yours?"

"Nothing . . . no business except, Tunafish, if I catch her, I'll kill her."

"Oh come on, Devlin. I'm almost twice your age."

"It won't always be that way. Don't you like me anymore?"

"Of course I do, but you're getting to be a pain. Dammit, Devlin, you're a girl. G-i-r-l. You should be doing the things they do. What business do you have coming home every day with a whole new set of bruises." Then he paused, "How many broken arms have you had?"

"More than you," she said defiantly.

"Christ, Dev, that's nothing to be proud of."

"Tune . . ."

"Yeah, what is it?"

"Can I come to practice to watch you?"

"I guess so."

"Wow," Devlin shouted, "I'll be there every day from now on."

The reports of John Travis's escapades at St. John's, Houston's premier private school, could not be ignored. The headmaster asked to meet with Vonnie and L.C. and suggested that he be withdrawn from school and sent elsewhere. Much against Vonnie's wishes, L.C. decided to send him to San Marcos Military Academy for "difficult" boys near San Antonio.

One might have thought that John Travis would not have gone willingly, but curiously, he was more than happy to be rid of his mother and to be removed from the constant reminder of his father's disappointment in him. On the determined day, with his bags packed, he was driven to school by Manuel the butler.

Devlin tried to say goodbye, but he rebuffed her. Tune tried as well, but John Travis ignored him. Tune was enough of a subject of his rampant envy, and somehow he blamed Devlin for subverting any affection L.C. might have shown him. There was no logical reason for it, except that he made it so. Thus, John Travis took the first step out of the family influence and environment.

Vonnie viewed the situation tragically. She buried herself in her bedroom and her poetry. The forlorn memories of her childhood, the precious toys and souvenirs were kept on careful and meticulous display in her most private and personal chamber. No one dared to enter. No one cleaned or made up the room. She remained there alone, sitting on the window seat, staring at traffic, and writing a new poem every day.

In the view of the other girls at school, Devlin was something of a freak. She was a tomboy. She was different and she didn't make friends. The cliques of girls were tightly closed to her.

Devlin was the subject of their eternal gossip. She knew what they were saying about her, and about her father, and *his* father. There were bad things that were said about him, ugly and unpleasant. Furthermore, Devlin still lived in Montrose, while their families had migrated to fashionable River Oaks, and their disdain was palpable. Devlin closed her ears to the gossip, to their chatter about clothes, vacations in far-off places, tales of unbelievable riches, and stories of their endless possessions.

Devlin became preoccupied with the fact that she was taller than all the girls and, at the same time, less developed.

"Devlin," Alma complained one afternoon in the kitchen, "you are only eleven. I myself did not have bosoms until I was eighteen. Now you see how big they are. I promise you, Devlin . . . you will have big bosoms too."

"Alma . . . I don't know."

"What don't you know?"

"There's something else . . . when I see some of the girls in the shower, they are beginning to have hair, down, you know where."

"It's not important, Devlin."

"Why not?"

Alma reached over and took Devlin's hand. "Don't you worry. When it is important, then God will give you as much as you need in time to please your man. Until that time, don't be concerned in the shower. It will not be for other girls that you will look beautiful. It will be for your husband."

"The hair down there, is it supposed to be pretty?" Devlin shook with revulsion. "My hair isn't dark enough to show, if it ever comes in."

"It will show, on your wedding day."

"What about *him?*"

"What *about* him señorita?"

"Is he having trouble growing hair down there too?"

Alma laughed. "*Probablamente.*"

Each afternoon Devlin rode her bike to the practice field to watch Tune. She became a fixture at each session. His teammates kidded him about his personal fan club. Then as Tune went into his sophomore year and became a star quarterback, there developed an adoring group of very pretty high school girls who came each day to watch him. Devlin sat alone, charting the plays and making notes so she could give them to Tune. She felt ill at ease, and embarrassed. She heard the whispering and laughter from the girls, and she knew it was directed at her, and she stopped coming.

The single redeeming fact in Devlin's life was Black Diamond. When she was thirteen, she began to hang around almost daily. The stevedores and the workers on the barges and tugs thought that she was an annoyance they had to tolerate; but little by little they spoke to her, and Devlin's insatiable curiosity about what each of them did and how they did it was both agreeable and flattering. More than that, they discovered that once Devlin was told something, she never forgot it. More often than not, after school, Devlin rode her bike the considerable distance on difficult streets, or managed a hitch to spend the afternoon hours at the channel.

Devlin learned to operate the forklifts and the marine legs that carried the huge containers from the pier to the sheds. She sat for hours in the two-man cabs of the huge 150-foot cranes, perched high above the ground. Little by little, she learned the function and how to operate every piece of equipment, the clam-shell buckets, the straddle carriers, the top handlers. But it was on the tugs of Black Diamond Harbor and Towing that Devlin felt most at home. In the beginning, she was a passenger only. Then, as an "ordinary seaman," she chipped and painted with the rest, and then as time went by, she learned the language of the "able bodied seaman," his skills and assignments.

She loved the smells and the sounds. She liked the rough men and the salty talk. At first she was a toy, then a curiosity, and finally, Devlin was viewed with healthy respect by the stevedores, the foremen, the equipment operators, the captains, the crews who came in contact with her. Devlin's eyes sparkled with pleasure. She didn't give a moment's thought to the fact that she was a teenage girl in the company of some of the roughest men in Houston. Every one of them adored her. Any one of them would have killed for her.

As time went on, Tune's career as a campus hero assumed legendary proportions. He was hardly ever seen around the house on Montrose, and though Devlin read every single piece in the papers about him, and kept a box full of clippings, she seldom went to the games. When Tune graduated from San Jacinto and went to S.M.U. on a football scholarship, his reputation skyrocketed. Not in years had a freshman played varsity quarterback at S.M.U., and instantaneously become a star. Then in 1964, everything changed when Tune announced that he was joining the Marines to go to Vietnam.

The last time that Devlin saw Tune was at Black Diamond, the day he appeared in uniform to bid L.C. goodbye. Devlin was fourteen, dressed in grimy jeans and workshirt. Her face was smudged unrecognizably and her hands were covered with grease. Devlin never forgot Tune's laughter when he saw her. She never forgot the incredibly handsome figure of the Marine, who quit football for another kind of heroics. That was part of Tune's nature.

Tune embraced L.C. as Devlin moved away and returned to her forklift. She bit her lip with a mixture of pain and anger. She had always been too young, and too late. That was the way it was. She had to accept it. It was a fact of life, the same as her small breasts, her height, and the fact that after all the biggest problem was that she had been born a girl.

By the time John Travis completed preparatory school in San Antonio, he had assumed the role of an evil sultan among his classmates. Through a combination of favors done both for his fellow students and for teachers, he managed to carve out for himself a quiet and comfortable fiefdom in which all of the school served him. John Travis had the gift of finding ways to make money. He arranged marijuana buys, brought whiskey and other contraband into the school, and even supplied prostitutes for a number of students. He loaned money "six for five" (six dollars returned in a week for five dollars lent), and could manage any kind of scam, from the securing of tests to the fixing of grades.

When John Travis entered Rice after completion of prep school, he had attained his full growth. He was a huge man, six foot four, weighing over 230 pounds. Despite his weight, he was agile and might have made a football player or wrestler had he had any interest. From the beginning of his college career, John Travis continued as a fixer and dealer, expanding his activities by scalping tickets for sports events, and handling bets. John Travis did all these things with considerable finesse. He was a rogue, with a curious charm, and people liked him despite his venal ways.

John Travis's native intelligence was more than enough to get him better than passing grades in his classes. His teachers were grudgingly convinced that were he to attend classes and apply himself, he would have become a top student. But John Travis had no interest in that at all. He held court each day at a large round table in Sammy's, the campus cafeteria, like a Godfather meeting his supplicants. His pockets were stuffed with large bills, and he was continually buying and selling. In the little universe of campus life, if you wanted anything done, from an abortion to buying dope, from buying and selling stolen airline tickets or transistor radios, from hookers to examination questions, John Travis was the man to see.

It took only one incident to change all that. A narcotics bust took place at his apartment. Federal officers discovered two ounces of cocaine and a kilo of marijuana. John Travis was destined to spend a lot of time in jail. In 1966, the maximum penalty for marijuana possession in Texas was life imprisonment, and the penalty for possession of cocaine would have nailed the door shut.

Were it not that L.C. Younger was a millionaire who could afford the best lawyer in Houston with the best connections, that's what would have happened. L.C. never discussed the details with the lawyer, but the case was thrown out of court. L.C. never even discussed with John Travis the how and why of his infraction. His silence was more punishing.

John Travis returned to live in the house on Montrose and to work at Black Diamond. He applied himself as best he could to life in the harbor, performing his work grudgingly at first and then with skill. It didn't matter, since L.C. had made up his mind about his son before he was one year old. John Travis was a Younger, but L.C. made no pretense of his antagonism. For his part, John Travis, try as he could to break through his father's resistance, finally gave up. Although he continued at Black Diamond, he appeared to some strangely dispirited. But anyone who looked closely could tell that John Travis was a smoldering fire.

During her last year at the fashionable Kinkaid School, Devlin blossomed. L.C. had always thought her beautiful, but everything about Devlin was idealized in his mind. The moment that changed Devlin's own concept of herself occurred on the docks at Black Diamond.

A stationery salesman came to call on the office manager one day. He was overheard making a number of suggestive remarks about Devlin. Unfortunately for the salesman, an employee mentioned the incident to L.C., and that was enough. L.C. came storming out of his office, down to the main floor, past desks of frightened secretaries, until he faced the hapless salesman.

L.C. grabbed him, turned him around, and proceeded to beat him unmercifully. In minutes, L.C. stood over the salesman, hardly panting from the exertion. The salesman was bleeding and barely conscious.

That day, L.C. realized that Devlin was a young woman, remarkably beautiful and appealing to men. The employees at Black Diamond had enjoyed her companionship as a friend. Now they understood how L.C. would deal with them should they entertain any other thoughts of her. That night, L.C. made the decision which would send Devlin away to the University of Texas. She cried desperately when she heard it.

Devlin mounted the stairs after dinner, and spent the rest of the night in her room alone. She hated being sent away, but a part of her mind noted with some pleasure that the salesman had thought of her as pretty and sexually attractive.

With a curiosity that should have come years earlier, Devlin took off all her clothes and stood for almost an hour in front of the mirror in her room. Naked, she turned and twisted to see her reflection at every angle. She was eighteen. Her bosom was small but attractive. Her waist was long, as were her legs. The color of her hair, the bright ginger that she had detested for so long, because she was the only one she had ever known to have hair that shade, now contrasted interestingly with the turquoise-green of her eyes. She felt her skin, and it was warm and soft. She touched under her arms, and the tiny wisps of hair were delicate and sensual. Devlin examined the hair on her crotch. Somehow there seemed as much as the other girls. Alma had been right in telling her that it would come in. Thank God.

Devlin wasn't bored for a minute during the process of self-examination. It had been a long time in coming. She knew how badly she

38

had felt for years about being a girl. She was less sure now. She had yet to really understand it, and she had the feeling that going to Austin wasn't going to be much help. She looked at her hands—they were large for her body, made for work. Devlin thought about leaving home and was incredibly sad. She searched through her record albums for a Ray Price favorite, and put it on the turntable. She sat on the floor, her knees tucked up under the chin, and thought how well the words expressed how she felt.

> I've got heartaches by the number,
> Troubles by the score,
> Every day you love me less,
> Each day I love you more . . .*

Things were changing, and Devlin wasn't altogether sure she was happy about it.

5

In Houston, girls of good family go to the University of Texas in Austin. The last week of August 1969, just before classes started, was the week during which sororities mounted their finest efforts to attract the most promising new girls. Even as Devlin drove up to Madison House in her red Eldorado convertible, a present from L.C., a pretty young coed, blonde and bouncy, with heavily lacquered hair, wearing a demure flowered shirtwaist dress with a Peter Pan collar, beamed at her.

"Hi, I'm Peggy Sue Cartright. I'm a junior and I want to welcome you to UT. I know who *you* are. Our spy system in Houston told us you were coming. You're Devlin Younger . . . and my goodness, you sure are pretty." She whispered confidentially, "There's only one sorority for you, Devlin. Kappa has all the prettiest girls by a mile." She laughed coquettishly. "Don't look at me—I'm the ugliest of them all."

Reaching to grab Devlin's suitcase, she found it was heavier than she had expected. "My," Peggy Sue sighed, "you sure are pretty. I never *did* see hair that color before."

Devlin smiled as Peggy Sue trudged off carrying the heavy weight that Devlin had managed easily. Peggy Sue turned and gasped, "That your Eldorado out front?" Devlin nodded. "My daddy has six . . . in different colors."

At five foot ten, Devlin seemed like a delicately poised, barely weaned young animal. Her close-fitting jeans and cowboy boots, her tiny rear, perched high, made her look like a young filly, all legs and tiny bottom. She looked so different from the other girls clustered in the lobby that one might have thought her the prototype of a splendid new species, newly born, still wet in her mother's fluid. Devlin walked like a businesslike cowgirl to the back of the convertible, opened the trunk, easily hefted one of the suitcases over her shoulder, and placed a second under her arm. She sighed at the thought of what lay ahead and walked through the open door to the reception desk. Three other girls were waiting to sign in as part of the cumbersome registration procedure, uncertainly supervised by a gray-haired housemother.

Peggy Sue Cartright trudged up the two flights of stairs to the room to which Devlin had been assigned. Devlin followed, muttering to herself. "Damn, damn, damn. They won't get me into dresses . . . they won't get me to lacquer my hair, and they won't get me into any damn sorority." Peggy Sue brightened as she put down the suitcase. "Gollee, Devlin . . . what do you have in here, horseshoes?"

"Just my boots. Should I have brought *my own* horseshoes?"

"Oh gollee, no. Nobody pitches horseshoes . . . did you think that we did? I hope that won't be a disappointment to you, Devlin, I don't think any of the Kappas pitch horseshoes, but I'll ask if you like."

Sweeping down the hall were a pair of young women, wearing towels around their midsections, headed for the shower. Peggy Sue looked at the retreating figures disdainfully, "Kappas always wear bathrobes."

Devlin snorted, "I always go naked."

Peggy Sue laughed, then stopped. She hoped Devlin didn't mean it. Carefully, the blonde opened the door. Inside the bedroom, a thick-waisted, pouty-faced young girl lay on one of the beds, her feet stretched over the end as she spoke on a telephone.

"Mama, the drapes don't fit, and the bedspreads don't go with the walls. I told you time after time that the flowered print will not go with flowered drapes, but you wouldn't listen to me."

The dark-haired young girl looked up at Devlin unbelievingly and continued her conversation. Devlin threw her suitcase on the bed and began to open it. "Mama, the other girls have all kinds of Papagallos that I don't have. You remember the pair that I wanted to get at Neiman's— the hot pink with the grosgrain bow . . . well, they are *very* fashionable, and the girl in the next room has two pairs like that, in case one of them gets stained or something. Mama . . . listen to me. She has three other pairs that they don't even *have* in Neiman's, at least our saleslady didn't show them to *us*."

Peggy Sue watched unbelievingly as Devlin's suitcase disgorged, among underwear and shirts, six pairs of worn jeans and an equal number of worn and scuffmarked boots. She whispered to Devlin, "You have more clothes downstairs in your car, don't you?"

Devlin shook her head no, "Just my hi-fi, and some Ray Price records and stuff. What kind of clothes do you have in mind? I only wear jeans and boots."

Peggy Sue shook her head unbelievingly.

"Mama, you go to Neiman's and give them a piece of your mind, and then you find that pansy decorator who got you to buy those flowered drapes and you tell him that if I stay here, I want to wallpaper my room.

Mama, it doesn't make any difference whether I have a roommate or not. I'm not going to live like a pig for my first year at college."

The pouty-faced brunette hung up and turned to Peggy Sue. "What sorority are you in?"

"Kappa," she whispered breathlessly, "we're the best."

"Uh-huh," the brunette continued, "that's what they all say." Then she turned to look at Devlin. Through tight lips she muttered, as she stuck out her hand, "You my roommate?"

Devlin put her hands on her hips and smiled, "I don't give a fart in a windstorm for flowered wallpaper or drapes, and I don't know what damn Papagallos are, and if I were your mama, I would take you over my knee and beat the living daylights out of you." Then she smiled sweetly, "Yep, I guess I am your roommate. My name is Devlin Younger."

The brunette gasped, "My goodness." Devlin chuckled.

Peggy Sue was red with embarrassment. She had never heard any girl use an "F" word before. Goodness, she thought, what am I going to tell my sisters? What are we going to do about this girl, who is clearly the most beautiful girl on campus? Kappa has *got* to get her, and it's all my responsibility. Peggy Sue stuck out her chin. If it's the last thing in the world, I will get Devlin Younger into proper clothes, and I will get her to use proper ladylike language, and I will make sure she is a Kappa, or I will die in the attempt.

"Devlin," she said, "I'll go now and let you get organized, and I'll come by and pick you up at five. We're having a little get-together at the sorority house, and I want to show off the sisters. You'll love them."

The Kappa girls and the girls in the other sororities were transfixed by Devlin, but horrified as well. While all the sisters and invitees from the freshman class appeared in classic shirtwaist dresses, dainty Villager prints, and matching shoes with tiny bows, Devlin's scruffy jeans and boots made her an object of intense curiosity. In the Chi Omega house, when a tray of melted cheese Fritos was passed around, another invitee whispered to Devlin, "Be careful how you pick them up. They make the melted cheese spill over everything and one of the sisters watches to see how you handle it." Devlin smiled and grabbed a sticky handful.

At the Theta house, Devlin spied a plate of chocolate eclairs. None of the invitees disturbed it, except Devlin. A hawk-eyed sister watched as Devlin helped herself to two, ate them hungrily, and licked her fingers.

At the Pi Phi house, tea was served in very fine china. Devlin went into the kitchen, got herself a warm Coke, unhinged the cap, and sipped it as she stood staring at the chattering females, and then left.

Devlin decided that she had had it with sororities, but Peggy Sue was not to be daunted. She came to Devlin's room and sat on the bed to have a heart-to-heart with Devlin.

42

Devlin stared at Peggy Sue. She noticed her heavily teased hair, frosted blonder than before, false eyelashes that made the room seem smaller, and the fussy Liberty print dress and matching shoes. Devlin sat on the corner of the desk, waiting and watching.

"Devlin, you know how much I like you, and all the other Kappas do too, but there *are* a few things that we thought you ought to know. First of all, you are only hurting your looks by wearing those beat-up jeans and boots all the time. You have such a pretty figure, that would go so well in the *nicer* kind of clothes."

"You think so?" Devlin inquired.

"Oh, yes." Peggy Sue was cheered by the warm response. "I'd love to take you shopping this afternoon on the drag. Sally Gee has wonderful things, and I noticed that you don't have pierced ears. Everybody does . . . and I can take you to a place that has wonderful little pearl stud earrings, like everybody wears. And Devlin, forgive me if I sound critical, the girls noticed that you don't wear a brassiere, and it shows. You know what I mean. Scarboroughs' has some very pretty Vassarettes, like everybody wears, with underwires . . . you know, for proper separation."

Devlin nodded dumbly. She was sure that Peggy Sue's voice could cure insomnia.

"Now your hair, Devlin. It's so pretty, and the color *is* remarkable . . . but we all wear falls to anything that's important, like the final formal just before we announce the pledges."

Devlin had finally heard enough. "Peggy Sue, I want to thank you and the rest of the Kappas for all your interest. I loved the little tea sandwiches, and the cucumber slices. I loved the conversation about what my daddy does and what your daddy does . . . and I loved being looked over top to bottom to see whether all of my seams are straight. I don't have anything against the Kappas, or the Thetas, or the Tri-Delts, or anybody, but nobody is going to pierce my ears, or get me into those funny-looking shoes, or take me out of jeans, or make me any different than what I am. So, why don't you wait around for my roommate, Miss Pout-mouth, she'd love to pierce her ears and everything else she has."

Peggy Sue was turning beet red. It had been her idea to make Devlin over, to get her sisters to revise their opinion that this most beautiful girl in the freshman class at UT was also hopeless. She had put herself on the line. "I will get her to shape up," she had promised them all. "What are you going to do, Devlin? You can't live here without belonging to a sorority."

Devlin hitched up her jeans and smiled. "Who says? I'm going out to get drunk, and then I'm going to have the damn gooiest taco that God invented, and get it all over my mouth, and my jeans, and then I'm going to throw up."

43

Peggy Sue ran, and never returned.

For the next two months Devlin dutifully attended classes. More often than not, Devlin overslept, and on those days she threw a raincoat over her naked body and raced to class, sleepy-eyed and unconcerned.

Devlin consumed more than her share of Lone Star beer each night at local honky tonks where she danced the Cotton-eyed Joe, and palled around with the campus radicals and the rowdies who seldom if ever went to class. Devlin's red Eldorado was a fixture at Barton Springs, where she and her friends would go to swim day or night. She was one of the pranksters who climbed the Texas Tower and painted the top of it black and blue. Devlin was a ringleader of the group that placed alligators in the East Fountain.

Her instructors were dismayed. She never did her assignments, but somehow managed to get by. The fraternity boys, usually only attentive to sorority girls, were almost impossible to remove from her presence. The jocks, the radicals, the rowdies crowded around her endlessly, looking for some sign that any one of them pleased her.

The truth was that nothing about UT pleased her.

In the quiet of the night, alone in her room (Lindsey Verhalen, the pouty brunette, had moved out weeks earlier), Devlin lay awake more often than not. School wasn't for her. Why had her father refused to allow her to do what she wanted? Why had he insisted that she be someone she couldn't be—a lady? Devlin thought endlessly about her room at home in Houston, and about her being a fish out of water at UT. She wasn't meant for college, and the thing she was meant for was unattainable. In the many phone calls with her father, Devlin found him absolutely unmovable.

She had been in school for seventy-eight days, and fourteen hours. It would soon be Thanksgiving, and the others could look forward to the excitement of the football game of the year, Texas versus the Aggies. Devlin hated the Aggies, and she hated the Longhorns, and she hated the fact that she hated everything, and she was so miserable that she could die.

It was three in the morning, and as Devlin figured it, there would be only another one thousand and thirty-four days until she graduated, or twenty-four thousand eight hundred and sixteen hours . . . and by the time Devlin started the mental arithmetic for the number of minutes *that* meant, she was asleep.

44

THE DORMS were a beehive of activity on Thanksgiving morning. From outside her door, Devlin could hear the whoops and shouts of girls going to and from the bathroom. Shouts could be heard of girls needing to borrow some special something to wear. Devlin sat on her bed, back to the wall, her long legs bent, as she cradled the white telephone on her lap, a legacy from her departed roommate. She bit her lip with determination and picked up the receiver to call home.

On the first and second ring, Devlin nearly hung up, but by the time she decided, it was answered and she heard her father's voice.

"Daddy . . . I wanted you to know that I'm coming home."

"Be happy to see you, Devlin, we're having Thanksgiving at around two o'clock."

"Daddy . . . you won't like what I have to say."

"Tell me why, little girl."

Devlin hedged, "Will John Travis be there?"

"Dunno, he may and he may not. He's free to come and go as he pleases. He knows he's been invited, but what he does with himself is a solemn mystery to me. Do you want to tell me your news now?"

"It'll wait."

"Okay, well, there'll be a surprise for you when you get home, someone . . . "

Devlin was interested, "Tell me *now*."

L.C. chuckled, "That'll wait too."

The conversation was over, and Devlin placed the phone on the night table beside her, took a deep breath, and continued with her packing. The news could wait till hell froze over. Devlin had been expelled from UT.

Last Saturday night Devlin had been part of a gang that went to the Armadillo, a huge barn of a nightclub on Barton Springs Road. The cavernous room, once an armory, would normally hold four or five hundred drinkers and dancers. This night, the weekend before the Aggie game, revelers had begun to gather a week ahead. Even the locals, the good old country boys, the radicals and the rowdies who were already there, made the Armadillo their pivotal place for a good time. A crowd of nearly a thousand pushed and shoved goodnaturedly at first, and then with a little more energy, until the interior became a solid mass, moving to the beat of the music.

Devlin got drunker than usual, danced more than usual, and fought off more busy hands than usual. Fights broke out to the left and right of her, but Devlin cheerfully ignored them. Later when tempers were really flaring, Devlin gathered up her group of seven. Somehow, in twenty minutes of frantic goodbyes, after last-minute kisses and swallows from proffered beer bottles, they all managed to get outside to the parking area. One of the girls was seduced into heading up to the top of Mount Bonnell. There, she and the fellow with her would discuss the meaning of life, meanwhile getting as much of it in the flesh as would be available in the back seat. Three others decided to go to Dirty's on the drag for hamburgers. Devlin had a fine idea.

"Jeb," she said slowly to her companion, an ex-Vietnam veteran, "do you have a gun?"

"Sure Devlin. I've got one, two, three, four. What do you want to do? We could catch a boat to Vietnam?"

"Where is it?"

"Vietnam? West, keep going west, and make a right turn at Australia."

"No, Jeb, just one of your guns. I've got an idea."

Jeb pointed Devlin in the direction of his trailer park home, and some minutes later he escorted her inside. Jeb quickly forgot what he was looking for, and instead surrounded Devlin with his arms and kisses. "Jeb," she insisted as she pushed him away, "that's not what we're here for."

"Devlin," he drooled, "I forgot. Why are we here?"

"Your gun, Jeb, your gun."

"Don't shoot me, Devlin, I just did what any red-blooded man would do." He rummaged furiously through a foot locker in the cramped interior. Out came khaki socks, a garrison belt, and finally a .45. He handed it gingerly to Devlin. "It saved my life, Devlin."

She looked at him questioningly.

He laughed, "I shot myself in the goddamn foot. Tell me, Devlin, are you gonna shoot Richard Nixon? We can drive to Washington in your car, and maybe you'll let me, you know . . . "

Devlin led him out of the trailer and to the Eldorado. "No, Jeb, something better. We want justice . . . Texas justice. Jeb, I'm going to kill five hundred cans of hairspray."

46

Jeb stumbled and muttered, "Good idea."

It was two o'clock in the morning when Devlin parked outside the Kappa house. She sat back on the top of the seat of the convertible and surveyed the street. It was quiet. Then she got out of the car and walked unsteadily up to the front of the building, holding the .45 at her side. She turned back to see if Jeb was still in the car. He was asleep on the seat. Shrugging, Devlin raised the pistol and, with both hands, squeezed off the first shot. The sound cannonaded and the recoil knocked her on her backside. A huge glass crash testified that she had hit something. Then, seated on the grass, her legs apart, Devlin squeezed off five more shots, each followed by a crash and a crescendo of screams. Lights went on all over the building. Devlin, seated on the lawn, roared with laughter. She turned as she heard the sound of the Eldorado starting. Jeb had made off with her car. Killing someone was one thing. Shooting up the Kappa house with the richest girls on campus was real trouble.

Minutes later the Austin police converged around Devlin's bemused figure, guns drawn, anticipating almost anything but what they found.

As Devlin drove down Guadalupe Street, the back seat and trunk full of her belongings, she ran smack into the revelry of Aggie and Longhorn fans, hanging out of maroon-and-white and orange-and-white-painted cars, respectively. The shouting, the blowing horns, the blaring of bugles and the "S" turns the cars made as they crisscrossed the streets nearly drove her frantic. It was a damn conspiracy on her last day in Austin. The ogling eyes, the ringing cowbells, the waving banners and the shouted sexual advances were unpleasant and embarrassing. She turned angry as Aggie fans circled their cars around her, preventing her passage. She would be sentenced to this terrible fate on her last day unless . . .

The unless was clear. Devlin gunned the Eldorado and pressed down on the horn. Turning the wheel violently, the Cadillac mounted the sidewalk. For five blocks, Devlin drove like a demon possessed, scattering pedestrians as they heard her coming their way. Finally, Devlin reached 15th Street, turned right and headed toward Interstate 290.

On the outskirts of Austin, Devlin stopped the car for a moment at the side of the road. She was hungry and she was angry. She wanted to cry but refused to allow herself to do it. Releasing the brake, she returned to the highway and began to gather speed. The wind whipping through her hair was a welcome diversion. The chill in the open convertible made everything almost bearable. Then as an afterthought, she fiddled with the radio and tried to find something that wasn't about the afternoon's football game.

She listened to a gospel station as she drove.

Now the Eldorado was past the towns of Hempstead and Waller, and

Devlin could see the outskirts of Houston in the distance, across the huge flat plain. It was a brilliant fall day, and the sunlight danced on the downtown towers. The population of Houston had grown enormously, even in Devlin's lifetime. People said that by the year 2000, Houston would be the biggest city in the world. Devlin wasn't sure of that, but she was certain when she got home she would find more trouble than the city had stirred up to date. The radio continued, "Sweet Jesus." Then the program was interrupted for the score at the Aggie game. Football, Devlin reflected, was as important as God in Texas. But *nothing* could save her.

Bell Park in the Montrose section of Houston with its gas lights, two fountains, running stream and bridges is a beautiful reminder of the impressive past of the neighborhood and its former elegance. In 1969 it no longer had its former luster. The huge Palladian mansions, the brick-fronted Georgian houses that distinguished Montrose Boulevard and made the wide, palm-lined avenue one of style and reputation, existed no longer.

In the 1920s these mansions were the homes of lumber, cotton, and banking millionaires,.who vied with each other in building grandiose dwellings. It was at that time, in the year 1925, when L.C. Younger was not even thirty, that he built the elegant, white brick mansion that he still occupied. It had a two-story facade with white stone columns. Inside, there was a spacious central hall with a tile floor. A carved wood banister led from the hall in a sweeping curve to the upper floor. On the ceiling of the two-story hallway was an enormous skylight, decorated with colored glass, made to form the shape of a tugboat. The bright Houston light flooded the room with the rainbow-colored symbol of L.C.'s success.

Even though the Montrose section lost its reputation by the start of World War II, L.C. refused to move. Most Montrose mansions were torn down and replaced by gas stations, bars, and small apartment houses. Montrose turned into a counterpart of New York's Greenwich Village, full of odd-looking and improbably dressed characters. The new and exclusive section of River Oaks had long since become the elegant place in Houston, with its large estates, rolling lawns, protective plantings, and newly constructed mansions. River Oaks had its own country club and shopping area and, most important, its very carefully controlled list of residents.

Now, at one-thirty, Thanksgiving day, the red Eldorado slipped under the side portico of the house on Montrose, and Devlin bounded out. Girding herself for the onslaught, she took the precaution of entering from the screened side door. At the top of the three steps was the huge old-fashioned kitchen that she had loved as a child. Alma was bending in front of the oven.

"Alma, *que pasa?* What's for dinner?"

The heavyset woman stood up quickly and took Devlin in her arms. "Señorita, now it is really Thanksgiving." She turned to call into the pantry, "Manuel, come quickly. Señorita Devlin is back home."

A dark-jacketed man came into the kitchen, his face full of smiles. "You will stay with us a long time?"

"If my daddy will let me, Manuel." Devlin walked to the oven, and carefully opened the doors. She smiled as she saw the turkey, the pies, the candied potatoes. "I can't wait, Alma." She asked seriously, "Who is coming for dinner?"

"I don't know, señorita; your brother and another person. Señor Younger didn't say who."

"Will there be enough to eat?" Devlin laughed.

Manuel smiled, "Señorita, there is always enough to eat when you are in the house."

"That is true, señorita," Alma declared solemnly. "You make the sun shine here."

Devlin laughed. "Don't tell John Travis, he's convinced that it's him." She turned and opened the door of the pantry. In a gesture that was practiced, she pulled out a Coke and in the same movement opened the bottle on an extended nail, and pulled on a warm swig of the sweet beverage. "I've got to get my courage up, Alma."

The cook looked at her with curiosity. "I'll tell you about it later. I have my stuff in the car, but it can wait till after dinner." Still brandishing the Coke, Devlin swung through the kitchen door to the hallway and walked across the center hall to where she knew her father would be, his study.

It was a clutter of souvenirs, photos, ship models, and newspaper clippings. A huge central table was piled high with books and magazines, and against the wall were a half dozen files and an ancient black safe. Against the wall, between the windows that faced on Montrose, L.C. Younger sat behind a huge rolltop desk. As Devlin walked in, she saw her father peering intently at an equipment catalog.

"You buying a new toy, L.C.?" She looked at the photos, "I like those Briggs-Weaver diesel lifts, but I'd get me the diesel instead of the electric or LPG. They're more economical." Devlin nodded to herself, satisfied that her judgement was sound. Her father stared at her, unsmiling.

L.C. Younger at 69 was an immensely handsome man. He had a weatherbeaten face and long sinewy legs and arms. He looked more like a horse wrangler than either a sailor or a businessman. As he stood up to hug Devlin, there wasn't even the suspicion of fat in his lean hard body. Sun, wind, and the elements had sandpapered his face with fine lines. He had a challenging face, ruthless and sharply hawklike. His eyes were keen, piercing, and hard as carbon steel. Devlin's comments, intruding on his jealously held prerogatives, did not please him. Still, he smiled as he took her in his arms and embraced her. "What's your news?"

Devlin pulled herself away from him, "Later, L.C., why spoil a perfect day?" Before Devlin had to make any more conversation, Manuel appeared at the door and announced dinner. L.C. led Devlin across the hall. Devlin stood aside, looking at her father. He carried himself like a captain. He was the center of every group, the focus of every eye. She felt his firm grasp around her waist as he led her into the dining room, and she felt the thrill of being in his presence that she had always sensed. Yet, he had been the one to send her away, to refuse her admission to his own preserve, the only area she really hungered for, Black Diamond.

"Tell me about it now," he insisted as he sat at the head of the table.

"Only if you tell me who's coming," Devlin teased. The exchange was interrupted by the entrance of Devlin's mother and John Travis.

Vonnie Younger had once been beautiful. Even today, the evidence could still be seen. She was tall and slim, but her eyes were those of a sad and frightened woman. Whatever fire there had once been in Vonnie Younger was no more. The present held nothing for her; she simply was occupying space and passing time. Even her clothes said as much. She wore a no longer stylish pale pink chiffon dress with a tiny floral pattern. The length of the skirt was unfashionable. The matching pale satin T-strap shoes belonged to another era. Her hair was a curled bob of the 20s. Vonnie was a woman who had retreated into the past, and into her poetry. Devlin knew that her mother wrote a poem every day. Although she never read a single one aloud, nor had any member of the family ever seen one, Devlin was certain her poems were all her mother really cared about.

Vonnie approached Devlin and bent to kiss her. "Devlin, how good of you to come down from Austin for Thanksgiving. I'm sure you're making some handsome beau absolutely forlorn, but you've made your family happy."

Before Devlin could stand and return her mother's peck, Vonnie floated past and took her place at the foot of the table. John Travis spied his sister, "Devlin, you're looking like a grimey workhand. Don't you dress up for anything?"

Devlin sighed, "John Travis, how come you always know the right things to say to a lady?"

"I do know the right things to say to a lady, but for sure, you don't know the way to become one."

Devlin looked at her father, "Good old John Travis. It's always a holiday when I see you."

John Travis sat down silently. Devlin glowered at her older brother. His huge, hulking presence cast an unrelenting chill. As if in reproach to L.C.'s Western shirt and string tie, John Travis wore Eastern business clothes. There was nothing Texas about his attire. His inner resistance to his environment and his family made everything about him foreign and cold.

Devlin reflected that she had made a bad choice of a day to look for understanding and forgiveness from her father for her shortened career at UT. Finally Manuel broke the quiet as his wife opened the kitchen door for him. He carried a huge silver tray with the turkey. At the same time, as if by an unspoken signal, Alma quietly placed an open bottle of Coke at Devlin's place.

"Dammit, Devlin," John Travis sputtered, "don't you drink anything but that stuff?"

"I like it."

"Warm?"

"Why not?" She smiled. "That's the way it comes out of the cow, John Travis. Why don't you try it. It might just clear up your disposition, and maybe some of your adolescent pimples."

"What do you mean by that?" he asked menacingly.

"Why, John Travis, I can see you don't have pimples. All the world can see you don't have pimples, but you've got them in the worst place, inside."

"Damn you, Devlin."

Devlin laughed and lifted the bottle to her lips. There was a ring at the door. Devlin looked at the place set on the table beside her. L.C. interrupted. "Devlin, I want to tell you some news and I want to hear yours." Devlin nodded dully.

The door from the hall into the dining room opened, and Devlin let out a gasp of delight as she saw a Marine officer stand in the doorway. She instantly jumped out of her chair and raced to greet him. Shamelessly she grabbed him and kissed his face repeatedly.

"Whoa, Devlin," Tune Richards said, fending her off, "what the heck are you doing?"

"Tune, darlin' Tune, you're back from Vietnam, and look at all those medals," Devlin cried with extravagant pleasure. "L.C., what a wonderful surprise."

The Marine freed himself from Devlin's arms and walked to the head of the table. "L.C., happy Thanksgiving, and to you too, Mrs. Younger." Then he turned to John Travis. "John Travis, you sure are looking self-satisfied, and you haven't even eaten the turkey yet."

John Travis looked at the handsome blond-haired man with a mixture of anger and envy. "Lieutenant Tune Richards, United States Marines, how in hell can we still be winning the war without you in Vietnam?"

"The answer is we're not, but they don't want anyone with as much shrapnel in his leg as I have. They think it weighs down the boats."

Vonnie viewed Devlin's display of affection toward Tune with

51

curiosity. She smiled and pursed her lips to murmur a greeting, but it passed unnoticed in the midst of a conversation that she felt incapable of joining. It confused and embarrassed her. Unheard, she whispered, "Tune, it's good to have you back with us."

L.C. motioned to Tune to sit down. He seated himself next to Devlin, and she stared at him with such love and admiration that Tune blushed. "Devlin," he remonstrated, "eat your food." Dutifully Devlin turned away, but in between forkfuls, she peeked at him and grinned like a big and beautiful Cheshire cat.

Tune sat eating silently. His tall, athletic frame was superbly clothed in the Marine uniform, and his bright blue eyes and dimpled smile were devastating. He cast an eye at Devlin. She had grown into a young woman since last he had seen her, and he was conscious, very conscious, of how beautiful she had become.

L.C. returned to carving and refilled the plates of Devlin and Tune. Then he served himself, and after Manuel and Alma offered the side dishes, L.C. turned to Devlin. "Okay, Devlin, tell us the bad news."

Devlin gulped and proceeded to tell the story of her escapade at the UT. Tune smiled as he listened. "You really did that, Devlin?"

She was thrilled at his wonderment. Proudly she smirked, "Yep, didn't miss a shot."

Vonnie interrupted, "I don't like you playing with guns, Devlin. You might have hurt someone."

Devlin looked at her mother, who had already returned to her food. L.C. continued cutting his meat. Devlin took that as a good sign. "L.C., you need help at Black Diamond, and you know that I'm good at it. Is it a deal?"

"Devlin, you're gonna go to school," L.C. said forcefully.

"L.C. I can't stand those girls and I'm not cut out for that kind of thing. Besides they expelled me."

"Expelled, hell, I'll get you in any place I want."

Devlin was stirred with anger. "L.C., please, let me go to work for Black Diamond." She looked at Tune as if she had spoken too freely in front of a stranger.

L.C. put it to rest. "Tune is one of the family."

Devlin was near tears, "Please, L.C., give me a chance."

"The answer is no. John Travis is a disappointment." He looked at his son who stared back with a cold knife of hatred.

"Tune is going to take over," L.C. said quietly. "It's all set. He and I talked it over yesterday. He's gonna start on Monday. He's the man I want."

Devlin started to say something, then she turned to Tune, and her father, and then back to her plate as she began to eat mechanically. She continued eating in silence. Vonnie looked at her daughter. "Devlin, you're eating too fast."

John Travis wordlessly got up from the table, his face a mask of violent anger. His feelings about the man he faced, his father, were hopelessly mixed. John Travis had yearned for his father's recognition, but it had never come. He knew this ramrod of a man looked at him as lumpish and dumb. His father had despised him from the very beginning.

The sorrow and tragedy of his situation overwhelmed him. He turned to his father and shouted, "I hope you die, old man." The four of them stared at the back of the retreating figure. Moments went by before they returned to eating. Devlin lifted her Coke to take a drink; her eyes were filled with tears. They could hear the door slam as John Travis left for good.

7

SOME PEOPLE in Texas felt that the year 1969 was memorable because the Manned Spacecraft Center in Houston sent a man to the moon.

On the other hand, Houston society judged 1969 to be remarkable because of the marriage of John Travis Younger to the daughter of Melvin Jurdam, Harriet Jurdam, granddaughter of Big John Jurdam, founder of the Texas National Bank, and heiress to the Jurdam fortune.

That Melvin Jurdam, Harriet's father, was the sworn enemy of everything that walked with the name of Younger was a given fact. That Harriet Jurdam was exceedingly plain, fifty pounds overweight, given to hyperventilating and victim of a constant postnasal drip, added to the mystery. Harriet would not of her own sake have attracted many men, but her money *would*.

Texas has an honorable history of maiden ladies with fortunes who have been quite content to live out their lives unmarried, doing civic good for the community. Such a life had been expected of Harriet by her mother and father and the city of Houston.

In early December, less than three weeks after John Travis Younger walked out on Thanksgiving dinner at his home, cursing his father, the wedding between John Travis and Harriet Jurdam was scheduled to take place at St. John's Episcopal church. The family of the bride, and society in Houston, was given only one week's notice.

The church had never been so jammed. Melvin Jurdam's friends and business associates were obliged to attend. Despite their uncertainty whether it would be less painful for Melvin if they didn't, curiosity got the better of their wives. *They* wouldn't miss it. Many in Houston would have killed for a seat. It was the most unexpected event since the virgin birth of Jesus.

The reason for such speed was clear to anyone within whispering distance of the tale-teller. They said that John Travis Younger had gotten poor Harriet Jurdam pregnant, and he was doing the honorable thing by marrying one of the richest heiresses in all of Texas. Harriet's very best friend, pretty Sue Lingen, homecoming queen at UT five years earlier and thrice married herself, was waiting in the vestry along with the other bridesmaids. Sue Lingen was matron of honor and unofficial historian.

Even in the solemnity of church, Sue Lingen never stopped talking. Standing next to her was a woman who was fascinated by Houston, enchanted by the wedding of John Travis Younger to Harriet Jurdam, and riveted by everything that Sue Lingen had to say. Laureen Tuttle, her companion, was a reporter for the *New York Times* who just happened to be in Houston the day of the wedding. She met Sue Lingen at a cocktail party and, in the course of nonstop listening, became intrigued by the folkways of Houston. Laureen telephoned her editor and convinced him to let her stay an extra day to do a story about Houston society. With notable New York prejudice, her editor mumbled something about "What society?". Laureen bit her tongue, and she got permission.

It was noon on Saturday. The church was so packed that Houston matrons had difficulty breathing. Part of the draw was the belief that being left out would be a mortal sin. It would be a benchmark for all time—a way of keeping track, "three years after the Jurdam wedding." Equal in importance was the wonder at what Harriet Jurdam would look like as a bride. Would there be enough tulle and satin in all of Texas to cover her up? Could they make a veil opaque enough so that Harriet could look passable?

Then there were the men, young and old, who couldn't wait till they saw John Travis Younger in his morning coat. He would be a huge bulk, but more importantly, they wanted to see the man who had the nerve to impregnate Harriet Jurdam. Imagine, they said, sticking your dingus into *that*. Such a man might not be too picky, but he sure as hell was going to be rich.

Time was hanging heavy. The church continued to fill up. God only knew where the new arrivals were able to find a place to sit. It was now a half hour after the appointed time, and Sue Lingen was irrepressible. Laureen Tuttle listened and wrote.

"Now, the only sororities that are *anything* are Tri Delt, Kappa, and Chi Omega. I was a Kappa, and Harriet was a Kappa. Kappa takes only the pretty girls but they made an exception for Harriet, because of her mama, and her mama's mama. They were all Kappas."

"Now, if you're a man, do you have to go to the University of Texas too?" Laureen Tuttle inquired.

"The man . . . well, that helps a lot. The man needs to have money and power, and his family needs to be, well, like owning land is a big thing here. Of course you can go into ranching or what have you. Oil, of course, is the number one thing."

Laureen continued to note the answers. People on either side of the two of them were disturbed by her chatter, but Sue Lingen was irrepressible. She was so *proud* of Houston, and the reporter promised to put *her* name in the paper, a New York paper.

"Are there people whose reputations are so unsavory that they wouldn't be welcome into Houston society?"

"Why sure, take John Travis's father, L.C. Younger. Well, he's rightly rich, I guess, but he doesn't own any land, at least not that I know of, but he did things on the way up that nobody here in Houston can even talk about. I mean, he really *did* them."

"What kind of things?"

"I don't rightly know. They was before my time. I'm only twenty-two. I don't know too much about the port of Houston. Goodness knows, I've got enough trouble keeping track of the people who are in oil."

"Go on."

"Oh," she blurted, "I could go on for a day. Well, Harriet was a debutante, like all of us who are society, and she came out the same year I did."

"If you are in oil does this make you a member of Houston society?"

"No, money cannot buy you in at all. Money won't get it. It has to be family heritage, so to speak."

"Then you can do anything and still be in society, provided you're old family?"

"I guess so. That certainly doesn't apply to the Youngers. God knows who *they* are, cause my mommy and daddy have been trying to figure this out from the first we heard about it a week ago."

"Do you mean that all of this was arranged in a week?"

"Why certainly, they weren't going to let the poor little baby be born without a wedding. Would they now? You wouldn't do that, even in New York City, and we all know how *loose* you people are." Sue Lingen smiled and waved to friends all around.

In the master bedroom of the Melvin Jurdam house in River Oaks, a very tearful Harriet was still not fully dressed. Her mother and father, he in a frock coat and ascot, she in a pink organdy floorlength dress which Sakowitz had made for her in a rush, were angry. Their daughter, and fate, had conspired to make them a laughing stock.

"I thought you were a virgin, dammit," Jurdam spit.

"Daddy," Harriet cried, "this is not going to do you any good now. I used to be a virgin. There was only *one* man."

Martha was sitting on the bed smoking a cigarette, nervously flicking the nonexistent ash. Melvin turned to look at his wife. "Don't you give a damn?"

56

"Of course I do, darlin', but what the hell do you expect me to do? I'd like to reach in and tear that egg out by its roots, but I'm her mama, and I shouldn't think such dreadful thoughts."

Harriet flinched when she heard her mother.

"Do you know what the son-of-a-bitch had the nerve to demand . . . demand, mind you, not ask, not discuss . . ."

"You've been over it a thousand times, Melvin. You're a very rich man, and what difference does it make?"

"Dammit, a home here in River Oaks—that's nothing. Control over Harriet's trust funds, so he can invest them. He thinks he knows more about investing than I do. He wants that and he wants to be a vice-president of the bank. Hell, it'll be a disaster. Who knows what else he'll figure out."

Martha Jurdam sighed resignedly. This was not the first time she had heard her husband curse his fate. He hadn't stopped even to sleep. "Younger is a venomous name and a viperous family. You know all about them, don't you?"

"Yes, papa."

"L.C. Younger is bad blood. The whole family is."

"Papa," Harriet cried, spoiling what was left of her mascara. The black lines down her face made her appear ridiculous. "I've heard the last of your complaints. I'm not a particular beauty. You and I know that even with all your money, there aren't a lot of young men asking me to marry them, and dammit, I was the one to make myself pregnant, so I could get John Travis." Between sobs, she shouted, "He's not the prettiest man in the world, but he's a man."

They watched stunned as Harriet picked up her full skirts, lifted them high above her waist, showing her huge thighs, and the straps of her girdle. Before they could say anything, she lay down on the bed and raised her legs high above her head, against the wall. "I put my legs up in the air, against the wall for one whole hour after he did it to me, hoping that his itty-bitty sperm would get to my egg. I got myself seduced the night that I was the ripest. I took my temperature five times that day, and if John Travis is going to marry me because of my money, or because I'm knocked up with his baby, then I say, more power to him."

Harriet continued, her voice somewhat muffled by the weight of her body on her chest and her vocal chords. "Now, I don't want to hear another damn word. Mama, you get on your feet and help me to look pretty, and papa, you better mind your P's and Q's, because I'm carrying your only hope for immortality—your grandbaby. So shut up now, the both of you, and help me to get down from here."

Harriet lowered her immense body from the wall, where she had provided her parents with an extraordinary show-and-tell. She had clearly ended the conversation. Melvin Jurdam adjusted his tie with finality as Harriet's mother proceeded to tidy up her daughter.

Back in church, the wedding party was hot and irritable. Laureen Tuttle was overjoyed that she had stayed in Houston. Her pencil was flying with the flood of information that Sue Lingen continued to provide.

"Well, there's such a thing as cafe society, but that isn't your real Houston society at all. Dallas has *that* kind of people, but not Houston."

"What's the difference?" Laureen demanded, looking around at the overdressed group in church.

"Sakowitz, naturally," Sue Lingen answered as if she heard the question. "Aren't they beautiful? They have Neiman Marcus in Dallas, but I consider their things trashy by comparison. You were asking about cafe society, well, those are the fast crowd, the ones who travel all over, and make a big show of their money, and buy outrageous things."

"Like at the opening of the Shamrock Hotel?"

"Well, yes. My mamma said they had some movie stars there and of course she went, because it's so much fun, and Glenn McCarthy is such a remarkable man. But now Houston is really going places. Those of us in society really consider that sort of thing showy. Did I ever tell you about Kinkaid? I think that's Houston's and, I guess, Texas's finest school. You've got to go to Kinkaid before you go to the University of Texas."

Laureen shook her head. "Does anybody go north?"

"You mean to Chicago or St. Louis? No, I don't think so."

Sue Lingen gushed on. "The real leader of society is a wonderful woman named Ima Hogg."

"*What?*"

"Oh yes. Didn't you know?"

"No," Laureen tried to explain, "what I mean is that her real name? Who would name a person *Ima Hogg?*"

Sue Lingen replied seriously, "Her mama who was Sarah Stinson, 'cept they called her Sallie, and her daddy James Stephen. But her daddy named her after the heroine in a poem that was written by her uncle, Thomas Elisha. Folks always call her Miss Ima. She's real musical. Taught piano, did you know that? She built us a symphony orchestra and everything."

Laureen was insistent. "But *Ima*, you know how that sounds. Maybe you're mispronouncing it. Maybe it's *Eema.*"

Sue Lingen was indignant. "We know how to pronounce our own names here in Houston, Laureen. I would consider it a favor if you let us pronounce our Texas names the Texas way. We don't try and interfere with the way you pronounce your New York City names. You can do that any darn way you want to."

In a small room adjacent to the main entrance of the church, John Travis sat with his best man, Troy L. Davis. Young Davis, who was a crony from as far back as the days in the school in San Antonio, had been John Travis's devoted acolyte then, and had continued with him during

58

his short and inglorious career at Rice as one of his merry band. Now he was nervous; he paced and smoked cigarette after cigarette.

"Christ, John Travis—you're sitting cool as a cucumber. This here wedding is not about to happen. I kid you not. Buddy, it's going up the flue. Her daddy hates your guts, and I'll bet they ain't gonna let her marry you."

The prospective groom sat in a comfortable stuffed chair. He filled it out handily. Smiling, he paused from sipping a Dr. Pepper and smiled. "She'll be here." He considered other matters and attacked them. "Troy, we should talk about the subdivisions I'm planning. I'm sure as hell going to want to start construction as soon as Harriet's property is legally mine. I want to see the architectural designs in six days. Don't take any delaying shit from anybody. We're talking muscle. I'm going to be a big man at the bank, and I can throw my weight around pretty good."

Troy shook his head ruefully, "It'll never happen."

"You mean the subdivision?"

"Yeah, that . . . and the marriage."

"Hell, you still don't know me very well." He laughed and sipped at his drink. "I thought that old man Jurdam might get a little antsy on this whole deal, so I got Harriet to make up a little story about how she was the one who wanted to get pregnant, and how she tricked me."

Troy was speechless. "Why the hell would she say that?"

"Simple . . . cause I happen to be as good in the saddle as my old man, better 'n him, according to some of the same whores we fucked . . . and poor little Harriet . . . sweet, ugly old Harriet and I have been fucking for the last twelve months, every day and in every way. I've got to tell you, Troy, that old girl just loves it . . . and I don't think there's another stud in Texas who can do the things to her that I can. I told her, 'Harriet, honey, you and me better marry, least I take my business someplace else.' So, Troy, I figured out a story for her to tell her folks."

John Travis smiled broadly. His best man burst out laughing. "You mean she's not pregnant?"

John Travis concluded, "Not as far as I know, unless her daddy fucked her too. Just sit yourself down and have a Dr. Pepper. She'll be coming along right soon."

In fifteen minutes, the organist was instructed to play the processional. John Travis and his best man walked reverently down the long aisle of St. John the Divine, to the unbelieving stares of three hundred guests, and the poorly disguised grins and titters from the ushers and bridesmaids. Moments later, as John Travis waited solemnly, Melvin Jurdam escorted his huge daughter Harriet down the aisle. Harriet smiled happily. She got just what she wanted.

If anyone had told Devlin she would be in a floorlength, white crêpe de chine dress with bare shoulders, sporting a dab of Arpège perfume down her décolletage, she would have given that forecaster a very hearty laugh. But now she leaned forward, feeling Tune's body as they danced in the Continental Room of the Shamrock Hilton on Christmas Eve.

Others on the dance floor, older than they, paused to watch the fairy-tale couple. Devlin's ginger curls, her glowing face, and her deep green eyes made her look like everyone's dream of a Texas beauty. Tune looked like the perfect prince.

Devlin was more beautiful than a nineteen-year-old had a right to be. Tonight was her birthday, and as with every other night since Thanksgiving, she was spending it with Tune. It had been Thanksgiving when Devlin discovered her own sexuality. She had long forgiven herself her continued virginity. The girls at Kinkaid and at UT were led to believe that there were certain men on whom Devlin had bestowed sexual favors. It was a conscious deception to avoid another instance of her being different. There had been no men.

Devlin's untouched virginity was obviously not for a lack of young men interested in her. It was not even due to her inability to recognize a potentially friendly and caring lover. It was simply that Devlin never thought about it at all, or if she did, she considered that there were so many other things that were more important, more interesting, and more agreeable. Surely Devlin had no possibility of comparing, since she was completely untried.

But she did know other things. She rode like the wind, a daredevil on a horse. She drove any car with studied casualness, one hand on the wheel, with a sure eye for speed and distance and a willingness to test herself against good or bad fortune.

Lust for a man's body, the craving which typified many of the girls she knew, was unknown to her. Even the exploration of one's own body that she knew occupied other girls in the privacy of the shower, or in bed in the darkness of the night, was an activity that Devlin didn't even consider. When she looked at her body, it was something that was *there*. Nothing more. It was, in her view, neither remarkable nor appealing. She had the insight of an unformed child, and felt uncomfortable with the notion of becoming a woman, and so she resisted strenuously all evidence to that effect.

To say that Devlin did things like a man would have been wrong. It would have been closer to the truth to say that Devlin did all these things like herself. Devlin was of a new breed. She was not man, nor woman, nor man-woman. She showed the courage and constancy that men associate with themselves, never women. At the same time she was a woman-in-waiting—a girl on the verge of becoming.

The key to Devlin's heart was available to no one until the moment that Tune appeared that Thanksgiving Day at the Younger house. At that moment, Devlin understood that she had been waiting all this time for Tune.

60

That Thanksgiving Day the two of them sat together late into the afternoon. Somehow the entire household had vanished. They talked animatedly, seated on the couch in the old-fashioned living room. Devlin took Tune's hands in hers for a moment. Their warmth and sexuality was something Tune never expected. Tune had marveled to himself, seeing Devlin after so long, when he was attacked by the butterflies of her kisses as she rushed to greet him. He realized that he really didn't know her anymore. She stood tall, formed, incredibly female and beautiful.

"Tune, you don't know how I missed you."

He laughed, "You didn't write, you didn't send a snapshot, and you didn't knit me a sweater. How come you can say you missed me?"

Devlin smiled. "Come on now, you are being dumb or failin' to understand a simple 'down home' girl on purpose. I didn't miss you while you were away. I miss you now, for all the times I could have been with you when you were away."

"You mean if you hadn't seen me now, then you wouldn't give a damn about me at all."

"That's the ticket. You're not so dumb after all."

"Devlin," he said seriously, "what are you planning to do?"

She was silent for a moment. The holiday afternoon was coming to a close. The servants had disappeared, and there were no lights in the darkening shadows of the house. "Tune, if I sound brazen, please try and understand. I've really been waiting for you . . . oh, how I've been waiting for you. You can't ever know. Tune, I've never been with a man. I know that may surprise you. It's not modern, and you've been all over and seen so much . . . but what I want to do now is take you by the hand, and lead you up the stairs to my bedroom . . . and I want to close the door and I want to undress you, so I can admire your fine body. I want to look at it, and touch it, and taste it with my lips. I want to rough up your hair, and feel every warm and dark place on you. Then, I want you to take my clothes off and I want to lie with you, and have you hold me for a little while to take away my fears, because I have them. I'm talking in a way that I never thought Devlin Younger could talk over a life time . . . and when I'm calm, and you've kissed me and held me against your fine body, I want you to show me everything that I have to know to please a man."

Devlin's green eyes shone mysteriously in the dark as they gazed into Tune's. Without another word, she stood up, her hand in his, and led him from the living room up the huge marble staircase to the second floor. There were no lights in the house, nothing to disturb Tune's concentration on the electricity of her touch and the sweet smell of her breath as she nervously held him close to her. The two of them walked to her bedroom door and she opened it. Devlin stepped inside and gently led Tune into the dark. She reached behind her and turned the lock,

61

and came slowly into his arms. As she pressed herself against him, she felt his excitement, and it made her breath come deeper and faster.

Stepping back, Devlin proceeded to undress Tune, surely and quietly. As she removed his clothing her hands played on his skin.

Naked, Tune reached down and lifted Devlin in his arms, and carried her gently over to the bed. He lay down alongside her and held her to him, and then he proceeded to undress her.

Devlin, for all her courage, lay rigid and uncertain. As she felt the touch of Tune's smooth fingers outline the crease of her mouth, and felt him kiss the softness of her neck and the gentle swell of her breasts, Devlin sighed deeply. Her entire body relaxed and opened to him.

Slowly Tune's hands began to explore the tiny curves, the back of her legs, the inside of her thighs. Softly and sweetly Tune kissed her shoulders and her nipples. Slowly, ever so slowly, he began to caress and skillfully touch the soft tender place between her legs.

Devlin opened her eyes and smiled at the face above her.

"Now, Tune . . . do it now."

GIROUX FRÈRES were merchant bankers whose position on Wall Street was unassailably at the top. Former Secretaries of the Treasury, Supreme Court justices and one ex-Vice President were members of the prestigious partnership. It was one of the oldest such institutions, and it was steeped in the mythic lore of the financial center. The building it was housed in was constructed in 1885. The partners had no private offices, no secretaries, and no chrome and leather desk accessories to bring the antique furniture into the twentieth century.

Claude Giroux, its most senior partner, was a man in his late forties, tall, gray-haired, and dressed in the best tradition of the consummate English banker: Saville Row suit, Turnbull and Asser shirt, Sulka tie, and Lobb shoes. Furthermore, he wore, invisibly, his estate in Tuxedo Park, his handsome daughters who went to Miss Porter's, and a wife who was Chairwoman of the most important New York charities.

Giroux Frères specialized in changing the face of business by mergers and public underwriting. The profits of these undertakings were almost immoral, since in every instance, at the end of the line, the public had to pay a huge premium for the right to own a piece of each of these new enterprises. If the new company prospered, it would be in the market to take over other companies. If it failed, then Giroux Frères could convince someone else to take over the failed enterprise. It was a function as coldblooded as packaging meats: Every part of the animal served as food for someone, and the merchant banker was chief butcher in the abattoir.

Claude Giroux was a man who believed in ideas, and one of the bright young men hidden in a dark corner of his office had put together an analysis of new opportunities in the southwestern Sun Belt. The port of Houston was singled out for special consideration. The research selected the Black Diamond Harbor Company as uniquely situated to provide this extraordinary business opportunity. Acting quickly, Claude Giroux had reached L.C. Younger and fixed an appointment in Houston.

Claude considered himself a master in dealing with individuals who had built their own businesses, whose egos had to be served, and who finally could be convinced, after an elaborate and painstaking campaign, to sell their businesses to the public. Their net reward was retirement with tens of millions of dollars, a liquid estate, and the prestige of an announcement in the *Wall Street Journal* that the transaction was "facilitated through the efforts of Giroux Frères."

Claude Giroux had never been in Texas before. He frequently said to himself, thank God, he didn't have to. Even though many of the mergers and banking enterprises that Giroux Frères arranged, dealt in Texas oil and petrochemicals, Claude Giroux made it a practice to stray no further from Wall Street than he had to. In addition to the folders on L.C. Younger and Black Diamond, which he had in his briefcase, he had asked a junior assistant to compile data on Houston and its relationship to its sister city, Dallas. He realized he might need a smattering of this information to satisfy local prejudices and appeal to hometown fervor.

As he sat on the front seat of the United flight, he scanned the report. The overzealous young man had headed the document with a quote from a nineteenth-century visitor to Houston. "Try to remember, Hell and Houston both begin with an 'H'."

Dallas, the report continued, has four seasons: summer, winter, and something different. Houston has two, the beginning of summer and the end. Houston's humidity, it stated, is capable of destroying metal, plastics, and one's soul.

Dallas is a city run by bankers who understand the nature of the world and recognize Copernicus, Galileo, and the law of gravity. On the other hand, it stated, Houston is a city run by lawyers with a shifty eye and hand who can turn words and facts inside out, as easily as turning a contract upside down, thus deriving new meaning for the hieroglyphics, according to need. Houston has no city zoning—a taco stand can be built next to a church.

The report talked about Houston's phenomenal growth, its population mushrooming. By the middle of the next century, Houston, it stated, would be one of the four largest and most important cities in the world. Then, to complete the report, which went on for pages, there was a list of statistics that compared Houston to Dallas. Houston, it reported, outdistanced Dallas in the number of "adult" bookstores, exterminators, victims of venereal disease, beauty salons, welfare recipients, murders, traffic deaths, and funeral parlors. Dallas had more parks, furriers, Rolls-Royces, private clubs, health food stores, and police officers with college educations.

64

Claude Giroux was not amused. He assured himself of one thing—
the young comedian who prepared the report had no value to Giroux
Frères. He would be fired as soon as Claude found a telephone.

The trip in a limousine from the Houston Intercontinental Airport
was interminable. Grudgingly he admitted that the airport was spanking
new and immense. What troubled Giroux was that he was away from the
familiar sights and sounds of New York City and Westchester.

He checked into the Warwick Hotel. His secretary had been instructed to find him a hotel that would be comfortable and conservative.
The Warwick, refurbished and redecorated twice since its first incarna-
tion on the outskirts of Houston forty years ago, was now an island of
green in the city that grew around it. On his arrival he collected a series
of messages at the desk. Then as he walked to the elevator he saw a tall
figure in cowboy clothes sitting in the lobby. The man stared at him. The
moment he walked into his suite, the telephone rang.

"I'm in the lobby," the voice said, "I saw you. Okay if I come up now
and get this thing over?"

Giroux flicked his thoughts to the tall, wiry cowboy he had seen in the
lobby. He shook his head in wonderment. Someone should have put a
photo of L.C. Younger in with all the other research. "Of course, Mr.
Younger. I'm pleased that we could see each other so promptly. The
suite is 901."

Without another word, the phone clicked dead, and before Claude
Giroux could prepare himself, the bellman deposited his luggage, and as
he opened the door to leave, L.C. Younger stood at the doorway.

Giroux was stunned. He knew that the man he faced was almost
seventy years old, but he had the face of a man much younger. When he
shook L.C.'s hand, he was struck by its remarkable strength. Electricity
seemed to pour out of his body. L.C. doffed his Stetson and placed it on
the coffee table. He wore a dark-gray Western suit with decorated
pockets and a gleaming pair of lizard boots. A black string tie was at his
neck, and as he sat down on the couch, Claude Giroux could see a huge,
handsomely tooled belt and silver buckle at his waist.

Caught thoroughly off balance, the New Yorker sat in the facing
armchair. He picked up a phone and started to dial room service.

"Don't bother calling for anything," L.C. commanded, "I won't be
here long."

Giroux sighed. He was on the verge of losing control of the situation.
Throughout a lifetime he had learned that the opening salvos were the
ones that determined the engagement. His carefully nurtured presentation had just been eliminated by his companion's refusal to deal in a
traditional way.

"Mr. Younger, I'm very grateful that you've taken the time out of
your busy day to see me."

L.C. looked disinterested. He stared around the living room of the suite as if checking it against something else in his mind. Giroux was very ill at ease.

"Can I order up some Jack Daniels, Mr. Younger? I know it's your favorite bourbon."

L.C. stared at him coldly. "Yeah? What else do you know?"

"Well, Mr. Younger, our people have had an eye on you for some time. We are convinced that Texas is only just beginning to find its way in the world, and it's our conviction that Houston is the place to put our money."

L.C. listened.

"Now Texas has more of everything than any place in the Union—minerals, oil, timber, manufacturing, and climate. Dallas has been the center of commerce and banking for many years, but my guess is that in five or ten years from now, Dallas is just going to be another spot on the map, and Houston will become one of the world's greatest cities. We have experts in every field of endeavor in Giroux Frères . . ."

"Who the hell is 'Frères'?" L.C. interrupted.

Giroux smiled. "My family is French, and the word just means 'brothers'." Giroux smiled indulgently.

L.C. placed his cowboy boots on the coffee table. If Giroux were surprised or shocked, he showed no emotion. L.C. examined his face. He was testing.

"What do you want with me?"

"Well, Mr. Younger, we have visions of what kind of empire Houston can become, and we believe that you can help us, and in all humility, I believe that we can be of considerable help to you."

"I'm not interested," L.C. remarked tonelessly.

Giroux was shocked. "You haven't heard my proposal, Mr. Younger."

"I know what your proposal is, Giroux. You are looking to build a big damn public company, feeding off Texas, and Houston is right smack in the middle of it. It has the oil, and through me, it has the port. I'm sitting right at the top of the bottle, Giroux, I'm like a damn cork. I control what comes in, and what goes out, and with those big damn tankers that are being built, the railroads are going to be dirt, simple dirt as far as moving oil is concerned. We'll probably be able to move it for half . . ."

Giroux nodded. "You understand absolutely, Mr. Younger, but that would be just the beginning. It would be a service industry for all the commodities in Texas. We'd build refineries alongside the Houston Channel for the oil. We'd build warehouses and conversion plants for petrochemicals, and everybody who planted, or dug for even a turnip, would have to convert it and ship it through us."

"Who would own it, Giroux?"

"Why the public . . . but of course, Mr. Younger. You would have

66

enough stock to exercise control. Giroux Frères has the financial resources to accomplish this. I'm certain, Mr. Younger, that you would become one of the most important men in Texas in five years, and certainly one of the wealthiest."

L.C. stood up. "Thanks for your time. I don't like anybody looking over my shoulder, Giroux, and that's no offense to you as a person, with all your French ancestors. That goes for anybody."

Giroux jumped to his feet. "Mr. Younger, you haven't even heard half of what I have to propose."

L.C. was at the door. "I heard the worst part. The rest of it wouldn't convince me."

"Mr. Younger, please take my card. It has my office and home number on it."

"What should I do with that?"

"Mr. Younger, don't be abrupt. Just think about it."

"Thanks for the offer."

"Keep the card, Mr. Younger, and give it some thought."

L.C. looked exasperated, but tucked the card in his pocket and walked out of the suite. He had a sweet young thing at his apartment at the Rice, and there was no sense keeping the lucky girl waiting. L.C. waited at the elevator to ride down to the lobby. He tried to remember her name, but couldn't. All he remembered was that she had a very shapely bosom. The elevator arrived and L.C. walked to the rear and placed his Stetson over his crotch. He wasn't being polite to the ladies in the car, just careful about exposing his arousal which jutted insistently out of his tight-fitting cowboy pants.

Claude Giroux was livid. He had traveled two thousand miles, inconvenienced himself no end, and spent a total of five minutes with a man who failed to show him even the simplest degree of politeness. He swore softly to himself, something he had promised never to do, never to lose the ability to examine dispassionately each and every alternative, and conclude a transaction that was based on reason.

If Giroux Frères couldn't find an existing company to capitalize on, then surely it, and he, had the resources to create one. He swiftly looked through his briefcase. He hoped he would find an attachment which listed the names and backgrounds of companies and men who were competitors of Black Diamond. It was providentially there. List in hand he sat resignedly in a chair and picked up the phone. He began his calls.

The offices of the Black Diamond Harbor Company had never moved from the very first. Other companies, smaller than Black Diamond, had moved their headquarters away from the channel to one of the showy new downtown buildings. L.C. had never wanted to be too far away to see the men, machines, and the work that Black Diamond did. The antiquated offices were on the second floor of a sprawling shed which had long ago lost its usefulness in storing merchandise. The immense corrugated metal frame was rusted and stained. In summer, it sopped up the sun's fierce heat, and in the winter it was bone-chilling cold. During the early days, an open or closed window was the only answer to the vagaries of the weather.

A huge open space with partitions that separated the departments was the main office of the company. In deference to 1970, L.C. had installed insulation in the roof, and window air conditioners. None of those things helped very much. L.C.'s own office had not changed in the past forty years. The plasterboard walls, the warped, unpainted floors, and worn walnut furniture were as bare and unrelenting as he was.

This morning L.C. walked down the long corridor between the desks, down the rows of each department. The men and women seated there nodded and saluted him with the wave of a hand or the raise of a head. Once he had known each and every one of them, but that was a long time ago. Now he knew fewer and fewer, and he felt more and more remote from the living entity that he had nurtured for nearly a half century. Hiring and firing were under the control of his general manager, Captain Biff Stevens, a former tug captain who had served a long apprenticeship under him, and was hard-headed and disciplined. When L.C. opened the door to his office, he found Stevens sitting in the chair opposite his desk.

"L.C., got a minute?"

L.C. took off his coat and Stetson and hung them both on a stand behind his desk. He nodded.

"Tune Richards." It was a statement.

L.C. was alert. "What about him?"

"Now, L.C., I don't want you to fly off the handle . . . and I'm only saying this for your own good."

L.C. faced Stevens menacingly. "Spit it out."

The smaller man gulped, "Hell, L.C., I may be wrong, but I don't think he has it."

"Explain what you're telling me."

"Look, I know who he is, and what Tune means to you, but you're asking him to be everything Royce was, and then some. He's been here almost two months, and he's learning, and the men like him . . . the men like him too much. He jokes with them, and he drinks with them, and he's telling them war stories about how it was in Vietnam, and football stories, about how it was at SMU, and that's not going to move a damn boat on the channel or from here to the end of my bathtub."

"He's learning."

"Look, L.C., it's going to take him years to know enough about Black Diamond to make it work. Most of the stuff is in your head, and in mine. It's not on paper. It ain't in a football-play book, and it ain't in some damn military manual. It's in your gut. You've got to run this operation

68

knowing when and how to kick ass. Nobody ever gets fired in the Marine Corps, and everybody on the football field has to answer to the coach. Shit, L.C., there ain't no coach here. Tune just wants to be one of the boys."

"Just shut up."

Stevens was shocked. L.C. had never talked to him that way before. "I'm only telling you like it is," he muttered.

"It ain't that way. Tune Richards is the son of the man who was by my side for twenty years. Royce had more guts than any ten men. That man, Tune Richards, played football with broken bones, when he could hardly walk. Tune Richards is a damn hero in the U.S. Marines, and he's got the damn Silver Star and Purple Heart to prove it. That ain't shabby. Don't you tell me what the man is good for. If you don't like it, get the hell out."

Stevens sat silent, cursing the first words that he said, angry that he had even laid himself open to L.C.'s wrath.

"And what's more . . . that man, Tune Richards, is going to be my son-in-law, and marry the most precious thing in the world to me."

Stevens smiled. The conversation had gotten back to personal matters, and the storm had passed. He had his chance to reverse the damage he had done. He stood up and grinned. "Congratulations, L.C. I'm sure glad. When is it going to happen?"

L.C. smiled. His mind had wiped the criticism away. "I don't know, soon, I hope. Just as soon as I let them both know that's what I have in mind."

L.C. grinned and reached into his desk drawer for a bottle and two glasses. Stevens saw the gleam in his eye. Everything would be the same as before, except he would have to find a way to nurse Tune Richards along, if Tune was ever going to act like the boss, that is, when L.C. stepped down. Stevens smiled to himself as he held the glass for L.C.'s steady pouring. That might not be for a hundred years, and that was okay by Biff Stevens.

Vonnie Younger had no idea what caused her to pick up a copy of the *Houston Journal* that morning. It had never been her habit to pay any attention to the news of the world nor of Houston itself. That would have disturbed the self-preoccupation which filled her life. Hidden in a small paragraph about local events was an item which stated that Gardner Land, the poet, was in Houston and would be reading his poetry at a gathering that afternoon. It gave the time and the address of Miss Jessica Hungerford, hostess for the occasion.

In her tiny apartment in Isabella Court, a Spanish-style relic on the outer fringe of downtown Houston, Jessica Hungerford made ready for the few people she expected. She managed to hide the unmade bed with a flowered spread she had inherited from someone whose name she had forgotten. She tidied up some of the overflow of magazines, rinsed out some of the glasses that dotted the tops of furniture, grasped a pile of bills on her desk, and in resignation threw them in the wastebasket. The dishes in the sink posed too big a problem for her to face. Jessica decided to let them remain as they were.

Jessica Hungerford was in her late fifties. Her hair was hennaed, and her full figure was usually wrapped in a huge shawl which she dramatically pulled around herself. The years had not dealt kindly with her, nor had life. A native of Houston, Jessica had gone to New York to become an actress. Somehow she managed for several years, never finding any work as an actress, but making a host of friends in the netherworld of New York's Greenwich Village. Back in Texas, Jessica became the Houston connection for her Village friends, and friends of theirs who passed through the city from time to time. She performed little favors for them, put them up, and somehow managed to eke out a living by being ready and helpful to all of their needs.

Most of Jessica's days and nights were spent on the phone. Although she callously tossed away many of her bills, she would pay Southwestern Bell. Each night, her New York friends phoned her. She sympathized with all their complaints, listened to their problems, and somehow this amateur psychotherapy helped them get through the long nights. For Jessica, it kept the connections alive and made her feel vital to the lives of her friends. Almost as important, it fed her constant gossip, which provided her with delightful tidbits of information that kept her interesting to talk to, both on the phone and in person.

When Vonnie Younger walked tentatively into Jessica's apartment, she was at the beginning of a great adventure. She seldom went out of the house, and this special trip was to hear a reading of a poet she had admired—the esthete Gardner Land.

Jessica made her way to the door. Her heavily rouged cheeks and obviously dyed red hair gave the impression that she was auditioning for the Lotte Lenya role in *Three Penny Opera*. Vonnie gazed around the room as she entered. Less than ten people were present. She wondered which of them was Gardner Land.

"So happy to see you, do come in," Jessica trilled.

Vonnie stood hesitantly at the door. "Where do I pay?"

"Oh there's no admission charge at all, my dear. All we ask, later on, is that each of the people at our little get-togethers make a contribution . . . for the food, and all." She smiled sweetly at the somewhat stupefied Vonnie Younger, who was staring wide-eyed around the room.

"How much is that?" Vonnie asked.

"Oh, whatever you can afford. Five or ten dollars . . . or two or three, if you haven't got that much."

Vonnie felt pressured to reply, "Oh, I want to pay the most. I'll pay ten dollars."

70

She reached in her bag for her change purse. Jessica took little interest in this forlorn figure, plain and colorless, and badly dressed in a shapeless sack. To Jessica, Vonnie looked like a pale imitation of a '20s film star like Vilma Banky or Thelma Todd who chose to go no further. As Vonnie looked through her handbag, searching for her purse, she muttered, "I'm Vonnie Younger . . . Vonnie Moore Younger . . . and I love Mr. Land's poetry."

Vonnie finally located her very full purse and gave Jessica a ten-dollar bill from a large roll of bills. Jessica renewed her interest as she folded the money, placing it down the front of her bosom. "Would you like to meet our guest of honor?"

Vonnie nodded violently, as if anything short of excess might be unresponsive. Jessica took her cold hand and led her into the middle of the circle of men and women.

"Gardner, I want you to meet Vonnie. She's an old friend of mine, and I want you to be particularly nice to her. She *adores* your poetry, and you two will have a great deal to talk about."

Gardner was in his late twenties, but he looked even more boyish. His hair was curly, and he wore it excessively long. He was dressed in a silk shirt, open to his belt, long velvet knickers, black stockings, and patent leather pumps. He moved daintily, with a pursed mouth and fluttering hands.

"Dear lady, I can't tell you how much I delight in meeting you. When Jessica invited me to Houston, she said that I would find many treats. Dear lady, I'm satisfied in knowing that one of them is you."

The afternoon sped for Vonnie Younger like Christmases and birthdays when she was a child. The profusion of sights and sounds bedazzled her. She thrilled to the mellifluous voice of Gardner Land, who read his poem "Xanadu" three times as a special treat for her. She revelled in listening to the bright chatter of her new-found friends, who didn't say a word directly to her. She sipped the cheap wine and devoured the cheese and crackers that had never tasted so good.

It didn't occur to Vonnie that these effusive young men were homosexuals, nor that Jessica was a lesbian, and that more than likely she was the sole heterosexual at the afternoon's reading. She only saw that these people were vibrant, exciting, fascinating, and like none of the conventional people she knew, or even the roughhewn types that L.C. occasionally brought to the house on Montrose.

The sight of Vonnie's full wallet encouraged Jessica to extraordinary lengths in making Vonnie welcome. Her demeanor inspired Gardner to ask about the ungainly woman, who stayed near him constantly and who stared at him with utter devotion. Gardner learned that the plain and unattractive visitor had money and might be a possible benefactor. He decided to use her infatuation for his benefit.

"You won't be offended if I call you Princess, will you?"

71

Vonnie flushed with embarrassment. "Why me?"

Gardner flung out his arms dramatically. "I was struck by a regal quality in you, by a remarkable charm and hauteur which I truly recognize. Princess, you seem to me, *souffrante* and *malheureusement triste*. Nothing would please me more than to see a tiny *sourire* on your lips. Will you smile for me?"

Vonnie didn't know what he was talking about. She did know that it was French, and that made things even more exciting. "Are you staying in Houston, Mr. Land?"

"Princess, how many times have I asked you to call me Gardner, pul-lease, *s'il vous plaît*, Gardner it must be."

Vonnie whispered "Gardner," and then she blushed.

"Houston? Alas, I don't know that I can afford to, sweet lady. I have just about run out of funds, and I will have to find some means of getting some in order to do anything."

"Oh, my."

"Yes, it's sad," he underscored, looking dolefully in her eyes. "Do you think that perhaps you might be of some help?"

"Oh yes, I have a great deal of money, and I would so much like to help you Gardner. Sort of like being a patron of the arts. Would ten dollars help?"

The young man recoiled. "No, dear Princess, ten dollars wouldn't even begin to help me. I am staying here with Jessica, and if I were to remain in Houston, then I would want to find a place of my own, so I can continue to write, and also . . ." he added meaningfully, "so I can continue our chats and warm contact."

Gardner placed the back of his hand gently against Vonnie's cheek, and brushed it slowly back and forth. She reddened. Slowly, he edged her into a far corner, and he stood between her and the rest of the room, his back to it. He continued his melodic talk. How wonderful it was that he and she had met. They were easily and simply soul mates. What a remarkable woman Vonnie was—and she wrote poetry too. How nice!

As Gardner talked, he gently insinuated his knee into the fold of Vonnie's dress, so that it pressed deeply into her crotch. Without changing his conversational tone, he moved his knee up and down in a firm and insistent massage. He continued his conversation, never stopping in his movements. Vonnie was petrified. She had never had a sexual encounter like this before. She reddened and tried to ignore his action. Could it be by accident? Perhaps it was. She had just met this young man hours ago. She looked over his shoulder and saw the half dozen others in the room in conversation. Then she shuddered as she felt Gardner's hand on her crotch. Vonnie didn't move. His silken hand moved up. The tip of his finger reached "that place." His finger delicately insinuated itself against the cloth of her dress and panties, and flirted on her clitoris, moving deliberately.

Gardner didn't stop his low conversation, talking softly and detachedly. Slowly, the sensation of his moving finger turned her into a mass of jelly, making her unable to do anything but close her eyes and to blank out everything but the incredible sensation. She was wet and hot, and her breath was coming low and long. She was afraid to open her eyes, for fear it was a dream, or worse, for fear that someone or everyone was watching.

Then it was too late. Vonnie, standing in the darkened corner of the room, found herself shaking from the orgasm. It had never happened before.

Her eyes remained tightly closed for minutes. She stood, unable to move as she felt his finger slip away and her dress fall into place. There was quiet for a moment, and then the voice of her companion.

"Princess, I do hope that I can count on your help. I so much would like to stay in Houston, and two hundred dollars would give me a nice start. Okay?" He smiled.

Minutes later Jessica Hungerford moved slowly toward her. Vonnie searched through her purse for her checkbook and pen. She had already ascertained that Gardner would accept a check, and that they would meet three days hence for lunch. By that time, Gardner would have found, he said, a convenient apartment where he could work, learn to love Houston, and listen to some of Vonnie's own poems.

Vonnie had just put her pen and checkbook away as Jessica arrived smiling. "Now, Vonnie, you've discovered us and we've discovered you. I want you here every week for one of my afternoons, and I want the two of us to get to know each other truly well. *Toi, cherie, tu es d'accord?*"

Vonnie nodded in quiet pleasure. Jessica smiled sweetly.

9

DURING the next month, L.C. busied himself with the kind of details at Black Diamond that he had long since delegated to others. He had the luck and the eye of the inspector, and each thing that he observed pleased him less.

The routine inspections he made of the tugs and barges, the freight handling equipment, the transit sheds and the terminal facilities showed him how lax everyone had become. That things had always been that way was not a matter L.C. chose to consider. Each observation of the tugs and barges showed up equipment that was faulty, repairs in need of making, and men who were not doing their job. Ashore on the stevedoring operation, he found men on the hold crew sleeping on the job, operations of the huge cranes imperiling the containers, equipment in need of maintenance. Each day brought new terrors to everyone at Black Diamond, with the exception of Tune.

Despite Captain Biff Stevens' keen observations of Tune, L.C. paid him no heed. There was one rule for Tune and another for the rest of his employees.

At home, L.C. dealt with Vonnie, Alma, and Manuel with stony silence punctuated with sharp bursts of temper. Only Devlin escaped his anger.

All this was L.C.'s reaction to the wedding of John Travis to the daughter of Melvin Jurdam. From the day of the announcement of the wedding, every trace of his son was eradicated from L.C.'s life. Every single one of John Travis' possessions was carried out to the backyard. He built a huge mound of his son's school books, souvenirs, old clothing, and childhood trophies. Then L.C. ordered that gasoline be poured on the pile. He lit a match, tossed it at the mound, and turned away. Every trace and memento of his only son was now consigned to oblivion. The last vision he would have of John Travis would be a flaming pyre.

During the same month, Tune and Devlin were together constantly. Only they were free of the contamination that L.C. felt touched everything in his life. And yet Devlin could not get over the feeling that she too was on trial and that L.C.'s patience with her was wearing thin.

Looking back on her recent life, Devlin remembered that the night of her birthday, dancing at the Shamrock, was the turning point. From that time on, something had changed. Less than a month following Christmas, Devlin and Tune lay in bed in Devlin's room. Devlin found herself humming a song she barely knew. At the time, she gave it no notice, but days later, she remembered the title of the tune she hummed. It was a Peggy Lee song, "Is This All There Is?"

That night in January as Devlin lay back in bed, she stared at the ceiling. Tune smoked a cigarette disinterestedly.

"Dev, I'm gonna be gone for about a week or ten days."

Devlin was silent.

"Did you hear what I said?"

"Yep, I did, Tune. You're going to be gone for a week or ten days." There was an edge to her voice.

"Don't you want to know where I'm going?"

"I know."

"How did you find out?"

"You told L.C. and he told me. You're going hunting with a bunch of the guys. Go ahead. Leave tonight."

Tune turned his head and looked across the bed. "What's bugging you? Didn't you like it?"

"Like what?" she asked, understanding exactly what he meant, but refusing to play his game.

"You know, *doing* it."

"Tune, I don't know whether I did or not. I'm so screwed up in my mind that I don't know whether I'm coming or going."

He sat up. "Right, that's one thing that I want to talk to you about, Devlin. You've got to grab hold of yourself. L.C. says that when you and I get married, if you want to go back to school here in Houston, that's okay, but *he'd* rather have you home making babies. Frankly, I would too."

Devlin bit her lip.

He stubbed out the cigarette. "You're thinking. I know you're thinking."

Devlin reached over to her bedside table and switched on the lamp. Tune blinked. "Why did you do that? I like it better in the dark."

"I don't," she almost shouted. "Let me ask you when you and L.C. started consulting about my future, all by yourselves?"

"What's got into you, Devlin? You know I work for L.C. and we talk from time to time."

"Did you tell him that you were *fucking* me?"

"Dev, you know *I* don't, and L.C. . . . Just don't use that kind of language, please. It doesn't become you."

"What *does*, you bastard? Having you and my father decide what I should do with my life, and you deciding how you're going to spend yours and what part of it I should play? Do I get a vote?"

"Of course you do, Dev. L.C. said that he'd give us any kind of house you wanted . . . in River Oaks or anyplace else for that matter, and you can decorate it any damn way you want, and spend as much money as you want. Christ, that's really one hell of a wedding present."

Devlin clenched her fists. "And *that's* the proposal that I get from you, Tune Richards?"

"What do you mean?"

"Is that how you ask me to marry you?"

"Oh, hell, Devlin, don't go acting that way. We both know that it would make L.C. the happiest man in the world, and we'd make a great couple. You didn't complain about us in the sack up till now."

"That's not enough Tune. I haven't the vaguest idea what other men are like. You were the first and the only one. I know I wasn't yours, but that's not what's bothering me, Tune. You and L.C. don't really know me very well. If you think that I'm planning to settle down and become L.C.'s pet babymaker, you're wrong. I'll tell you one thing, Tune, I finally realized how come no one disturbs us while we're making love, here in my own room and my own house. It never dawned on me, Tune, L.C. himself is pimping for me. He knew from the first what was going on. That goat can smell pussy at a thousand yards."

Tune recoiled at the phrase. He hadn't even given L.C.'s participation any thought, but when Devlin mentioned it, he knew she was right.

"What's wrong with your father wanting us to get together?"

"Tune, that's my point. Something is wrong with L.C. arranging our lives."

"Look, Devlin, I don't think that you're feeling good, and I don't think that this conversation is getting us anywhere. Why don't we just take a raincheck on it, and we'll talk about it tomorrow. Maybe you should talk to L.C.?"

"What for?" she cried. "Is he getting a piece of your action?"

Tune got out of bed. He furtively took a peek at Devlin's blazing green eyes as he began to dress. "You ought to be sorry you said something like that, Devlin. Tonight is only one night, and I think that we ought to make allowances for a lot of what we've been saying. You'll feel better about it tomorrow."

Tune zipped up his pants hurriedly. He wanted to leave as fast as if he were running from the sheriff. "Look, I'll give you a call tomorrow, and see how you feel."

Devlin didn't say a word as Tune closed the door behind him. A few moments later she put on a robe and slippers, went to her bathroom, and brushed her hair. She stared at her face in the mirror. For the first time she paid attention to her eyes. They seemed haunted. She didn't like that at all. Then she left her room to walk down the hall. It was almost eleven. She saw a light under the door of her mother's room. She knocked on the door and entered.

For over twenty years Vonnie Younger and L.C. had not shared the same bedroom. The night that L.C. had taken Vonnie by force and made her pregnant with Devlin had been the last time that L.C. entered her room.

Vonnie lay in her high four-poster bed. The room was dark except for a bed lamp with a tiny bulb attached to the backboard, barely illuminating a book she was reading. Devlin had never realized how protected her mother had made her room. Tall, lined drapes cut out every bit of street noise. Inside this cocoon was a slice of time harking back to the furnishings of her childhood. The chaise and the standing lamps, the chiffarobe had belonged to Vonnie's mother. Here, she was a child again in surroundings that were familiar and safe.

Vonnie, in a high-collared white lace nightgown, smiled at her daughter. "Darling . . . do come in. I'm so glad to see you."

Devlin was surprised at the warmth of her mother's greeting. She walked to her bedside and sat on the side of her bed. "Mother . . . I need your advice."

Vonnie patted Devlin's head as the young girl leaned her head against her shoulder. "Tune asked me to marry him, mother."

"I see." It was said thoughtfully, without any emotion.

"Mother, he's handsome as the dickens, and L.C. thinks the world of him, and all the girls have their eye on him, and I'm so confused."

"Do you love him, Devlin?"

"Mother, I don't know. Would I know if I did?"

Vonnie smiled. "I loved your father, in my own way, and *I* knew it . . . and everyone else that I ever spoke to or read about seemed to know it, Devlin. If you don't know it, my dear, the answer may be that you aren't in love."

"L.C. wants it, mother. He wants me and Tune to be together really bad."

"Devlin . . . you're my daughter too." There was pride in her voice.

"Mother . . ." Devlin trailed off, not sure of what to say. She hadn't ever had a serious talk with Vonnie in her life.

"I know that you think that I favored John Travis, and I expect that I did, Devlin. He was my first, and he was all that I had."

"There was L.C."

"Oh, Devlin, you know L.C. as well as I do. It wasn't only his other women. It was that Black Diamond was more important to him than anybody. I needed L.C. in a way that he couldn't understand. He's a strong man. I know that I'm weak and fearful. This room . . . you can see

77

I wouldn't really care if I never get out of it. But L.C. could have helped me. Little by little, I might have learned to see what it was like outside. But it wasn't to be, Devlin."

Devlin took her mother's hands in hers in a simple and involuntary move. They were cool and long and graceful. The skin was soft, like her own. Devlin wondered how much more of her mother there was in her. This was the first time that she had ever considered that.

"Do you think Tune will make me happy, mother?"

"Devlin, what ever happened to your great plans to work in Black Diamond, to make your way and prove yourself? You could do it."

"Mother, you know L.C."

"Devlin, I thought I knew you."

"But we never talked, mother, how could you know me. I never confided in you." Then Devlin blurted, "It was all my fault. I only looked to L.C., and you've been here right along."

"Devlin, I don't think that I've been a good mother to you. I'm not sure how good I was for John Travis either, but maybe tonight I can be a good friend. You're very special, Devlin. I admired you from afar, always afraid to come near you, and it was wrong. A mother shouldn't be afraid, but I was, and one of the things I admired about you, Devlin, was that you never showed fear—even though I could tell in your eyes from time to time that you were . . ."

Devlin looked up into her mother's face. "You could tell."

"Devlin," Vonnie concluded, "be afraid and do it anyway. I don't know if Tune is worthy of you, but I do know that if you are going to marry someone, it shouldn't be to please L.C. It should be to please yourself. I love you very much, Devlin. I'm afraid of so very much, and this is the first time that I haven't been afraid to say what I feel."

Vonnie couldn't see the tears in Devlin's eyes as she clasped her to her breast and held her. Neither of them said a word for a long time until Devlin broke the spell and kissed Vonnie's cheek. She took the book from her mother's hand and placed it carefully on the night table and smoothed the covers of the bed. Vonnie watched her beautiful green-eyed daughter silently as she felt the protective spell that Devlin cast over her. Vonnie had surprised herself with the advice she gave Devlin. It had just come out. She wondered how much of her new-found courage came from her own new life—the secret she now shared with Gardner Land.

Devlin opened the door to let herself out. Vonnie's voice trailed her, "Good luck, Devlin." She closed the door behind her, and strode briskly to her room. Devlin was busy for hours before she turned out her own light and set her alarm. By the time the house was awake, Devlin had made herself a cup of coffee and eaten a pair of sugar doughnuts that were well past their prime. The doughnuts tasted better than anything she had ever eaten in her life.

Devlin took a look around her at the familiar sights of a lifetime. On the kitchen table was a sealed envelope for L.C., with a note inside that said that she was leaving to learn more about herself. A second letter was on the table for Tune. It said virtually the same thing.

She knew that neither her father nor Tune would understand a word of it. They would only be angry, and that was okay. She felt better about everything in her life than she had ever felt before. She hadn't the vaguest idea of what was in store for her, only that she felt free. She had said her goodbyes to Vonnie last night or rather Vonnie had said them to her.

Devlin opened the kitchen door and viewed her gleaming red Eldorado loaded with everything she wanted to take. She hadn't packed much, but being unencumbered was another mark of her freedom. Whatever she really needed was inside her.

Devlin let herself out the kitchen door as she heard Alma approach. By the time the Mexican woman was in the kitchen, staring at the envelopes, Devlin was driving out onto Montrose, heading toward the freeway.

She smiled to herself as she switched on the radio. It was winter, chilly and damp. The radio said the temperature was forty-two. Devlin pressed the button on the dash and the canvas top began to retreat into its compartment. The rush of air against her face was invigorating. She had no idea where she was going, but certainly it wouldn't hurt to get there faster. She pulled out of the growing traffic as the white-yellow sun began to generate a bit of heat. Devlin found a rock station and settled down to driving. She drummed her hand to the music as the Eldorado pulled away from the traffic beginning to clog the freeway.

When Claude Giroux caught the flight from Houston to New York, he was both grateful to be returning to familiar territory, and disappointed at the angry results of his meeting with L.C. Younger. He was also hoping that he had come up with a solution, or rather that a solution had presented itself to him.

There was no way that Giroux could keep his presence in Houston secret. The financial marketplace is worldwide, and as given to gossip and the quick dissemination of rumor as a country club. Within three hours of his arrival, the phone began to ring in his suite with invitations from prominent financial and social leaders in Houston. Giroux sighed that he would have to invent excuses for his stay in Houston. He did not care to make it easier for his competition to finesse his carefully planned assault on the port of Houston. If L.C. Younger, his natural link to the port, would not participate, so be it. There would be others.

Giroux politely disengaged himself from invitations for dinners, lunches, and cocktail parties which would be instantly organized in his honor. His excuses were lame, but even if they had been more reasonable, he was sure that they would not be believed. Deception and guile were as much a part of Wall Street's advocacy of new projects as suspicion and skepticism were part of the marketplace. The simple reason for Giroux's unhappiness stemmed from contemptuous disdain that L.C. Younger had displayed toward him. He hadn't experienced that kind of rejection since he was a Harvard freshman and the upperclassmen had made life difficult for him. He was highly sensitive to the cavalier dismissal that Younger had shown not only toward his proposal, but to the 200-year-old tradition and importance of Giroux Frères.

He fended off all invitations with the singleminded purpose of finding a replacement in whom to place his trust. Within hours, the first of these possible alternatives was in his suite, and the first of a series of frustrating interviews took place. To all of them, the owners of ware-housing, towing, and stevedoring companies, he made proposals. To a man, each of them rejected the promise of future power and money, both gifts that Claude Giroux was quite capable of bestowing on them. None of this seemed to make any difference to the toughminded men who prided themselves on their independence. Claude Giroux was not the first Wall Street slicker who had wanted a slice of Texas.

Claude Giroux's dossier of research had balance sheets, profit and loss statements on each of the companies these men owned. Giroux made outright offers to several of them for control of their companies, at prices far in excess of their actual value, but there wasn't even a flicker of interest.

At the end of the second day, dining on room-service food, drinking room-service whiskey, Claude Giroux was about ready to give up his project. He was stymied at how to get a hand-hold on this great enterprise that he envisioned. In its history, Giroux Frères had accepted occasional losses in transactions that turned sour, along with huge profits in ones that matured. That went along with the investment of risk capital. What Giroux was not able to accept was his dismissal by Houston. That rankled.

The phone rang before he had a chance to call the transportation desk and arrange a flight out.

"Mr. Giroux . . . you don't know me, and I'm not on your list of people to talk to, but I think that I've got what you're looking for."

"Who is this?"

"Never mind for the minute, Mr. Giroux. I'm downstairs in the lobby, and I've been waiting for you to clear out the rubbish you've been talking to. Now, you've seen it all, and you'll be able to appreciate better what I have to offer. Okay to come up?"

"Yes," Giroux answered hesitantly at this unexpected encounter. He did not appreciate meeting people he didn't know, or going into discussions he was not prepared for.

80

"I know your suite number." The phone clicked off.

A knock on the door followed moments later. When Giroux opened it, a tall sandy-haired young man in his middle thirties stood before him. The man was dressed in work clothes: blue denims and heavy shoes. He didn't appear to be the sort of person with whom Giroux usually did business, and Giroux's face showed it. But there was something about the man's intense eyes that made Giroux think twice, and he decided to let him in.

"Glad you changed your mind." The man walked confidently into the suite and sat down in an armchair near the coffee table. He motioned to Giroux to take a seat. Giroux was mildly amused. His guest was taking charge.

"Mr. Giroux, I know why you're here, and who you talked to, and what you said and what you didn't say."

"How do you know?" Giroux asked testily.

"I'm in charge of the port, Mr. Giroux—not so that I own it, or anything like that, but nothing goes on from here to Galveston that goes against me, and nothing goes on that I don't know."

Giroux smiled at the arrogance of the young man but stopped when he saw his steely eyes.

"I'm secretary-treasurer of the Port and Seaman's Local, Mr. Giroux. The president and vice-president do what I tell them to, and the men do the same. When I say that I run the port, I mean it. You've been talking to the wrong men. You want to buy Gulf and Houston Towing? You want to pay less than the offer you made? I'll get it for you. Interested in getting the Houston Storage facilities—tanks and grain elevators? Just put the money up, and I'll see that you get it."

Giroux smiled. He reached for the bottle of scotch on the table and poured some for himself, then caught the eye of his companion and poured a second glass for him. He sipped it momentarily, then he stared at the young man. "You must have a name and some credentials. You talk awfully big."

"My name is John Dowie, Junior. I come from a family that once controlled all the shipping in the gulf. My father was the one who was king, until some time ago, when he lost everything, and he died penniless and very angry, Mr. Giroux."

"Angry at whom?"

"Angry at the first man you spoke to, Mr. Giroux. Angry enough to try and kill him, and angrier that he couldn't do it before he died."

"So you went about your career in the port the other way?"

"You're wrong, there is no other way. There's only one, and that's power. Now, the power is with the men who do the work. I knew what I was doing. I was biding my time, Mr. Giroux, waiting for something. I didn't know it was you. I wasn't filled in till a while ago, but it was you I was waiting for, and for you, there's only *me*."

Giroux smiled indulgently. "You seem like a serious and intelligent young man, Mr. Dowie, and I have no doubt that you run a very tight union local, but heading the kind of operation that I have in mind calls for organizational ability, proof of being able to build something out of nothing, and proof that the man can do the job. Now the men I talked to all run successful businesses. L.C. Younger, to my eternal displeasure, runs the port, or our researchers say that his control is substantial."

Dowie laughed. "Mr. Giroux, I'm proposing that you write down what you want accomplished in the first stroke. Which companies you want to buy and for how much. Don't be generous. The price will be right, and after I have the deals you want, then I expect you and your Wall Street friends will deposit the money in the bank to pay for it. I'll tell you how to gain control of every single thing in this port and on the gulf to make your dream come true. All I want is my share, and I want to run it."

"What do you think is your fair share?"

"I always let the customer decide, Mr. Giroux, and one of the important things that your association will do for our new company is to be free of any—I mean *any*—labor problems. You'll find that our employees will be happy to make our enterprise a successful and profitable one."

Giroux liked the sound of what he was hearing. He picked up a pad and pen and began to write. "You know that I'll have to check you out, Mr. Dowie, before anything really happens . . . and we'll have to have the financial controls we need. You sound very ambitious and that's fine . . . but order and experience are what makes these enterprises pan out in the end."

Dowie shook his head. "I know you and your family, Mr. Giroux. I've done my own checking. The founder of your line was as big a crook as ever went to jail, but he did it the smart way and the daring way. Money isn't everything, Mr. Giroux. Men are. I'm the man for you, and I'll prove it."

"Then when you have, what are your plans for L.C. Younger?"

Dowie laughed. "Mr. Giroux, not my plans, first *our* plans, and then my private ones—very private and very personal. Some day, when we have more time, I'll show you some pictures of my father, when he was in his prime, and then one which will disturb you, his dead body after his set-to with L.C. Younger and his gang at Black Diamond. Please keep writing, Mr. Giroux, and put down your private telephone number. I'll have news about the first deal in a few days' time."

Giroux didn't believe what he was hearing. He'd never heard such arrogance in his life, but something told him to test it. Many important discoveries that had made Giroux Frères very rich came from hard-heads with what sounded like very inflated ideas.

Furthermore, John Dowie knew more than any of Claude's friends on Wall Street. The first Giroux in America had been a man such as the one he was with—an ambitious, young working man with ideas and daring and a willingness to skirt the law.

John Dowie was right about that. He might be right about other things as well. Claude continued writing.

Moments later, in the hall, John Dowie smiled to himself. He had always known that the way to power was through the union. He had been helped along the way by some powerful people, and he had some debts to pay. The men who helped and guided his way to the top were not playing games, but he wasn't either.

They would help him and he would help them.

Then, he would help himself and settle a very old score.

•

Sue Lingen had been as pleased as punch at the story on the Jurdam wedding in the *New York Times*. Her name was mentioned three times, and even though there was no picture of her alone, she was included in the group photo that was taken at the wedding luncheon.

It was a shame, Sue Lingen thought, that the picture hadn't been in color, because she had looked wonderful in the pale blue picture hat that she wore and her Sakowitz dress with the underskirt of taffeta and overskirt of net, were very flattering. Still and all, even though some of the other people who were mentioned in the article were angry as bedbugs, Sue Lingen thought that it showed off Houston society to the snobby New York people, and proved once and for all that Texas could hold its own with any place.

Harriet Jurdam Younger was *sooo* happy. You could have cut her up sideways with a cake knife and served her for breakfast. When she and John Travis left to go on their honeymoon, Harriet threw her bridal bouquet from the top of the stairs, and guess who caught it. Sue Lingen caught it. It wasn't as if she *needed* a husband, or even wanted one. Three divorces had taught Sue Lingen that it's easier picking a dress than it is a husband, and one should take as much time finding a mate as one does in finding a dress at Sakowitz.

When Harriet and John Travis returned from their European honeymoon, Harriet was ecstatic. Somewhere along the way, she explained to her daddy, she became *un*pregnant, but he was not to worry. She was sure, she said, as it was the first time, it would be again. Harriet, never one to brag or put on airs, told Sue Lingen how grand it was at the very fancy Paris restaurants, and how even grander it was in the very fancy Paris hotels. John Travis, Sue Lingen concluded at the time, must be an absolute bull, because to hear Harriet Jurdam Younger tell it, he just *never* stopped wanting it, and after he had it, wanting it again. Sue Lingen shook her head in disbelief, and smiled sweetly at Harriet

Jurdam Younger. Brides needed that kind of indulgence from their friends, particularly when they were as inexperienced as Harriet.

But now it was different for Sue Lingen. This was the fourth time that she had gone to meet the person that she was now heading toward. The first time came after a dinner party that she gave for the bride and groom. It was only right that their new River Oaks friends entertain the new couple in the community. It was no special event, the dinner party that Sue Lingen gave for Harriet and John Travis, just some of the nice people who were friends of everyone's. Sue Lingen had the party at the country club, because ever since her last divorce, she disliked entertaining in her big house, the one she got as a wedding present from her first husband.

During the dinner, each of the men changed places after every course. Sue Lingen had seen that done in Beverly Hills at a party and thought it was just a wonderful idea. Right after the beef Wellington, John Travis, whom Sue Lingen had never talked to really intimately, sat next to her.

Lo and behold, before there was much conversation about where the couple went and the sights they saw on their honeymoon, the kind of questions that make conversation, Sue Lingen felt John Travis's hand reach for hers under the table. Heaven knows, it was not the kind of thing that she expected, but if someone was going to take her hand, then she might just as well give it to him. It seemed that John Travis had something in mind. It was for Sue Lingen's hand to massage his *thing*. Somehow, and it wasn't easy at a dinner party, his thing was outside his pants, and it *was* big. It wasn't hard or anything, just *big*. For the sake of curiosity, Sue Lingen kept her hand right where John Travis put it, and kept it there, just hugging and squeezing it right through the salad and dessert.

It was lucky that they were in a very dark corner of the club, and that nobody was really paying attention to her end of the table. Sue Lingen could have gone on hugging and squeezing for a long time, because she admitted to herself, she *really* was getting excited. Suddenly, Sue Lingen dropped her earring, accidentally on purpose. It didn't create much of a stir when she bent down on the floor and began a thorough search for it.

In any event, under the table, in all the commotion, she really took a shine to John Travis's manly erection. She didn't do anything really bad to it, just a few sweet kisses and a couple of quick ladylike licks, and just one mouthful around its mighty top. She could tell, when she finally came up for air, smiling sweetly at John Travis, that he was really aching.

So, it was easy to see that they both wanted to keep that first date at the apartment that John Travis had at the Rice. Just like his father, L.C. Younger, she understood. But not the same floor. And clear as a bell, Sue Lingen understood that Harriet Jurdam Younger was not just whistling Dixie when she talked so outrageously about the kind of stud John Travis Younger was.

And it wasn't as if Harriet Jurdam Younger were her best friend or anything. Sue Lingen didn't think that she was being disloyal. Harriet would just have to figure it all out for herself. After all, if Harriet hadn't bragged so much about John Travis, Sue Lingen wouldn't have even been curious and would have minded her own P's and Q's.

In all her days, Sue Lingen had never, ever been at a loss for words. It wasn't only because of the first time when Sue Lingen did that naughty thing to John Travis under the table. There were the other times that just took Sue Lingen's breath away. She still remembered the heavenly excitement that came her way, time after time, on only one little bitty afternoon.

Now, she stood expectantly in front of the door of John Travis's apartment at the Rice. The door opened and John Travis stood there shaking hands with a man she had never seen before. He was tall, red-faced, and kind of common. But John Travis smiled at him, shook his hand, and put one hand on his shoulder.

"I knew he'd be interested in what you had to tell him. That's why I wanted you to see him. Damn funny name for an American. At any rate, you're started, and when your new company gets going, you know which bank to put the money in."

The other man replied earnestly. "John Travis, you won't regret it."

John Travis smiled. "I don't already."

John Dowie politely tipped his hat to Sue Lingen as he left her at the door. Sue Lingen didn't care who that was, because she was really hungry to get into bed with her incredible stud. Playfully, she reached down and grabbed at his thing.

And do you know that it was semi-hard already, and just *immense*? Imagine that!

10

TERRY JORDAN had been working at Carmine's even before her divorce from Staff Sergeant Fred Jordan. The sprawling bar on Marback Road in San Antonio catered largely to the Air Force men stationed at nearby Lackland. She and the three other cocktail waitresses on her shift worked from four in the afternoon till two in the morning, by which time under Texas law all drinks had to be put away. Terry, born Teresa LoBianco, was raised in Asbury Park, New Jersey. Her runaway marriage to Fred Jordan when she was only seventeen came to very little good, except that Terry Jordan discovered Texas, and in Texas she discovered Rodeo.

Even before her divorce, the five foot three, dark-haired pixie hung around the local stock breeder in San Antonio, and spent weekends traveling to such distant places as Poteau and Vian, Oklahoma; Hereford and Wertham, Texas; and Torrington and Casper in Wyoming just to be near the cowgirls on the professional circuit.

Where other Texas girls had lived rodeo from the moment they were old enough to walk, Terry had to learn a lot in a short time. She quickly eliminated from the events she considered those which required a lifetime of experience on a horse. Barrel racing on a quarter horse "can chasing," and roping or goat tying "nanny whamming," were skills that Terry thought it was too late in life to learn. The event that caught her eye and inflamed her passion was bull-riding. All she had to do was stay on!

Each afternoon Terry went to a nearby stockman, and for five dollars he let her ride as many of them as she could catch, for as long as she could last. Day in and day out, Terry kept at it. The contractor and his helper thought she was insane. The bulls tossed her around like a bag of cement, but despite the constant pain and bruises, Terry found that she had the will to master the animals. All she needed was to stay on for nine seconds—it took Terry two years of bruises to do it for the first time.

Devlin had been working at Carmine's for over eight months, and from the first she and Terry hit it off. The two roomed together, sharing a tiny trailer. Terry's irreverent spunk and sense of humor took Devlin through the early dark period of being on her own.

One Sunday night Terry returned to the trailer they shared from a rodeo in Santa Fe, sporting twenty-five stitches on her forehead. With a smile, she plunked herself down on the bed, reached in her pocket, and brandished a check in front of Devlin's face.

"Gollee . . . what a time we had."

"Terry, what happened to you?"

"Oh, hell, Devlin, nothing." She laughed in her pain. "You should a' seen the bull."

Then she stood up in the tiny trailer and relived her ride on a monster bull named Snow Cloud. "And do you know, Devlin, I took fifty-three points on that mother, and I got me third prize. Look at it, honey. Fifty dollars."

Devlin sighed, "Terry, you spent three times that in expenses."

"Devlin, one of us in this trailer is full of poetry, and the other is full of vinegar. My old Sicilian grandfather used to say something about people like you Devlin."

"Yeah? What did he say?"

"How the hell do I know, Devlin? I can't speak a word of Italian, and the only wop that I know is in my stomach. God, what I wouldn't give for spaghetti carbonara, or veal piccata. I gave up an awful lot, Devlin—my whole damn heritage to become a Texan, but one thing you ain't gonna do is make me like Mex food."

"You'll never make it then, Terry," Devlin laughed.

"I'll make it. Just you wait and see. I'm gonna change the face of Texas."

Devlin surveyed her cuts and bruises. "Also your own."

"I'm gonna bring religion to you heathen. We gave you pizza—but you didn't take to it. For Pete's sake, Devlin—if you Texans don't shape up, I'll bring in the Mafia."

She winced with pain and lay back on the bed, holding her side. "I think I cracked a rib."

"Terry, why don't you give it up?"

"Devlin, baby, it's my life." She sat up with an effort. "Honey, you don't know what it does to me . . . not only the excitement of the rodeo, and the thrill of fighting that big damn mother of a beast . . . but the feeling of being part of the life of the girls I meet. They're the best people in the world, Devlin. You met them. They're my friends. They understand me . . . and I understand them. They'd go to hell for me if I needed it." Then Terry brightened. "Besides, Devlin, I saw a red satin shirt that I'm saving for. It cost one hundred dollars and you have to wait three months for them to make it." She held up the check. "Look, baby, I'm halfway to that shirt. Even with my expenses for the rodeos, and the doctor bills and all, I figure that I can afford it in time for the finals in Fort Worth."

Terry fell back and closed her eyes. Devlin moved over beside her and held her hand. She knew there was nothing she could do that hadn't been done already to ease the pain. All Devlin could do was to show Terry that she stood behind her. Terry smiled wanly and murmured, "You understand. Are you *sure* you're not Italian?"

It was Saturday night, closing time. Devlin's feet ached, and her lower back felt like a bag of potatoes. She smiled in spite of her fatigue as she saw Terry approach the dressing room where the girls hung their clothes. Here they could snatch a moment or two of privacy away from the customers at Carmine's, or better yet from Carmine himself. The ever present owner was a short, greasy-looking, baldheaded man in his late fifties who sported a single rope of black hair which he carefully folded back over his scalp. He was perpetually angry and endlessly suspicious. But jobs were scarce, and the girls, including Devlin, had become used to him.

In the tiny dressing room, Devlin began to remove her bunny outfit. The push-up bras were supposed to make the girls look sexy. The cotton tails, which the Playboy Club could have sued about, were Carmine's idea. Only Devlin's remained. The customers at Carmine's took to removing them whenever they felt playful, meanwhile grabbing as much flesh as they could in the process. Although Devlin's red hair and long-limbed body were much admired, curiously, the men were more attracted to Terry and the other girls, who were cuddly and well rounded, and ducked and weaved and had flirtatious things to say. Somehow the customers at Carmine's got the feeling that Devlin was unapproachable, and as far as Devlin was concerned, that was all to the good.

The other girls finished dressing and wordlessly disappeared out the side door. It seemed incredible to Devlin that as closely as they worked, there was no intimate contact among them. They competed for tips and tried to get each other to handle the shit work if something spilled or if there was a problem. When the ten-hour shift was over, they vanished.

Standing patiently outside would be men from Lackland hoping to make a connection. That was always the most trouble—fighting one's way out of Carmine's, and on a weekend it was worse. Some of the girls had dates. Terry's boyfriend Emilio would be waiting for her, and Devlin would be going back to the trailer park.

Devlin stepped out in the dark first, avoiding the three airmen who began to close in on her. A white-suited man in his thirties, tall and darkly handsome, moved into the light. It was Emilio.

"Get lost." He bit at the servicemen.

They looked at him and took his measure. The look in his eyes was unmistakably dangerous. The airmen moved away, and Emilio took Terry's arm.

"Good night, Devlin. See you when I see you."

"Terry, if I decide to go out, I'll leave the key in the usual place."

Emilio whispered to Terry. She nodded and came over to Devlin. "Honey, Emilio says that if you'd like, you can come along with us. I won't mind. He's all man, and you'd have a good time. We can have anything we want to eat and drink. Come on, Devlin, honey, let's party a little."

Devlin shook her head. "Terry, you go on. I don't think that it's my kind of thing."

"Whatever you say, honey, but I'm telling you that you're missing out on a good thing, and Emilio would like it."

Terry walked back into the dark to rejoin her companion and they walked to his car. Devlin went further into the parking lot to rescue her Eldorado. She hoped it would start. It needed a new battery and a new set of plugs, neither of which Devlin could afford. It wasn't something she relished, being stuck in the outskirts of San Antonio at three in the morning.

Eight months earlier when Devlin left the house on Montrose, she was happier than she had ever been. At first she had felt at a loss, having gone off into the unknown without a final confrontation with her father. She imagined a thousand final confrontations with L.C., but even in her fantasy, none of them was satisfactory. Eventually she recognized that she was playing a familiar game with her father in seeking to confront him. If she really meant what she said—that she wouldn't let him control her life anymore—then she had to work it out by herself. L.C. was not about to hand over control to her. Nor would the statement of Devlin's intentions do her a damn bit of good, no matter how angry it got L.C.

As she drove away from the house at seven in the morning, it didn't concern Devlin that she didn't have much money. Money had never been something she worried about. It had come as automatically to her as breathing. But, after Devlin stopped for gas, she looked in her wallet. All she had left was eleven dollars and change. Life was certainly going to be different from now on.

Some inner magnet led Devlin off the freeway and onto one of the lesser traveled roads. It turned out to be the road to Sugarland, along route 90A, one of the oldest east-west trails blazed by Indians and widened by the Spanish explorers. It led from the flats of Houston's pines into level, open prairie which—with the exception of timbered Brazos and Colorado bottoms—extended all the way to Hallettsville, halfway to where Devlin had decided to go, San Antonio. The countryside was rich, and even though it was near the end of January, the very earliest of spring wildflowers had begun to appear. In less than a month, there would be a profusion of blue and orange across the plains that would dazzle the eye.

The day was sparklingly beautiful when she arrived in San Antonio, and Devlin found herself along the banks of the river of that name, following the serpentine beauty along the downtown Riverwalk. Below the level of the street, the jade-green water twisted and turned, as buildings crowded almost to the water's edge. In other places, oaks and evergreens, oleanders and cypresses grew in rich profusion. Dozens of stone bridges arched over the water. Sidewalk cafes abounded, and Devlin sat down to enjoy the freedom of a city at peace with itself. The sight of the slow-marching strollers and the glint of sunlight on the river were hypnotic.

San Antonio is like a pearl in a perfect martini. A city full of history, it is also full of beauty, and a mixture of its Mexican heritage along with the bustling energy of Texas. More than its palm trees, its banana plants and the residue of sleep from its nineteenth century past, San Antonio is a mixture of old and new, of ox carts carrying produce to market, of intercontinental missiles, of broiled *cabrito* and McDonald's hamburgers.

It was lunchtime, and the tables began to fill. Devlin took a look at the menu, and decided that common sense and caution would not allow her to spend three and a half dollars on a meal—she had to find a job, and then a place to sleep. The *San Antonio Gazette* had an ad for cocktail waitresses, "experienced, long hours, big tips." That brought her to Carmine's, to Terry, and to the trailer park.

When Devlin awoke that Sunday morning, she poured tomato juice for herself from an open tin in the tiny refrigerator. Briskly she set about cleaning the trailer, washing the dishes and putting them away. Terry was a good soul and she did not question Devlin about her past, but it was simple for anyone to realize that Devlin was new to the life of a working girl and needed to learn how to live independently and frugally.

Devlin didn't know about matters as simple as how to wash her clothes in the laundromat or how to accept dates with overeater airmen—promising them unspoken treats after wolfing down steaks, finding a convenient excuse to deny them what they felt they had paid for. Devlin learned how to get by on almost nothing, how to promise the trailer-park boss the rent week after week with new and extravagant tales, meanwhile using the money for some crazy extravagance.

Devlin once thought she had come to understand the life of the average working slug during the summers at Black Diamond. She realized that she had been kidding herself. With a protected home to return to every night, it made no difference that she was doing brute physical work on the docks. That was only physical exercise for her body. It gave her the illusion that she was like everyone else. How wrong she had been! Devlin began to recognize the reality of working for survival, the way each of the women around her did. Unlike Devlin, they had no way out.

Sunday afternoon, after Devlin had tidied the trailer, done the laundry, and purchased the groceries they would need for the week, she heard a knock on the door. It was Emilio. Devlin let him in.

"Where's Terry?"

"Look," he said as he eased himself into a chair, "Terry got herself into a little jam last night after she left me. She kept a date, and the date got a little rough on her. She's in the hospital. She's okay, and it's gonna be fine." Devlin was panicked. Terry was her lifeline.

"Don't get upset now, Red . . . Terry's fine, and she's got the best of care, a private room and all, and don't get yourself all steamed."

For the first time, Devlin surveyed Emilio. He was a mixture of Anglo and Mexican blood, handsome and cold as ice. Devlin thought that he really hadn't *had* to come and inform her. That was okay.

"You wanna go see her?"

Devlin nodded, grabbed her denim jacket, and followed Emilio out to his car. It was a handsome white Continental with sheepskin-covered seats and loads of ornamental chrome. As Emilio started the car, the air conditioner and stereo came on together, and they pulled away from the trailer park in a hermetically sealed cocoon.

Devlin sat silently for a moment, feeling Emilio's look. "What about the guy who did it?"

Emilio sniffed, "I got them, two of them. Beating up on chicks is not the kind of fun that I'm gonna permit anybody. Terry is a good kid, and she decided that she wanted to go on this date, and that's her business. I don't interfere, but like I say, I got these two, and I took care of them."

Devlin stared at him. "Did you kill them?"

Emilio laughed, "Christ, no. I just showed them that any girlfriend of mine deserves protection, and that's what she got." He laughed again. "Now, I'll admit that when they woke up, they might 'a wished they was dead, but in the meanwhile, they ain't."

Devlin sat in silence as the stereo sound surrounded her. It felt good to be driving in cool comfort. She wished that she had the money to repair the Eldorado—the dents and dings as well as the ignition and plugs. The repair shop refused to extend her any credit. Emilio drove to the main entrance of the hospital and left the car in a no-parking zone. He led her to an elevator, which was jammed with nurses, doctors, and visitors. Emilio muscled his way in, making room for her, and then muscled his way out on the third floor. He led her down the corridor to a semiprivate room. There in the white afternoon light she saw Terry lying in bed.

Her eyes were virtually closed. Her face was puffed and blue, swollen beyond recognition. Her arm was in a splint, and the bruises that followed down her neck indicated that they extended down her body.

Devlin stood over the bedside, too shocked to speak.

"Terry," Emilio announced, "I brought the redhead with me."

Terry managed a greeting, "I don't like to have you see me this way, Dev."

Devlin began to cry. "Oh Terry, honey, how could they do that to you?"

"Dev, I won't be able to buy that red satin shirt." There was a long moment's pause. "Otherwise, it's not too bad, Dev . . . not too bad. I won't be going back to Carmine's for a while, a long time . . . but Emilio is taking good care of me, and everything is going to be okay. Be nice to him, Dev . . . for me . . . won't you. Emilio is a great guy, and I want him to be happy while I'm out of action . . ."

Devlin was confused by the request. "Terry, are you sure you're okay? What do the doctors say?"

Emilio interrupted, "She's gonna be fine. Just take a while till the bruises heal, but everything is gonna be okay, don't you worry."

A nurse entered and saw the group. "It's not visiting hours, folks, and the young woman is really not up to seeing people. I'd appreciate your leaving."

Terry mumbled, "Devlin, keep Emilio company. If it wasn't for him, I don't know what I'd do."

Devlin shook her head in wonderment.

"Promise you will, Dev."

"Sure, Terry, you can count on it."

Emilio led Devlin out of the room and they retraced their steps out of the hospital. Outside, Emilio held the door open for Devlin, snatched a parking ticket off the windshield, and threw it away.

"How about a steak, Red?" he asked.

Devlin shook her head in recollection of Terry, and looked at Emilio with interest. "Sure, Emilio, you pick the place. I haven't had a steak in three months, two days, and ten hours." Devlin laughed. It was absolutely true. She was famished and shocked. A drink would do her good, and Emilio, for all his strange and mysterious ways, had surprised her with his care and attention to Terry. He didn't have to be that considerate. Terry appreciated it, she could tell. And Terry wanted her to keep Emilio company in her absence. She felt herself thinking about the clothes she was wearing.

Emilio caught her eye and laughed. "Don't worry, Red, you look good enough to eat any place in this town." Devlin smiled and turned on the stereo. For the first time in months she was looking forward to something, even as a result of Terry's misfortune. She turned to look at Emilio's face. It hadn't changed expression from the moment he came to pick her up at the trailer—even at the sight of the outrage to Terry's body.

IN Claude Giroux's life he had never done anything, ever, that defied convention, until he met John Dowie. Giroux had done everything that a patrician gentlemen should: gone to Harvard, been a member of Porcellian, married a socially proper and financially sound young debutante—the right homes, clubs, friends, and occupation. There was never any doubt about Claude's vocation. There had always been a place for him at Giroux Frères. Even though his own father, who would have headed the firm, died years ago, Claude's uncle quite properly made room for him, as Claude's father would have wished him to do.

Claude was certain that his daughters, aged seventeen, eighteen, and nineteen, were virgins, as certain as he was that they had properly come out as debutantes and that they would marry appropriate men.

Claude and his wife had an understanding which called for separate bedrooms. Neither Claude nor his wife Dulcima had any interest in sex. They were not even like a conspiratorial brother and sister. They were more like chairpersons of separate committees, who had no function together except an occasional exchange of information.

One day Claude suddenly discovered that instead of more money, what he really wanted was fun. He had been robbed of it as a boy, robbed of it as a man, and he considered that he was in danger of losing it for all time. This revelation struck him after he met John Dowie, when he quickly inferred that through Dowie he could be involved in activities that some might consider to be somewhat naughty. John Dowie was the Huck Finn to Giroux's Tom Sawyer. Claude was captivated by the aura of secret danger that surrounded his accomplice.

It was clear that John Dowie was a pirate, willing to take on extraordinary risks and tasks, and to deal with them in the most direct and effective way. Through John Dowie, Claude himself had become a highwayman, dealing in unknown peril that gave him a delicious conspiratorial thrill.

Dowie phoned him days after they met in Houston to inform him that Claude's first test had been accomplished. Dowie had negotiated a price on this first acquisition so favorably that some would have doubted the reality of it. When Giroux asked Dowie just how he accomplished his deal, Dowie replied simply, "I'll tell you anything you want to know, Mr. Giroux, but I'll say this, some of the things I do you *don't* want to know about."

Claude listened. He was excited and intensely curious. "Is this one of those times?"

"Yes, Mr. Giroux, this is one of those times."

The holding company was to be named "HOUCORP." Its first acquisition was the purchase of controlling interest in Houston Stevedoring Company, a highly sophisticated organization of men and machines, capable of unloading anything from specialized bulk cargo, including grains and ores, to the most complex kind of containers. They had even loaded an entire zoo for shipment to Taiwan. This acquisition was an important cornerstone for the new company, with its new equipment, efficient manpower, and fine reputation.

Houston Stevedoring was run by the Demeret family. Roy Demeret, a man in his fifties with considerable wealth, was from an old Texas family. Demeret's son, Roy Junior, was in his late twenties and had a reputation as a playboy. Roy Senior had pulled his son out of half a dozen minor scrapes.

John Dowie was well known to Roy Demeret as the bane of his existence across the bargaining table. Consequently Dowie had no trouble in getting to see Demeret the next day. Dowie explained that he was speaking for an associate who was interested in acquiring controlling interest in Houston Stevedoring. Demeret thought Dowie was joking. Where in hell would he get the kind of money needed to buy Houston Stevedoring and how in hell did Dowie have the nerve to come sniffing around Demeret's preserve?

"Mr. Demeret, now, I've been polite and nice, and I've offered you a good deal."

"Dowie, I don't like you, and you know it. It's enough that I have to deal with you in union matters. I should throw you out on your ass. What the hell do you think your membership would say if I told them you were looking to doublecross them?"

"Mr. Demeret, I don't know *what* they'd say. All I can say is that when I hear from you next time, I'd sure like your second thoughts on this subject, and I'd sure like your answer to be yes."

Demeret stood up angrily and told Dowie to get out. Dowie smiled broadly, gracefully lifted his large bulk from his chair, and left.

Dowie hadn't expected anything different to happen at the meeting, but he had to let Demeret know the price he expected to pay, and having done that, the rest of the transaction was put in motion. The key to the riddle was Roy Junior, and Roy Junior's highly refined taste for very young girls.

May Ann Seibel was not yet thirteen, even though she looked and acted considerably older. Roy Junior was wild about her. She was the youngest girl he had ever been with, and May Ann was also the most perverse. She appreciated Roy's attention, his gifts, and the drugs he gave her, and she led him a merry chase.

The night after Dowie's meeting with Roy Senior, Roy Junior was entertaining May Ann in his apartment. High on cocaine, they were also in the throes of making love. A knock on the door went unheard. Then the door was opened with a passkey. Two men made their way into young Roy's bedroom, one of them carrying a 20-gauge shotgun. Without any ceremony, they pushed the bedroom door open and switched on the lights.

Roy Junior jumped at the brightness. May Ann sat up in bed. She saw one of the men and cried out, "Daddy." Then she broke into tears.

The man with the shotgun raised it to fire at Roy Junior. The other man stepped in the way and forced the barrel aside. Roy Junior looked at the younger man. A glimmer of recognition flitted across his face. John Dowie, his adversary of the docks, could save his life.

"John, tell Seibel that I'll pay him whatever he wants."

The older man sniffed and raised the shotgun again. Roy Junior begged, "Please don't kill me, I'll make it up to you."

Dowie smiled, "Call Roy Senior, and tell him to get over here right away, and tell him to bring his pen."

Dutifully Roy Junior, naked and exposed, picked up the phone and dialed. May Ann took the bed covers and wrapped them around herself. She walked over to the man with the shotgun, and sobbed in his arms.

In fifteen minutes Roy Senior was in his son's apartment, and in a half hour, he had reached an agreement to sell HOUCORP fifty-one percent of the stock of Houston Stevedoring.

What really convinced Roy Senior was the obscene view he had of May Ann's father. The man had the barrel of his shotgun stuck two full inches up Junior's ass during the entire transaction. Roy Senior would continue to be in control of operations on a daily basis. Roy Junior would live, and there would be peace on the docks from the union.

May Ann disappeared into the bathroom and reappeared dressed, looking like the schoolgirl she was. She shamefacedly made her way out of the apartment, followed by the two men. The three of them waited at the elevator. When it arrived, they rode down silently. Dowie led them to his station wagon parked fifty yards away from the entrance. When the three of them got inside the car, May Ann exploded with laughter.

"Mr. Dowie, did you see Mr. Demeret's face when he saw that big fucking gun up his son's poop?"

Dowie smiled, then he turned to the man in the back seat. "Lloyd, see you tomorrow."

The man in the back placed the shotgun on the floor, eased himself out of the car, and closed the door. May Ann paid him no attention. Then John Dowie started the car and drove away.

"May Ann, you were real fine tonight."

"You really think so, Mr. Dowie?"

"Yep, you were worth every penny. I already gave your mom the money I promised."

She smiled, "That was a lot of money to pay. I had fun, Mr. Dowie. Where did you get the man who was supposed to be my daddy? He don't look nothing like me."

Dowie laughed, "Demeret wasn't in any position to compare blood-types, honey. He did his job and you did yours."

May Ann smiled and moved closer to the driver. She put her hand on his thigh and ran the tip of her fingers slowly and sexily toward the inside of his crotch. Dowie smiled and removed her hand. "No need for that now, May Ann, you're through for the night."

The girl smiled, "It's not for *anything*, Mr. Dowie, just for fun. We could stop someplace and do it in the back."

Dowie pressed on the gas pedal and laughed, "Never you mind, May Ann, you did your good deed for tonight. I'll take you home, and you and your mom can figure out how to spend the money."

May Ann sighed. As far as she was concerned, she would have done the whole thing for nothing. When Mr. Dowie came around and made her mom the proposition, she was all for it, and her mom was too. It wasn't as if her mom thought the whole thing with a grown man was a big deal for an almost-thirteen-year-old girl. Her mom had started just like May Ann had, at practically the same age, and it didn't hurt her none. She still liked it, and she had a good time with men who brought her things and paid her good money every time they came to the apartment for dates, day or night.

But it wasn't anything like the kind of money that May Ann earned for *one* night's work. That was really something. Ten thousand dollars for screwing a rich jerk who had almost passed out anyway, and who wasn't that good in bed to begin with. May Ann sat in the corner of the front seat and gazed out the window at the Houston traffic. Tonight was really a score, and something she could tell her own daughter about, when the time came.

Gardner Land had discovered two things in Houston that made life worthwhile. The first was someone who was prepared to subsidize him in a manner to which he was suited by taste, and the second was a charming "friend" who happened to be the best lover he had ever known. It would have been convenient for Gardner if he had been able to find both in one person, but to find the answers at all, even in two people, was quite satisfactory.

96

The person who was prepared to provide him with the luxuries of life was Vonnie Younger. Since that afternoon tea in Jessica Hungerford's apartment, she had been his constant telephone companion and also his guest on frequent afternoons at his own apartment. The man who filled his life with ecstasy was David, an ex-Green Beret and now a gym teacher in an elegant Houston parochial school.

Gardner hadn't placed a pen to paper during the past five months. He felt that he owed himself a good time for once in his life.

On afternoons that he had nothing to do, he dropped in on Jessica. She was delicious to dish the dirt with. He had never before been able to have an intimate friendship with a lesbian, but Jessica was different. She was jolly and motherly, and she didn't parade her superior dykedom in front of you, as if it were a crime to have a cock, and anyone who had one should be put away.

Jessica was different. The one thing she was, unfortunately, was businesslike. She demanded her cut for the introduction she made to Vonnie. Gardner had parted with almost a thousand dollars in commissions. There was no formal agreement on what Jessica's portion should be of what Gardner received from Vonnie. What he passed on to Jessica apparently pleased her, and since it represented only a tiny fraction of the money he received, it pleased Gardner too.

One afternoon he was seated on a chaise in the corner of Jessica's living room, licking his fingers. Jessica had thoughtfully provided some jelly doughnuts for him, along with the tea she was preparing. Gardner, without waiting, had taken the first bite. It squished all over.

"You certainly get the juicy ones," he called into the kitchen.

"What are you talking about?"

He laughed as he sucked on his thumb and index finger. "Oh, my God, I made a funny. I didn't mean what you thought I did. I'm talking about the jelly doughnut."

Jessica appeared with a pot of steeping tea. She hadn't dressed for the day yet, and Gardner thought it distasteful to see her in hair-rollers and a nightgown. A scarlet satin robe covered her bulk, but the sash that came with the robe was lost, and Jessica used an electric extension cord. She smiled as Gardner stared at her.

"The ultimate chic, Gardner. This of course is Houston and not Paris. I hope you don't mind. I consider you one of the family."

She sat down in an armchair opposite and placed the tray with the pot and cups on a table between them. "Thank you for the coffee table, Gardner."

"I didn't know I had given you one."

"It comes by way of your patron."

"Oh, her, isn't she a scream?"

"I wouldn't know," Jessica said matter of factly. "You seem to be taking your meal ticket very lightly."

He said confidentially, "You know she writes poetry."

"Oh, no."

"Yes, and you wouldn't believe it. Third-grade children write better stuff than she does. But I moon all over it, and congratulate her as a talent, a talent, of course, that needs nurturing."

"Naturally, and that will take time."

"Yes, Jessica, and money."

"She has a lot, I understand."

"Well, it seems as if *everybody* in Houston does, darling Jessica, except thee and me, but I'm trying my best to relocate more of the worldly goods. I think that Karl Marx had the right idea, but the notion of giving it away to those gruesome-looking peasants and factory workers . . . He should have arranged to give it to people who would have fun."

Lifting the lid, Jessica peered into the pot to see if it was dark enough. She poured two cups. Gardner helped himself to four spoons of sugar and milk. "I just love those doughnuts, Jessica. I must buy some and bring them home to David."

"I'll write down the address. Does your patron know about David?"

"Of course not, do you take me for a fool, Jessica? Does Macy's tell Gimbels?"

"Quite right."

"Her husband, Jessica, he owns the entire port of Houston. Every boat, and every single shipment that comes in here, it's all his. I went down there to take a look, and I must say that he has some giants of men working for him. My mouth watered."

Jessica looked at him drily. She hated fags. God, they were all alike. They had no stability and no dedication to purpose. Their minds were always in their mouths or between their legs. At least lesbians, she considered, were into long-term relationships, and could behave like grown-up people. Fags, damn their eyes, were always looking for something different to eat. She smiled at her phrase. It was true in every way. "More tea?"

"Yes, it's so good. I love loose tea. Nowadays everybody is using tea bags, and they *are* dreadful. Don't you think?"

"Gardner," she said as she poured, "do you have any difficulty in keeping your patron in line? If so, perhaps she might prefer the company of a woman, and I could help you there."

"Oh, you mean sex? God no. Let me tell you one thing, Jessica. I've never had any trouble making love to a woman, whenever it was necessary. Thank God those occasions were very rare. You just close your eyes, and, well, you know . . . but this one is different, unbelievably different. I can't make her out. We haven't done a damn thing since the first day, you remember that day that I read my poetry, the day I met her."

"You were diddling her in the corner, I remember. Very good idea of yours, Gardner."

"Thank you, Jessica. I thought so, but since that time, she hasn't let me put a hand on her. I thought if she liked a 'handy' then, that's what I'd do, and maybe even a few licks and a promise, if you know what I mean. For the sort of money that she's paying for her happiness, it wouldn't hurt for me to stick it in a couple of times, but every time that I suggest something, she puts her hand on mine, takes it away from under her dress and murmers, 'Gardner, you and I had something perfect, and I'll never forget what that was. There's no way,' she says, 'to improve on that blessed moment . . . and so, I must deny myself, Gardner . . . and you must deny yourself, for all times . . . till eternity . . . it has been all I ever dreamed of . . . .' "

Jessica guffawed. "You're making that up."

"Cross my heart, Jessica. You know that between us there are no secrets. I'll tell you one thing, and I never thought it would happen to me. When she says that, she gets me excited. I look down at my cock, Jessica, and the damn thing is hard as a rock, and I'm scared, Jessica, that I may rape the bitch."

Jessica shook her head. Now she had finally heard everything.

For Vonnie the past months had been like a dream. She had never been happier. It had, of course, all stemmed from that remarkable afternoon that she had spent at Jessica's. Listening to Gardner recite "Xanadu" and his other poems had fulfilled a prayer she secretly nursed: to get close to a creator of poetry, someone like herself whose purpose in life was to distill from the experiences of the day—the simple, the prosaic, the mundane—and, with God-given talent, create an appreciation of life that others could feel.

Vonnie had this feeling all her life, which accounted for her commitment to write a poem each day. She had copybooks full of her poetry locked in her heart as well as in a suitcase in the bottom of her closet. How banal her poetry used to be before Gardner opened her eyes. He had shown her true beauty and brought her to the marriage of words and feelings. Vonnie's body burned with the memory of the divine transport she felt that first afternoon.

She knew when she got home that it had been a religious experience. But, since she had never known it before, she was worried that she might have had something of an ejaculation. The idea filled her with dread until she got to a private place and examined herself. Thank God, it had been nothing like that. At that point Vonnie's lack of self knowledge convinced her it must have been a religious experience.

At home with L.C. and the servants, Vonnie's fear of each new day had vanished. She accepted the obligation to manage the house, much to

Alma's surprise. She was now an occasional dinner companion for L.C. when he was home rather than eating in her room. But these were just intervals in her life that occupied her between her times with Gardner.

Vonnie was happy when L.C. was out of the house, even when he was at his apartment at the Rice. She had known about that, almost from the very beginning. How thankful she was now that L.C. had that distraction. It had been more than twenty years since L.C. forced her to make love to him. She prayed that he would continue to leave her alone. The purity of her relationship with Gardner would be hard-tried if L.C. were ever to intrude his physical presence on her.

The money—oh, she was spending it recklessly. Thank heaven that she had her own. But that was what money was for. It was able to give her something beyond measure. Vonnie Younger was a happy woman. She was even beyond caring about the break with John Travis. She had a full and a rich life, and Gardner Land had made it all possible.

In her reverie the telephone rang. Gardner was on the line. From the beginning, she had warned him not to phone her at home. Their meetings at his apartment had been planned ahead. She had phoned him, never the reverse. But as time went on, he began to phone her. She always rushed to answer it before one of the servants.

"Vonnie?"

"Oh, Gardner . . . I'm so happy you called. We're not scheduled to meet until tomorrow, but I've been thinking about you all day. I've been writing down my thoughts in my diary, and you know what they are . . . ."

"Vonnie, please, something important has come up, and I'm going to have to leave town, maybe go back to New York."

Vonnie cried out in pain. "Gardner, you can't, I won't let you."

"I've got to, there's no choice, Vonnie."

"You can't go, Gardner. When are you leaving?"

"Tonight. I'm just packing now."

"Gardner, I'm coming to see you."

"Vonnie, you can't, I really mean it. I'm leaving Houston, I mean right away. I just can't face it."

Vonnie's mind was made up. She was not going to let her happiness escape her this way. She was steely in her resolve. "Gardner, stay where you are until I get there. It will only be fifteen or twenty minutes. Now promise."

From the end of the phone, Vonnie heard, "I promise." Then she hung up and quickly changed into a street dress. Her mind was made up. She would do whatever was necessary to safeguard this joy in her life, so late, so pure, so perfect.

Vonnie shook violently from the fear that engulfed her. Gardner must not leave her.

After three unsuccessful marriages and three successful divorces, Sue Lingen had worn out more caterers, florists, and interior decorators than any girl in Houston.

Sue Lingen's first husband was "Small" Ty Wimpers, who owned seventy-eight thousand acres of prime Texas land. His father, "Big" Ty, owned three times that amount of land and was a damn sight more charming than his son. Small Ty, six foot five, and capable of downing a six-pack of Coors for breakfast, and eight more by the time dinner was ready, had very little interest in any practical matters. He didn't work. He watched game shows on TV and went to bed very early in order to get the ten hours of sleep that he thought necessary to keep him in shape.

Small Ty had been a diffident lover during their courtship, but Sue Lingen had just thought he was being courteous. Marriage had slowed him down even further. They had made love only twice in the six months following their honeymoon. Small Ty admitted his inattention, but excused it by saying that he was tired and that he would get around to it in his own good time.

To still Sue Lingen's constant criticism, Small Ty brought his wife a vibrator that he picked up in a New Orleans sex shop. He laughed as he handed her the giftwrapped package.

Sue Lingen was furious. The instrument was larger than Small Ty's modest equipment, and she didn't think it at all funny that the vibrator was black.

The next day she filed for divorce.

Her second husband was a very handsome, very polished polo-playing Virginian who had come to Houston to promote the sport and get some of the local millionaires to become patrons. He was gallant, well mannered, and very social. "Tige" McCauley was said to have had affairs with some of the most desirable and famous women in the world. It was rumored that Tige was on very intimate terms with three members of the royal family, the daughter of a secretary of state, and the mother of the most famous debutante from Grosse Point.

Tige said yes when Sue Lingen asked if he'd like to marry her, and he said no when Sue Lingen asked for a divorce. It cost her father, T.W. Lingen, three million dollars to get an affirmative answer, after less than nine months of marriage.

She tearfully told her parents that she wanted out when she discovered that Tige was a man in name only. His valet looked after Tige's clothes, his tack, his appointments, and his love life. What was more, his valet *was* his love life.

Sue Lingen's third marriage was scarcely more than a weekend romance. The chauffeur who drove her around Manhattan for three days of shopping was awfully nice, and very good in bed. He sped the two of them to Greenwich to get married after a riotous few hours in the back seat of the stretch Cadillac he drove, which he parked in a dark corner of a garage near Bergdorf Goodman's. When Sue Lingen discovered that he was not much fun outside the limousine, daddy rescued her from the entanglement by getting him a stretch Mercedes of his own, with TV, hi-fi, telephone, and tinted-glass windows.

After a suitable period on the singles market, with entrée into the world of fun open again to her and affairs with some of the husbands of her very best friends, Sue Lingen decided once more to get married. Beaux were not always available, and sometimes the husbands of her friends were with their own wives. Sue Lingen's parents had lives of their own, and they were putting a lot of pressure on her to marry, settle down, and raise a family.

This time she was clear about what she was looking for. She wanted someone she could be seen with, a solid kind of man, someone she could go to Homecoming Day at UT with, someone she could go to the country club with. She wanted someone who would drive the other girls wild with jealousy. They had all married stodgy types who were interested in making money and doing whatever daddy wanted them to do. She wanted a hero who had *no* daddy.

Sue Lingen picked Tune Richards, and before he knew it, he asked her to marry him. She acted surprised and nodded. Then she soul-kissed Tune Richards. That was the same night the two of them made love for the first time. She considered that, for a hero, he wasn't bad, but give her the villains any day. They really knew how to deal with a girl.

John Travis would still be available to her from time to time. She would have to reserve a place with him, because she knew that John Travis had every girl in town. How many had he been through? She knew for a fact that half the girls in her bridge club had fucked him, and probably ten times that number. Tune was a good sort. He wasn't society, but Sue Lingen was enough for the two of them, and Tune was so damn trusting that she knew she could have a handsome husband and as many lovers as she wanted.

Nicest of all, her parents were finally happy. Her daddy had always wanted a football player in the family to go with him to the games, someone on the inside. A minor problem was that Tune worked for that son-of-a-bitch L.C. Younger. That would have to stop. But T.W. Lingen was willing to wait. He could use a son-in-law in his business, but he would find out how the marriage was working before committing himself. It was easy enough to get his daughter divorces by the dozen, but having a son-in-law in the oil business with him was a very serious matter, and one that would have to prove out first.

Meanwhile, Sue Lingen called up all her favorite stores and gave them her patterns to register once again. She had used up her first and second choices in china, glassware, and silver with her earlier marriages.

Too bad they hadn't come up with new patterns to interest her. She hated to repeat, but on the other hand, Spode was beautiful and Gorham's Medici was a handsome silver pattern, even if she had used it before.

Then there were the caterers, decorators, fabric choices, upholstery decisions, paint and wallpaper choices that faced her all over again. What a bore!

Meantime there would be a nonstop series of parties to celebrate her fourth marriage, and in between she knew that she would have to find some free time to see John Travis.

As a matter of fact, she thought she would call Harriet Jurdam Younger, and get the inside story about what was happening in her life. She would make a lunch date with Harriet, and spend the afternoon with Harriet's husband. Sue Lingen liked the sound of that.

She felt warmed by the thought.

12

EMILIO LOPEZ seldom if ever smiled, and beneath his light olive-colored skin, his dark eyes, and jet black hair was a disposition of cold cynicism that nearly terrorized Devlin at first. In a short time, that terror put her under his domination, as it did many women.

The evening they left Terry Jordan at the hospital was the beginning of Devlin's indoctrination into the netherworld of San Antonio, and her flirtation with danger that barely allowed her to come out alive.

Each place they went that evening they met people who greeted Emilio with deference. He got the best tables, the best service, to the point of being obsequious. Paying for dinner and drinks at a nightclub they visited later, Emilio flashed a huge roll of bills. His tone was imperious to waiters, his manner distant with equals, and his conversation virtually nonexistent with Devlin. The first sight of Emilio's garishly decorated apartment in a modern complex on Austin Highway nearly made Devlin laugh. When he turned to stare at her, she barely suppressed her reaction at what assaulted her eyes. White shag rugs, huge three-dimensional fabric paintings of nudes, ornamental Persian tables, heavily upholstered white furniture covered in clear plastic, an elk's head over a fake fireplace, garishly colored artificial flowers in earthenware pots, and immense stuffed animals. On the console TV sat a large framed picture of Jesus with eyes that followed her wherever she walked.

The bedroom had framed centerfolds from *Playboy* on the walls, a mirrored ceiling and wall, and a huge pile throw on a heartshaped bed. Emilio made no demand of Devlin that she approve its appearance. Its very presence articulated his pride in the way it looked.

The apartment, like everything else about Emilio, was makeshift and expensive. He was a kid who adored expensive toys, threw away the

104

instructions on how to operate them, and kept them around as reminders that he could own them, and as many more as he wanted.

"Can I fix you a drink?" he asked.

"Sure, Emilio, scotch." He made his way to a console which sprang to life at his touch, extending itself and revealing glasses, liquor and ice automatically.

"How long have you been in this apartment?" Devlin inquired.

He paused for a moment and stared at her. She wondered if he suspected some underlying criticism. When he found none, he filled Devlin's glass and poured Cognac for himself, and walked toward the couch where Devlin sat. "I've been here about four years. I have other apartments around town."

It was as mysterious an answer as she had ever heard. Why would anyone want to live in different apartments? Emilio sat next to her and swallowed some of his drink. He looked at her with cold eyes.

"What are you doing here in town?"

"It was something personal, Emilio."

"Yeah, what?"

"I don't like to go into it. It doesn't make any difference. I'm here, and I like what I'm doing, and there's no hurry."

"Yeah, there's no hurry. You come from money?"

Devlin reddened. "I guess so."

"You either do or you don't. There ain't no 'guess so.' "

"Yes, my father is a rich man."

"What the hell are you doing here?"

"Emilio, I don't want to say that it's none of your business, but that's exactly what I'm saying."

He took her wrist and pressed on it. It was an angry gesture. The pressure hurt, and Devlin didn't know whether it was in response to her refusal to answer or another means of displaying power. That was crazy. She couldn't believe that anyone would react that way. Yet, the pressure continued.

"Emilio, please, you're hurting me."

Slowly he loosened his hold. He was incredibly strong.

"You know about Terry?" he inquired.

"What about her?"

"I tried to get her off the habit, but there was no way. That was the reason she took those dates, and that was the reason she got beat up. Never had enough dough to keep up with her buys. You ain't on H, are you?"

Devlin was confused. Terry a user of heroin? She didn't believe it, but why would Emilio lie? There was no reason for it. Terry's whole life was rodeo and keeping fit. It made no sense. She sipped her scotch, "What do you do, Emilio?"

He laughed and stood up. He motioned to Devlin to follow him. She didn't understand. "Come into the bedroom," he said matter of factly. "I think I'll fuck you."

As Devlin looked back on her experience with Emilio, that had been the moment she could have avoided the problems that arose. At that moment Devlin surrendered control of herself in response to a cold, mechanical being, who from that instant dominated her.

Looking back, Devlin thought that the reason was her loneliness. Her defense against all men had been so complete that not one of them had breached it. Emilio had, with his thoughtfulness for Terry. For that she trusted him and would give herself to him. Another thought that did not occur to her was that Emilio was as cold and forbidding as L.C. himself.

Even though Devlin loved her father, she feared him too—feared his disapproval and the withdrawal of his love.

Devlin put down her drink and submissively followed Emilio to his bedroom.

Devlin's experience with men had been limited to Tune. Since that time there had been no one. Her sexual discovery had been later than other young women her age, and yet Devlin found it natural for her. She also found it natural that there had been no stirrings, no need for a bedmate from the time she arrived in San Antonio. Yet, she felt obliged to follow Emilio's lead, on his command. In the bedroom, she began to undress.

There was no romance to this moment. She fleetingly recalled the first night when she had rushed into Tune's arms like a loving puppy, felt his stirrings, and abandoned herself to his exploration. Devlin felt alone and vulnerable as she stood naked in front of the ugly bed, seeing reflections of herself in the wall and ceiling mirrors. She felt a metallic taste in her mouth. The skin on her body seemed to hold a static charge.

She turned as Emilio emerged from the bathroom. He was naked. Devlin felt only fear as he lay on the bed in the bright light, waiting for her to join him.

Hesitantly she moved to the bed, her eyes still staring at his hairy nakedness. She murmured, "The lights."

"Leave them," he commanded.

She lay down next to him, uncertain of what was expected of her, or for that matter what would happen to her when Emilio was aroused. Devlin closed her eyes. Why was she here? Why was she doing this? It was too late to do anything but feel terror.

When Devlin awoke Monday morning, shafts of sunlight were shooting under and around the blinds. The sun played on the bedclothes, and she turned to see Emilio's body stretched out grotesquely on top of the sheets. She rose from bed and made her way to the bathroom and closed the door. She stared at herself in the mirror, and splashed water on her face. She felt brutalized by the cold water, the way she felt about her entire body. There was not a moment's pleasure that she could recapture. The lovemaking had been forceful and punishing. Devlin felt an ache from the pounding of Emilio's hard body against her.

She knew at once what it seemed like to her, as her mind went back to the days she had worked at Black Diamond. She grimaced at the allusion in her mind. She had learned the expression and she had learned how to do it. It was called "screwing cotton." Old river hands taught it to younger men and then to the next generation. The practice of placing huge cotton bales in the hold of a freighter was as much a skill as piloting the channel. Screwing the cotton simply meant forcing more cotton bales into the hold of a ship than it was intended to carry. Last night she had been used as a reservoir for Emilio. He had positioned her and handled her exclusively for his satisfaction. Devlin was to be filled, and she had been, time after time.

As the lovemaking continued through the night, Devlin found a secret pleasure in teasing and denying him. His anger was something she kept not more than a fraction away. Her control over his near frustration was something she began to like.

Emilio had the final thrust to her parry. She submitted a last time to his angry demand. Then he quickly fell asleep. In the dark, for the longest time, Devlin felt her own anger rise. He hadn't paid the smallest amount of attention to her. He was a beast, she thought, and yet she felt an extraordinary degree of satisfaction in his very coldness. Devlin was comfortable with that. It was familiar.

Moreover, Devlin felt that this night she had climbed out of the role of a girl, and by her entrance into Emilio's perverse and dangerous world, her break with home was now final.

Over the next few weeks, Devlin saw Emilio frequently. She still waited on tables at Carmine's. Some nights, and she never knew when, he would be waiting for her at the back door. Those nights were full of strange surprises. Emilio made his rounds of clubs and bars downtown. Some of them were in the center of town on Durango. They were low-class dives, with strippers and B-girls. Emilio and Devlin would sit at a rear table and inevitably be joined by the owner or manager. Never once did he introduce Devlin to the men who sat with them. It was a strange underworld that Devlin knew contained drugs and prostitution.

Devlin's Eldorado was put in good repair, courtesy of Emilio. It felt good to have the symbol of her freedom back once again.

Terry returned to the trailer park from the hospital. She was still badly bruised and black and blue. Devlin was shocked when she saw her and guilty at the reminder that she had moved into Terry's territory with Emilio.

Her friend was silent and withdrawn. She seldom spoke, and when she did, she was almost impossible to hear. It seemed as if the heart and fire had been taken out of her. Terry had been through a terrible physical ordeal, but something more had happened to her. She knew that Carmine wouldn't take her back until she had completely recovered. Devlin watched as Terry vainly tried to use makeup to cover her bruises. Curiously, although there was no way to mask them completely, what gave her away was the frightened look in her eyes.

As soon as Terry could drive, she left early in the afternoons for undisclosed places, coming home even later than Devlin returned from Carmine's. Devlin knew that she was going on "dates."

Life at Carmine's was routine. The acknowledgment came from everyone that she was Emilio's girl, and it gave her status with Carmine and the other cocktail waitresses. There was a flurry of excitement one morning when Devlin read about Emilio in the paper. He had been brought in for questioning by the police in connection with the murder of a known drug dealer. Devlin didn't hear from Emilio that he had been released. Her first knowledge of it came that night, when he stood waiting for her outside Carmine's.

As they drove away in his Continental, Devlin thought of inquiring about his arrest. But it was none of her business. She had accepted Emilio for what he was, and she knew that he would have no patience with her curiosity. Moreover, Devlin was not only unwilling to find out, she was frightened about the truth.

Emilio drove them downtown to a nightclub he frequented. The "Eskimo Pie" was dark and noisy. A topless dancer on the bar's counter was moving wildly to the beat of a record played at maximum volume. Crowds of men stood at the bar, drinking.

Devlin made her way behind Emilio to the back, avoiding the staring eyes of customers whose lusting looks disturbed her. A man was already seated at their table. He looked young and earnest and very much out of his element. Devlin, for the first time in all the weeks she had been with Emilio, was introduced to him. He looked at Devlin strangely.

Emilio ordered drinks. He reached into his pocket for an envelope and handed it to the man, who quickly placed it in his coat pocket. The man stared once again at Devlin. Then, she recognized him. His name and photograph were in the morning's newspaper. He was the assistant district attorney who had released Emilio from custody. There was no evidence of wrongdoing, he had said. The investigation was continuing through other channels and other parties.

Moments later, Emilio turned to Devlin. "Stay here with him. I'll see you in a day or so."

The man smiled embarrassedly. Devlin understood what was happening. She was the last part of the payoff. She glared back at Emilio, "I'm going with you," she said.

Emilio grabbed her wrist. Devlin felt the intense pressure of Emilio's hand as he twisted it. She was in terrible pain. What was happening to her? How had she gotten into this situation?

With a swift brush of her arm, Devlin knocked over the drinks on the table. In the split second that Emilio reacted, he released her hand.

108

Devlin sprang to her feet and raced out of the nightclub.

The same lusting eyes viewed her with interest as Devlin pushed her way through the crowd at the bar. She went out to the street. First she ran, then she walked quickly to avoid attention in the direction of the Palacio del Rio in the hope of finding a taxi. Devlin looked over her shoulder, fully expecting to see the white Continental speeding down the street behind her.

She crossed over the stone bridge spanning the river and made her way to the front of the hotel. A sleepy-eyed driver was jostled awake. Devlin got inside and held her breath.

She gave the driver the address of the trailer park, and he stared back at her. Sullenly he dropped the flag on the meter and headed out of the center of town. Devlin's mind was reeling. She had been playing with fire. What a fool she had been. How had she gotten herself into this situation? She would leave San Antonio tomorrow. Where could she go? Anywhere, but never to make this kind of mistake again.

The traffic at one in the morning was light. The taxi arrived at the gate to the trailer park. Devlin paid the fare, got out, and walked through the dark aisles toward her trailer. The Eldorado was at Carmine's. She would have to go there tomorrow and pick it up. She would get there early, better to be out of San Antonio as soon as possible.

The few electric lights at the heads of each aisle barely lit her way. She nearly stumbled in a deep rut in the darkened path. The trailer park was quiet. The night-shift workers at the bases were on their jobs. The rest of the park's population was finally asleep—the older retired couples, the workers at the base, the non-coms and enlisted men who lived off base with wives and children.

Devlin shook her head with wonder as she neared her trailer. Why had she left the comfort and protection of the house on Montrose. There had been no need for her to do anything she hadn't wanted to. Tune? She could have handled the situation with L.C. She had really screwed things up to a fare-thee-well. It had been almost a year since she left home. She would phone L.C. tomorrow morning, and maybe, just maybe, she would go back.

She opened the door to the trailer. The interior was ablaze with light. Emilio sat directly in front of her on a chair. Terry sat opposite on the bed. For a moment, Devlin considered running.

"Sit down, Red, I want to talk to you."

Terry was crying.

Devlin seemed undecided. Emilio stood up and positioned himself between her and the door.

"Emilio, leave me alone, and get the hell out of here." Devlin was quivering with rage and fear.

Terry stared at her. "Devlin, you should have done what Emilio wanted." Her voice was toneless.

Emilio advanced on Devlin as she sat on the bed. "Terry's right, Red, you should 'a done what I wanted you to. You're no better than any other whore. You made me look stupid tonight. The guy would have settled for a feel or a hand job. Red, you made me look dumb. I don't *like* that."

"Get the hell out of my way, Emilio. I'm getting out," Devlin muttered.

"You're not going anywhere till I tell you to."

Devlin sat shaking with fear. My God, what was happening to her? Where was the protection she had always been able to count on?

"Are you going to go back to this guy tonight, Red, and tell him you're sorry and that you made a mistake?"

Devlin spat out the word, "No."

Emilio slapped her across the face. It stung fiercely.

"I didn't hear that, Red. I'll ask you again."

Terry interrupted, "Devlin, it was Emilio that put me in the hospital. It wasn't those two guys."

Devlin sat immovable, her eyes streaming. She remembered the sight of Terry bruised almost beyond recognition. Terry's words had paralyzed her.

"Are you gonna do as I say?" he shouted at her.

Devlin sat dumb with fear.

Emilio raised his fist and smashed Devlin across the face. She fell to the floor from the blow. He kicked her with the point of his shoe, then leaned forward and pulled Devlin by the hair, and held it, while he readied another blow at her face, and then Devlin screamed.

●

Devlin steadied herself for the first of ten stitches she required in the emergency room of the Santa Rosa Hospital. The cut had been frozen, so there was no way that she would feel the stitches. The intern was young and professional, and Devlin had been given a sedative to calm her. Standing opposite her in the emergency room was Terry, who had driven Devlin to the hospital.

Earlier when she lay on the floor of the trailer, she heard Terry plead with Emilio to leave. It would only get him in more trouble, she implored. "The redhead isn't important," she said. Finally Emilio made the decision to leave after he heard the people gathering at the entrance to the trailer. He turned, adjusted his jacket and tie, and opened the door. He elbowed his way through the crowd outside that had heard Devlin's screams. As Emilio left, Devlin heard Terry shoo them away. "It was nothing," she said. "Nothing at all."

Terry helped Devlin into her VW and drove her to the hospital. Devlin was silent and angry. She hurt badly and was bleeding. What was worse was that she hated, for the first time. If she had had a gun in her hands, she would have killed Emilio Lopez.

The night air quieted her on the drive to the hospital. She spoke to Terry, "Why did he beat you?"

"He said I held out money on him."

"Did you?" Devlin asked.

"Yes," she said simply. "I wanted that red satin shirt so bad, Devlin. There were the finals in Fort Worth . . ."

"He said that you were on drugs, Terry."

She nodded. "I had to, Devlin, it was the pain, so much pain after the bull-riding and all. It helped, and I had to go on dates for Emilio to pay for it . . . ." Terry's voice trailed off in sadness.

After the intern cleaned her face, Devlin looked in a mirror. She looked bruised, but she had gotten off cheaply. Terry had only taken Emilio's money, but Devlin had taken his self-respect. She had made him look like a fool, and he wouldn't forget it. She had been lucky. Now, there was nothing that she could do but leave San Antonio. Terry read her mind.

"You better get out of town, Devlin."

Devlin nodded. "What about you?"

"I've got no place to go. Emilio will take me back, and I'll get back into rodeoing before long. It's okay."

Devlin pleaded, "Come with me, Terry. I owe you an awful lot."

Terry shook her head. "Forget it, Dev, another time. Do like I say. Get out of town." She turned and was gone. Devlin stood up. She felt dizzy. The intern tried to steady her.

"Maybe you better not leave."

She shook her head and walked out the door of the emergency room. She had her car keys and her wallet. She couldn't go back to the trailer for her clothes. Almost a year after she arrived in San Antonio, with less than ten dollars, she was going to leave with about the same amount of money. If she were lucky, the Eldorado would still be parked behind Carmine's.

Devlin walked to the street corner of Pecos and Houston. It was nearly dawn. She was cold and hungry, and she hurt. The first priority was to get her car, a cup of hot coffee, and then, get out of town. She stood beneath a street light, just as it automatically switched off for the daylight hours. She waved her thumb at a passing car. Miraculously it stopped, and a young Air Force second lieutenant opened the door for her. He was on his way to Kelly Field. He knew where Carmine's was. As crazy as it sounded, he would drop her off in front of the place.

He said, "You know of course the place is closed."

Devlin nodded.

As he drove, the lieutenant began to make conversation. "I know it's none of my business, but what's a pretty girl like you doing out on the street this time of day, and all beat up the way you are?"

Devlin started to cry. It had been a long night.

The lieutenant changed his mind about talking and turned the radio

111

on. He was very anxious to be done with his good-samaritan offer and get this young woman out of his car. However pretty she might be without her bruises, the redhead clearly spelled trouble.

13

THE WARDEN at Huntsville State Prison was damn happy to be rid of T-Bird Johnson. T-Bird, tiny and wrenlike, with a perpetual stubble of a gray beard that never seemed worth shaving, or even capable of being shaved, should not have been sent to Huntsville for assault with a deadly weapon, when the victim hadn't even been hurt. In T-Bird's case, he committed the same offense three times, and all on the same man, with equal results, no pain or punishment except his own. What compounded the problem was that the man T-Bird chose as the continuing object of his violence was the sheriff of Uvalde County, in which the city of Uvalde is situated.

T-Bird's defense each time was the same, "The son-of-a-bitch cheated me." Weighing all of 125 pounds, brandishing an ax handle the first time, a tire iron the second, and a fence post the third time, T-Bird was no match for the 250-pound sheriff, who took the matter seriously, particularly since each time he was waylaid in the dark, in order for T-Bird to gain an advantage. It was not the third attempt that the sheriff was anxious to punish. It was the fourth try he wanted to prevent. The first time, T-Bird got off with probation. The second time he got a suspended sentence, and the third time the judge threw T-Bird into Huntsville.

By the time he was fifty-five, T-Bird Johnson had led an extremely checkered life. His nickname stemmed from his service with the Thunderbird Division which came out of Oklahoma. It achieved an impressive record of valor and heroism in World War II. Although it was essentially an Oklahoma Division, soldiers from other states served in the 45th, among them cartoonist Bill Mauldin, whose cartoon characters Willie and Joe became the best known G.I.s in the war. T-Bird claimed every day in his life that Mauldin had drawn Joe, the tiny one, as a copy of himself. T-Bird kept a cellophane-covered copy of his favorite Willie-and-Joe cartoon next to a photo of himself in uniform.

T-Bird, in addition to his work in the prison library, was a self-proclaimed defender of the oppressed and the disadvantaged. His interest was the righting of wrongs. Others in prison—jailhouse lawyers—would spend days and weeks researching law books and carefully compose writs and pleas for themselves or for other inmates. T-Bird had bigger causes.

T-Bird instituted suit against the entire prison system for overcrowding and faulty nutrition, and other suits to correct the insufficient pay for the work performed by prisoners in the factories and farms of the Texas Correction System.

The warden cursed the day that the U.S. Supreme Court gave federal and state prisoners direct access to the federal courts. T-Bird kept a running correspondence going with like-minded prisoners in other states. By the time T-Bird was paroled, he was on the verge of having the entire penal system of Texas declared unconstitutional.

On an April morning in 1971, at seven in the morning, T-Bird left the Huntsville gate. He wore a prison-issue suit of gray tweed and heavy cordovan shoes. All his possessions were in a large paper sack. In it were copies of pleas and writs that he had composed during his two-year stay, some clothing, and a hand-worked object that T-Bird had lavished the best part of those two years in shaping, polishing, and tending. It was a "doodlebug."

In the distant past of mankind, men, impelled by the necessity of finding water, discovered that certain persons with the gift, holding a wand, would cause the wand to dip and quiver as a sign of the presence of water. Some thought that the magic wand was a branch of the staff that Moses used on his pilgrimage in Canaan. In the Americas, a fork of willow or hazel or peach, in the hands of water witches, could discover the precious liquid.

When oil was discovered, the water witch moved to the oil fields with the conviction that knowing the elements of water, fire, and earth, his wigglestick could divine oil as easily as water. As time passed, and doubters saw the tiny rod in the midst of the huge array of derricks, pumps, refineries, the wigglestick man turned to a more scientific-looking instrument. The switches of willow were jettisoned in favor of elaborate metal contraptions. These were called "doodlebugs," and the diviner a "doodlebugger."

It was on Route 10 later that day that T-Bird spied a stunning ginger-haired girl standing near a fire-engine-red Eldorado convertible at a service station. A truck had given him a lift this far. Something about the sight of Devlin Younger stirred the divining rod in T-Bird's soul. He marched to the service station, and after watching her pay the attendant for gas, T-Bird made his typically gallant introduction.

"Miss, my name is T-Bird Johnson, and I just got out of prison. I would like very much to have a ride with you in your handsome Eldorado. I know a fine restaurant very near here run by a dear friend, Mrs. Foley, in the town of Seguin. If my memory serves me they have liver and onions today, okra gumbo, snap beans, cabbage, sweet potatoes, and homemade rolls. It's modest in price, and I am good company, and besides, I hope you won't take it amiss if I tell you that I'm deeply in love with you, and hope to convince you to marry me."

Devlin laughed deliciously. Her face was alight from T-Bird's irrepressible smile. Devlin had planned to drive to Houston and home as quickly as possible, but Seguin was not much out of her way. More to the point, she really didn't want to go home, even though she felt defeated by the experience in San Antonio and dirtied by her experience with Emilio.

Devlin looked at the funny little man. His eyes danced, and he smiled broadly at her. He was in seventh heaven, and there was an extraordinary goodness about him that radiated affection. She started the car and headed in the direction of Mrs. Foley's.

The town of Seguin, Texas, with its neat, shaded streets, and pretty homes, many of historic note, is situated near the Guadalupe River. Even though it got its name from Juan Seguin, a staunch Texas patriot, the tiny city was settled to a great extent by the massive German immigration into Texas in the 1840s. The Whipping Oak opposite the courthouse on the square, a three-inch iron ring still embedded in the tree, secured thieves and wifebeaters for public lashing. As a tourist attraction, however, for the last twenty-five years the Whipping Oak has been overshadowed by the extraordinary kitchen of a gray-haired motherly woman legendary throughout Texas.

Bustling from the main dining room of the white frame house into the kitchen, a round, fresh-faced woman in her sixties, spelled by two young teenage girls, her grandchildren, toted plates, swung in and out among the customers carrying refills of food, empty plates back into the kitchen, to the steady hum of fifty diners. Over-sized eighteen-wheelers were parked down the street. Cars and pickups formed a cordon along the treelined street in front of the old building. Two places emptied as a pair of truckers left behind a stack of empty plates. T-Bird ushered Devlin to the bench. He held up a five-dollar bill, the price of two lunches. One of the young girls snatched the bill from his hand, piled the dirty dishes on the tray, dabbed at the table with a wet cloth, and set down two plates, knives, forks, and spoons wrapped in paper napkins. With a quick move, T-Bird shortstopped the collard greens, watermelon rind preserves, and speckled butter beans with salt pork, spooned out portions for himself and Devlin, and set himself up in position to signal for the other delicacies.

Devlin began to eat. The men in the room scarcely paid attention to

115

her. Everyone in the room was submerged in a flood of home-cooked food that made her head swim with its variety and flavor.

"You serious you just got out of jail?"

"U-huh. Ever been to jail?"

Devlin smiled, "Not yet, but I'm still young."

"It's an enlightening experience, young lady. It teaches you that *not* all corruption is out here where you can see it. Some of it is left in jail for us poor sinners who get caught. You see, my problem is that I left some important work in Huntsville, and I'm sure that what with the diversions of the world outside, I may not get around to reforming the prison system."

Devlin wiped her chin. "How are you planning to spend your time?"

"A pretty young woman like you never has to worry about who's going to take care of her, but I'm five foot two inches tall. I had to lie about my height just to get into the war, and then I had to lie to get *out*, but I've got to admit that if my face isn't my fortune, then my doodlebug is, and I'm planning to finally make it big."

Devlin reached for the pitcher of milk, poured a glass for herself and T-Bird. "What's a doodlebug?"

"Ah-hah," T-Bird shouted triumphantly, "got you where I want you. It's my magic to find oil, that's what it is."

"Then you'll drill and be rich?" She smiled.

"Devlin, I will use your given name, because I like you, and perhaps I can ask your daddy to stake me to the drilling costs?" He added conspiratorially, "I'll even marry you if I have to." He laughed uproariously.

"T-Bird, that's the best offer I've had in a long time. I don't speak to my daddy, and all I have is title to that red beauty outside, and about six more dollars to my name. I had to leave my clothes and things in San Antonio, and I'm in worse trouble than you are."

"Devlin, let me be your guide to the world. You've got a car. I need transportation. You've got six dollars. That's almost as much as I have. You need company, and so do I. But even though you have beauty, my God, do you have beauty, there is one thing that makes us come out even, and that's my doodlebug."

Devlin laughed, "Where are you headed?"

"Uvalde, there's a man I know who runs a poker game there that I think I can bust."

"It's waiting for you?"

"It's waiting for *anyone*. I'm the one that's been waiting for *it*, and then with a couple of dollars, and my doodlebug, I think that I'll just buy me some leases, and maybe I can convince you to sell your Eldorado for something more economical to operate, and you could put the difference into drilling for our well."

"Our well?"

"Of course, Devlin. I took my integrity along with me to jail, and now

I have it back in the free world. When I say partners, I mean it. No ninety-ten, or eighty-twenty, I mean right down the line."

A teenage girl lifted T-Bird's plate and put down three kinds of pie. He dove into the apple and started on the peach.

"Can you sure enough find oil?"

T-Bird grinned.

"Can you sure enough win at poker?"

He chuckled and chewed.

"How far is Uvalde?" Devlin asked.

T-Bird looked at Devlin's pie plate. "Ain't you going to eat your pie?"

Devlin carefully piled up the pies and added three thick slices of white bread. Then she wrapped them in her napkin. "T-Bird, if we're partners, you won't be offended, will you, if I say that I've never seen you play poker, and tonight if you lose your bank roll and mine too, I'd like to have something for breakfast."

T-Bird stood up as tall as five foot two would allow, pounded his chest, and smiled. "Devlin, have confidence. This is your lucky day. Uvalde is the way you just came, 80 miles past San Antonio."

Whatever else could be said about T-Bird, Devlin had to admit that he was a nonstop conversationalist. As the miles flew by, Devlin felt a keen anticipation about the adventure. She put behind her the lingering thought that her search for freedom had been a disaster, and that she had been too big for her britches. Only hours before she had been tempted by the thought of going home, making her apologies, and resuming the life that L.C. had ordained for her. She would be a submissive daughter, a perfect wife, and somehow her cravings would be stilled. Other girls seemed to be happy with that. They lived conventional lives. Not one of the girls she knew at UT or in Houston would have done what she had done. She had spent the best part of a year drifting.

Yet as she drove, she realized that it had not really been a disaster. She had nothing to show for her dramatic flight from marriage with Tune except herself. She had been happy, for the most part, working at Carmine's. She had learned a lot from Terry and even from Emilio. She learned that there were people, outside the protected atmosphere of well-brought-up young women, who lived lives that were routine and hard-working. The prospect of a paycheck and friends were the things that kept them going. Beers, a burger after work, and an occasional movie had been the limit of her extravagances. But that was enough. She learned that the palship of two women fighting to stay afloat was very precious, that the quality of the friendship she had with Terry was something special.

Maybe it wasn't completely fair since Devlin always had a parachute to safety—L.C. Terry had none. Even though Terry was forced to use sex to survive, she still had a dignity and honesty that Devlin had not seen in some of the girls she grew up with.

Devlin *had* come away with something.

117

Something else had been accomplished in San Antonio. Devlin knew now what it was. It was not enough to run away from something. She had to run toward something. She hadn't found that yet. She smiled to herself as she heard T-Bird declaim on a hundred subjects: the amount of furniture produced by the Texas prison system in its factories last year, and how they could afford to pay the prisoners a minimum wage; the value of vitamin C in the diet, and how supplementary doses would help reduce prison colds, inflammation of the joints, and keep hair from falling out. Something about her small companion felt right to Devlin. T-Bird had said that this was her lucky day. It might just be.

"Devlin, I'm going to teach you everything I know about the oil business, because I have this great legacy, which I should leave to someone before I die."

"Okay, T-Bird, that's a deal. And when you've told me everything you know, then just disappear, but leave me with all your vitamin C."

He laughed.

"Where are you going?"

"First thing I want to do is find the man who sent me to jail."

"Look," Devlin said, "I didn't sign on for a vendetta."

"Devlin, the first thing you've got to understand in the oil business, is that yesterday was then, and now is now. R.D. Stanhope is our ticket. Also, he runs the poker game I'm looking to bust. Also, he has an eye for pretty girls, and you won't do me no harm, and also, he's the most crooked man in all of Uvalde County."

"But you said he's the sheriff."

"Was—but no more. Devlin, you don't understand, eviltry is no respecter of high or low places. A man is more apt to be a crook when he has great opportunities than when he ain't."

Devlin smiled, "Which way?"

"When we get to Uvalde, head south on Route 83. When you see the biggest, fanciest ranch you ever seen, then you know you've arrived."

Uvalde, in Southwest Texas, is near the great state's natural line that separates the hills and plains. The Balcones Fault—a fracture in the earth's crust—wanders from the Rio Grande near Del Rio east to San Antonio, and then continues in a meandering way the entire distance to the Red River in the northeast.

Halfway between San Antonio and Del Rio lies Uvalde, a city of less than 15,000. It was settled in 1853, under the protective guns of nearby Fort Inge, and not far from the protective cavalry at Fort Clark. It has had a violent and colorful past. Indian fighters, gun fighters, and lawmen have swept through the territory. But now in the foothills of Uvalde county, there are ranchers raising cattle, goats, and sheep.

Elsewhere in this sparse and rocky landscape have been the homes of famous men, fierce and independent. Pat Garrett made Uvalde his residence, as did a fast gun named John King Fisher. Legend has it that the gunfighter placed a sign at the crossroads leading to his ranch. The sign read: "This is King Fisher's Road! Take the other."

Elsewhere in Uvalde County, a sign on the outskirts of the thriving little city of Hondo greets travelers: "This is God's Country Please Don't Drive Through It Like Hell."

As Devlin's Eldorado approached its destination, T-Bird sat perched like a sparrow high atop the front seat. Any short stop would have tossed him precipitously in the air, twenty yards away, and cracked his skull. He didn't care. He was as much aquiver with excitement as his doodlebug might have been in the presence of oil.

During long nights in Huntsville, lying in his cell, T-Bird dreamed about former Sheriff R.D. Stanhope. T-Bird had repeated fantasies of dropping R.D. in a pot of boiling oil, or stringing him up by his toes over a lime pit, or holding him under the water of the nearby Nueces River.

"I'm gonna get that fella," he muttered half to himself and half out loud. Devlin wrinkled her brow. She hadn't signed on with this tiny bantam of a man to become a partner in murder.

T-Bird let out a whoop. There it was, a handsome spread, sitting serenely on a rise, a long low series of ranch buildings, adobe in color, planted in oak around the house, with tall cactus marking the road to its entrance.

Devlin brought the car to a dusty stop in front of the main building. "You're not going to do something that will toss you back in Huntsville, are you?"

"Me? Who me?" T-Bird asked innocently. "Gotta know, Devlin, that I ain't the first to try and kill R.D. Stanhope."

Devlin cried, "But what has he *done*?"

T-Bird curled his lip. "The son-of-a-bitch never loses at poker. That's what he's done."

The ranch house door opened and a tall, heavyset man in his fifties, weighing over 250 pounds, emerged.

"T-Bird, they let you out of jail. Come on in, you son-of-a-bitch." T-Bird's nemesis roared with pleasure.

The sight of T-Bird, standing next to the immense figure over a foot taller than he was and twice his bulk, was amusing. R.D. shook T-Bird's hand with a huge paw that all but enveloped his. As he performed this ritual, R.D. stared at Devlin with a sexual fascination that was almost embarrassing. Devlin blushed to the roots of her hair, then walked up and extended her hand.

"Mr. Stanhope, I'm T-Bird's partner."

The huge man laughed. "You're the only thing that T-Bird's ever had that I envied him. Everything else he's had I've won from him at poker or sent him off to Huntsville."

"You sent him to jail!" Devlin challenged.

"Sure, and I'll do it again. This little fellow nearly took my head off."

119

T-Bird nodded happily.

"But you stole from him."

R.D. laughed. "Did he tell you that? Hell, I stole from everyone else, but I never stole from this little fella. He's too easy to win from at poker for me to bother with anything that crude."

Devlin still wasn't sure. R.D. let the two of them into the spacious entrance hall, and then into the curiously appointed living room. With all R.D.'s money, he liked to live as his fantasies dictated. The room was full of cowboy gear on the walls, paintings of western scenes, and the furniture was appropriate for a frontier whorehouse. Ornate Victorian sofas, tufted in red silk, red velvet drapes, and a floral-figured carpet were throwbacks to a life that R.D. was too young to have lived. He was perfectly prepared to commemorate it today, and he obviously had the money to finance the trip into the rollicking western past.

"R.D.," T-Bird asked, "you've got a game tonight?"

The huge man nodded, "Sure, just like usual."

"Can I get in?"

"You got any money?"

"Nah, but I've got something better than money," he said fiercely.

"I've yet to learn what that is." Then he turned to Devlin. "This old bastard hasn't introduced us proper. You know that I'm R.D. Stanhope. Call me R.D. What do they call you, darlin', besides beautiful?"

Devlin smiled. R.D. was a thief and a rogue, but he had the kind of charm that men like him always have. It was the reason that T-Bird was back. She wasn't sure that R.D. hadn't stole T-Bird blind, and maybe a thousand more like him, but so great was the lure of these men, that the force of their personalities always brought the suckers back. Perhaps their sheer size overwhelmed people, like a tidal wave.

"I'm Devlin Younger, R.D., and I'm happy to meet anybody that T-Bird says stole from him."

R.D. laughed. "Then you don't believe my poker-winning story?"

"Hell, no, R.D.," Devlin laughed, "I'd sooner believe that there were two Christmases in every week than think that you'd leave anything to chance."

"Miss, when I play poker, there's nothing that I leave to chance."

Devlin smiled, "Then I guess you'll deal me in to tonight's game?"

"It's not for ladies."

"R.D., there are no ladies in Texas, just those who pretend to be. I'm a woman, and I've come to believe that you noticed that from the first minute you saw me."

R.D. was embarrassed for the first time in his life. He quickly recovered, but not before he recognized that Devlin Younger had something to say, and was prepared to say it.

"T-Bird, what do you have that's as good as money?"

"My doodlebug, R.D. It took me two years, three weeks, and two days to make, and it's guaranteed to find oil."

R.D. smiled. "We'll see." Then he turned to Devlin. "Little lady, if you'd like to change or something, one of my servants will go and get your things, and take you to a room. You *are* spending the night."

"Seeing we don't have more than twelve dollars between us, R.D., I take your invitation with pleasure, and seeing that I don't have anything more to my name than what I'm wearing, this is not going to be a fancy poker game."

R.D. eyed Devlin. "You'll tell me the story sometime of how you came to lose all your pretty things, maybe I can help. I like helping lovely ladies. Your friends are mine, and your enemies are mine too. I can be a dangerous enemy."

Devlin rose, and smiled seductively, "I think, R.D., you can also be a dangerous friend."

For the second time, R.D. reddened. Now that ginger-haired, green-eyed beauty had done it to him twice in a row. Dammit, he liked it. It made him feel young.

"Devlin, you come on in, and I'll show you your room myself." Then R.D. turned to T-Bird, "Come on, you old bastard, you can hole up next door, and let me see that damn doodlebug of yours. I may be able to use it to open up bottles of beer."

There may have been more charming rascals in Texas than R.D. Stanhope, but not many. There may have been better poker players than R.D., but very few, and the evening proved to be first a disappointment to Devlin, and then a disaster. Had it not been for her experience on the docks with the hard-drinking, card-playing stevedores and swabbies, she might have lost the Eldorado, her boots, her belt buckle, and everything else.

As it was, one of the friends that Devlin made at Black Diamond was a poker-playing freak, who found in Devlin a most apt pupil. Afternoons, when he should have been working, he spent his time behind bales of cotton, instructing Devlin in the niceties of the game. It would have been moderately useful for anyone, but especially so for Devlin, who was blessed with a natural poker-playing gift. She learned the rules, the odds, and the play from him, but the one thing that Devlin couldn't learn was the soul of the game. Two people at the table had that from birth. Devlin was one. R.D. was the other.

The players were men who arrived around eight in the evening. There were five in all, plus R.D., Devlin, and T-Bird. The men were simple working stiffs. Two of them were still on the sheriff's staff. Another was a small rancher from Del Rio who made the trip especially every week, and the others were local men. They were shocked to a man when R.D. introduced Devlin to the game. It had never been done, but if anyone were to do it, it would be R.D. The men minded their manners and their language. But Devlin's cutthroat approach and professional hand on the deck gave them an indication that they had better watch their cards.

121

As the game progressed, by his insight, personality, and presence, R.D. began to assert his influence over the game. He had advanced T-Bird a thousand dollars against the doodlebug, and T-Bird gave Devlin a hundred dollars of it to play with. For all his enthusiasm, T-Bird was a willing and hapless victim. He called when he should have folded. He raised when he should have called. He folded when he should have stayed. Devlin saw this with despair. Whatever the value of the doodlebug might be, her partner of twelve hours was a bad poker player and a willing victim.

R.D. played a brand of poker that was as near to an exact science as brain surgery. He observed every pore in his opponent's face as if he were able to chase the shadows of thought beneath the cool surface of their eyes. Devlin sat with her cards, keeping even, but reading R.D. with continued admiration.

At three in the morning, the game was called. Devlin had loaned T-Bird back her stake plus her winnings, and he had lost it. The big winner was R.D. At the door, the men tipped their Stetsons to Devlin and shook her hand. They were full of compliments on her poker. They hoped she'd be at the next game.

T-Bird was full of woe. He had lost his doodlebug and his hope of a stake. He had shamed himself in front of Devlin, for all his bragging, and he was angry. He stormed upstairs without saying goodnight. Devlin started to follow. R.D. stopped her.

"Devlin, come on into the living room, and let's have us a beer. I want to talk to you."

Devlin was wary, "About what?"

"Miss Younger, I'm old enough to be your daddy, and I sure wish I wasn't. You know that you lit a fire in my old body, but I don't have the engine to keep it burning and that's a fact. But there are two things I can do for you, and myself. First thing I can do is make a suggestion on how to play a little better game of poker than you do. It's all in your body, little lady, not your mind. It's like dancing or making love. The second thing I can do is to help you get some money together and get yourself a stake. I made me a pile of money because I found out where the oil is. I never left home, never drilled a hole, never put up a well. All I do is to buy and sell leases. I buy 'em cheap and sell them dear. It's as simple as that."

Devlin took off her boots and tucked her legs under her on the couch. R.D. put his legs up on the coffee table and took a swig of Lone Star. Devlin smiled and lifted her own bottle. She settled in, feeling she was at the start of something very important. She knew what R.D. meant about poker. She knew what it meant to make love to Tune by the book—without feeling, without meaning. She knew that there would be a man someday who would let her abandon the ghosts and the voices that made it mechanical, like playing out a technical game of draw poker. She had seen the joy on R.D.'s face as he received his cards, studied them, sat back and reflected, and pursued the pleasure of the contest. He felt it, and she would too, sometime.

"Devlin, there's money all over Texas, and it's all in pieces of paper. I know it, and don't ask me for a minute *how* I know. Hell, I'll tell you. I got me the finest ring of spies all over the state in the offices of geologists of the big oil companies. Those nice fellows do their hunting and testing, and looking and sampling, and examination of the land, and then they figure out where the oil companies should go to acquire the land. Only favor they do is to tell me the same thing they tell the people they work for. Gives me a chance to get there soonest and fastest. But it don't suit my style to go out, running around all over Texas buying up leases—so if you'd like a job of work that I think you'd be good at, I can give you a stake. You can take your fine-looking car, and your fine-looking face and handsome figure, and try to sweet-talk some of these worthless dumb ranchers out of the leases on their land, and then I can turn them over to the oil companies, so *they* can get what they need."

Devlin smiled. "I like it, R.D."

"Good," he smiled, "I thought I could talk business to you."

"We'll talk the deal now, if it's okay, and I'll talk for T-Bird and myself."

"T-Bird? You don't need him."

"You're wrong, R.D., I'm doing it with my heart and not my mind, like you told me about poker. Besides, if I cheated him, what would you think of me? I'll tell you what you'd think of me. You'd be waiting around to find out when I figured it was your turn. R.D., I won't do that to you, and I'm gonna watch that you don't do it to me. Now, let's talk deal, and after we put it on paper, I want to fix you up some *huevos rancheros*. I am not fixing to go to bed tonight, so you better get yourself ready to eat and talk. I want to know everything you know, about oil and poker."

R.D. smiled. "That's a deal." God, how he wished he were ten years younger, or even five. Still, he figured, having Devlin working for him was the next best thing to having her in bed. Hell, that just showed how stupid he was getting at his age. Nothing would be as good as having her in bed. He sighed, and the two of them headed for the kitchen. From the rear, R.D. eyed her high-waisted form, her long legs, and her tiny, high-pitched rear. The filly with the ginger hair and green eyes.

Ah well.

14

US HIGHWAY 80 and Interstate 20, along the towns of Ranger, Abilene, Big Spring, Midland, Odessa, and on to Pecos, cross the inhospitable land of West Texas. At Abilene, startlingly clean and bright on the rolling plains, one enters a land of small stands of timber, endless vistas on the broad flat horizon, air so sharp and clear that it can make you use your car heater in the morning, and your air conditioner in the afternoon.

Midland and Odessa are the two capitals of this oil-rich region of the Permian Basin, an area where not too long ago lone sentries stood guard over buffalo hides stacked on top of rises of land, free of trees and scant of any real vegetation.

Midland, Texas, a city of over fifty thousand, is the oil capital of this area, with over five hundred companies, serving oil and the oil fields, located in the tall towers of the city. This is the Permian Basin, likened to an inland sea of oil which floats incorrigibly under parts of the entire region. The first wells were discovered in the 1920s, and only a small part of this underground ocean has been tapped. Yet a hundred thousand wishful drillers have failed to find the key to the unwilling jigsaw that puts riches under parts of it, and dry holes under others.

When Devlin's Eldorado pulled into the Holiday Inn on East Highway in Big Spring, T-Bird got out their bags and carried them to the office. Devlin parked the car as he went to the registration desk and checked in.

Hours before, as the miles fell away behind them, Devlin inquired, "How have we been doing?"

"Devlin, we're doing fine, just fine."

She smiled at him, "Tell me how fine, T-Bird." It was a game they played together, and had for the last ten months, ever since they left Uvalde with five hundred dollars in their pocket. T-Bird, with his

124

encyclopaedic recall of names and figures, had kept an instant running total of their finances. To conserve money for the first months, they slept in the Eldorado, and then they shared a single hotel or boarding-house room. Devlin did the cooking with a hotplate she bought from a secondhand store. T-Bird was fit to be tied. "We had better food than this in Huntsville, Devlin. I'm gonna eat better than this or I'm gonna go back to jail."

"All you have to do is attack R.D. another time, and he'll put your ass right back there."

"He cheated me," T-Bird said unhappily.

"At poker?" she asked.

"Yeah."

"T-Bird, nobody cheated you at poker but the Lord. If there ever was a bad poker player, then you are numbers one, two, and three. It is a crime against nature to give you a poker hand. It's like giving a baby a loaded gun to play with."

"He should 'a given us more of a stake."

"R.D.?"

"Yeah, five hundred dollars and he's making God knows what on us."

"T-Bird," Devlin said with a smile, "you don't know what that man is doing for us. He's giving us a college education at no cost to us. Five hundred dollars. If I had it, I would have given *him* the money."

"Yeah, why?"

"T-Bird, can't you see where it's taking us?"

"Yeah, West Texas, that's where. I never liked this part of Texas myself—dry, dusty, and the people here ain't that friendly."

"T-Bird," she cooed, "how much money? Where are we?"

He sighed, "We have three thousand, four hundred and forty-five dollars, and we done paid all our bills, and we have another shipment of leases to send on to R.D.; for which he will owe us another seventeen hundred dollars. All told, we've got five thousand, one hundred and forty-five dollars."

Devlin added, "And what I can sell the Eldorado for."

T-Bird looked at her, "What can you sell the car for? Why would you want to do that?"

"Because I just wrote a letter to R.D. along with the leases, telling him that we quit. We're going into business for ourselves. I told him to send back your doodlebug, and keep the money you owed him for the poker game. I thanked him for everything he did for us."

"Everything he did. Hell, he threw my ass in Huntsville."

"He brought us together, T-Bird."

"Well, I'm not so sure that was a great idea. I don't like to think that you made that decision without me. I been protecting you a lot, Devlin, and I was just thinking that maybe I'd go out on my own, and hit it big."

"T-Bird, what was the biggest stake you ever had?"

"A lot, I don't remember."

"Bet you it was less than we have now."

"You don't know nothing."

"You'll be honest, won't you?"

"Listen, Devlin . . . I hit it big lots of times. I had women . . . and cars . . ."

"How much?"

"I once had two thousand dollars, but I blew it in one night on two ladies."

"T-Bird, please listen to me. You and I can make it very big together. I feel it in my bones."

"Hell, Devlin, it's been all *you*. I don't do a damn thing, just keep you company, and sit on the porch and pull out a bottle of whisky and whistle."

Devlin could see that he was feeling unappreciated, that she was acting as the leader and not upholding the equal partnership. Devlin understood that she needed him more than he knew, and more than he needed her. She was only learning to use her wings. True, it was Devlin who sold the ranchers and their wives a bill of goods—the idea of signing leases with them, when nobody else was able to accomplish it. It was Devlin who played with the kids, who talked women's talk with the women, talked serious with the men, and told them how she hoped that the money they would earn would give them a better life. The men looked at her and saw the kind of girl they wanted their daughters to be, and the kind of girl that they wanted their sons to marry. Then there were the lonely men, who were widowers or lived on their own and missed the warmth and comfort of a woman. Those men took to Devlin as they would to a sister or a daughter.

Devlin never let their interest go beyond friendliness. She'd sing songs in the firelight at night, tell them stories about her daddy, stories about the early days of Texas, stories of her pride in the state, its people, its independence. Listening to her was like a revival meeting, and Devlin would do that too, sing gospel, join with them as they prayed, and walk away the next day with a lease to the oil-drilling rights on their property.

T-Bird never doubted that it was Devlin that made the ranchers respond. There was nothing artificial in the way she dealt with them. She was just being a woman—caring, interested, and doing the things that only a woman can do to make you feel good and happy and praise God that in the Garden of Eden He bothered with Adam's rib.

They walked up the stairway to their rooms in the Holiday Inn in Big Spring. Devlin kissed T-Bird on the cheek. It was late. She didn't know what T-Bird had in mind for himself, but she was exhausted, and tomorrow was a big day. It was the day that they were to start business for themselves. Her dreams would be full of plans for the Younger-Johnson Oil Company.

126

T-Bird smiled. From his five feet two, he stared up into Devlin's green eyes and smiled. "I think I'll take the car and go into town—get a beer or something."

"Goodnight, T-Bird. See you tomorrow early for breakfast. We have to get there by ten."

Early the next morning Devlin dressed in a sheepskin-lined jacket to keep warm in the twenty-degree cold. She knocked on the door to T-Bird's room. There was no answer. She knocked again—still no answer. She tried the door. It was unlocked. Lying across the bed, dead to the world, was T-Bird's fully dressed figure, face down and spread-eagled. An empty bottle of bourbon lay on the bed beside him. His snoring was too loud for any single sleeper. There was no way of rousing him.

Devlin looked at her watch. She would leave without him, but she needed the key to the Eldorado. Devlin looked through the pockets of his pants, in the bathroom, and on the floor of the bedroom without any success. She looked at her watch and panicked. Her appointment with the rancher was for ten, and it was an hour's drive from Big Spring. She hadn't had as much as a cup of coffee, and she was ravenously hungry. More than that, she was angry. She considered that the keys might be in the car. She ran outside to the parking area. There was no Eldorado to be seen. Now she was really in a stew and mad as hell.

She turned to the entrance of the hotel, hoping in some fantasy-laden way for her car to appear by magic. Instead, she saw an old Chevy pickup, caked with mud, clanging with loose metal, steam into the entrance. A tall, gangling young man in his twenties got out and walked slowly to the office. Devlin rushed to intercept him. As she reached him, she stuck out her hand.

"Hi, George, you fixin' to go to the dance tonight?"

The young man stopped, stared, and smiled. He had no more notion why this beautiful young lady was stopping to talk to him than the man in the moon.

"Lady, I think you got me mixed up with somebody else."

"I'm so embarrassed," Devlin muttered. She began to invent things madly, "I'm the sister of John Travis Younger, and he's the best friend of a man he said is he best dancer in all of Big Spring. You see, I'm here to find a dance partner for the All Texas Two-Step Dance Competition that's going on in Abilene . . . ." Then her voice trailed off. He looked at her with more interest.

"You *do* dance, don't you?" she asked.

The young man looked bewildered. "Look, I ain't that friend of your brother. I'm somebody else." Then he grinned a big grin, as if the notion of stealing this heavenly looking filly right out from under somebody else had just occurred to him. He stuck out his hand and said shyly, "I'm Billy Bob, what do they call you?"

127

Devlin smiled in return. "I'm Devlin Younger." She had her transportation. "Billy Bob, I know you've got business, but this friend I was
supposed to meet was going to take me out to a ranch near Knott, off of
Route 87. You don't suppose you could just postpone your business and
help a lady in distress?"

He smiled, "Sure, I could. I'd prefer the company of a pretty lady to
what I planned to do anyway." Before he had finished his speech, Devlin
hopped up inside the pickup and sat waiting for him. Billy Bob, all six
foot four of him, ambled around and swung into the driver's seat. The
pickup lurched forward and then settled down to a steady speed of
thirty-five miles an hour. On the way out of town, Devlin saw a
half-dozen truck stops and diners. God, she was hungry.

She looked at a Thermos on the floor.

Billy Bob caught her eye, "I'd offer you some coffee, Miss Devlin, but
I finished it on the way in. Matter of fact, that was the reason I was
stopping at the Holiday, to get a cup of coffee. I can drink a gallon in the
morning. Wish I had some right now, but I guess you're in a hurry.
Sorry about this rig of mine. It don't go no faster."

Driving north on Route 87, the pickup bounced along, the motor
missing firing every so often. Devlin thought it should be warmer in the
cab, but the windshield was broken, and huge gusts of cold air shot up
inside. She was cold, she was hungry, and she was miserable. Looking at
her watch, she knew that she would be late.

Over the past months, Devlin became a known person in the cities
and towns that fed off the oil fields. In Texas that could be anywhere.
Devlin had spent the best part of the last three months in East Texas and
had secured leases for R.D. Stanhope from ranchers and farmers who
thought they had been blitzed by a red-headed angel. Devlin was like a
German Panzer division after she learned the ropes and got started. The
phone buzzed back and forth to Uvalde with new reports of her success.
R.D.'s booming voice took it all in stride. He had always been certain of
it. He could pick 'em.

One night a couple of lease hounds, a few drillers, and Devlin filled
out a poker game in a small club in Waco. It took until two in the
morning for Devlin to clean out one of the drillers and one of the
leasehounds. The leasehound was busted and wanted a chance to get
even. There was no money showing, and Devlin was not about to take his
I.O.U. What he had left, he said, was a valuable lease on almost 500 acres
in Howard County, just northwest of Big Spring. What's more, he had
the geological report that went with it. Devlin took a fast look at the
promising report, scanned the lease, and loaned him a hundred dollars
against it.

It took only one game, a blizzard of a game that Devlin picked. It was
seven card high-low, with the lowest of the three hole cards wild. Three
cards were dealt before the betting began, two down and one up. The

seventh card was dealt down, and the lowest of the down cards and all like it were wild. It took only two minutes for Devlin to win the pot with five aces, a perfect hand, and for anyone superstitious, and Devlin was, she had the feeling that the gods had smiled down on her. Someone had wanted her to win the hand, the pot, and the lease.

She tucked the geologist's report and the lease in her shirt, slid back her chair, shook hands with the losers, and took off. This was the sign that she had been waiting for. With this she and T-Bird could go in business for themselves. Only the next morning, as she showed what she had won to T-Bird, did she look carefully at the lease. T-Bird pointed out that the lease called for drilling five years after the date of the signing. On the top page, the lease read one date, three years hence. At the tail end, the lease read another date, less than a month away. Devlin looked at the top date carefully. The son-of-a-bitch had used ink eradicator and changed it.

Devlin screamed bloody murder. He had her. Not only had he passed off a no-good lease to stay in the game, but Devlin loaned him one hundred dollars to buy his lady friend a birthday present, or so he said.

It wasn't till Devlin checked the geologist's report further, and the results of drilling in the neighborhood over the last year, that she realized that only the lack of time could prevent her from drilling in one of the most promising fields in Texas. She wondered why the man in the game had never done anything with the lease, and in the face of that, she set out with T-Bird to try and convince the Conroys—Thornby and his wife Sadie—to extend the lease.

When she first phoned, Mr. Conroy was reluctant to see her, but Devlin was insistent. He had specified this morning, and this morning only at ten. No other time would be convenient and that was final. Now her happy-go-lucky driver of the pickup was talking incessantly as Devlin tried to urge him and the vehicle to move faster. Nothing helped with the reluctant machine, and it was now half past ten. Devlin was heartsick. In her mind's eye, she saw the Conroys staring at her, pointing to the time, and turning her away. That no-good bastard T-Bird had caused it all. She would kill him.

Finally Devlin saw a sign that marked the Conroy ranch. She looked at her watch again. She was almost an hour late. Billy Bob chirped along as he pulled into the dirt road that led to the farmhouse. He shifted gears, and as he did, the pickup shuddered to a halt and died. Devlin flung open the door and began to race the hundred yards to the small white frame house. Behind her, Billy Bob was cursing and kicking the motor. He called after her, "I'll take you back to town, Miss Devlin, so's you can pretty yourself up for tonight."

Devlin was out of breath when she came to the neatly planted yard. She managed to catch her breath and walked up the three concrete steps to the door and knocked. After a suitable period, she knocked again. She heard sounds and opened the door hesitantly. From inside she heard a TV. She walked from the tiny hall into the living room, and she saw a man and a woman watching a TV game show.

"Mr. Conroy, it's me, Devlin Younger."

The gray-haired man turned from his chair, "You're late, young lady."

The woman added, "We're watching the TV."

"I can wait," Devlin replied. She stood uneasily in the hall, wondering what they would say if she went into the kitchen for something to eat. Anything. A piece of bread or a slice of cheese. She didn't have time to think about food any longer, because in minutes the gray-haired man, tall and wiry, walked into the room, followed by a plump-faced woman. When Devlin saw the woman, she thought her face was familiar. She must be mistaken. This was the first time she had ever met the Conroys.

"Mr. Conroy, I'm Devlin Younger, and I'm darn sorry I'm late, and doggone sorry that I broke into your TV-watching. I love that show too."

Devlin saw the blank look on the Conroys' faces. She hoped that they wouldn't challenge her lie.

"You're late, young lady," the man broke the silence.

"You kept Mr. Conroy from doing his chores so we could watch the Hollywood Squares," the woman stated flatly. The two of them stood at the door of the living room. Devlin decided to wait them out. Their stares were cold and unfriendly. She had never seen people as unwelcoming in all of Texas.

Suddenly, Billy Bob came bounding in the room. Devlin saw his smiling face and figured that this was the last straw. The dumb bumpkin had ruined everything with his damn pickup, and now the Conroys would toss the two of them out. Mrs. Conroy turned to the young man. "Billy Bob," she said, "you got back sooner than you thought. Why don't you take a ride over to the Jenkins place for your dad?"

Devlin was thunderstruck. Billy Bob? Your dad? She smiled at the gawky young man, and walked over to him. She put her arm around him. No wonder Mrs. Conroy's face was familiar. She was his mother. "Billy Bob, I didn't know these were your folks. You kept that a secret, and after all we're keeping company together and going dancing tonight, you're not going to forget me now, are you Billy Bob?"

The young man grinned so hard his teeth could have fallen out on the floor. "Ma, this here is Devlin, and we're gonna enter the dance contest. She's my friend. It was all the fault of the pickup, I just got to get that thing fixed one of these days."

Mrs. Conroy looked at the two. She saw a handsome Texas girl, who her dear son had somehow corralled. Nothing was too good for Billy Bob, and that was for darn sure. Devlin could tell by that look. Mrs. Conroy smiled at her husband. "Thornby, why don't you tell this pretty young lady to sit down and spell awhile, it's just impolite to keep her standing there, and Billy Bob, why don't you go into the kitchen and fix us up some coffee—you and coffee, I know you both, and if this here is your girl, she's gotta be in love with coffee too."

Devlin grinned. She was saved for the moment and in prospect of getting something to fill her stomach. First things first. As she sat down on the couch next to Billy Bob's father, she pulled the lease from her pocket. Conroy took the lease from her hand.

"Golly, you don't have *that* lease, do you? Every three or four months that darn lease comes back here or a copy of it. Was it some slim man with greasy slicked-back hair around five foot and a half, with a space between his teeth, you got this from?"

Devlin nodded.

"Sorry you went to this much trouble young lady, this here lease is a forgery. The man wanted us to sign a lease for the oil, but I never liked him, never wanted to and never did."

"But where did this come from?"

"Dunno, he must 'a signed it hisself. Neither Mrs. Conroy nor me ever signed the darn thing."

Devlin was destroyed. All her hopes were shot. "If this isn't any good, would you sign a lease now—for the future?"

Conroy shook his head, "Lady, I'm sorry, I would have, but I already done it with the WESTEX Petroleum people, they're the biggest around here. Sorry you came all this way for nothing. I showed 'em a copy of this lease. There's dozens of 'em, and just to avoid trouble, they said the new one would start at the end of the date. It's only a month away."

Devlin was heartbroken.

"Mr. Conroy, I got this lease in a legitimate transaction . . . and maybe you and I and Mrs. Conroy can figure out something. After all, Billy Bob and I are going dancing tonight . . . and I don't have any place to go, or any way to get there." Devlin smiled her prettiest, "You just have me prisoner around your lovely house. I can make myself real handy in the kitchen . . . and since it's just near lunch time, why don't you and Mrs. Conroy go watch some TV awhile, and I'll just fix us up something to eat. Don't you worry. I'm a pretty darn good cook and I'll clean up anything I spill."

They looked uncertain but changed their mind as Billy Bob appeared at the door and grinned at the chance to be alone with Devlin. Ma and Pa Conroy took the hint and walked back into the parlor.

Devlin was playing for time, but she had no idea where she was heading or what further use there was in hanging around.

15

"YOUR FOLKS like pancakes?" Devlin inquired.

"Sure, Devlin, I'll bet they'll be great."

Devlin began searching for a bowl and milk, studying the instructions on the side of the package. Then, rousing a frying pan and shortening, she began the adventure of making pancakes. There was a mess a yard wide of spilt batter, burnt shortening, and badly scorched pancakes piling up, until Devlin wiped her forehead with her sleeve and smiled at Billy Bob.

"Why don't you tell your folks lunch is ready?"

Devlin pulled some plates out of the cupboard and arranged them on the kitchen table. The first disappointment came when Mr. Conroy walked into the kitchen, surveyed what he was about to eat, and muttered unhappily, "Pancakes." The second disappointment came when Mrs. Conroy walked into the kitchen, took a look at the monumental mess, and sniffed. Devlin hadn't concerned herself with the problem of finding syrup or jam or something to put on them, or any kind of meat to serve with them. She smiled proudly at what she had accomplished, a nearly charcoaled pile of soggy pancakes. The Conroy family sat down dutifully to see what they could eat. It wasn't much.

Devlin had spent her time thinking about the lease problem, and when Mrs. Conroy started to make some drinkable coffee, Devlin brought up the subject.

"Mr. Conroy, I have looked at more leases in my lifetime than people twice my age. I've got to tell you that I'm a smarter person than my pancakes make it seem."

The older man smiled. His stomach would never be the same, but the pretty girl at his kitchen table was a feast for the eyes. He didn't go much for women being in business and being around rough types in the oilfields, but Mrs. Conroy said that times were changing. She told him

132

that his favorite TV person, Mary Tyler Moore, ran her own business, making millions of dollars, and he had thought for the longest time that she was just simple little Mary Richards.

"The way I see it," Devlin continued, "if you, Mr. Conroy, will give me the month still owing on your lease, I think that I could start work on the well. Now a lease says that it remains in force for a term of five years and as long thereafter as oil, gas, casinghead gas, casinghead gasoline or any of the products covered by the lease can be produced."

Conroy nodded. Billy Bob nodded. Even Mrs. Conroy, who was on her feet stirring up coffee in a flat-bottom pan, nodded. They were listening, but not really understanding. Devlin continued, "A lease says that operations for the drilling of a well for oil or gas must be commenced on said land on or before . . . and we both know that nobody can drill a well in four weeks, but," she smiled sweetly, "what if the *operations* began right away, like bringing pipe, and setting up the rig, and stuff like that, then as far as I'm concerned, Mr. Conroy, *operations* are underway."

Billy Bob laughed out loud, "Glor-ree, you are a smart one, Miss Devlin, on top of looking prettier than a bouquet of flowers. Daddy, you listen to what she says. What do you want to do business with them big boys at the WESTEX for? Besides, what did they give you for a royalty? One-eighth, that's all they gave you."

Devlin waited in silence.

"Tell you what, Miss Devlin, I don't want to appear no smart trader, but I'll bet daddy will let you have the lease good and proper for the four weeks, if'n you was to increase the royalty from one-eighth, to, say, like one-tenth, or maybe even one-twelfth."

Conroy smiled broadly. He was aware that his son Billy Bob, for whom he had little hope, was pulling a sharp deal, and he was proud of him for the first time in his life. First he brought home this pretty girl, prettier than any girl *he* ever saw when he was Billy Bob's age, and now he was trading with her for a bigger share of the royalty than the WESTEX folks were going to give.

Devlin smiled and slapped her hands on the table. "Tell you folks what I'm gonna do, since you've been so fair with me. I'm gonna raise the royalty to something unprecedented in the history of all Texas oil dealing. Hold onto your hat, Mr. Conroy, Billy Bob convinced me to give you not one, but *two*-sixteenths."

Devlin sat back smiling and sweating. Maybe they would never figure it out, but it seemed an honest deceit, and it made the Conroys so damn happy, happy enough to shake hands deliriously all around, and happy enough to sign the damn lease one time again, this time for real, right there on the kitchen table. Devlin had three ball-point pens with her at all times for such an occasion. She smiled broadly and put the signed lease back in her pocket. Mrs. Conroy, distracted by all the good things

133

that were happening, almost forgot that the boiled-off coffee was scorching the bottom of the pan, and nobody was going to get a drop to drink.

Almost worst of all, Devlin's stomach had been so full of butterflies, she didn't even have the satisfaction of eating one of her inedible pancakes. She looked at her watch. It was two in the afternoon, and all that she had gained was a tiny piece of breathing room. Somehow, she had to begin drilling on her lease in twenty-eight days, or everything would be lost. As it was, she knew damn well that the WESTEX folks, a damn big outfit, were not going to sit still for her playing fast and loose with their lease. But dammit, their lease wouldn't begin for six hundred and seventy-two hours.

Devlin stood up. "Billy Bob, if you would take me back to town, then I can get myself fixed up tonight for the dancing. There is dancing tonight, isn't there?"

Billy Bob looked stupefied, "That's what *you* said, Miss Devlin. I thought you knew. Me, I know that there'll be dancing Friday in Midland and Odessa, but gollee, why wait for *that*? I'll sure as the dickens take you back to your hotel, and just hang around till you're ready, and then we can go to a real restaurant and have us a meal, and maybe take in a movie—and the same thing tomorrow night, and Thursday, and then," he smiled joyously, "we can go honky-tonking Friday."

Devlin smiled bravely. She had to get back to town to start work on the problem of the drilling, and she would need all the goodwill and cooperation in the world from the Conroys. "That sounds like a swift idea, Billy Bob."

Mrs. Conroy gave Devlin a big hug, and Mr. Conroy grabbed her around the shoulders and grasped her warmly, "Hope there's no hard feelings, Miss Devlin, about our sharp dealings—that two-sixteenths royalty, and all."

Devlin shook her head sharply, "What's fair is fair, Mr. Conroy." They smiled happily as she and Billy Bob headed for the pickup truck. It would still go no faster than the 35 miles an hour it made coming to the ranch, and unless she could find her Eldorado, this was the only transportation there was. Her stomach was growling from hunger. She hadn't had a single thing to eat since she got up, and this wasn't the time to stop and get something. She made her way inside the pickup. Billy Bob turned the key and the motor ground out the sound of an unwilling start. Devlin closed her eyes in pain. Billy Bob turned the key once again, and the pickup came to life, shaking and trembling like a leaf in the rain.

"Wahoo," Billy Bob shouted, "I got me a girl, and I got me and mine a fancy royalty, and I'm going dancing, and I done never danced before, and I never thought life could be so damned sweet when I woke up this morning."

The pickup lurched forward in its stuttering way.

Devlin had plenty of time to concentrate on her problem on the way back to Big Spring. She knew that if drilling actually began during the next four weeks, then she could keep drilling, and the lease would be good until the well showed up dry, or she struck oil. The WESTEX folks would have fits, but that was the way it was. On the other hand, the lease said that she had to commence operations, and that could mean a lot of different things. She didn't really believe that she could get pipe on the land and convince anybody that was drilling. Still and all, it was something that she could try if all else failed. What Devlin needed above and beyond anything else was a partner, a drilling operator who would put up his rig for a part of the return on the well. Every fly-by-night wildcatter had that same idea, and tried to get a driller into a deal, but drillers were too damn smart for that. Let the wildcatters go broke trying to find money to pay the drillers. The drillers would be around today, tomorrow, and for a hundred years, while the dumb wildcatters went from dry hole to dry hole.

Devlin considered that there might be a way to interest a driller by putting up some of the cash for the drilling. If she sold the Eldorado, plus the other money she and T-Bird had saved, then that might be as much as twelve thousand dollars. Not the world, but maybe enough to put down. Of course, if there were a decent-sized poker game in town, with a little luck Devlin thought she might just increase that stake. But games of poker that size, and ones that would admit a woman, were scarce. She looked at her companion, whistling happily. No man could have used Billy Bob and his lust for her the way she had unmercifully done, but on the other hand, being a woman did have its advantages.

The pickup arrived at the Holiday Inn, and Devlin headed for T-Bird's room. Billy Bob happily volunteered to stay downstairs just as long as Devlin wanted. He was in no hurry to leave. He pulled a Captain America comic book out of the glove compartment and began to study the well-worn pages. Devlin left him, and walked up the stairs to T-Bird's room and knocked on the door.

T-Bird opened it. He looked gray and drawn. Devlin expected some sign of life, but it was just a remote flame.

"Dammit T-Bird . . . what the hell happened to the Eldorado? I had to find another way to get out to the Conroys' place. You have an accident . . . or the car break down?"

T-Bird looked concerned. He pursed his mouth. "Devlin, I know that you and I are partners, and your good luck is half mine, and that makes me happy . . . and my good luck is half yours, and that thrills me with pleasure . . . and if'n the luck turns bad, then we just share and share alike."

Devlin stared at him.

"Devlin, I just happened to lose it at poker."

"You *what?*" she shouted.

"Them cards, I thought that they were running my way, and I held two pairs in the last hand, jacks and kings . . . well, you don't want to hear about that." His voice trailed off, and Devlin sank down on the bed. She was near tears, "T-Bird, it wasn't your car."

He smiled wistfully, "You and me is partners, ain't we?"

In moments Devlin discovered that not only had T-Bird lost the Eldorado, but he also had bet and lost all the cash they had. The only thing remaining to them was the money that Devlin had in her room, all of one hundred dollars. Devlin felt totally crushed. She suddenly thought of R.D. Stanhope. She picked up a phone and called Uvalde. The conversation was short and brief. R.D. was happy that Devlin had won a lease for her and T-Bird, and he knew that the field was promising. He had already received her last leases, and the notice of her quitting. Since things were that way, she was on her own, and big enough to make her own success or failure. He ended the phone conversation quickly, only to add that he had sent the doodlebug on to T-Bird in Big Spring. R.D. hoped it would help. Now, it appeared that all was *really* lost. Devlin had burned all her bridges behind her.

She heard the sound of an auto horn and looked out the window. From below she saw Billy Bob standing beside his pickup. He shouted happily, "Miss Devlin, just wanted you to know that I'm still waiting, just take your time. I got all night."

For whatever it was worth, Billy Bob Conroy became Devlin's constant companion. It was as if he had gladly taken up the job of being Devlin's chauffeur and slave. He bought her the first meal she had during that long day, and happily invited T-Bird to join them at a local restaurant. T-Bird couldn't make much sense out of the young man, and Devlin was still not speaking to T-Bird, so it became a triangular conversation with Billy Bob serving as the person who passed conversation on from Devlin to T-Bird, and vice versa. Billy Bob wasn't discommoded in the slightest. "I don't know how you folks talk to each other when there ain't a third person present, but I just want you to know that I consider this here very enjoyable. Ain't very often that I have two people caring to talk to me, and listening to what I have to say."

The next morning, Devlin went to the Big Spring National Bank. She held onto the lease and the geological report. Finally, after waiting an hour, she managed to see the president, Amos Stuckey, a small, waspish man in his late forties. He wore a light-blue polyester suit and a black string tie, rimless glasses, and had an almost bewilderingly staccato speech. Translated, he was very quick to the point: Banks are not in the business of investing money. He was in the business of *lending* money to local people, not foreigners. Moreover, said Mr. Stuckey, every scoundrel in Texas wanted to borrow money to drill for oil on the sure thing that his lease had more oil under it than Spindletop.

Stuckey looked at Devlin and struck an icy chord, "Young lady, I don't know what you think you're doing trying to drill for oil. You hardly are dry behind the ears, and women have no damn place in that business at all. You put in your time, miss, and come see me in twenty or thirty years." Amos Stuckey smiled toothily, "What makes you think that anybody in this world could start drilling in less than four weeks? It would take a month to locate the supplies. Do you know, young woman, just how tough it is to find casing and pipe? Do you know that anybody with a drilling rig has work for the next year? And do you know, young woman, that you are wasting my time?"

Amos Stuckey was not very helpful.

Devlin walked out of the bank building. Billy Bob was lounging in the doorway, "Where to now, Miss Devlin?"

"I want to go to a telephone, and get a bunch of dimes, and make some calls."

Billy Bob led her to a nearby supermarket with a pay phone out front, and Devlin began her search through the Yellow Pages of Howard County for the names of drillers. Surely if Stuckey were right, there wasn't going to be one she could convince to work for nothing, but on the other hand, she wouldn't know until she tried. She began to phone, and little by little, she came to the conclusion that Stuckey, that horrible little man, was absolutely right. When Devlin was able to get the drillers on the phone, they quickly cut her off when she asked if work could start right away.

Devlin thought that it would be better not to mention that she didn't have enough money to pay for the drilling, or even her hotel room. She didn't concern herself that Billy Bob was not only her transportation but, in addition, her life-line for food. Thank God he appeared to be hopelessly in love with her. Devlin didn't like to think about it, but what if Billy Bob suddenly wanted her body in return? She shuddered at the thought.

Devlin stopped at the Denny's next door to the Holiday Inn. She searched her pockets and found two dollars in change. She had considered the possibility of trying to borrow money from Billy Bob, but that didn't seem to be a good idea. "Hell," she thought, "this lease is a curse. I can't do anything with it, and I can't do anything else till I prove that I can't." Devlin sat down in an empty booth. Her place on the table was full of dishes. Someone dropped a dish tray on the table and began to clear them away. She looked up and saw T-Bird. He smiled sheepishly at her.

"Damn, T-Bird, what are you doing here?"

"I got a job as a busboy, they needed someone, and I'm not doing any other good, so I took it. We need the money, and besides, I get my food, and I can sneak you some." Then he leaned over and whispered to her, "The hamburgers are damn fine."

Devlin laughed. The news made her day.

"I'll have twenty-five dollars by the end of the day, Devlin, enough to get started in a poker game I heard about."

Devlin nearly shouted, "You again?"

T-Bird was shaken, "No, not me, Devlin. You this time. I asked, and they don't mind if a lady sits in. I think that's mighty white of them. Of course, I didn't tell them that the lady is a pretty girl, but when you show up, it'll be enough time, and Devlin, I got my doodlebug in the mail from R.D., and I'm gonna sell it and buy back your Eldorado. As for the rest of the money that I lost, Devlin, I am so damn sorry, I could bite my toe off."

She put her hand in his and looked in his face. He was crying. "T-Bird, we're still partners. Go see if someone will bring me a burger and fries, and a Coke, warm from the bottle."

He smiled and carried off his tray of dirty dishes.

Devlin had a rooting section composed of T-Bird and Billy Bob Conroy as she sat in on a small-stakes poker game that night. West Texas has laws against drinking—unless you belong to a private club, the rule is to bring your own bottle. West Texas also has laws against gambling. But there must have been some magic in the air that night, because in a period of six hours of nonstop poker, Devlin came away winning better than seven hundred dollars. She also was able to sidestep a half dozen proposals of marriage, and other less respectable liaisons. At two in the morning, the three of them—Devlin, T-Bird, and Billy Bob—left the private club on Gregg Street where the sign in the front room stated, "No Gambling Allowed," and boarded the pickup in which they drove back to Denny's.

"Devlin, can't we go someplace else? I get the fidgets when I walk in here. They're like as not gonna give me a white apron and a tray and tell me to clear the tables."

Devlin laughed. "T-Bird, just tell them you're quitting. I've got to get something to eat, and also I've got to get to a ladies' room. I didn't dare leave the table during the whole game, 'cause I felt it might change my luck. Order me some scrambled and fries, and you order yourselves what you want. It's coming out of the winnings, and T-Bird, we're gonna start making the preparations for drilling 'cause I have a feeling our luck has changed."

T-Bird's effort to get back the Eldorado was to no avail. The new owner, a local barber, loved it and wouldn't sell it back at any price. He proudly drove it each day to his barber shop, just opposite the Howard County Courthouse, and parked it in front so that the local bigwigs could see it with envy. The barber, a detestable man, T-Bird stated, laughingly invited T-Bird and Devlin to come for a ride with him in *his* car any time they wanted.

Devlin and T-Bird had enough money to survive for a while. Devlin knew that eventually she would have to go back to the poker table. The losers wanted revenge, but she wasn't in any hurry. There was no telling when her luck would change. She couldn't win all the time. It was T-Bird who came up with the notion that provided their next step.

"Devlin, you know that there's a lot of used equipment for drilling, and used pipe around. It don't do anybody much good, just useful for scrap, the worst of it, but maybe if we got somebody to lend us an old drill, say one of the portable jack-knifes, we could park in on the lease, and there ain't nobody could say we're not ready to drill, and if we could just spud in the well, we'd be home free."

In Odessa T-Bird found what he was looking for. In a graveyard of broken machinery with thousands of feet of used pipe and rusted parts of drilling equipment, T-Bird found a rascal of a man, Red Stennis, a roly-poly scoundrel, as wide as he was high, willing to make a deal on anything, no matter how bruised or beaten, and who could make a profit on soiled Kleenex.

On the eighth day of the four-week lease, T-Bird phoned Devlin in high glee to come to Stennis's junkyard. It was salvation. Devlin's personal transportation, Billy Bob, was not available, so she managed to thumb a ride part-way with an Air Force sergeant attached to nearby Webb Air Force Base who was driving a troop carrier.

Staff Sergeant Tony DeVito was enchanted with his passenger. He would have driven Devlin to the end of the world if she had asked him to. He tried every which way to make a date with her that night, or any night, but the best he could get was a promise that Devlin would telephone him at the base. She had a jealous boyfriend she said, as he dropped her off in front of Stennis's junkyard in Odessa.

DeVito implored her to phone. He would take on as many jealous boyfriends as she had. He was a New York boy, in a faraway lonely place in West Texas. He would commit suicide, he swore, unless Devlin said yes. He would turn over military secrets to the Russians, to the Chinese, unless Devlin promised to phone.

Devlin laughed, "You New York boys do have your big-city ways."

"Then you love me the way I love you, Devlin?" he asked hopefully, as he ushered her out of the high cab of the truck. "More," she returned, "more than you, till the end of time, till hell freezes over."

"Then you'll marry me, Devlin?" he smiled.

"Of course, Tony, but then you'll fall in love with my pretty sister, and you'll have nothing more to do with me."

"Your *pretty* sister?" he asked incredulously.

"Uh-huh," she murmured dreamily, "I mean really pretty. Not like me. My family almost threw me away when they saw me. They said, 'Why aren't you pretty, like your pretty sister?' "

Sergeant DeVito laughed, "You got yourself a deal. I'll save your pretty sister for my ugly brother, meanwhile, you're the one I want."

He waved as the truck pulled away, and Devlin walked into the junkyard, moving in the direction of a small wooden office where Red Stennis sat waiting for the deal of a lifetime, or so he said. T-Bird had already surveyed the portable jack-knife rig—or the parts of it that remained. It had been built by a machine-parts company in Houston in 1950, and as far as the oil business is concerned, twenty years is several lifetimes ago.

Devlin shook hands with the proprietor. His handshake was soft and wet, and the grin on his face was not reassuring. He was measuring her interest to match his understanding of why anyone in her right mind would want the pile of junk he now proposed to sell.

Once the jack-knife had been mounted on its own truck. No longer. Devlin walked out into the yard and saw a pile of twisted and rusted metal. It might have been alive once, but no more. In the middle of the mounds of parts and piles of oil-field junk, it was no more distinguishable for what it once was than if it had been compressed in an avalanche.

Devlin wrinkled her brow and looked at T-Bird, "What do you do with this thing?"

T-Bird was concerned about Devlin's reaction. He thought she would be overjoyed. "Needs some work, Devlin, but it's a jack-knife and can do the job."

"Your business associate has been telling me what you want to do, little lady, and you've got a real winner in this here piece of equipment."

Devlin turned and stared at his unctuous smile.

"You'll guarantee that, Mr. Stennis."

"Why sure. This here jack-knife has drilled more producing wells in Texas than any other piece of equipment. Some folks want me to donate it to the Smithsonian Museum, you know the one in Washington where they have the space capsules and Lindbergh's airplane, but I told them that its time ain't come. It's got a useful and productive life ahead of it."

He nodded his head vigorously.

"Can you put this into working condition?"

"I *could*, Miss Younger, and I'd be glad to, but you see that ain't my business. My business is dealing with the 'A number-one' previously used tools and equipment in the oil business. Letting others live, that's my motto. The fellas who can put this here beauty into working condition, and it ain't no big deal—well, those fellas are friends of mine, so it wouldn't be right, if I stepped on their toes. Live and let live. That's my motto. There ain't enough money in the world to make me go against my principles."

140

Devlin smiled. She waited patiently for the rogue to end his sales talk. The problem was that neither she nor T-Bird knew the first thing about how to go about fixing it, or what that would cost.

"Mr. Stennis . . . this drill is a little beauty, but my associate and I aren't interested in making it work. See, we want it for decoration. What we're about to do is start a Petroleum Museum in Big Spring, like the one they have in Midland—but better, and what we thought was that you might want to donate this drill, and we would put it in its own special place, and put a great big sign on it that says it is the gift of that well-known benefactor and philanthropist, Mr. Red Stennis of Odessa, Texas. Think what pride in accomplishment this will be for you and your children in generations to come."

Stennis leaned against a post. "Lady, I don't like to talk mean in front of the opposite sex, but you are full of bull."

Devlin smiled, "And you *too*, Mr. Stennis. Tell you what, I'll give you a hundred dollars for this piece of junk, cash money."

Stennis bit his lip in what first seemed like anger, then he smiled, "Make it two hundred, and you've got yourself a steal, little lady."

Devlin smiled, "A hundred and a quarter, and a sign that says, donated by that great philanthropist and lover, Mr. Red Stennis."

"Done, little lady. Is there anything else you'd like to buy?"

"T-Bird, is there anything?"

"No, Devlin. By the way, Red, I'll tell you where to deliver it."

Stennis roared, "You own it, you figure it out. This hunk of junk could be moved by itself if you put an atomic engine under it."

Devlin laughed, "Mr. Stennis, can I use your telephone?"

He looked at her. "First I want to see your money."

Devlin smiled, "Sure thing, Mr. Stennis. T-Bird, pay the man, and I'm only making a local call."

T-Bird reached into his pocket and counted out the money as Devlin walked to the junkyard office. Inside, the desk was littered with catalogues and bills. A few ancient files stood opposite, and an open copy of *Playboy* sat on the middle of the desk. Devlin dialed a number and waited.

"Am I speaking to Sergeant DeVito?" she asked sweetly.

The voice at the other end confirmed it. "Devlin, you missed me," he said happily.

"Well, yes, but I had a question to ask you."

"Anything, and forget about your sister. You're the one I want."

Devlin laughed, "Tell me, does the Air Force have cranes and flatbed trucks?"

"Sure, how many do you want?"

"Just one of each."

"Do you want them to lend or to keep?"

"How many years in jail is it to *use* them?"

"Nothing, if it's government business, and about ten years if it isn't. Why, what's your problem?"

"I need to move, Tony."

"How about a U-Haul, Devlin—a crane and flatbed aren't exactly used for beds and couches. It's kind of overkill."

"Well, my things are a lot bigger and heavier than your typical hi-fi, Tony. When you see it, you'll understand."

"Okay, you got it."

"Are you sure?"

"Sure I'm sure, do I kid around? Now, one other thing. What about dinner tonight?"

Devlin laughed, "Okay, you got it."

"Are you sure?" he asked.

"Sure I'm sure," she replied. "Do *I* kid around?"

16

THE PRESIDENT of WESTEX Petroleum in Midland would not have telephoned the main office of Holson and Nichols in Houston, had they not perceived a problem. Holson and Nichols was the largest and most important law firm in Houston, with particular interest in problems that related to the oil and natural gas business. With three hundred lawyers, and branch offices in Washington, Riyadh, Zurich, New York, and Paris, Holson and Nichols was the single brain-cell conductor that eased the problems of the multinational Texas-based companies it represented.

Frank Holson, the senior partner, had been a U.S. senator, and Wayne Nichols had been governor of Texas, a president-maker, and mover in the Democratic Party. To balance things out, Frank Holson held equivalent power in the Republican Party.

WESTEX was not one of the big seven, but as far as Texas was concerned, it was one of the big ten, the next group down that was exclusively involved in petroleum drilling, exploration, and refining in Texas, Oklahoma and the gulf. They had no holdings in Venezuela or the Middle East, but with a sales volume of five hundred million dollars a year, WESTEX was no slouch.

Dan'l Simon, a junior partner of Holson and Nichols, was the man selected to go to Midland, thirty-five miles away from Big Spring, and deal with the problem. In the five years since Dan'l graduated from the University of California law school in Los Angeles, he had made a substantial mark. Dan'l, twenty-eight, had graduated summa cum laude, and Law Review. He was a dark, handsome, and intense city boy who had been captain of the UCLA Bruins basketball team, organized anti-Vietnam demonstrations, burned his draft card, and demonstrated in Chicago in 1968 during the rioting at the Democratic Convention.

Dan'l Simon would appear to have been one of the last men on earth to be recruited by Holson and Nichols, and Holson and Nichols would

143

presumably have been the last place Dan'l would have cared to go. As editor of the Law Review, he had received offers from every major California firm, and even the snobbish New York Wall Street firms bent over backward in their attempts to seduce him. Recruiters for those firms totally ignored his radical political views. Dan'l was too smart and too personable to pass up.

From the very earliest when Dan'l's teachers observed the curious spelling of his name, he had been asked, "How come?" Dan'l had smiled and shrugged his shoulders, "My mother made it up."

By the time he considered changing it to the more traditional "Daniel," every computer in California had locked in on the spelling, and he had learned conclusively that you can't win against IBM or your mother.

For reasons that confirmed Dan'l's smartness, it was his conviction years ago that the world was running out of oil, and those who controlled it would be top dogs, and the lawyers who controlled the people who controlled the oil were going to be top, top dogs. His interest in Houston was clinched by the fervor of the Houston fans. In all the years that Dan'l had cheered the Dodgers in Los Angeles, and had whipped up his fellow man's passion for the Rams and the Lakers, given up his guts rooting for Elgin Baylor, Jerry West, Maury Wills, Sandy Koufax, Merlin Olsen, Jack Snow, and Roman Gabriel, he had never seen fans like the Houston fans. They clinched his affection for the city.

When Dan'l went to Houston for his interview with two senior partners at Holson and Nichols, they took him to dinner at the Gusher Club, high in the tower of the Petroleum Building downtown. Dan'l sat quietly while the two men extolled the beauty and future of Houston, the religion of Big Oil and Big Business. The year was 1968, and Lyndon Johnson had just renounced his bid for reelection to the presidency. Dan'l scared the pants off his prospective employers with a fervent plea for George McGovern. Conversation at dinner stopped. An embarrassed silence would now keep pace with a hasty dinner and early retreat.

But then something happened.

From across the huge, luxuriously appointed dining room came a wild whoop. Bearing down on the three of them was a handsome young man, his eyes full of excitement, his arms outspread. He was tall and blond, and more importntly, he was Jamie Lord, son of Tarquin Lord. The Lord family was as old as Texas, and almost as rich as all of it. With interests in construction, ranching, oil, and banking, the Lords appointed governors, suggested senators and befriended presidents. Jamie Lord, blue-eyed and incredibly handsome, whooped again, and came over to the Holson and Nichols table, grabbed Dan'l Simon, hugged him, and nearly threw him on the floor.

144

"You son-of-a-bitch, what the hell are you doing in Houston?"

Dan'l laughed. "I'm heading a consortium to buy you and your pappy out, then we're gonna jail you, nail you, and throw you out of Texas. This place is too good for you. Jamie, why the dickens didn't you tell me how great Texas was?"

Jamie Lord sat down uninvited. He looked warmly at Dan'l and spoke to the men at the table. "I don't know what your connection with this shyster is all about, but whatever he says, you can believe." The two men introduced themselves respectfully to Jamie Lord. Jamie smiled, "We give Holson and Nichols our business here in Houston, but we'd rather have a Dallas firm." He laughed, "Better class of people." Then he got serious, "Let me tell you about Dan'l. He and I and a hundred others were on the summer Olympic team in Tokyo. He saved my damn life, and I guess Dallas should be grateful. Hell, the whole state of Texas should be grateful, maybe even the world."

The two men eyed Jamie Lord with wonder. Dan'l Simon was becoming more interesting by the minute. "I was in the fifteen hundred meters, and came in a bad sixth, but Dan'l here was captain of our basketball team, and we became friends. I got into a little mess in Tokyo, on the Ginza they call it, and Dan'l here bearded the lions—the Tokyo Mafia—the Yakuza they call it. Well, the son-of-a-bitch got me out of there, when otherwise I might have been sliced up like that Japanese raw fish. Remember, fella?"

Dan'l nodded and smiled. Then he addressed the men. "You know, Houston ought to have its own basketball team in the NBA."

The men looked at each other. Their clients would be thrilled if Holson and Nichols were instrumental in doing that. Houston had the eighth wonder of the world, the Houston Astrodome, and its hunger for sports was almost insatiable. What's more, its fans were crazy, wonderfully crazy. As Jamie Lord turned and left, one of the men addressed Dan'l, "Mr. Simon, I don't have your history, but you were on Law Review?"

Dan'l smiled, "Yes, I was editor, and Phi Beta Kappa, and I've got a bone spur that bothers me a little and I smoke an occasional joint, and my politics are a little suspicious, but I'm probably going to be a good lawyer. I sure as hell want to be, and I like Houston."

The men smiled, "Do you think you could be helpful in getting Houston an NBA franchise?"

Dan'l laughed, "I haven't the vaguest idea, but if you want me to, I'll figure that one out in my spare time."

The men laughed. They liked his style, and they wanted Dan'l Simon in their firm. He would undoubtedly cause them more than a few sleepless nights with his very un-Houston ways, but editor of Law Review was the most prestigious honor in law school. Phi Beta Kappa was not

145

bad, and he was a damn jock and maybe, maybe Houston could get a basketball franchise in the NBA. One of them inquired, "Did you see the Bluebonnet Bowl game on TV, by any chance?"

Dan'l grinned. "You bet, the first one they played in the Astrodome. What a great place. If I remember, SMU beat Oklahoma twenty-eight to twenty-seven, and if I remember, your son caught the winning pass for SMU. You must be pretty proud."

The men breathed deeply. What a winner! Dan'l Simon would not get out of Houston, nor the Gusher Club, without making a commitment to work for Holson and Nichols.

By the time Dan'l Simon arrived in Big Spring in 1973, Houston had its NBA basketball team. The San Diego franchise moved to Houston in 1971. Dan'l was at every home game and died each time Houston lost, which it did with considerable consistency. At work, Dan'l Simon was considered by the senior partners at Holson and Nichols to be one of their brightest finds. He personally represented many of their major clients in corporate law and litigation. Dan'l understood the ebb and flow of government and its relationship to oil. His politics hadn't changed. You could not get him started talking about Richard Nixon without putting your fingers in your ears, but despite Dan'l's outspoken ways, he was a huge success. Socially, he cut a wide swath among the prettiest girls in Houston. His near-par golf, class-A tennis, and his refusal to talk Texan, as most of the newly arrived Texans tried to do, made him much respected by the people who knew what was what in Houston. Dan'l Simon was a legitimate adopted son.

WESTEX Petroleum's president asked Holson and Nichols to send someone to Big Spring to clear up the mess that Devlin Younger was causing on a piece of land just outside Big Spring. It involved only five hundred acres, they said, but they were very promising. This Devlin Younger was trying to steal the lease from under the eyes of five-hundred-million-dollars-a-year WESTEX. Holson and Nichols assured its client that they would take care of it. They would send someone in whom they had utmost confidence.

When Dan'l Simon arrived at Midland Airport on the Texas International commuter plane, he had filled himself in on as much of the detail as WESTEX's house counsel had on the Conroy lease. The young lawyer in the Midland headquarters of the oil company had carefully acquired the lease from the owner of the land. Title had been searched to insure that Conroy was empowered to grant the lease. Payment of a bonus on signing had been made. The bonus check for five hundred dollars had been presented, cashed, and the lease had been recorded. The forged lease had been noted, and a copy enclosed. It ran to the date of the WESTEX lease. The date of the start of the WESTEX lease had already come and gone. Efforts to get Devlin Younger off the land had been for naught.

Copies of correspondence were enclosed in the file. Letters to and from Devlin Younger. Dan'l noted with amusement the first two of them.

WESTEX PETROLEUM
Midland, Texas

March 13, 1973

Dear Mr. Younger,

This is to inform you that despite repeated demands by our drilling supervisor, Mr. Walon Thomas, that you remove your equipment and personnel from the premises of Mr. and Mrs. Conroy, on Leasehold #735, in the town of Knott, in Howard County, you have refused.

Your suggestion that you are in fact drilling an oil well pursuant to a lease which you hold is specious and false. We contest the fact that you have a proper lease, and furthermore, if said lease should be declared proper, that you in fact have commenced drilling on that lease.

Notice is hereby given that you abandon said premises no later than March 19th, or we will have no recourse but to pursue all available remedies under the law.

Very truly yours,

L. Carter Dixon III

YOUNGER-JOHNSON OIL COMPANY
Holiday Inn
Big Spring

March 15, 1973

Mr. Carter Dixon III
WESTEX OIL
Midland, Texas

Dear Mr. III,

First of all, you are all wet. Second and third of all, agree with the first. Mr. T. Conroy acknowledged that the lease which I won from a leasehound, Goober Smathers, in a poker game in Waco, Texas, in December of 1972, is better than his poker. As a matter of fact, almost anything is better than his poker, except Goober's honesty.

In any event, Mr. Conroy signed another lease which gave me the right to drill before your lease could take effect. The laws of this great state of Texas allow that if I and my partner drill, we can continue to hold the lease. Furthermore, if we are lucky enough to strike oil, then our lease will continue until we squeeze the last drop of precious stuff out of the land. So be it.

As for our drilling, we went to a huge expense and brought in a fine portable jack-knife rig, which has brought in more wells in the past twenty years in East and West Texas than any rig that WESTEX has at its disposal. After all, experience counts for something, and this rig is one of the most experienced in all Texas. It's a little slow, and needs a kick in the tender places from time to time in order to remember how it did it way back then, but Mr. III, age and tradition are very important to us, and who's to say that there should not be a premium paid to the slow and steady. He did win the race.

The last mistake you made is that I am not Mr. Devlin Younger. I am therefore female and will respond to all means of gaining my attention except, "Hey you! Get off my land!"

Please go on about your business, and I will go about mine, slowly and painstakingly, drilling in the precious land of West Texas for what I hope will be one hell of a gusher, and make all this trouble worth while. Your prayers would be much appreciated.

Most sincerely,

Devlin Younger (Miss)

Dan'l's eyes followed the course of the remaining correspondence as it became less polite. The final sheet of paper was a copy of the court-ordered writ, obtained by L. Carter Dixon III in behalf of WESTEX requiring Younger-Johnson Oil Company to vacate the land. Dan'l was to appear in Howard County Court the next day on behalf of WESTEX to request that the court enforce the writ.

Devlin had completed a month of the most back-breaking work she had ever attempted, but in the course of it, she discovered that she had never been happier. Somehow T-Bird had been able to locate a trailer, which Billy Bob's pickup pulled to the Conroy place. Devlin and T-Bird made their home in it. Nothing, but nothing, was going to drag Devlin off her lease, not even the frigid cold in the ten-degree nights of West Texas. Devlin slept in the tiny bunkbed hardly meant for a woman five foot ten, but T-Bird had it worse. He slept on the floor.

During those days, the two of them became closer than Devlin had thought possible—closer than T-Bird had ever been with any other human being. "Devlin," he said one night, "if it has to end tomorrow—if they throw us off the land—if we never drill, and if we drill we only hit a dry hole, then I've had the best of it. I've been a partner of the best damn woman ever to set foot in Texas, and I've been like a real person in the oil business, instead of just hanging on the side, hoping for crumbs and doing my little deals. We're in the oil business, Devlin. Don't you ever forget that."

There was no electricity in the trailer, no plumbing, and no way to keep warm; still, Devlin and T-Bird managed to stretch the little money they had left further than they could have living at the Holiday Inn. When the Conroys invited them in for a meal, it was a celebration. Mrs. Conroy, remembering the disaster of Devlin's cooking, made chicken-fried steak, hot biscuits, and yards and yards of coffee. Keeping Billy Bob at a distance became a little easier, what with the attempt to repair the jack-knife rig and get to spudding. He lent a hand and went out on

148

midnight raids with them to see if parts could be begged, borrowed, or stolen.

Tony DeVito and his buddies at the air base were the best of friends and helped more than could be imagined. Tony even managed to convince some of the base metal-workers and mechanics to figure out a way to get the jumbled mess of parts to fit.

One week after Devlin's lease had in fact expired, the first boring took place, and on that first day, with six men from the Air Force, an auto mechanic from Big Spring, and a part-time worker for a driller in Odessa, the first pieces of casing were placed around the spudding of the core. From that time on, each day Devlin managed to make a little more progress when the drill could be coaxed or beaten into cooperation. By the time the first writ was handed to her, Devlin's rig had drilled to forty feet. By the time she was due in court, the spudding had gone to seventy feet.

At the beginning of her correspondence with WESTEX, Devlin hoped that the big oil company would somehow lose interest in her. In her heart she knew that was just wishful thinking. Big companies, she knew, did not like to be interrupted in the course of their profit-making. Particularly oil companies. The first exchange of letters with L. Carter Dixon III had a humorous touch. Devlin surveyed the exchange with a little pride. She wasn't certain what "III" looked like, but he sounded like a dumb ass, and in her letters, she noted with some pleasure, she was getting the better of him.

But then the court writ came, and Devlin could no longer consider the matter funny. Billy Bob took her to Big Spring to find a lawyer. There were several, but when they heard about her case, and learned that Devlin had no money to pay them, their interest flew out the window. The day finally arrived when Devlin had to face up to the problem. In the Howard County Courthouse on Monday at ten A.M., Judge Nathaniel Cameron would decide on the matter of *Westex Petroleum* versus *Younger-Johnson Oil Company*.

The Howard County Courthouse is one of the most impressive buildings in the town of Big Spring, occupying a square block in the middle of downtown. Apart from the court, the building headquarters the police, the city jail and the office of the mayor.

On the day of the trial, the usual business of the city of twenty-five thousand was being conducted. WESTEX's lawsuit had very little significance to the general public and the small courtroom had no spectators except for Billy Bob Conroy and his mother and father. WESTEX Petroleum's representation was extensive: L. Carter Dixon III, one of his associates, a thin young man who nervously chewed on pencils, and Dan'l Simon were the legal brain-trust arrayed against Devlin and T-Bird.

149

Also in attendance were two of WESTEX's vice-presidents, gung-ho business school tyros who seemed to have brought not only computer programming to West Texas but also a taste for Brooks Brothers clothes, button-down shirts, striped ties, and brown cordovan shoes. The two of them looked as if they were in uniform.

At five before ten, everyone but Devlin was present. At exactly ten o'clock, Judge Cameron walked through a rear door from his chambers. The clerk asked everyone to rise, and just as the judge sat down and adjusted his glasses, the outside door opened and Devlin arrived, breathless. In her hand was a container of hot coffee and in the other was a half-eaten doughnut.

Judge Cameron stared at her then turned away. Devlin found a place to sit at the end table alongside T-Bird, and stealthily began to undo the soft cardboard top of the coffee container. It didn't want to budge. The judge stared at her occasionally. Stealthily, she placed the sack and the container on the empty chair next to her, and returned to it from time to time to try and open it. Devlin bent down below the eye level of the table and took a bite of the doughnut. When she emerged she managed to chew silently but with a hefty wad still in her cheek.

Across the way, L. Carter Dixon III stared incredulously at the sight. On the other hand, Dan'l Simon had a completely different reaction. From the moment he turned at the sound of the courtroom door opening, from the second he saw Devlin's incredible face, the green-eyed beauty with ginger hair, her long limbs scooting down the aisle, from the moment he saw her impish expression and enchanting smile, Dan'l Simon was in love.

It wasn't the whimsical jolt that Dan'l might have associated with the casual "clung" of a usually imperturbable bachelor. It was an atom bomb! Devlin's green eyes put him into a state of shock. He had seen Italian art, and all he could liken her face to was a Botticelli angel. Her hair mystified him. It had highlights of tangerine, which made the curls that surrounded her apricot skin sparkle with tiny halos. They moved as she did, and when she moved, it made him silly with despair. The knobby-kneed, unsteady newborn fillies he had admired reminded him of Devlin's long-legged gait. Furthermore, the work jeans and jacket that she wore, the scuffed and dirty boots that came from below the frayed ends of the denim pants, were absolutely beautiful.

To say that Dan'l Simon was smitten would be an understatement. When Devlin apologized to Judge Cameron for the fact that her container of coffee had spilled on the floor, Dan'l was certain that her melodious Texas voice had been scored for him alone.

For a brief second Dan'l considered resigning his job as counsel for WESTEX and defending Devlin Younger's hopeless case. It lasted no longer than a brief second, because Dan'l Simon conjured up visions of a thousand impediments to his meeting, talking, and courting Devlin

150

Younger, not the least of which was his solemn obligation to throw her and her partner, that tiny wisp of a man T-Bird Johnson, the hell off WESTEX's land.

"Miss Younger, Mr. Johnson, I see that you are not represented by counsel."

Devlin rose, "We can't afford to hire one, your honor."

L. Carter Dixon III rose, "Your honor, I object to the statement by the defendant. It is meant to be prejudicial to our case by attempting to appeal to the court's sympathy."

Dan'l pulled Dixon down into his seat. Things were not going as planned, Dixon was making a fool of himself.

"Miss Younger, the court has no sympathy. This is Howard County and not one of your big city playgrounds. You are a grown woman and you are here on a serious matter. If you think that you can defend your interest without a lawyer, then that is all well and good. If not, then that's too bad." He spied Devlin's last remaining piece of doughnut, "There will be no more eating in this court."

Devlin swallowed the last piece with a gulp.

Dan'l rose, "If your honor please . . ."

"Who are you, young man?"

"I am making an appearance in behalf of WESTEX."

"What about his other one?" pointing to L. Carter Dixon III.

Devlin eyed him with seeming disinterest. Dan'l fleetingly caught her eye. "I am Mr. Dixon's associate, your honor, and I am presenting our case."

"Where are you from?"

"Houston, your honor. Holson and Nichols."

"I don't mean that, young man. I mean where do you come from?"

"California, your honor."

The judge turned away in disgust. It was clear that he didn't care for many people—locals, strangers, downstaters, or Californians. Devlin smiled.

"Your honor, we have submitted a bill of particulars of our claim against Younger-Johnson Oil, and we believe that the case stands on that document. The plaintiff requests that you make a decision based upon that document."

"I read it," Cameron sniffed. Then he turned to Devlin. "What do you have to say for yourself, miss?"

"I don't know what a bill of particulars is your honor. My partner and I thought that we were coming here to talk things over, in Texas style, and figure out what really happened. We aren't big for papers, but we are big for the truth, and that's all that me and my partner want you to hear."

"Then you're requesting that I deny the plaintiff's request."

"Yes sir," Devlin nodded, "about everything."

151

Dan'l smiled. The judge snorted and blew his nose, "Plaintiff's request denied. Counsel for the plaintiff, present your case."

Devlin sat down and smiled.

In a workmanlike way, Dan'l Simon proceeded to call T. Conroy to the stand. He identified a copy of the lease that was dated more than five years ago. He stated that he hadn't even gotten the dollar that the lease had provided for, nor had he signed it. It was a forgery. He identified the lease that WESTEX entered into, which he agreed he signed. He admitted that he received the five hundred dollars bonus for signing.

Dan'l asked him if he had signed a new lease with Younger-Johnson for a period of four weeks, and if he had received the dollar of consideration. He admitted that he had. Had he told Miss Younger that he had already signed a lease granting WESTEX the rights after four weeks? Yes, he had. Had he in good faith believed that a well could be drilled in four weeks' time? Conroy smiled, "Not really, but she's such a pretty gal, and my son is real interested in her. I thought I'd do her a small favor."

Devlin rose. "Mr. Conroy, did you and your son negotiate with me to increase your royalty from one-eighth?"

"Yes," he said proudly, "Billy Bob got you up to one-tenth, and then we went up to one-twelfth, and you finally came back with two-sixteenths. Billy Bob ain't no fool."

"Mr. Conroy," Devlin continued, "in your opinion, you considered it impossible for a well to be drilled in four weeks?"

"Yep, but you're so pretty, I said okay."

"Mr. Conroy, is it your opinion that you got a better deal in negotiating me to two-sixteenths royalty, rather than one-eighth?"

"Yessirree," he said proudly, "twice as good."

Judge Cameron snorted.

A continuing parade of exhibits was introduced: land searches, geological findings, the cancelled check given by WESTEX. It was completed in an orderly and professional fashion, until the mass of exhibits had been through the alphabet twice.

Judge Cameron turned the exhibits over to the clerk, and after he listened to the boring recital from Dan'l Simon, he looked at his watch and addressed Simon. "Counsel, do you have any more testimony?"

"No, your honor."

"Okay, then we'll break for lunch. Court will reconvene in two hours."

After Judge Cameron left, Dan'l Simon walked over to Devlin, who was preparing to leave with T-Bird. "Miss Younger, I wonder whether you and your partner could talk to me for a few moments. Perhaps there's a way of settling this matter for all parties. WESTEX are good people, and I'm authorized to speak for them."

Devlin looked into his brown eyes. She was expressionless. Then she brightened, "Maybe you'd like to go into partnership with us and put up the money for the drilling?"

Dan'l laughed, "For two-sixteenths of the royalty?"

Devlin smiled, "I was thinking about four thirty-seconds."

T-Bird shook his head. "Devlin, I'm gonna go to the barber, and then grab a beer. Why don't you and this fella have lunch. At least WESTEX will pay for that."

Dan'l Simon was overjoyed, but he managed to keep the excitement from his face.

"I was thinking of splitting the check, Miss Younger, but if you insist."

"Tell you what, Mr. Simon, we'll cut cards for it, or play a hand or two of poker for lunch—and anything else you have in your pockets."

Devlin led him out of the courthouse, and across the square to a small lunchroom. On the way she passed T-Bird sitting in the barbershop. Standing next to the curb was her captive Eldorado convertible. Devlin ran her hand over the metal and rubbed her elbow in the chrome.

"Do you do that for all Eldorados, Miss Younger? Part of your service?"

"No, Mr. Simon, just red ones."

This was not going well, and lunch went worse.

"Miss Younger, you really have no case to speak of. The lease calls for your drilling a well, not preparing for one. The drilling rig that you installed on the location wasn't even working by the time the lease expired, and that was critical."

Devlin was eating a very badly cooked burrito and sipping a Coke. She nodded. "What should I pay you to let me leave town, Mr. Simon?"

He was stunned. "No, we're prepared to make a significant payment for you to release your claim, and we'll forget about our claim for damages caused by the delay."

"That's mighty nice." Devlin seemed disinterested. The Coke in her hand was cold. She had asked for a warm Coke, but that was the way with Texas. Things were going to the dogs.

"How much?"

"Ten thousand dollars, Miss Younger."

"No thanks."

"We might do better."

"How much?"

"Fifteen." Simon was authorized to go to twenty thousand dollars, and that would be his next and last step. It would go something like this. "I'm not authorized to go a nickel more, Miss Younger, but if you say yes, then I'll plead with my people to get you another couple of dollars, maybe seventeen or seventeen-five. Okay?"

"Look, Mr. Simon, you can take the money and WESTEX and the rest of this nonsense and stick it where the sun don't shine. I broke my rump getting that lease to work. I got me a drill, sure it ain't the best, and I got it working, and I got it spudding, and I like the looks of that land. Besides, T-Bird's doodlebug spoke to him like a fairy godmother. It sang him a song, like the one that they sang to Snow White, 'A dream is a wish your heart makes.' That movie never stopped making me cry, Mr. Simon, and Snow White got the prince. How's that for American enterprise? I'll play you any kind of poker for ten, fifteen, or twenty thousand dollars. I'll put up my lease against half of WESTEX, 'cause I know that I've been honest about what I've done, and one thing I know in my heart is that I've got a good shot to make it. WESTEX isn't giving away doodley-squat, and we both know that the Conroy place, or somewhere near it, is sitting on a damn ocean of oil. Mr. Simon, I'm gonna swim in that gooey black stuff, and WESTEX can stuff it. Here's the check. I generally leave fifteen percent for good service."

Dan'l Simon was not happy. He had hoped for better; he wanted to settle that lawsuit. Twenty thousand would have been a cheap settlement, even the fifty thousand he had recommended, but that was over. Furthermore, his interest in Devlin Younger as the angel of his dreams was over too. She was one tough cookie, and he didn't like her at all.

In California, girls didn't talk to men like that. He had some regrets, because in California girls didn't look like Devlin Younger, no matter what the chamber of commerce said.

WHEN Devlin looked in the window of the barbershop on her way back to the courthouse, T-Bird was gone. Still parked in front was her Eldorado, serving as a reminder of how things can go wrong.

On the other hand, the Eldorado she no longer owned was only one of the many parts of her life that had failed to jell when she set out on her own. She scuffed her boots on the pavement and ran her hand over the hood as she stared at the reminder of her follies. What right did she have, a twenty-two-year-old girl, to play games with a multimillion-dollar oil company? She had been brusk and impolite to their lawyer. It had only been a mask to still the anxiety she felt about the court case. She had been too proud or too stupid to find a lawyer to represent her. The judge was right. She should have and could have found a way to get one. She had attempted and failed to make an end run around WESTEX. They finally had her, hands down. She hadn't started drilling till after her lease expired, and even then, the spudding of the well, at the rate that it was going, might not be completed until the next Ice Age. She had conned Billy Bob and Tony DeVito and a carload of Tony's Air Force buddies to get the jack-knife rig working, and what was worse, she had taken a decent man, T-Bird, and given him a fantasy to tie onto that she had no right to promise.

Devlin thought of the life she left behind. A week ago, she had caught up with the news of Tune's marriage. Sue Lingen? Good Lord. What a girl to hitch up with! Poor Tune. Wonderful Tune. Tune, the man who had introduced her to womanhood, and with whom she might have had a marriage, a home, a family. She had left L.C. and Vonnie behind. It was as if they were on another planet. Correction. They were where *they* had always been. It was *she* who was on another planet. She was in space, weightless, incapable of forward motion, bound to suffer the fate that she had foolishly selected for herself—rootlessly wandering in a hostile environment, one that she had no natural gift for, and one that would not wait for her to adapt to.

Devlin walked up the outside steps of the courthouse and then the second flight. As she walked down the corridor toward the courtroom, she saw a familiar face. It belonged to Amos Stuckey, the president of Big Spring National Bank. The little man stopped and stared at Devlin, then walked in her direction.

"Miss Younger, what are you doing here?"

"I'm in court to defend my lease on the Conroy property."

He looked surprised. "Do you mean that you still own it?"

"Look, Mr. Stuckey, that's for the court to decide. The WESTEX folks are planning to lynch me. The supply people I bought pipe and casing from on credit are after my hide. The Air Force is investigating my illegal use of its equipment and personnel. I understand that I can't be court-martialled, just executed." Then she smiled. "Apart from that, everything's fine."

"Hmm," he murmured, "I remember when you came in for a loan, Miss Younger. You know, of course, that people come in every day of the year with hairbrained schemes for finding oil, and of course, I didn't mean you any ill will, and I'm sorry if I sounded sharp, but you know how it is."

Devlin was bewildered. Why the dickens was this little man spending so much time with her? "Mr. Stuckey, what are you trying to tell me?"

"Well, Miss Younger . . . I thought you knew . . . but in any event, since I didn't know that you had any position on the Conroy land, there was no reason for me to look you up . . . and I guess you've been too busy to hear the news."

Devlin fairly shouted, "What news?"

"Why, Miss Younger, not three hundred yards away, across on the east side of the road from the Conroy place, WESTEX struck oil. Now I guess you know the way things go in one of these fields, if you were to dig an offset well on your land, just opposite, you'd have oil too. How much more or less I couldn't say, but the WESTEX find is a very big one. It's the first in the area."

Devlin seized the banker by the arm. "That means that if the lease is mine, you'll lend us the money to drill?"

The little man laughed. Devlin saw a row of perfect teeth, without a single imperfection. "Absolutely, Miss Younger, it would be a pleasure. After all, we *were* the first people you came to, so we should have the business."

In the face of his overbearing grin, Devlin let out a whoop and raced down the hall to the courtroom. She pushed open the door without a thought. Judge Cameron stared at her, as did the others in the court.

"Miss Younger, I hoped that you had learned a little decorum from your time with us this morning. I told you that there would be no food in court. I failed to tell you, because I felt that every grown adult knows, that behavior in court does not allow for playing tag."

"I'm sorry, your honor," Devlin said penitently as she moved to the table to sit next to T-Bird. She took a pad and pencil and scribbled, "OIL!" T-Bird took the pencil and wrote, "What about it?"

Judge Cameron interrupted. "Miss Younger, as counsel *and* defendant, do you have any witnesses to call?"

Dan'l Simon and L. Carter Dixon III glanced at her with little interest.

"No, your honor, but I do have a statement to make."

"Go ahead, Miss Younger."

Devlin moved to the front of the table, her back to T-Bird and the opposing counsel. Judge Cameron was the only audience she wanted, and the only one she needed. She felt the eyes of the men in the courtroom on her as she began to talk. Not for one minute had Devlin considered what she would say, nor had she rehearsed it. Just as the way she felt, she had to come on naturally and honestly.

"Your honor, you've seen pictures of our lease that WESTEX has shown you. It shows a rig on the land, supplies, and men to work it. As far as the law goes, as of today, I don't think anyone would quarrel with the fact that drilling has commenced, even if it is kind of slow. Your honor, that machine won't work more than a half-hour at a time without a talking-to, or fixing this, or trying to find out what ails it. But the law doesn't say that the hole has to be drilled overnight, just that drilling has commenced, and as long as it's commenced, the lease would be good until we came up dry. Then, and only then, the WESTEX folks could take over and try their luck."

Judge Cameron seemed to nod assent. Reassured, Devlin prepared to continue. On the other hand, the judge might have been reacting to a stomach cramp. Devlin proceeded anyway, in the hope that her first assessment was right.

"The trick then is to find out when the drilling actually did commence. Was it when the first bit dug a few grains of sand in the ground? If that's all we did, then we didn't do it in time. Because I admit that the corings didn't start popping out till after our four weeks were up. But, your honor, it's like an accident. If there's two cars coming down the highway in the same lane at a hundred miles an hour, when does the accident happen, and when could you tell that an accident was about to happen? You knew the accident was gonna happen when you saw those cars, even though they were a quarter of a mile away. You knew that an accident happened when those two cars met with just a millimeter of contact. You wouldn't have to see those two cars crumbled like accordions on the side of the road to know there *was* an accident."

Devlin turned to see Dan'l Simon and his associate looking thoughtful and concerned. That reassured her.

"Your honor, it's like kissing a pretty girl. You know you're going to kiss her, and she knows you're going to kiss her, before your lips even touch, even when they're inches away, and that's why I say that the day we bought the drill and made arrangements to have it delivered to the site was the day we commenced work on that lease." Then Devlin sniffed. "Where *was* the hole in the ground? The WESTEX people are gonna ask. I say to them that a hole in the ground is nothing. Describe it. What color is it? What does it taste like? What does it look like? Can you put it in your pocket or take it to church?" Devlin fleetingly thought that she had finally found her calling. Even if she lost the case, she would become a lawyer and save the lives of criminals. Damn, she said to herself. I'm not gonna lose this case.

"Your honor, the only way you could describe a hole, is if something else is in it. What I'm saying to you is that we had something else in our hole on the Conroy lease. We had a hole full of sand, and we're getting that sand out just as fast as we can. Drilling is continuing every day."

Devlin turned and sat down. She grinned at T-Bird and he seemed too stupefied to respond. She turned to the two WESTEX vice-presidents. They looked angry and mean. Mean, Devlin thought, mean as cat shit.

"Miss Younger, I assume that the case for the defense is concluded."

Devlin smiled outrageously at the judge, flirting in a way that would have seduced a fire hydrant. "No," he answered for her, "I don't think that there's any more necessary . . . not at all." Then he added, "You're from what part of Texas, Miss Younger?"

"Houston, your honor."

"Not from California?" he inquired pointedly.

"No sir, your honor, from good old Texas, as long and as far back as I can remember, and my daddy, and his daddy before him. We're proud of the courage that people in our state show to take on anything and anybody, at the Alamo—you know your history, your honor." Devlin crossed her fingers at the outrageous chauvinism.

"Yes, Miss Younger . . . my people fought at the Alamo. We're a proud and fighting people . . . and we'll take on anybody, and anything—no matter how big."

Judge Cameron stood up. "I find for the defendant." Then he grinned wickedly at Devlin. "Come on to my house tonight, Miss Younger, my wife will be happy to make you a meal. She's the best cook in Howard County."

Devlin let out a whoop heard for a hundred miles. She grabbed T-Bird and hugged him so hard he could barely breathe. Then she picked up the pad and put it in front of him.

"Devlin, dammit, calm down."

"Look at it, look at it, T-Bird. The WESTEX folks struck oil just across the way from us. That means we've got oil, too. The bank wants to lend us the money. T-Bird, you go find that barber and offer him anything he wants to get my car back, you hear? And we're gonna have dinner with the judge and his wife tonight. After all, it isn't every day that the most beautiful, nicest, most decent judge in all of Texas can listen to my bull and make us rich."

Dan'l Simon took all of it in. He had had no idea that WESTEX had struck oil. It would have made a difference to him. He would not have insulted Devlin's intelligence with the offer he made. She would take him for a fool, or a scoundrel, probably both. WESTEX had tried to pull a fast one.

There was hardly time to try and explain himself. Dan'l Simon took L. Carter Dixon's arm and led him out the courtroom.

When Devlin arrived back at the Conroy's place, she met stonyfaced stares from Mr. and Mrs. Conroy. They had heard about her triumph.

"You pulled a neat one on us, young lady," Conroy said.

"Mr. Conroy, what do you mean?"

"Billy Bob wanted one-tenth instead of one-eighth and you talked him out of it."

"I sure did, Mr. Conroy."

"Then you talked him into one-sixteenth, and then into two sixteenths."

"Yes," Devlin said.

"Girl, I just found out this afternoon that two-sixteenths is the same thing as one-eighth. I think that you did a bad thing."

Devlin looked around. Mr. Conroy snarled, "You won't get your hands on our Billy Bob. He knows about you and your fast-talking ways. He's gonna go back to his old gal, before he met you, leastways, she talks to him straight. Don't you think you can get out of anything now, young lady. You're gonna drill that well, and the rest of them around our land. Mrs. Conroy and I are gonna want all the money we can get for our royalties. She and I are going to California—Hollywood. She wants to go and see Johnny Carson and all those shows, and the Universal Pictures tour, so you better find someone else to make your chicken-fried steak and biscuits, young lady, 'cause her and me and Billy Bob are out of your life, for good."

Devlin turned and smiled to herself as she walked out of the house. When things go right, they really go right.

It didn't take Devlin very long to understand the complexity and seriousness with which the professionals attack the business of drilling a well. After she made arrangements with the bank, drillers who had been too busy and too occupied to even consider drilling for Younger-Johnson were only too happy to submit bids and go to work. The difference was that the Conroy lease consisted of over five hundred acres of what was now understood to be a huge find of oil. The discovery well, the first one that had been spudded in, would only be the first of dozens that the lease would spawn. That work would be very profitable for drillers.

As the days progressed, Devlin began her education in the process of working a lease. Hard-looking men, driving big semitrailers and flatbeds, arrived daily with the supplies necessary for drilling. Long sections of pipe (the "stem" that would follow the process of drilling down into the hole) along with tons of girders and equipment arrived collapsed on flatbeds and were erected to form a skeleton tower over a hundred feet high in the air. An enormous concrete "cellar" lifted the floor of the derrick above the ground and exposed the machines which did the drilling. On the cellar, the drillers positioned the stem, forcing the mud into the hole for core-testing, and drained the water that would be encountered from the underground tables. Hundreds of thousands of dollars worth of equipment and supplies came in a never-ending stream from Odessa and across the state, as the quiet talking men set about doing their jobs.

Ten yards away from the derrick, connected by an outside walkway and an enclosed passageway, was the engine house containing the drilling engine. Devlin was never far off as she watched the men handle the machinery, baby the giant pipe and fittings with controlled strength, and drill deep into the ground for the oil they all assumed to be there. Even with the conviction that her discovery well would be an offset for an already proven well, she knew there had been mistakes and missteps before. Not every offset well would come in.

The drilling that had been done by the raising and dropping of a walking beam, which hammered the casing into the ground, had been replaced by a huge rotary bit. Days and nights—three eight-hour shifts were working. Drillers dipped hands into the bailings as they came out of the hole. Devlin saw, inquired, and learned how the samplings were being taken and logged to determine the makeup of the entire field, if and when this discovery well was found to contain oil.

How deep would they have to go? The WESTEX well was over seven thousand feet. This might be the same, or deeper. Yet they were making progress, and Devlin saw how the bit had to be "dressed" frequently as it succumbed to the pounding and the pressure against hard sandstone and limestone.

Devlin stood and watched as work stopped and a dozen or so ingenious fishing tools were lowered to find some tiny piece of machinery that had come loose from the drill, thousands of feet down in a seemingly bottomless hole. It would prevent further drilling unless it were found. Devlin held her breath. It could be the terrible end to her discovery well, unless it were found.

One day that Devlin marked in her memory, a control head was put on the top of the casing, a heavy fitting that screwed on the top of the

160

string of what was now almost a mile of pipe. She watched as it was tested, to let the tools in or out of the hole, and closed to fit snugly around the drilling line. From the control head, several pipes fitted with heavy valves could conduct the oil to the field tank that had been built close by. When Devlin asked its name, she was told that it was called a Christmas Tree.

Later that day, at four in the afternoon, a quiet descended on the site. Her attention was riveted to the men on the platform. Their movements, once forceful and swift, had now turned into slow and watchful gestures, hardly dealing at all with the line and the rig, as if they were waiting for something that none of them could ascribe to core samples or tests. It was just the feeling of oil men who had at other times presided at the birth of nature's gift.

Devlin watched with awe as she saw the line slacken, and moments later, a spray of gas and oil began to sizzle around it at the control head. The Christmas Tree began to vibrate, and she heard and felt what seemed to be a tumultuous shaking of the ground, as one of the oil workers opened a valve, and a stream of oil shot high up into the air. It was convulsive and majestic.

Devlin was too shocked to react, but she felt T-Bird grasp her around the shoulders with a grip of iron. She had struck oil, and as the drilling boss moved over to where she stood, virtually petrified with awe, he said the words that she had prayed to hear, "Miss Younger, it's a big one, a damn big one. You've hit it damn, damn big. Congratulations."

The Stampede on Snyder Highway, just on the outskirts of Big Spring, had never in all its days, or since, seen a blowout like the one Devlin threw that night. Talk about honky-tonking with a vengeance, the inside and outside of The Stampede was the scene of an incredible celebration.

It took Devlin just an hour to stop at one of the stores on Main Street and buy herself a new shirt, new Acme boots, tan Lee pants and jacket, and a new Stetson. For anywhere but Big Spring, it would not have been called dressing-up, but for this city of twenty-five thousand, Devlin was going to look her best. T-Bird went to his favorite barber, the man opposite the Howard County Courthouse, who treated him with new-found respect. He, like everyone else in town, had heard about the strike that afternoon. He, like everyone else in town, had been invited to the blowout that night at The Stampede.

Three bands—Hoyle Nix and his fiddle, Lefty Frizzell and his group, and a third that came all the way from Abilene—played for the waltzing and two-stepping that started at nine and ran all night. In West Texas, things close up at two in the morning, but when the sheriff and the judge are in attendance, and still dancing to "If You've Got the Money" and "Mom and Dad's Waltz," and everybody is sopping up cases of Jack

Daniels and Coors, then there isn't any worry about the law closing things down.

Even L. Carter Dixon III was there. Devlin thought it only fitting that he be invited to her victory celebration.

"Mr. Dixon," the telephone conversation started, "I'm Devlin Younger, you remember, we met in court."

"Yes, Miss Younger . . . I don't think that we have anything to say to one another."

"Well, one thing, Mr. Third, I want you to know that we struck oil today, and that you and your vice-presidents are invited to a blowout tonight at The Stampede. No hard feelings."

"I don't know what to say, Miss Younger."

"Just come. Don't say a thing."

"I don't know whether WESTEX would want me to."

"The hell with them." And Devlin hung up.

Not only did WESTEX agree to L. Carter Dixon's appearance at The Stampede, but his boss, and his boss's boss and the representatives of a dozen other oil companies were at The Stampede that night. While everyone else was dancing, drinking, and having a good time, each of them was trying to corner Devlin.

By the time that evening was over, WESTEX had made the top offer for her lease, ten million dollars, and Devlin gave L. Carter Dixon III a big kiss on the lips and told him "no." If it was worth ten million to WESTEX, Devlin was certain it was worth many more times than that to her and to T-Bird.

At six in the morning, there were only a half-dozen people left at The Stampede. The sheriff and the judge with his wife and family had left a long time earlier. Devlin was dancing with the bewildered L. Carter Dixon III, who was hopelessly confused and quite certain that he would be fired.

"Third, just loosen up and tell your people that we're still negotiating."

A few others from the lease were still there, and the music they danced to was no longer provided by the bands. Only the juke box remained alive and well. T-Bird had long since departed with two ladies. Devlin watched him leave with one on each arm. She was happy for her partner. She looked at his retreating figure weaving out of the huge barnlike structure and thought about all that had happened to them since the beginning of their partnership. He was so full of love for her, and she for him, that her eyes filled with tears of happiness.

A little later she and L. Carter Dixon III were the only two left. She kissed him on the cheek, "Third, I'm hungry. I could eat the biggest damn breakfast in the world, are you game?"

He nodded and the two of them helped each other out of the empty dancehall. The place was a shambles, Devlin noted with pleasure.

Everyone had had a helluva time. It was the best damn party ever given in West Texas, and that meant that it had to have been the best damn party ever given anywhere.

Devlin walked unsteadily to her Eldorado. It was hers once again. During the weeks of drilling, she had lavished love and care on it, standing behind a genius of a body man in Odessa as he nursed the dents and dings back to perfection, and repainted and polished every inch of it.

The sun was beginning to appear on the horizon, and on this April day, even though it was near freezing, Devlin felt the warmth of the sun's rays. She started the motor.

L. Carter Dixon III sat down beside her patting himself to keep warm. Devlin pressed the button to take down the top. She put the car in gear, and with the wind whipping around them, the radio tuned to the country music of KBYG, she drove to Denny's next to the Holiday Inn.

Farmers and oil workers were already gathered. She caused every eye to turn. L. Carter Dixon III burbled on cheerily as he ordered coffee quickly to restore his circulation. Together, they devoured stacks of pancakes and fried eggs, toast and bacon, and more coffee. By the time they finished breakfast, more people were in the cafe. Devlin was barely conscious of the talk that was spinning around her. They knew who she was, and she smiled cheerily and sleepily at them, raising her coffee cup to accept their congratulations.

L. Carter Dixon III paid the bill and led Devlin outside. She gave him the keys to the Eldorado, and instructed him to care for it with his life and return it to her later. She would be going next door to the Holiday Inn and, finally, to sleep. He nodded, and when Devlin kissed him again, he reddened. Devlin reflected that maybe after a year or two of working on him, III might not be a bad person after all. She watched as he negotiated the Eldorado out of the parking space and she headed toward her room in the Holiday Inn.

The sun was up. It was seven o'clock, and Devlin walked into the office for her key. The sleepy-eyed young man handed it to her along with several messages. She walked outside and around to her room. It was chilly, and she wanted nothing more than to sleep all the way through till tomorrow. Finally, she reached her door, managed the key, and opened it. It was even colder inside. She turned on the heat and pulled the bedcover around her as she sat on the bed.

In the light of the bed lamp, she looked at her messages. They were all the same, but left at different times. They all read, "Phone L.C. Younger in Houston." For a moment or two Devlin thought that it could wait till later, but the number of messages indicated that it was important.

As she lifted the receiver and began to dial the familiar number, she wondered how L.C. had tracked her down. She hadn't been in touch with home for over three months. She wondered, too, what was *that* important. Devlin looked at her watch. It was seven-thirty, not too early to call. L.C. would be awake.

The ringing stopped and she heard Alma's voice.

"Alma, it's Devlin. How are you and Manuel?"

"Miss Devlin, señora." Her voice broke off in sobs. Then there was silence as the phone was left unattended.

"Devlin . . ." It was L.C. on the line.

"L.C. . . . what's wrong?"

"Devlin, get home right away."

"Daddy, what's wrong?"

"Your mother, Devlin, she got mixed up in a scandal. She's dead. They're going to bury her tomorrow."

"Daddy," Devlin screamed. "What happened? How did you find me?"

"Everybody knows about that business of yours in Big Spring. If it hadn't been for you, your mother would still be alive. If you have any interest in your family, come on back. If you don't, stay where you damn well please."

Then the phone connection was broken.

18

IT had taken Vonnie Moore Younger just one afternoon to fall under the spell of Gardner Land. It had taken a little longer for Gardner Land to recognize that Vonnie Moore could be his ticket to a highly comfortable life in Houston. It happened when Gardner learned that the terribly plain, terribly shy, and incredibly smitten lady was married to an enormously rich man.

The early gifts that Vonnie gave Gardner were, in his view, pitiful. In response to the first afternoon at his poetry reading in the apartment of Jessica Hungerford, Vonnie reached into her wallet and wrote him a small check, "to tide him over until he got his royalties in the mail from his publishers."

It wasn't much later when Vonnie began to understand that much more was expected of her. In the beginning she was uncomfortable and unwilling to spend substantial amounts of money on presents to Gardner. It struck her as unseemly and embarrassing to go into one of the better men's stores at the Galleria to buy Gardner a sweater or jacket, but as the days progressed, she was proud to see him dressed in her gifts. Then she began to indulge herself, buying him more and more extravagant things. In the space of one month, Vonnie bought Gardner a two-thousand-dollar Patek Philippe watch, several Cardin jackets, two handsome English-cut suits, shoes, custom-made shirts, a gold cigarette lighter, and assorted other items.

When Vonnie asked once about the watch and lighter, since she hadn't seen him use them, Gardner admitted shamefacedly that he had been forced to sell them. His publisher had reneged on the money, and Gardner was nearly destitute. Vonnie thought for a moment and decided to give Gardner an allowance each week to ensure his solvency.

What did Vonnie get out of this arrangement?

Afternoons, when she could manage it, she met Gardner in his tiny apartment. He was always handsomely gotten up, in one of the many robes that Vonnie had bought for him. Gardner was a young Oscar Wilde, his hair curled, a lace handkerchief inserted in his sleeve, scarf tied at his throat. Always there was a kettle on the boil, ready to serve Vonnie one of his favorite teas, Twining's Russian Caravan, which "a friend" had sent him from Fortnum and Mason in London.

Tea was ceremonial. The dishes were chipped and unmatched, but the routine of the service was practiced and perfect, almost as if he were serving a dowager dutchess. As Gardner poured, he chatted about the world. Buried as he said he was in Houston, somehow he knew more about the rich and famous of the world than anyone she knew. It was as if Vonnie had been able to tune into the life of a girlfriend her own age, indulging in teenage gossip about the scurrilous happenings of movie stars and the famous in Houston.

When the first cup was served and the milk was poured, and Vonnie bit into the scones smothered with Tiptree jam, she relaxed in happy ease. There they were, the two of them, alone together and friends. Later, after Vonnie listened to the gossip, she read Gardner another of her poems. Gardner was at all times intent on her words. He would repeat a line or a phrase that particularly appealed to him. Then he would smile, cross to where she sat, and kiss Vonnie on the cheek, holding her face in his hands. "It's our secret, Princess, just how sensitive you are. Someday, the world will know of your talent and your sensitivity. Yes it will, and perhaps someday you will give me permission to read selections of your poetry to the public, perhaps in Town Hall in New York or when I appear in other places across this land . . . Princess, someday, will you allow me?"

Vonnie smiled and blushed. "Someday, Gardner . . . someday."

Later, Gardner read other poems to her. Vonnie's favorite was Swinburne. Almost without fail, she made Gardner recite a stanza which carried her through till their next meeting:

> From too much love of living,
>   From hope and fear set free,
> We thank with brief thanksgiving
>   Whatever gods may be
> That no life lives forever:
> That dead men rise up never:
> That even the weariest river
>   Winds somewhere safe to sea.

Vonnie Moore Younger was shameless in her adoration of Gardner. In addition to the thousands of dollars worth of gifts and money, Vonnie liked nothing better than to cook and sew for him into the long afternoons, while he read or watched television. It bothered Gardner in the very beginning that Vonnie was forever about, hardly giving him room to breathe, but the deal he made was not demanding, and for the most part it was acceptable.

Gardner was free of the obligation of earning a living. He was out of the New York City rat-race, but the best part of his arrangement was his friendship with David.

It was largely through David that Gardner had his hand on the pulse of Houston society. He sniffed whenever he heard the gossip, because if David were to be believed, the young girls in the school he taught at were *doing it* to and with everybody in Houston, and everybody else was doing it with everybody else. He and David snickered with delight as they poured over the pages of the City magazine or the Houston papers, seeing in the society columns names whose intimate secrets were known only to their daughters, friends of their daughters, and finally to David and Gardner.

The only thing that Gardner didn't like about David was his rough way. All right to be "Mr. Macho"—Gardner had had his times with the leather boys, but David was in earnest. Anyone like David, who had been in the Special Forces by his own choice, was someone, Gardner considered, who just loved to hurt. Many were the times that Gardner had to excuse away bruises he bore as a result of David's temper. David was as charming and winning as ever a person was, when he wanted to be, and he was certainly the handsomest and most accomplished lover that Gardner had ever known.

Did Vonnie know about his friend David? There was no way of hiding it, he supposed, since even in the afternoons when he entertained Vonnie, reading her new poems and letting her cook and sew for him, the phone rang constantly with calls from David.

Vonnie had long ago abandoned caution in her relationship with Gardner. She was certain that if L.C. knew, he would kill her. That L.C. was, today and every day, in the middle of a tawdry affair with some little tramp, a prostitute or no better, was something that she and all Houston knew. But L.C. would not have tolerated for a moment, or even understood, the platonic relationship she had with Gardner.

As time went on, Vonnie found it easier to lie about her secret life. She had become a mistress of falsehoods, inventing excuses where she was going and where she had been. Not that L.C. was seriously interested in her goings and comings—they spoke very little, and it never would have come up. Vonnie had no need either to make excuses for Alma and Manuel, but she kept inventing new ones.

The money she lavished on Gardner was no problem in the beginning. Vonnie had always kept a savings account of her own from childhood. As time went on, the money became depleted, and in some deep recess of her heart, she understood that when that was gone, she would have a problem holding on to Gardner. But she had several thousand dollars left, and she wouldn't have to face that for a little while, or so she thought.

David made it a problem when he informed Gardner that he needed money. He had a situation, he said, for which five thousand dollars was an absolute necessity. It turned out that David had been picked up in a raid on a gay bath house, and the matter could be quashed by a lawyer with connections. It was either five thousand dollars or jail.

Gardner telephoned Vonnie directly one afternoon. He was in tears. Vonnie threw all caution to the winds and rushed to his apartment.

Gardner was seated on the sofa in his dressing gown, looking desperate.

"Princess, you are the finest person I've ever met . . . the very finest. Can I pour out my heart to you?"

Vonnie practically stopped breathing, fearful of what was to come. "Gardner, you know how close we are. There's nothing you can't tell me."

"Are you sure, Vonnie? Sometimes there are things, you know . . ."

"Gardner, trust me . . . please trust me."

"I will, Vonnie, but if you think the less of me, and if it makes you angry, you'll tell me right away, won't you? No secrets."

Vonnie crossed her fingers and placed one of them on Gardner's petulant and quivering lower lip. She saw a tear in his eye, and it frightened her. "Tell Vonnie."

"You know my friend, David."

"Yes," she said tentatively. "You know that I really don't approve of David, he's not *fine,* Gardner."

"He's changing, Princess. Some of the things you told me about him opened my eyes, and we've had some very frank talks, he and I. I told him that you are my dearest friend, and that what you said about him was only for his own good, and I know he's changing. But he's never had anyone who really cared about him, I mean, *really* cared . . . until me."

Vonnie was taken aback. She didn't understand the implications. "Gardner, what I want to do is find you some very nice young woman to marry. It would have to be someone who understood our special friendship. I just think that a handsome man like you shouldn't be a bachelor forever. I know that would mean my sharing you with another woman, but if she were the right person, she'd understand."

Gardner blinked. He didn't understand a word of what Vonnie was saying. My God, he thought, she doesn't even know that I'm homosexual. How can anyone be so stupid? How am I going to get the money for David?

"Vonnie . . . David is in trouble, and he'll go to jail unless I get him five thousand dollars."

Vonnie's mouth fell. Five thousand dollars was more than she had in her account. There was no way that she could find that much money without involving L.C. It would be the end of the world.

"Why do you feel you have to give him the money, Gardner?" she asked fearfully.

Gardner turned away. "He'll go to jail, Vonnie. I can't see him go to jail. They'll do things to him in jail, you don't understand."

Without another word, Vonnie went into the kitchen and closed the door behind her. She dialed a number and began an animated discussion. A little while later, she returned and sat down again. Her face was aglow.

"It's all over, Gardner. You don't have anything more to worry about."

"What are you talking about?" he demanded.

"Just that I spoke to David."

"You *what?*"

"Yes, Gardner, someone had to."

Gardner was livid with anger. "What did you tell him?"

Vonnie replied smugly, "Gardner . . . it's all over. I told you that I took care of it."

"Dammit, how?" he screamed.

"Gardner, don't lose your temper with me. I know what's best for you. I told David that you didn't want to see him any more, and that it was his problem if he went to jail, that I wouldn't give you the money to waste on him. That was what I told him."

Gardner slapped Vonnie across the face. Then he slapped her a second time viciously. "You dumb bitch, what do you think that you're doing with my life? *What do you think you're doing?*"

In a series of convulsions, Gardner lurched around the apartment, hardly understanding what had overcome him. He smashed dishes and lamps, and then sped into the bedroom. When he emerged, he held a .22 revolver in his hand. He advanced on Vonnie. Before she could say a word, Gardner Land fired five shots into her chest.

Vonnie Moore Younger was dead before the ambulance arrived.

19

AT nine o'clock in the morning, Devlin set out on the saddest journey of her life, the return to Houston for her mother's funeral. L.C. had been brutal over the phone. He had accused Devlin of being the cause of Vonnie's death. Her anger was dissipated by the overwhelming shock of the event.

In the hour that it was necessary for her to arrange the return of her car, and to shower and change, she managed to phone Tune. When she reached his number, she spoke to Sue Lingen, whom Devlin had never met.

"Devlin, this surely is you, now, no imposter. I tell you, Devlin Younger, I have heard so darn much about you, I feel that I know you already . . . like a sister."

"Sue Lingen, is Tune there?"

"No, he surely isn't, Devlin. He had business to attend to this morning, like he has almost every morning. I tell you that man works like a *demon*. He surely does. There isn't any reason in God's heaven why any man has to work as hard as he does. What's the fun of life, if all there is is work, work, work?"

"You heard about my mother?"

"Well, I tell you, Devlin, there isn't anyone in Houston who hasn't. I think it's a shame."

"Do you know how it happened?"

"All that I know is what I read in the papers, and I tell you, Devlin darlin', they are *full* of it. Where are you calling from? Guess you don't get the Houston papers, because if you did, then you'd for sure know what happened. They call those things 'love triangles' I guess."

"Who killed my mother?"

"Some person from New York. They'd been keeping company for

170

over a year, just about as long as you've been gone I guess, and nobody knew a thing about it. Leastways no one ever mentioned that your own mother would be involved with such a young man. Well, it seems as if this person, he's a homo, you know, was keeping company with *another* man, and your mother was the one who was in the *middle*, so to speak. Well, I tell you, they say women are jealous and will throw all kinds of fits when they're aroused, those fairies are the worst. I've seen some of them. I have a hairdresser I'm sure is one of *them* . . . ."

Devlin had had enough, "Dammit, shut up."

"Well, you don't have to be so high and mighty, now that you're rich on your own. We read all about it."

"My mother was killed . . ."

"Isn't anything you can do, darlin', to bring her back. What's done is done. You coming back for the funeral? I don't know *what* to wear. Of course Tune and I will probably have to go, what with his working for your daddy and everything. I do wish we didn't have to. Funerals are so . . . you know."

Devlin hung up. Sue Lingen sniffed into the dead telephone. She didn't like any one of the Youngers she had ever met, and she was fully prepared to dislike Devlin without a meeting.

The road back to Houston took Devlin south on Route 87, through the harsh, cactus-dotted land, and gentle sloping hills, dry and parched. It was early in April, and wildflowers painted magnificent patches alongside the long open road, nearly bare of traffic between the distant towns. Spring was in the air, with a quickening of the pulse through furrows that were dug into the difficult terrain. Low foliage of cotton had already begun to peek up from its seed beds.

Devlin passed through the town of San Angelo, heading south, mile after mile. The land was changing before her eyes. The mesquite and cactus gave way to a rolling landscape of green and shade trees, as she continued past Fredricksburg, nestled in a ring of hills. The quaint German town, carefully tended, sparklingly clean, gave way to other points of the road, Johnson City, and then the short distance on to Austin.

It had been about two years since Devlin had left Austin, and she wondered what the young women who had been her classmates might be doing. The recollections of what might have been were painful as she continued round the city, circling past the widening Colorado River, crossing the river, jutting on past the airport, campus buildings, and getting back on 290 for the last dash to Houston. It was the same trip that she had made Thanksgiving Day, almost a lifetime ago.

Late in the afternoon Devlin drove up to the house on Montrose and left the Eldorado under the portico. She went up the familiar stairs into the kitchen. The first person she saw was Alma, who grasped Devlin to her bosom.

"Señorita, don't believe what they say. Your mother was a good woman. She was a pure woman."

Devlin forced open the encircling arms, and walked inside the swinging door to the main hallway. There was no sound in the house, except for the scratching of a pen. Devlin followed the sound which led her into L.C.'s study.

Her father heard her step, and moments after she stood in front of his desk, he looked up.

"You're back," he said coldly.

"Daddy, where's mother?"

"At the funeral home."

"I want to see her."

"They won't show her to anyone. I told them not to."

Devlin stood impassive in front of her father, challenging him in a way she had never done before. "I'm going to see her."

L.C. didn't reply.

"Daddy, what happened? What happened to mother?"

"I don't want to talk about it."

Devlin burst into tears. "Daddy, don't do that. You knew mother better than anyone. You knew how timid and kind she was. She'd never do anything against you. There's got to be a mistake."

"There's no mistake."

"L.C., when is the funeral?"

"There isn't going to be one. Now you just mind your own business, Devlin, I'm telling you for your own good. There's no funeral, and that's the end of it. Your mother is going to be buried and nobody is going to be there, not you, or anyone else that's near to me."

With tears in her eyes, Devlin turned abruptly and walked out of the study, up the stairway to her bedroom. She shut the door and sat on the bed. For a moment she thought, then picked up the telephone. She asked information for the telephone number of John Travis and dialed. In a moment she was connected with her brother.

"John Travis . . . it's me, Devlin."

There was a moment of silence.

"It's me, Devlin. John Travis, say something."

"You're back in Houston."

"Yes, what happened to Vonnie?"

"Ask L.C., Devlin . . . he's the one to ask."

"Dammit, John Travis, what was she doing in a situation like that? Who is the man who did it?"

"It's in all the papers, Devlin. I don't need this kind of publicity in my position."

"What are you talking about, John Travis?"

"I'm executive vice-president of the bank, Devlin, and this kind of thing isn't good for me, or the bank."

"Excuse me, John Travis, your mother is dead, shot by some man we don't even know, for no reason that we can even figure out . . . a woman with lots of faults, but she loved us, John Travis. I know she did. I never really felt it until the last. She encouraged me to leave. She made me have the gumption to get out. She was your mother too."

"She's dead, Devlin, just forget about it."

"You bastard. Forget about it? You and your fancy new family, with all their tradition. You'll own the whole damn state of Texas before you know it, and you'll have sold your soul in the process."

"I've got nothing to say, Devlin."

"Are you going to the funeral?"

"I have to go to New Orleans on business, and they'll be all kinds of reporters there. For once I think that L.C. is right. Just bury her, and be done with it."

Devlin smashed down the phone. She redialed, waited, and the telephone was finally answered. It was Sue Lingen once again.

"Devlin, you must be back in Houston."

"Yes, is Tune there?"

"Of course, but you must come over to the house for tea one of these days. You really struck it rich, I understand. You've got to tell me all about it, and what it's like in the oil fields, the men and all."

"Please let me speak to Tune."

Sue Lingen's voice sounded hurt. She had so much more gossip.

"Hi, Devlin, back in town . . ."

The voice was familiar and reassuring. He had been the first man in Devlin's life. Over the telephone, the image of what he had once meant to her came back in waves. The bad times, the indistinct moment when Tune was wafted between her and L.C., disappeared on the phone. He was married to that dreadful girl. So be it, but they could still be friends, and Tune would find a way to help her.

"Tune, what happened to Vonnie?"

"Devlin, near as I can figure it, she was supporting this guy . . . Gardner Land, is his name . . . there's all kinds of checks and receipts for things she bought him. It started right after you left town."

"L.C. blames me for it, Tune."

Tune didn't comment. "Anyway, the best information that I have is that he wanted money, more money, and she refused, and he shot her."

"The two of them were together for over a year?"

"That's the way I hear it. That's what the papers say. You better watch yourself, Devlin, when they find out you're in town they'll be after you like buzzards."

"Tune, where is she?"

"The funeral home, I guess."

"Which one?"

"L.C. won't say."

"When is the funeral, Tune?"

"Devlin, I don't know. L.C. doesn't want anyone to go, and you know how L.C. is."

"Tune, she was practically a second mother to you. What difference did it make what she did? L.C. has been catting around every day of his life."

"Devlin, I still work for L.C. I've got to respect his wishes."

"Tune, that's the only thing you *do* respect."

Devlin looked at her watch. It was nearly eleven P.M. She was exhausted, but there was one more thing she had to do. She picked up the Greater Houston directory and searched for a name, and then dialed a number. As the phone rang, she looked at her watch again. It was not time to phone a stranger, but the person she called knew her a little, and she had a feeling that he could help. The phone stopped ringing and a sleepy male voice answered.

"Dan'l Simon?"

"Yes, who is this?"

"I'm Devlin Younger. You remember me, I'm sure."

There was a sleepy response, "Do you know what time this is, Miss Younger?"

"You're awake, Mr. Simon . . . and you're an attorney, and I don't know anyone else in town who can do what I want. I'll pay you for your services, but I need your help."

Dan'l sighed. He remembered Devlin Younger very well. He remembered the thirty-minute love affair he had with her in Howard County Courthouse. He also remembered the other Devlin Younger, tough, strong-willed, and tricky as an adversary.

"Yes, Miss Younger, but I can't represent you in anything to do with your oil business, it would be a conflict."

"No, it's not that. I want you to get me into jail, first thing tomorrow morning."

"Jail?"

"Yes, I don't know whether you read the papers about my mother Vonnie Younger. She was shot and killed by someone, and I've got to see the man who did it."

"I read the story, Miss Younger, but you've got to understand that I'm not a criminal attorney."

"Mr. Simon, if your law firm doesn't have the connections to get me into jail, and even empty out the damn place if you wanted to, then I don't know Houston. I'll give you my telephone number if there's any problem, but if not, then I expect to be at the jail tomorrow morning at eight. I want to see Gardner Land, more than I want anything. You do that for me, Mr. Simon."

"Yes, Miss Younger, I surely will."

"Thank you very much, Mr. Simon. I appreciate your help."

Dan'l Simon hung up and wondered whether Devlin Younger was back in his life. He didn't really need her, or want her, after the impression of her that he got that day in court. He held the phone in his hand for a moment, replaced the instrument, and set the alarm for six.

He had to make some early phone calls. No one but Devlin Younger would have the nerve to call him at close to midnight.

The police headquarters building at 61 Reisner Street was too small for its task when it was built in 1950, and twenty-three years later, it ministered to a city of over a million with incredible difficulty.

Opposite, across an empty plaza, was the line-up of storefronts occupied by bail-bondsmen. Nearby was the interchange on the freeway, newly built, which linked the once out-of-the-way headquarters to the center of the city.

At eight o'clock, Devlin's Eldorado pulled into the restricted parking place in front of the headquarters building, and she got out. Standing waiting for her was Dan'l Simon. Devlin looked considerably different to him in Houston than she had in Big Spring. She looked serious and older than the provocative child-woman he had seen briefly.

For a moment he thought to advise her that she would probably pick up a rash of tickets on her car, or perhaps have it towed away, but he thought better of it. Let her figure it out. He put out his hand and received a firm grasp in exchange.

"It's set up with the police, but there's no way of telling how cooperative this fellow is going to be."

"I understand, Mr. Simon."

"Your car?" he said questioningly.

"What about it?" Devlin asked as she walked up the stairs to the interior of the building. Embedded in the floor of the central lobby, a pink marble emblem with green and black inserts commemorated the building. Walking swiftly past were dozens of policemen, lawyers, and others who had business on one of the six floors of the building. Simon led Devlin to the elevator, and slowly the lumbering carrier took them both to the sixth floor—the location of the city jail.

They identified themselves and signed the log. A deputy led them to a visiting room, and shut the door behind them. Minutes later it was opened, and Gardner Land was led in, in handcuffs. The deputy opened the cuffs, removed them, and locked the door behind them. Gardner Land sat impassive, his handsome head poised in a condescending manner. He looked uncomfortable in jail clothing, workpants and shirt.

"Do you have a cigarette?" he asked.

Devlin shook her head and looked at Dan'l Simon. He reached into

175

his pocket and handed Gardner a pack of Marlboros and matches. The two of them watched as the prisoner lit one and put the pack in his pocket.

"You're her daughter?"

Devlin nodded.

"You don't look like her at all. You're very pretty . . . but I do think that you should do something about your hair . . . it should be much more off your face than you have it, but your eyes . . . they're quite lovely." He turned to Dan'l, "Could *you* be my lawyer? You look more intelligent than the one I have. What can they do to me? I'll die if I have to go away to jail in some place like Huntsville. That's where they send *everyone* don't they?"

Devlin could hardly believe what she was hearing. How could this man discuss her hair when he had committed a brutal murder? She stilled her anger, understanding that she wanted only one truth from him—what her mother had been to him.

"I can't be your lawyer, Mr. Land, and I'm only doing this as a favor to Miss Younger, this interview. The court has appointed a lawyer for you, and I'm sure you're going to get an adequate defense."

Gardner tapped the end of his cigarette and crossed his legs. For a moment the fire in his eyes came back. "Don't you believe it. They're going to hang me, or whatever they do. Of course I was absolutely justified in being angry, but I do think that *maybe* I went a bit too far." He looked at Devlin plaintively, as if he were asking for her understanding and forgiveness. Devlin was thinking. She needed to know about her mother.

"Mr. Land, my mother gave you expensive presents and money, didn't she?"

"Oh yes," he smiled, remembering the good times. "She was very generous, up till the end."

"What do you mean till the end?"

"Well, she knew about David and me, that he was in a lot of difficulty with the police. David was never far out of trouble, and he and Jessica really drained me dry. Even the clothes I got from Vonnie, I had to return, because Jessica was getting her rake-off and David was getting what he needed, and all I got was the dregs. I mean the merest dregs."

Devlin stared at him in disbelief. What could her mother have been doing with this man? He was a homosexual, and her mother was twice his age.

"Mr. Land, my mother must have liked you a great deal."

"Oh yes, she came over a couple times a week. She loved to cook for me, and clean . . . can you imagine that? And her poetry, can you imagine me listening day after day to her poetry? I was even willing to offer her sex, but that wasn't what she wanted. Do you know that she wrote a new poem every single day of the year?" Then he smiled

176

conspiratorially, "It was really dreadful, my dear, really dreadful, but she liked mine, and she liked me to read her Swinburne. Can you imagine Swinburne? And making chicken pot pie and meat loaf, as if anybody eats that sort of thing." Then he became sad. "I don't know if David will ever forgive me. He's out of a job now, because of the scandal and all, and I don't know what I'll do if David leaves me. It was all because of your mother, Miss Younger, all David needed was five thousand dollars, five thousand lousy dollars. What was it to her? I certainly showed her a thing or two."

Gardner Land sat smoking contentedly on his cigarette. He was in a vague state, hardly knowing where he was and what he was doing. Devlin stood up, and walked to the door. She knocked on it, to alert the deputy. Devlin stood aside as the deputy walked in and escorted Gardner Land out of the small room. Gardner paused at the door. "I take back what I said about your hair, it suits you."

Then he was gone. Devlin's eyes were moist. She had learned everything she needed to know. Vonnie had desperately wanted someone to care for, someone who needed her—and she found it. That was all Vonnie had wanted, all she had gotten from Gardner Land.

Devlin walked down the jail corridor with Dan'l, and was checked out by the policeman. They entered the crowded elevator, full of officers in between assignments. Silently Devlin walked out of the lobby and down the stairs to her car. A policeman was on the verge of writing her a ticket, but stopped as he saw her approach her car. Devlin paused and put out her hand to shake Dan'l's. "Thank you, Mr. Simon. Please send me a bill for your services."

Devlin got into her car, and drove west along the city streets. It had taken her almost an hour of telephoning this morning to find out in which of Houston's many cemeteries her mother would be buried. By the tenth call, she learned that L.C. had chosen Washington Cemetery, one that dated almost as far back as Houston had been a city. It was a ten-minute drive from police headquarters.

Devlin followed the route along Washington Avenue, past used-car lots, garages, small business buildings and single-family homes that now housed the poor. She passed black, brown, and white children at play in this very mixed neighborhood, a part of Houston's past that was now occupied by those who couldn't afford to live in its present.

Finally, she drove through an ornate entrance, and stopped to inquire about the site of the burial. She was early.

She stood patiently in the gray light of the morning, feeling the heavy moisture in the air, until a single hearse drove up to the graveside. The cemetery workers and funeral technicians busied themselves with the task of moving the casket and placing it on pulleys above the grave. They paid no attention to her as she stood near.

With businesslike precision they proceeded to lower the casket into

177

the freshly dug grave, without any concern, except for the simple mechanics of the job. These workmen were, apart from Devlin, the only ones to see the burial of Vonnie Moore Younger.

Quietly Devlin spoke the words she knew by heart from her freshman English course at UT, before all of this happened.

> That no life lives forever
> That dead men rise up never:
> That even the weariest river
> Winds somewhere safe to sea.

As the first shovelful of dirt tumbled on top of her mother's casket, Devlin walked slowly to her car, got in, and, with gathering speed, put Houston behind her.

20

THE NAMING of an oil well follows established practice. The name of the drilling company, Younger-Johnson, precedes the name of the land-owner, Conroy, and is followed by the number of the well. The official name by which Devlin's first well was to appear in the oil industry registry was Younger-Johnson Conroy No. 1. By the time Devlin returned to Big Spring, Conroy No. 2 was being spudded in, along with numbers 3, 4, and 5.

Younger-Johnson had taken over six rooms in the Holiday Inn to serve as offices for the company. Desks were purchased. Typewriters, file cabinets, copying machines, and telephones were installed. Accountants and secretaries, jammed into the small rooms, were trying to make some sense out of the incredible developments that had taken place.

Late one afternoon after everyone had left, Devlin sat on one of the hotel beds in the office she used, tossed off her boots, and opened a bottle of Jack Daniels. T-Bird held out two glasses, and Devlin poured them both great dollops of the amber liquor.

"T-Bird, what the dickens are we gonna do?"

"Get drunk, that's what."

"No, come on, you know what I mean. What are we gonna do with our lives?"

"Dev, I don't know about you, but I'm having the time of my life. Talk about a big man in Big Spring, why there isn't anyone on the main drag who doesn't tip his hat, bend down and flick the ashes off my shoes, smile and say 'howdy' to me. I get the best seat in restaurants. They hold up showing the movie until I get there, and when I want to go and take a pee in the middle, I just raise my hand, and the movie stops until I get back. I got pretty little gals coming out of my ears, and Devlin, you ask me what I'm gonna do?"

"This is a big *nothing*, T-Bird."

"What do you mean?" he asked angrily.

"I'm twenty-three years old, and do you know how much money I have in the bank?"

"The same as I got. How much is that?"

"T-Bird, the answer is I just don't know, it's so damn much, I can't even count. The WESTEX folks keep knocking at the door offering us more money than I thought there was in the world, and now the big seven are in the act, with their smooth-talking lawyers, and their Dapper Dan presidents and chairmen of the Board. It's as if I were homecoming queen." She held up a letter in front of T-Bird's face. "You heard of Exxon, T-Bird, a small company about the size of the Planet Mars. Well, they are proposing buying a half interest, I said *half interest* in the Conroy field for fifty million dollars. Do you know how much money that is, T-Bird?"

He swallowed his drink and poured himself another. "Devlin, I don't know, and I don't care. I can only wear one pair of pants at a time—I'm wearing the shoes I like. My room here at the hotel has its own toilet that flushes, and Denny's next door has great fries. What I'm thinking about doing is starting a fund to abolish the prison system in Texas. We should put our petty criminals out on the streets and our politicians behind bars."

Devlin laughed. "Okay, but I'm not a jailbird. I don't have that kind of outlet. T-Bird, I'm damn serious. Look at my hair, I haven't had it done in a month, my nails are bitten down to the nubbins, and I've holes in my jeans. I don't have a damn thing to wear except what I have on, and I could buy out a department store. I mope around like a sick cow except when I'm up to my armpits in mud on the lease, or working around the clock, looking at reports, organizing the new drilling, paying bills, and munching a steak every so often."

"Sounds pretty good to me. Want to play some poker tonight?"

"What for, T-Bird? If I lose a million, who cares, and if I win a million, so what. Besides, they run when I come to the table, they think that I make magic with the cards."

"Well, don't you?"

"Sure, can't you tell?"

"Want to go to a movie in Midland? Dunno what's playing, but you ain't been anywhere in months, so it's bound to be something you ain't seen."

"Nah, T-Bird."

"Okay, let's get drunk."

"T-Bird, that's not the answer."

"Well, what is?"

Devlin looked at T-Bird seriously. "I just want to start all over. I want to go back to the problem of trying to convince the Conroys to give us the lease, and the headache of trying to get a piece of drilling equipment, and the near disaster of what it was like to go to court facing extinction. That's what I'd really like."

"Roll back the clock?"

"Yep, that's it."

"You want to come back to the table and throw everything in the pot again, and start all over?"

"Sure, why not?"

"Do it, Devlin, don't sit on your butt watching them pump money out of the ground. Bet everything we have on the next play, and if that works, do it again, and if it doesn't work, then hell, we'll be right back where we started, without a pot to pee in. We can always go looking for leases for old R.D., and there's always a poker game for a stake."

"You'd do that, T-Bird?"

"You're damn right. Look, why don't you set up in Houston and start looking for more oil. This time we'll put up our own money, play it down the line, and see whether we can build us another Exxon. The only thing they got we don't have is a double 'X,' and they don't have any patent on double and triple letters in a name. There's twenty-five other letters in the alphabet that we can use when we get to be that big."

Devlin's eyes lit up. "Yep, do you think we could do it? I mean build up a real big-size company. T-Bird, there's no one else who knows me the way you do. Do I have the nerve, a twenty-three-year-old girl trying to fight it out with the men?"

"Dunno, Devlin, but you're smart, and you're lucky."

"It's worth a try, T-Bird, and if we fall on our faces, who the hell is gonna give a damn. We'll just start right over again. Speaking about luck, it's up to you, partner, but we haven't named the well yet and even though it's gonna be looked on as dumb, I'd like to call it Lady Luck Number 1."

"Fix me a drink, Devlin, and one more change, I want you to do for me. I think you ought to change the name of the company to Younger Oil—not Younger-Johnson."

"Why? You're my partner?"

"No more, Devlin. I didn't know how to break the news to you until now, but I want out. I truly do. I never said much about it, but for about three years I've had a real bum ticker—that was the reason they let me out of Huntsville, not because of anything else. They figured it would be cheaper if someone else buried me. Well, now I can afford it. Devlin, don't look so sad. I've had the best of it, the best. I want to stay right here in Big Spring. I made some friends, and they know me and respect me. I want to be near Lady Luck No. 1 and go take a look at it every couple of days or so, whenever I want, and when I go I want to be buried with full honors, right in the middle of the Conroy field."

181

Devlin moved over to T-Bird's chair. He sat with his feet on the desk, and his tiny frame for the first time looked fragile. She sat down on the floor and put her head in his lap.

"What's going to become of me, T-Bird?"

"You're gonna be the best and the brightest star ever to come out of Texas, and the prettiest. You're gonna have the time of your life indulging your every wish, spending money as if it were being printed especially for you with your picture on it, building up Younger Oil and having a ball risking everything, and if it don't work, then starting all over again, and doing it better. And I'm gonna put my share of the money into something good for people. And someday, Devlin, you're gonna find a man who is up to you, and then when you have a kid, I want you to name the first one after me, cause that way, I'll live forever."

"T-Bird?"

He laughed, "That ain't my Christian name. It's Wilbur. Can you handle that?"

"Yep, even if it's a girl."

Devlin rested her head on T-Bird's knee, and dared not move a muscle. She heard the quiet sound as he sipped his bourbon, and thoughts whirled around in her head. She would really be alone, and she was frightened. The person who cared and watched out for her, T-Bird, was not going to be there any more for her. But it wasn't T-Bird who had done the watching and caring. She had been the one. She needed someone to love and tend, someone to protect and defend. It had been T-Bird on whom she had lavished all of that. She would miss it, and she would miss him.

"I'll write," she said simply, "and you'll have to come to all the celebrations . . . you've got to promise to come to the opening of my new office, and my new house, and I'm going to make you meet all my boyfriends and have you tell me whether they're only interested in my money or my body. You're not going to leave me, T-Bird."

He smiled and brushed the curls on her forehead. "Never in a million years. Remember the name, Wilbur, like it or not, that's the deal."

Devlin laughed and got to her feet. "Come on, Wilbur, I'm gonna buy you a steak, and we'll take in a movie, and we'll get drunk, and I'll put you to bed, and tomorrow, I'm gonna start Younger Oil in its merry way."

T-Bird laughed with pleasure. "Let's git."

As rich as L.C. Younger had been, Devlin had never felt it. L.C. scrupulously avoided all the trappings of wealth that most others in Houston indulged in with careless abandon. For L.C., money was something to work with, not spend on pleasure. The symbols of his wealth were measured in the number of tugs he owned, the amount of shipping that Black Diamond handled, the number of its employees, the huge investments he had made in cranes, loading and unloading equipment, flags painted on the hulls of dredges and barges, the familiar Black Diamond symbol on almost everything that floated in the channel.

Devlin had never lived like a rich girl in the house on Montrose. Her interests had been in sports, playing the games the boys played and working on the docks. She found the three months at UT with the girls who lived rich and thought rich, an unqualified pain. Now, there were strange feelings stirring within her; she wanted to show the young women of Houston who had been so disdainful of her and her family just who Devlin Younger was.

Devlin knew people thought her pretty, but that, like so much about her, was one of the enigmas of her life. The mirror showed her clear skin, good features, hair of a curious reddish color, and eyes that had a greenish tint. She looked the way she looked. Big deal. Clothes had never been her interest. Jeans and workshirts fit everyone, and she hardly wore anything else. A place to live? That had never been a concern. While the girls at Kinkaid commuted daily from extravagant homes in River Oaks, the house on Montrose, in its seedy location, was as much a cherished place for her as if it had been a palace.

Now it would all be different. She had no history of self-gratification, no background in self-adornment, and yet she had the nagging feeling that she was missing something by not having the same urges as the young women she knew, the cravings for clothes, elaborate houses, handsome and elegant men. But, with the same degree of intensity that Devlin applied to Younger Oil, she decided that she would bring all those things into focus.

But where to begin?

First, she didn't have any idea what she needed to know. She would make a list. That always worked. But, with a pad and pencil in front of her, it was no easier. Someone was needed to tell her what to do. Then Devlin remembered the article that was written about John Travis's wedding. The writer, a woman from a New York paper, was a specialist in society news. That seemed like a good place to start. Locating the writer was not difficult. In several hours Devlin's secretary in the Big Spring Holiday Inn had Laureen Tuttle on the line.

"Miss Tuttle, my name is Devlin Younger, and I'm phoning you from Big Spring, Texas. Are you the same woman who wrote that article about my brother, John Travis Younger, and his wedding to Harriet Jurdam?"

"That's me, Miss Younger. How on earth did you ever find me?"

"It wasn't easy, Miss Tuttle."

"And how on earth did you ever remember that article?"

"I thought it was a very good story. It made John Travis look like a fool, but I always thought he was anyway, so I admired that part of it."

Laureen Tuttle laughed. "Were you at the wedding, Miss Younger?"

"Nope . . . I'm part of the black sheep side of the festivities. John Travis crossed over to the other side. The Youngers and the Jurdams are about as dead enemies as the Christians and the lions."

"How can I help you, Miss Younger?"

"Well, I'm twenty-three years old, Miss Tuttle, and I've been working all my life, which you will admit isn't too long. Now all of a sudden, I've come into a bit of money, and I don't know what to do with it."

"Miss Younger, all of us should have that problem. The newspaper business is not the most generous. Those of us who've been working in it for years wish that they could be in your position."

Devlin interjected, "I mean a *lot* of money, Miss Tuttle."

There was a long pause. "What do you mean by that, Miss Younger?"

"Well, I own quite a few oil wells, drilled them myself, and I guess that they're worth maybe a hundred million or more."

Suddenly Miss Tuttle's voice turned to honey. "Miss Younger, you have something in mind, please don't let me stop you. You did say millions, not thousands."

"Yes ma'am. You see, I'm planning to go back to Houston and set up shop there with a nice house and everything, and there are a lot of girls who knew me earlier, and who were pretty snippy, and my feeling is that I'd like to show them a thing or two."

"How can I help, Miss Younger?"

"Well, you could come down to Houston and work for me, organize getting my house in order, and organize some parties and other things, but it would have to be *my* style, Miss Tuttle, I'm Texas, and nothing else. I like to put my feet on the table. I ride hard, and I drive my car as fast as it will go."

"What do you look like, Miss Younger?"

"Do you mean am I plain? Does *that* make a difference?"

"Well, no, Miss Younger, with a hundred million dollars you could look like the hunchback of Notre Dame, but I was just curious. If I remember your brother, he was no great shakes. He didn't marry too pretty a young woman, either."

Devlin laughed, "Harriet Jurdam, I guess you could make two of me out of one of her."

"Well, what would you like me to do, Miss Younger?"

"Tell you what, I'll send an airplane for you today, and you come on down and meet me in Houston, and we'll see if we like each other, and then we can talk money."

"A plane? Do you have your own plane?"

"Not yet, Miss Tuttle, but after I hang up, I'm gonna call one of the dealers whose name I have and buy one, and I'll get it out to you right away."

Laureen Tuttle smiled and sucked in her breath. "I think maybe you can teach me a thing or two, Miss Younger. Where are you now?"

"Big Spring, it's a little bitty place in West Texas, but it's the place where I struck oil. I'll be in Houston tomorrow at the Warwick Hotel, and I'll have everything ready for you. So, is it a deal, Miss Tuttle?"

"You bet, Miss Younger."

"Call me Devlin, that's my name."

"Miss Younger, Devlin, you can call me anything you want to . . . just anything."

Devlin bid T-Bird goodbye later that day and got into her car for the drive back to Houston. Much of the drive was at night, and Devlin passed the miles away listening to the changing voices of Texas radio. All night, D.J.'s were playing Ernest Tubb and Lefty Frizell, and as the radio voices of the cities she passed faded into the new voices of cities she headed into, the country music sounds gave her a lift. Her heart was high with hope, and the task she set for herself was another mountain to climb. Life was good and she wanted desperately to enjoy it.

Two years ago, Devlin had known nothing about the oil business, and now she knew something about it, but more than that, she knew something about herself. She was happy being alone, and she realized it. T-Bird had been smarter than she was. She wasn't certain about his story of a bad heart. It might have been a graceful way of saying that he couldn't keep pace with where she was going, and he didn't want to try. Devlin would make it on her own, and that's the way it had to be.

The warm moist air of Houston sneaked up on her as she approached the city from fifty miles distance. It was still night, but the morning stars were in the heavens as the rosy glow of the sun began to spread gloriously. She should have felt tired, but she didn't. She would get to the Warwick by seven, shower and change. Yesterday she had phoned from Big Spring to make a breakfast appointment at 8:30. That would be the start of her business career in Houston. At breakfast she would meet Frank Holson, senior partner of Holson and Nichols. He had agreed to meet Devlin. He admitted how curious he was, particularly after the WESTEX case in which she had bested his client. Was she now interested in accepting WESTEX's offer to purchase her share of the Conroy lease? Devlin said no, but if he had no objection, maybe she might be willing to buy out WESTEX.

Frank Holson laughed, and when he hung up, he realized that Devlin Younger had not been joking. He promised himself that tomorrow's breakfast might be extremely interesting.

In every time, in every place, there are men so attuned to the needs of their leaders that they serve as the grand viziers, as chamberlains and ministers of kings and princes.

185

When the spirit of individualism and venture capitalism invaded North America in the nineteenth century, it brought with it the Fisks, the Vanderbilts, the Whitneys, the Morgans, and the Rockefellers. They in turn brought with them a new breed of individual, not unknown to princes—lawyers who could get the wishes of these new princes turned into reality.

Big Frank Holson was such a lawyer. He needed to ask only two things of his clients: What did they *really* want, and how much were they prepared to pay for it? The latter consideration was really academic, because if a client really wanted something, he was prepared to pay extravagantly for it.

Big Frank Holson lived up to his name. He was six foot three and weighed over 230 pounds. Try as he might to look well tailored in enormously expensive suits made for him by a Saville Row tailor, and custom-made shoes and shirts, it was an almost useless task. Big Frank had a way to turning a newly pressed suit or a handsome silk shirt into a pile of damp rags. His face was puddinglike, and his hair fell into an uncombed state no matter what. Overall, his looks worked like a charm, because he appeared to be only a "country boy," and his pincerlike strategies were unexpected and incredibly effective.

Frank wove his magic in many ways. He was one of the most charming of men. He and his wife entertained lavishly in their River Oaks home, their Hill Country ranch, and the apartment he kept in Washington. He was incredibly gallant to the wives of his clients, congressmen, cabinet officials, Supreme Court Justices. He had an encyclopaedic memory for the names, birthdays, anniversaries, hobbies, and tastes of everyone he met. He never forgot to send extravagant presents to everyone of consequence, never forgot to write fulsome letters of thanks for every little favor, no matter how small, never failed to remember to congratulate practically everyone mentioned in any newspaper for any good thing that happened to him or her.

But, as if that wasn't enough, Frank had a wonderful way of sizing up the basic point in any transaction and focusing in on it, even when the parties at interest failed to be able to isolate it for themselves. He was endlessly patient in nursing people to the point of recognizing the essential truths that he quickly understood. Eventually they got the point, and became convertees to Frank Holson's tutelage. And Frank never lorded it over his clients, nor the people he did favors for. He was always subservient, never failed to pay people their due, and consequently when clients and others came to him for advice, they left, having taken it and somehow convinced that they knew all along what to do, and Frank Holson had only confirmed what they already were certain of.

Frank's wife, Dolly, and his children were choice emissaries for his incredible salesmanship. Each of them was an example of the ideal way in which Frank Holson lived his life. Clients and others were as charmed by their perfection as they were by his own.

Unbeknownst to any of them was the fact that Frank was as manipulative of his family as he was of everyone else. Everything was a deal, a transaction, and he had so brainwashed everyone he dealt with, that they had long ceased to present any opposition to his grand plan. His grand plan was simply to run everything.

Frank Holson's goals could be your goals if you were a client of Holson and Nichols. With over three hundred lawyers in Houston and a special group in Washington, Holson and Nichols could weave magic spells, charm congressional committees, deal remarkably with the Securities Commission, head off anti-trust suits, and make things happen at the bequest of their clients.

It was curiosity that brought Frank Holson to breakfast with Devlin. He knew everything that he needed to know about her before they met, and her one-shot victory against a client was entertaining, but not conclusive. Still, he had sent one of his best men, young Dan'l Simon, to work things out in Big Spring. It hadn't been enough because Frank had not made a few phone calls to some of the people in Howard County who could have been helpful. But still, the young woman had been extraordinarily resourceful, and that had stimulated his curiosity.

The clerk at the desk telephoned Devlin's suite when Holson arrived. At his knock, Devlin opened the door. He stood stock still for a moment as he looked at her.

"They didn't tell me you were a beautiful lady, Miss Younger."

Devlin reddened. Somehow the challenge unnerved her, but she shook the lawyer's hand with a firm grip. Frank Holson held her hand several moments longer than she expected him to, certainly longer than was necessary. Devlin, dressed in her jeans, boots, and cotton workshirt, was a stunning inconsistency for Frank Holson. He was twice her age, married, with two children Devlin's age. But Frank Holson was unquestionably smitten. As he followed her to the already set table in the dining room, he stared at her tall, slender figure, and marveled. This was not at all what he had expected.

He held the chair for Devlin ceremoniously and then seated himself. Across the table, he stared at Devlin's green eyes and the ginger-colored curls around her childlike face.

"Miss Younger, it is a real pleasure to meet you. I must say that I never ran into anybody in the oil business as charming as you. You don't smoke cigars, do you?"

Devlin smiled, "No."

"Good," Holson said, "I was wondering if there was any imperfection, and I thought *that* might be it."

"There are some, Mr. Holson, but that's not one of them."

187

"Miss Younger, can I pour you some cream for your coffee?"

"No thanks, Mr. Holson. I took the chance of ordering an assortment of things you might like."

He lifted the plate covers, examining and surveying the scrambled eggs, sausages, bacon, biscuits, and the pots of coffee.

"Reminds me of breakfast on the ranch, going out on the range."

"Mr. Holson, you've never been any further out on the range than flying over in your Lear jet."

Frank laughed, "You got me there, little lady, but I do like my breakfast, and my coffee. Why don't we eat a little, and talk after."

Devlin sipped her coffee and watched as Holson fed himself. Notwithstanding his appetite, his eyes seldom left hers. It made her feel uncomfortable.

"You're not eating, Miss Younger?"

"I just drove in from Big Spring this morning, and I had my breakfast earlier. Please don't mind me, Mr. Holson."

He stopped. "Do you mind if I ask you a really big favor? I would dearly like you to call me by my given name, Frank. I think that we are going to be friends, and all my friends call me Frank."

He accepted it as if it were done. Devlin decided that henceforth she wouldn't address him by name at all. That would solve that problem. He settled back in his chair, lit a cigar, took a sip of coffee, and began to unwind. "Tell me, what did you have in mind?"

"I've been giving a lot of thought to what I want to do, and I think that maybe your law firm can be helpful to me."

Holson nodded and exhaled a cloud of smoke. "Go on."

"Younger Oil has very substantial assets, and I suppose that I could sit around and live very handsomely for the rest of my life on the money earned from what we have, but I'm not interested in that."

"What does interest you?"

"Taking chances interests me . . . and seeing if I can do it again."

He lauged, "What would that prove?"

"Simply that it wasn't a fluke, and that it wasn't just a piece of luck that made it happen. And one more thing, that I'm as good as any man in it."

Holson whistled, "Don't you think that you're trying to prove the wrong thing in the wrong way?"

"What do you mean?"

"Just that women and men *are* different, and that difference is put there by God for very real reasons . . . one of them has to do with biology, and the other has to do with mentality. Now, I know just from looking at you the things you're good at. You're a young woman, in the glorious bloom of beauty. A woman, I might add, who would be a fit consort for any important man. I see you in jewelry and furs, alongside a powerful man who could take care of you, make the world respect you and protect you. It wouldn't necessarily have to be marriage, because after all, this is the twentieth century, and marriage is only a piece of paper."

Devlin sipped her coffee quietly.

"Now the WESTEX folks are good friends of mine. They admire the little thing you did up in Big Spring. It took gumption to do it. You brought it off and you can cash in like a bandit. I know you have an offer from several of the major companies—don't ask how I know—but whatever that is, WESTEX will do twenty-five percent better. And you can have the best of everything, a beautiful life and exquisite homes. I know it hasn't been easy for you, Devlin, with your daddy being the kind of man he is. Lots of people look down their noses at the Youngers, but it doesn't have to be, not at all, and after that terrible thing that happened to your mother. What you need is someone to protect and advise you."

Frank Holson looked quite satisfied. As he spoke, his eyes seemed to devour everything that Devlin was. He puffed on his cigar to let his message sink in.

"Frank," Devlin said with a wide smile, "you can take that line of bullcrap and your shitkicking ways and get the hell out of my room. But before you leave, I'm telling you that you had better brush up on your technique. You aren't going to get this gal into the sack as your pretty little toy, and you're not going to get Younger Oil into WESTEX with all your down-home sweet talk. I wanted to see you because I thought that what I had in mind for Younger Oil could use a smart lawyer. Maybe, but that sure isn't you."

Frank Holson chomped his cigar. She had nailed him and she would regret it. That young pussy would regret talking to Frank Holson that way. He stood and avoided the fire in Devlin's eyes as he turned his back on her and walked out of the room, and out the door. He had never been so angry in his life. As he waited for the elevator, he felt his blood pressure rise, and the bile in his throat almost consume him. She had nailed him. The bitch had nailed him, and he would never forget it until he got even.

21

RIVER OAKS! In the year 1924, three Houston men secured an option on two hundred acres near the newly completed River Oaks Country Club. One of the three, William "Will" C. Hogg, the eldest of four children fathered by one-time Texas governor James Stephen Hogg, decided to add a thousand more to it, and turn it into a carefully controlled, perfectly designed community of "our kind of people."

"Tall Timbers," the original name for the area, was not a garden spot in the mid-20s. Muddy streets required the purchase of two truckloads of rubber boots for prospective customers during one 1927 sale.

Will Hogg conceived of less expensive homes protecting an inner core bounded by Memorial Park, Buffalo Bayou, and River Oaks Country Club.

The salesmen for River Oaks put out a brochure in 1924 which invited prospective buyers to "estates as once made Virginia famous," where "there's laughter and love, where there's a cool breeze in the summer and the pure air of countryside year round."

Fifty years later, River Oaks became synonymous with the protected, beautiful planned community which housed exclusive members of Houston society. One night in May 1974, all of River Oaks was up in arms, except the five hundred or so who were invited to Devlin Younger's housewarming party.

Not everybody dressed in costume for the party at "Fairlawn," the name Devlin gave to her estate. The ones who did had the best time; the ones who didn't kicked themselves for days. It was a night to remember, because the theme of the party was "Old Houston," and that was a pretty riotous time and place.

When Devlin bought her house, she inquired whether the mansion on the estate next door was for sale, too. When she discovered it was, she bought it and tore it down. She had the scarred land beautifully landscaped with flaming azaleas, and found a genius who was able to light the tall trees at night in an effect that copied moonlight, and she proceeded to make over the first house.

Laureen Tuttle, who now served as her social secretary, advisor, and voice of reason, was shocked at the wasteful display.

"Devlin, are you sure you know what you're doing?"

"Laureen, listen to me one more time. I'm twenty-four, richer than anybody can believe, and I didn't get that way by being chintzy or careful. The well I hit is called Lady Luck, and I guess that's what I am. I want you to know that if I was to lose it all tomorrow, I wouldn't give a damn. In the meantime, if I'm lucky, I can just keep pace spending it almost as fast as I'm making it."

Laureen Tuttle was defeated. She continued to watch the acquisitions build up. Devlin's Lear jet was refurnished and redesigned by a Long Beach firm that specialized in custom-made interiors for heads of states and Arab sheiks. The headquarters of Younger Oil was moved to a splendid set of offices on the penthouse floor of a brand-new downtown office building. Laureen had suggested a New York design firm to create a chaste and handsome metal, leather, and marble interior. Devlin wouldn't hear a word of it. She had seen a series of photographs of the interior of the Élysée Palace, the home and office of the president of France, and decided she wanted to copy its look. Months later contented workmen and designers, who were getting richer than they ever imagined on this project, considered it might take as long to build as one of the smaller Egyptian pyramids. They still had not put in place even the first piece of custom-made furniture.

Laureen surveyed the plans and drawings with horror. "Devlin, this is in the worst kind of taste."

Devlin sniffed. As she turned and walked off, she muttered, "Tell it to the president of France."

The night of the housewarming a parade of fine cars appeared in front of the high wrought-iron gates of Fairlawn. A score of parking valets, dressed in tailcoats and striped vests, took over each of the vehicles. A provocatively dressed, high-heeled maid, with a short black skirt, dark net stockings, and very low-cut bodice, poured champagne for the passengers who rode to the main house in an open tour bus, borrowed from the Universal Pictures studio tour and flown to Houston in a cargo jet.

As the guests arrived at the mansion, they were met by other maids and butlers who removed the women's furs, and held up hand mirrors so they could adjust their makeup and the men could adjust their fake mustaches, whiskers, and sideburns.

Fairlawn was loosely patterned after Washington's Mount Vernon, except that at Devlin's insistence the roof was raised to accommodate a twenty-foot crystal chandelier that appealed to her. Additional wings had been added so the mansion could have accommodated a family of thirty, their horses, and their horses' horses.

Laureen Tuttle sniffed, "Devlin, you're destroying the architectural purity."

"Laureen, I want an indoor swimming pool, and I want a place to grow flowers, and I want a couple of billiard tables, and a nice big place with its own bar to play poker. If you don't really think that it's nice and proper, well, maybe I'll arrange to put a striped tent over the whole damn thing."

Laureen commented regretfully, "A circus."

"Yeah," Devlin smiled with pleasure. "A damn circus."

As the guests filed in, they noted the three-story center hall had swags of the six flags that had flown over Texas. The huge crystal chandelier had been lit with almost a thousand long tapers. Minutes before the first guest arrived, a half-dozen men on ladders had completed the tedious task of lighting each of them.

From the distance the sound of an orchestra could be heard. It was country music, and the two-step was being featured along with the waltz.

Laureen was dismayed at Devlin's plan. "I can call Peter Duchin, Devlin, he's the most fashionable."

"Never heard of him, Laureen. They don't play his stuff on the radio much in Texas."

The hum of hundreds of voices, the clinking of glasses, and the shuffling of feet on the dance floor could be heard as the guests wandered wide-eyed through the palatial mansion. Not a single stick of furniture that Devlin had ordered for the downstairs was in place. It would all be delivered this week. Only her living quarters upstairs were complete. Devlin seized this moment in time to run riot in decorating the main floor for her party.

On the walls of the soon-to-be cardroom were large sepia prints of the sights of the city in bygone days. The Sweeney and Coombs Opera House on Fannin Street; the Old Houston Post Office with its huge rounded cupola, then at the corner of Franklin Avenue and Fannin; a street scene of two Negroes racing their drays in 1873 down the main street; a Negro magnolia seller; a street hawker with his bell and flag; the Lord's Cycle Club at Chenevert Street, when cycling was one of Houston's chief pastimes; Main Street in 1900, looking south from Congress Avenue, with buggies and streetcars.

A room off the main hall was made into a nickelodeon, with silent westerns run continuously. Another was turned into the Victorian parlor of a whorehouse, a re-creation of the most famous one on Congress Street. Scantily clad models, dressed in chiffon wraps and maribou throws over scanty underwear and sheer camisoles, posed on sofas. A photographer was nearby to take souvenir snapshots of guests with any or all of the young women.

In the ballroom, which would be Devlin's living room, the walls and ceilings were covered in silver foil. Garlands of magnolias festooned the room. Kerosene lamps, hanging from the ceiling, gave the ballroom a magical feeling, and the guests danced dances they scarcely knew— polkas, schottisches, and the two-step.

On one living-room wall was a wide bay window that faced the sloping lawn. Belled candles lit the expanse and dark-suited men would soon be shooting off a fireworks display.

On the lawn, a hot-air-filled balloon was tethered by ropes. Attendants were waiting for guests to take a high view of the city of Houston, a basketful at a time. Tiny Christmas-tree bulbs on the side of the balloon spelled out "Younger Oil Company." Of course, Laureen was horrified.

Finally Devlin appeared, surrounded by a crowd of men and women who were offering her their congratulations.

She was dressed in scarlet. A taffeta swag on her skirt outlined soft velvet of the same color, and a feathered boa was draped around her bare shoulders. Her narrow waist and long legs were sheathed in yards and yards of velvet and taffeta.

On the bodice of Devlin's low-cut dress was a fifteen-carat cabochon ruby, and on her wrist was a monstrously large, four-inch band of diamonds, sapphires, and rubies. Bulgari in Rome had sent a representative to Houston with a treasure trove of jeweled pieces for Devlin's selection.

Her face was aglow with pleasure; her green eyes sparkled with delight. Ginger-colored curls framed a smile of such intense pleasure that every guest could recognize that this evening a twenty-four-year-old woman had indulged her every whim. Even if no one else had a good time, Devlin was hugely enjoying this night of her life.

From the first, the event was a thunderclap on the Houston scene. No one had composed a party like this, and like it or not, this newcomer, Devlin Younger, had made a splash of her own.

Some in Houston would never forgive Devlin for this evening. She had done too much too soon. Whispered asides at the party told the story. They were openly full of praise, but among themselves bitter at the show of crazy extravagance from a newcomer only twenty-four, who had no background or tradition. The men, captivated by her youth and beauty, were brought down somewhat sharply when they realized that she was competing with them, and that for all her femininity, Devlin was a strong-willed, self-determining woman who scared them to death.

The guest list included every important person in Houston: bankers, lawyers, oilmen, ranchers, radio- and TV-station owners, newspaper publishers, political figures, heart surgeons, land developers and everyone in cafe society.

193

A score of young turks took sick from the nonstop champagne, hard liquor, and groaning board of imported delicacies, caviar and quail, patés and barbecued ribs, crêpes, and enchiladas, soufflés and chili.

At midnight a group arrived that *made* the party for the guests. A Hollywood company was filming a motion picture in Pasadena, just outside Houston, and the stars and directors appeared as if by magic. In Houston, where the success of parties is frequently measured by the star value of the guests, the arrival of David Hampton, the star of the film, was the crowning achievement of the evening.

Devlin came to the front hall to meet him and the others. They kissed as if they were old and intimate friends. This had been their first meeting, but no one watching would have guessed it.

"Devlin, how good of you to invite us. I wasn't sure until the last that I could get away. We're doing some night shooting, but I told the director that I had to get here. As a matter of fact, I even *brought* the director. We closed down the set, just so we wouldn't miss it."

A bearded man in blue jeans and boots stuck out his hand, "Miss Younger, you are really a showman—or a showlady—even for Texas; this is one hell of a party."

Devlin laughed, "This is just an introduction, the party waited for you all to come."

As if magnetically drawn to Hampton's presence by some secret signal, every woman gravitated to Devlin's side for introductions. Those who couldn't wait introduced themselves.

In every period of movie-making, a star of incredible magnetism emerges such as Robert Taylor, Tyrone Power, Cary Grant, Paul Newman, or Robert Redford. David Hampton was such a star. He had a slick and polished look; he was a "gentleman" actor, unlike the scruffy appeal of a Dustin Hoffman or Al Pacino. One almost expected him to put a cigarette into a gold cigarette holder and light up with a solid gold briquet lighter, and look off into the distance as the screen said, "The End."

David Hampton's elegance made women crumble. His appeal was not to teenage girls, but rather to the American women hungering for established values. In 1974, in the midst of the terrible war in Vietnam, and student rebellion, David Hampton was not the biggest star in Hollywood, but for the establishment in Beverly Hills, New York, London, and Paris, he was *the* movie star. Even though his box-office appeal to young moviegoers was questionable, there were always people who wanted to make a David Hampton movie. They were the traditional heads of studios who found his looks and manners refreshingly old-fashioned.

He was handsome in a dark Latin way, perpetually tan, and ineffably elegant. His manner of speaking appeared affected, since for no apparent reason he had a trace of an English accent. Dark-eyed, he could focus them on you unnervingly. But for the most part, his eyes and his spirit roved in concert. There was always another person, another opportunity behind the one at hand, and that was worth checking at all times. One never knew.

Surrounding David Hampton were stories of his affairs with some of the world's most attractive women—the daughter of a Greek shipping tycoon, a member of the British royal family, wives of society figures in Bel Air and Southampton. And now, David Hampton saw someone else he promised himself he would acquire, Devlin Younger.

Ignoring everyone else, he grasped Devlin's hand. "I hope you're putting this house for sale, Devlin."

"Why is that? I just bought it, and I'm fixing it up."

"You won't be using it much," he said matter-of-factly. "I think you'll be wanting to travel with me. I don't expect to leave Houston without you." He smiled playfully.

Devlin laughed at his effrontery. "You take a lot for granted, Mr. Hampton. Me."

"Not *you*, Miss Younger, *me*."

"Yes?"

"I don't think you've ever met anyone like me in your life."

"Why would I *want* to?" she asked with growing displeasure.

"Ah, I will have to show you slowly and carefully, so as not to overwhelm you."

"You think that I'll be overwhelmed?"

"You could be, others have been."

"How many of them?"

"Devlin, let's not talk about others. You're a very young and very beautiful woman, and from the appearance of this house, which I must add is in dreadful taste, you must be a very rich young woman."

Devlin withdrew her hand, "Mr. Hampton, I don't think that I like you. I won't ask you to leave, but I would appreciate your leaving *me* alone. Go spread your charm on the other ladies here tonight. From the looks of them, it would appear that they are all panting for your attention, or can't you handle them?"

"Oh yes, Miss Younger, you, them, and a million more like them, but I think that you have something quite individual, and I take upon myself the clear obligation of showing you the light of day. Look at those people dressed like clowns. Look at that room over there—a whorehouse, I'm sure—but whorehouses have to have some appeal, some sexuality. You make a mistake in being a copyist, Miss Younger, I could teach you how to be an original."

Devlin couldn't tear herself away from this arrogant man with the mean and malicious smirk. "Who arranged for all those second-rate people to come here?" he asked.

"What do you mean, second-rate?"

"Just simply that all these people seem to have is money. Now I admit that's an important consideration, but whatever became of grace, style, wit, elegance? Did that disappear someplace along the Great Divide? Tell me, Devlin, whatever grossness possessed you to advertise your oil company on that dreadful balloon?"

Devlin was exasperated, "Where do you come by your fancy manners, your elegant diction? Are you titled royalty?"

"God, no, Devlin. I learned it at my mother's tit. She was a saleswoman at Saks Fifth Avenue in New York, and we hardly had a sou, but I learned how to think the right things, appreciate the right things, and with my body and mind in harmony, I was able to accomplish much. You may have seen some of my films, perhaps you have, but I don't consider myself much of an actor . . . I am a personality. As I go, others go, too, and Devlin, like it or not, you'll find that you will be going with me." He laughed, "Have I frightened you? Don't be afraid, you'll enjoy the ride."

David Hampton turned from Devlin and walked to a group of anxious, starstruck women who elbowed their way to be next to him, to stand in the illumination that flowed from his brow.

At three in the morning, shaking their heads in wonder, the last guests entered the last Cadillac. A car valet, nearly asleep from the fatigue of racing hundreds of yards for distant cars, buoyed up occasionally by nips of coffee and stronger beverage, closed the door on the last couple to leave, a senator and his wife.

Dozens of waiters and maids were busy removing glasses, dishes, and ashtrays and sweeping the floor of the party debris. Several waiters found treasure—a diamond earring, a diamond bracelet, and a platinum watch. They pocketed them, considered turning them in, and then reconsidered.

A maid found a packet of condoms. Others found keys. The bartenders took their personal stashes of champagne and whisky bottles from under the bar and packed them with their uniforms.

Outside, the half-dozen technicians who flew down from Hoboken to install and operate the fireworks display on the lawn were trying to clean up the smoking remains which smelled more like the day after D-day than a costume ball. The lawn was scarred from the fireballs, some of which had landed and fizzed out instead of popping off celebratorily in the Houston night sky.

Neighbors in River Oaks, those who had not been invited to the party—who managed to survive the sounds of music, fireworks, and crowds on the lawn and the screeching of valets parking cars, and who phoned the police regularly, without success, to get the proceedings quieted—were now finally asleep.

The party was over, and Devlin in her stocking feet, holding her shoes in one hand and the hem of her dress in the other, managed the staircase with some difficulty, dodging souvenirs of the celebration that was now part of Houston legend. It had been a damn good party. Not the one that Laureen Tuttle had proposed: little finger sandwiches, stuffy black-tied people, quiet champagne-pouring. Laureen had finally caved in to Devlin's insistence that this party be Houston, not New York. If Devlin had had her way, she would have come in workshirt and denims, had the music of Lefty Frizell or Willie Nelson, and danced the Cotton-eyed Joe the night away. But that wasn't possible. She had a position to establish. She sniffed as she trudged along the deeply carpeted hall to her bedroom suite. She had set out to make Houston society sit up and take notice of her arrival on the scene. She clearly had done that.

Devlin remembered the stares, the candy-sweet smiles, the honey-dripping words of greeting from the young women and their escorts. The young women, akin to the sorority girls she had known at UT, were bewildered by her. Devlin's mansion was extravagant by even the most lofty standards of Houston's big rich. The party had been original in every detail, and most of all they were impressed at the arrival of David Hampton. Devlin had no idea why that man appealed to all the women at the party. Devlin found him unpleasant, egotistic, and arrogant. Who had invited him? Laureen? She would speak to her tomorrow about him. Right now, there was nothing that she wanted more than sleep.

Devlin opened the door to her bedroom suite. In the dim light from the dressing table, she thought she saw a figure lying on the bed. One more guest unaccounted for. Pausing at the door of her bathroom, she switched on the light and looked at the bed again. It was empty. Had she imagined something?

One of the features that Devlin had devised for her mansion was a bathroom suite of incredible proportions. An entire mirrored wall faced a sunken marble tub, reached by three steps. Devlin walked over to the mirror and looked at herself. She was exhausted, but the idea of taking a soothing bath seemed irresistible. She walked to the controls, and a surge of warm water began to fill the tub.

Devlin placed her jewels on a mirrored table, unzipped her dress and stepped out of it. She stood in front of the mirror for a moment. She had spent an entire night looking at a parade of Houston's young beauties, and she knew that they had all compared themselves to her. For the first time in her life, she had worn a very feminine gown, and Devlin realized that the women looked at her enviously, not to mention the men.

For almost all her lifetime, Devlin had not understood the appeal she had for men. She stepped out of her panties and walked to the tub. It was nearly full. She poured in bath oil and saw the spirited foam form a wonderfully soapy mountain. When it was full enough, and warm enough, Devlin turned on the radio, catching an all-night station. With the overhead spotlights making a rainbow of the bubbles, she stepped

197

down into the water. For the first minutes, she closed her eyes. The warmth and luxury were delicious. For a moment or two, she lay there, replete with the indescribable pleasure of relaxing and savoring the embracing water.

A sound caused her to open her eyes and look up. She saw David Hampton standing above her, smiling in an impudent way. He was nude.

"What the hell are you doing here?"

"Looking, just looking, until you invite me in."

"Hampton, get out of here or I'll call the police."

Without paying attention to what Devlin said, he kneeled down along the side of the tub, and brushed her lips with his forefinger.

"Devlin, my dear, I've been waiting for you since I saw you earlier. I've been resting on your bed. I saw an extraordinary woman when I met you—totally inexperienced in so many ways, perfectly composed to be a companion and lover for a man, but so rigid and fearful of contact that she couldn't allow herself to feel passion."

"I'm telling you to get out, Hampton."

"I'm not listening to your speech, Devlin, just looking at the rise and fall of your breast, and feeling the warmth of your breathing. I can see a difference in your nipples, even this early."

Devlin was numb from the fatigue of the evening. She wasn't fearful about this man poised above her on the marble ledge, just angry that he had the gall to impose himself upon her. But he was right. The intrusion, the effrontery of his entrance to her bedroom, into her bath, *was* exciting. Her eyes dropped to his penis, resting hugely, on the nest of his balls. Devlin felt him take her soapy hand in his and place it around its length. She felt his penis harden within her hand.

"I know what you want, even if you don't know yourself, Devlin. I told you that you would remember this meeting, and it's only just begun."

His penis was diamond hard. In an easy move he lowered himself into the huge tub, and lifted Devlin so she lay back against his chest, his penis jutting up between her thighs. Devlin's heart was pounding, and she closed her eyes, as she felt his encircling hand begin to massage her triangle of hair, then search and find the tiny nub, then caress it in gentle but insistent strokes. He probed inside her to feel her own wetness, and from behind, he inserted his penis inside her, and slowly moved his hips and pelvis to position himself. He kept one hand on her from above, preventing her from moving away in the water, forcing her to remain a part of him.

He caressed the nipples of her breasts. He whispered nonsense words in her ear, more like humming than like a language. Then in moments as he replaced his hand above the mating of his penis and her vagina, he caressed her with increased vigor. Insistently he pumped his pelvis with mounting fury and Devlin felt the first orgasm she had ever experienced. She thrashed in the water in a violent series of moves, and then lay still as she felt herself floating into a far-off place. She started to move upward in the water, but was restrained. He was still hard inside her. She moved to separate, but was held back.

"Devlin," he whispered in her ear, "we've only just begun. Smile, baby, you've just been baptized in the waters."

At noon that day, Devlin and David Hampton sat on the terrace of Fairlawn, eating a late breakfast. The movie company was going crazy over its inability to get in touch with him. They had phoned a half-dozen times. Though he was scheduled for a full day of shooting, he proceeded to eat his melon and eggs with gusto, not minding the inquisitive eyes of the butler and maid, who watched him eating in a huge terrycloth robe kept at the pool for visitors. He sat on a wicker chair facing Devlin across the glass-topped table. She held a paper in her hand, pretending to read as she sipped her coffee.

She was self-conscious, since she, as well as the maid, could see that David Hampton had nothing on beneath his robe. As he sat at the table, his legs spread apart, the terrycloth robe did not cover his penis. To make the matter worse, he conspicuously and unconsciously caressed himself.

Devlin was embarrassed, but thoroughly constrained. She drank her coffee in silence, although she could feel the stares of the servants.

Hampton put down the paper and smiled at Devlin, "Darling, I'll be finished with this ghastly film in three days' time. You be packed and ready to leave. You'll have a most agreeable time in Beverly Hills, I assure you. I think that I can promise you a splendid holiday, but don't count on returning to Houston for a while. It really *is* a ghastly place." Then he tapped his cup, "Darling, *will* you ring for more coffee like a good girl?"

Devlin reached for the bell, and stared down at his hand fondling his penis through the glass-topped table. She bit her lip at the realization that she would do exactly as he said.

22

FROM the start of Black Diamond, L.C. had scrupulously avoided hiring Mexican-Americans except in his home. At home, however, he employed them as cook and butler. But none worked at Black Diamond with Anglos, either on the water or as members of the stevedoring gang.

Eventually the federal government made it impossible for L.C. to maintain his prejudice, and he was forced by the government and the Union to hire them. Even though Mexicans now worked for him, it didn't mean that he would like them or show them the smallest courtesy.

When one of his warehousemen, Jesus Hernandez, had an accident that partially blinded him, L.C. instructed the insurance people to refuse payment for his hospital treatment and disability. The young Mexican, in his twenties, had been a troublemaker as far as L.C. was concerned, and he refused any assistance. L.C. was convinced that the accident was the man's own fault, and that the hospital and medical records were faked.

When Black Diamond received a letter from the Mexican-American Legal Defense League on the subject of Jesus Hernandez, it was turned over to Tune. The letter stated that the organization was representing Hernandez, and that unless he received satisfaction by a certain date, a lawsuit would be filed, and claims made with the federal government for discriminatory labor practices. The letter was signed Miss Constanza Juarez.

Tune telephoned Miss Juarez and in the course of the conversation was charmed by her manner. Something in her voice made him want to see her. Tune wondered, he said, if they could meet to discuss the matter. She agreed.

When Constanza walked into Maxim's, every eye in the heavily ornate restaurant turned toward her. Had she chosen to become a fashion model, it would have been a career in which she would have prospered. She was tall and dark; her skin was flawless and fair. Her features were a fine mixture of Mexican, Indian, and Anglo, with eyes almost too dark to be called brown.

She was dressed simply in a pale linen skirt and soft cotton blouse. Her bare arms and throat emphasized the opalescence of her skin. But the single quality that set Constanza above the crowd was the simple innocence she radiated. As she sat down at Tune's table, she held out her hand and introduced herself.

"I'm Constanza Juarez, Mr. Richards. I accepted your invitation to lunch, although I don't have any idea why we should discuss a business matter in a restaurant."

There was, he knew, no reason at all. The only excuse was his intense curiosity. It had been only her voice, now and before soft and melodic. His curiosity was coupled with the terrible restlessness Tune felt. He wasn't happy in his marriage to Sue Lingen. He had discovered that he was one of her collection of playthings, a handsome escort expected to be shown off as another of her many possessions. This young Mexican woman fed his fantasy on the phone. Now that he saw her, he was thoroughly captivated.

"Miss Juarez, I'm pretty new to this kind of thing myself, and I hope you won't blame me for trying to make this discussion a pleasant one. I know that you're representing a client, and Black Diamond wants to do what's fair, so just bear with me a little, won't you?"

Tune flashed her his most winning smile. It had worked on hundreds, thousands of coeds, Houston girls who had fallen into faints at his blue-eyed smile, his crinkly grin, and his all-American-boy good looks. Tune recognized that his luncheon companion was not impressed.

"Would you care for a drink?"

She shook her head. A waitress came and took Tune's order for a martini, and left a pair of menus. Tune began to study his, but Constanza left hers folded at her place. Tune finally noticed.

"Do you know what you want?"

"Yes," she said. "I don't want anything."

"Oh, come on, you can't be on a diet. Everyone is on a diet, but you don't need one."

"No, Mr. Richards. You insisted, for some reason I can't fathom, to meet me at this restaurant. I'm here, but that doesn't mean that I have to eat, or that I want to. Why don't you order, and then we can talk. I'll just have coffee."

Tune shrugged and gave his order, then sipped his drink.

"Mr. Richards, my client has been very badly treated by Black Diamond. You've seen the medical reports. Several doctors examined Mr. Hernandez. He has lost fifty percent of his vision. You carry disability coverage, and the insurance company will make payment, but only if it is job-related. Now, there were no witnesses to Mr. Hernandez'

201

accident, but you and I know, Mr. Richards, that it took place during business hours. Why are you unwilling to instruct the insurance company to pay?"

"Miss Juarez, we're willing to do that, but you see, Mr. Younger . . ."

"Ah, yes, Mr. Younger . . . the famous Mr. L.C. Younger."

"Well, yes, but he had some run-ins with Mr. Hernandez—he's seen him drinking beer on the job, and one time he thought he saw him smoking marijuana, and . . ."

"Did Mr. Younger complain because my client also has a hot temper and got angry when he was accused of those things?"

Tune twisted his lips, "Well, look, he wouldn't have got angry if he hadn't been caught red-handed. Now would he?"

"Mr. Richards, what about being accused unjustly? How would you feel? Kindly, friendly . . . cooperative? Your Mr. Younger is prejudiced against Mexican-Americans. Now, I see the whole picture. This is a way for Mr. Younger to get even. It won't work."

"Not at all, Miss Juarez, if you can get Mr. Hernandez to admit a few things, then I'm sure that we can clear this whole thing up in no time."

"Such as . . ."

"Such as admit who he got the marijuana from, and where the beer came from. Were there other Mexicans involved? And what are their names?"

"Idiot. I'm a dumb idiot. I knew I should never have come. I told you that Mr. Younger is mistaken. Hernandez was not drinking, and he wasn't smoking at the time of his accident."

Constanza stood up. "Mr. Richards, I have nothing more to say. Goodbye."

"Wait," he called, "I know we can work it out." All eyes turned, as the stunningly beautiful Constanza Juarez stormed out of the restaurant.

It took almost four weeks of campaigning on Tune's part with Constanza and L.C. to come to a resolution of the problem. A series of placating phone calls and explanatory letters finally got Constanza to a point where she was willing to speak to Tune over the phone. At the same time, L.C., almost a tougher nut to crack, was subject to a constant barrage of arguments from Tune to settle the matter. L.C. was a bear on the subject. Under other circumstances, Tune might have convinced him, but business had turned so bad that L.C. was continually in a foul mood, and angry at the world. Black Diamond's prospects had been progressively worsening. The new combination of HOUCORP, with its computers, high-pressure techniques, tie-in deals with the multinational corporations, and slick, slick managers, was too much for L.C. to deal with. HOUCORP was eating Black Diamond alive.

Eventually, Tune cornered L.C. in his office. All L.C.'s arguments had been met. The proof that Tune needed to clear Hernandez of the

202

charges of drinking and dope smoking had been found. L.C. sat fuming, angry at being deprived of this piece of vengeance.

"L.C., come on, this isn't important enough to fight about."

"Don't tell me what's important and what's not. Your daddy would have fought alongside me, not against me."

Tune shook his head in wonderment. He had never really known his father. Would he really have done that, despite the wrongness of L.C.'s position?

"Come on, L.C., I'm not *against* you."

"You a Mex-lover or something?"

Tune bit his lip. "L.C., do it 'cause I think it's right."

The old man just sat there, refusing to say yes, but unable to say no.

Tune walked out of the office quickly, choosing to interpret the answer which pleased him the most. He literally ran to a telephone and dialed Constanza's number.

"Miss Juarez, look, this is Tune Richards. I have some good news for you."

"Yes, what is it?"

"How about meeting me so I can tell you about it? It's a little complicated, but I think that I can give you what you want for Hernandez." He waited, "Sort of like a victory celebration." He waited for a moment or two longer.

"Where, and what time?" she inquired.

The bar of the Hyatt Regency was in the main lobby. Tune led Constanza to a corner banquette he had previously selected. He had chosen this particular spot in the busy hotel lobby for a reason. His task was to get Constanza off the defensive, and Tune hoped that the impersonal atmosphere would do it.

"A drink, Miss Juarez?"

"No, thanks."

"Champagne . . . I've already ordered a bottle, in celebration. You've got what you wanted, Miss Juarez. I sent a letter to the insurance company to make payment to Hernandez." Tune smiled in anticipation.

The waiter appeared with the champagne and ceremoniously opened the bottle. He poured two glasses. All around them the hum of conversation hung over the cavernous interior. Travelers, bellmen, and guests passed by in a continuous stream. Tune had been right to select this place. In a more intimate setting, Constanza would have been frightened off. As it was, she barely smiled and grasped the glass tentatively.

"This is my first champagne, Mr. Richards, but thanks for the victory drink, and for all your trouble."

Tune raised his glass. "Please call me Tune, Mr. Richards sounds like my father, and I'm not old enough—I think." Constanza smiled warmly.

He had won her over, at least so far. She relaxed in her chair, sipping the drink. "I think I prefer Coca-Cola." Tune was about to signal the waiter when she took another sip. "I've changed my mind. I think that I might get to like this."

The conversation was general. Tune's mood was joyous and conspiratorial. He told her how he had come to Black Diamond and how much of a contrary sort L.C. Younger was. Tough, but good-hearted, he said. She was amused at the anecdotes Tune told her about L.C., but in her laughter there was a hint of the resentment and anger she felt about him. The stories that emphasized L.C.'s toughness might be funny to some, but not to her. She had seen too much suffering by those who were forced to bend to the power of an L.C. Younger.

Cocktail time passed, and Constanza appeared anxious to leave. Tune looked at his watch. "Look, I know this is sudden, but I'm not doing anything for dinner, and I know that you didn't eat a darn thing the other time, and it would be a shame to waste a good invitation. I'm entitled to a raincheck. How about it?"

Constanza sat for a moment, undecided, and then she nodded. It had taken Tune a month of careful planning to get this far. It was worth it. He signaled the waiter, paid the check, and the two of them walked through the lobby to the front of the hotel. Tune retrieved his car from the doorman, helped Constanza in it, and set out in the direction of the southwest freeway, toward the Galleria. His choice was Tony's, where he had carefully reserved a quiet and discreet table. Some of Sue Lingen's friends might be at Tony's, but it *was* a business dinner, which he could explain and prove.

As they drove, Tune switched on the radio. He looked beside him at the enchanting face of his companion. The scent of Constanza's perfume filled his nostrils, making him too full of happiness to explain. He felt a hardness in his loins, just at her fragrance and the sight of the soft swell of her breasts under her light dress. He had never felt that way about any woman before. It would make problems for him, but he didn't give a damn.

For Constanza, this contact with an Anglo was unique and disturbing. She was only twenty-four years old, with an outstanding academic record at the University of Houston and its law school, where campus activities brought her in touch with the largely Anglo student body. She trod an enormously difficult path—competing at every level in the Anglo world, meanwhile keeping her identity as a Mexican-American.

Constanza lived with five younger brothers and sisters in a small frame house in the East-End barrio of Houston. The house had only two bedrooms; her mother and father shared one, and the younger children shared the other. Constanza slept on the couch in the family room, which in fact was where they ate and watched television, and where the children played. Her father, Luis, a clerk at an auto-parts store, took

Constanza to school each day. There were many days when she would arrive hours before class, because her father had to be at work early. Even as Constanza graduated law school, her mother was pregnant once again.

From her earliest childhood, Constanza kept in touch with her grandparents who lived in the small city of Matamoros, just across the bridge from Brownsville, Texas. On holidays she visited them, learning the ways of the old traditions that had changed for many of the Mexican families in Texas. When her grandfather died, the old woman came to Houston to live with them. The grandmother, a loving and gentle woman rich in the folklore of Mexican ways, taught Constanza to respect her heritage. Constanza's mother and father had become Americanized; they ate American food and followed American customs.

Constanza grew in years, in beauty, and in her scholarship. She was a devoted churchgoer, like her grandmother. The difficulties that she experienced at home came from her parents' disapproval of her dedication to the ways of her grandmother. Her father resented the woman. In anger, he sent the old woman away, and shortly thereafter, Constanza's grandmother died.

As she grew to young womanhood, Constanza dedicated herself to the Mexican community. For her, it was a debt of remembrance she owed to her grandmother. She worked at the office of the Mexican-American Legal Defense in a storefront in the heart of the Mexican neighborhood. Although weeks went by without her receiving full pay, Constanza, with only occasional help, began to establish herself.

Little by little she earned respect in the Mexican community, an environment where women are traditionally not looked upon favorably as authority figures. Constanza thought that in time she might run for office in Houston, perhaps the City Council, and then at some time in the future, perhaps the state legislature. She was young, and time would tell.

As she and Tune drove, Constanza looked at the lights of the buildings of Houston that hadn't been there a year earlier, and knew that in even less time, there would be more of everything. Houston, she knew, was a good place to live, if you were Anglo. If you were Mexican, it was not good. But times were changing, and perhaps she would be able to travel with the times. One day it could be useful politically to be Mexican.

Constanza saw her reflection in the window of Tune's Cadillac as they drove along the freeway. It was the first time that she had ever driven in such a luxurious car, a fine car, a remarkable car. She felt the soft upholstery under her hand. Her reflection in the window against the night sky reminded her that she was pretty. No. She was much more than pretty. Mexican men had said so, had been after her for years. Her girlfriends from the neighborhood were now married and fat with children. She had never been with a man. Never. Her grandmother had told her that she must be a virgin for her husband. She would fulfill that pledge. Her work in the community would help her do that. She would expend all her energies in her work.

Constanza turned to look at her companion, just as Tune looked at her. She felt fear. But she sensed it evaporate as she looked in her companion's eyes. He seemed kind and good. The Cadillac turned off the freeway to the down ramp in the direction of the Galleria. Anglo restaurants frightened her, with their beautiful furnishings, and handsomely dressed people. She would never be able to look or act like them, but tonight she would still her fear. This dinner would be an experience. If she wanted to run for council, she would have to know and deal with all kinds of people, and be seen in many different kinds of places. This evening could be helpful for her future.

The Cadillac came to a stop before the entrance, and a man opened the door for her. She waited a moment, unsure of herself. Then, Tune appeared at the car door, smiling, and offered her his hand. Constanza smiled at him in thanks.

"*Gracias, señor.*"

"*Me llamo Tune, por favor.*"

Constanza laughed at his attempt at Spanish. He held her hand in his, leading her to the entrance. That simple touch inflamed Tune more than he had any suspicion it could. He looked at her. "Constanza, I like that name, I am so happy that we can be together."

Constanza looked in his eyes and saw something that startled her. She suddenly knew what Tune was thinking, and more that he hadn't even dared to. For a moment, Constanza was so panicked she might have run, but the restaurant door closed behind her, an attractive hostess greeted them, and led them into the luxurious restaurant.

Constanza smiled tentatively when Tune began to look at the elaborate menu that the maître d' presented to each of them.

"Let me order, okay? I know what's good here."

She closed the menu, feeling relieved. Around her were rich, well-dressed, perfectly self-assured Anglos. She knew how poorly dressed she appeared and felt uncomfortable once more. Tune broke into her thoughts, "Tell me about how you became a lawyer."

She smiled and began slowly. Then, as she warmed to her subject, she found that she wanted to say more and more. She had never had so interested an audience. She looked at Tune's face from time to time, and noted the attention he showed. Slowing down momentarily when the food was served, Constanza kept up a merry chatter about her life, the cases she worked on, the people in law school, her professors, and finally, though she had told no one ever before, she told Tune that one day, perhaps, she would run for office in Austin.

He laughed, "You'll be the governor of Texas if anybody has any brains, or a senator in Washington, don't you kid me."

Constanza blushed. She had never dared to express her wildest ambitions, perhaps to be a congresswoman in the nation's capital. She smiled at his laughter over her confusion.

"Perhaps," she nodded.

Constanza looked at Tune more closely. He was handsome. Indeed he was. She had never seen so handsome a man so close. He was blond, blue-eyed, graceful in his ways; an Anglo, yes, but gentle and caring. She saw the smile in his eyes as he listened to her stream of conversation. He liked her, she knew, he liked her a lot. She could talk to him in ways that she could never talk to a Mexican man, who would never have wanted to listen to her, never understood or sympathized with her ambitions, never been pleased to hear about her hopes and her dreams. Tune was rich. She knew that he was very attractive to women. He undoubtedly had hundreds of them. He was important. Even though L.C. Younger, that tyrant, ran that big Anglo company, this man with her was important in it.

Tune said little about himself. He mentioned the war in Vietnam, but nothing about his achievements, nor did he mention that he was married. He might never mention that, he thought, or perhaps at some time in the future, but not now. Constanza smiled. She was happy, and she liked him. He could tell that she liked him, and that was what he desperately wanted.

Dessert and coffee came and went. He ordered more coffee, and then a glass of brandy. The restaurant was slowly emptying, and he had to do something. He had to say something.

"Constanza, I'll take you home."

"It won't be necessary, it will be so far out of your way. I can take a taxi from here."

"No, please, Constanza, let me take you home."

"I live with my family. It is a long way from here. You live in a different neighborhood."

Tune paid the check, stood up and helped her out of her chair. By the time they were at the entrance, his Cadillac was parked in front, the doors open. Constanza started to say something. Tune put his hand on hers, "Please . . . I really would like to."

She sat silently. The door was shut behind her, and Tune closed his door, and they drove off. Tune returned to the freeway and turned on the radio. The green glow of the dashlight and the fleeting headlights of the cars across the center divider cast quick shadows on both their faces. The radio was tuned to an all-night call-in show, full of nonsensical talk. It was a blessing. Tune was lost in his own thoughts, and Constanza didn't want to think at all. The chatter from the radio made their silence possible.

The Cadillac was quietly comforting. Tune drove down a ramp into the city, and onto the side streets leading into the Mexican neighborhood. It was home to Constanza, and foreign to Tune. The row of board houses, closely built; the refuse cans in front, some spilling into the street; the abandoned wrecks of cars alongside the curb; the dark-skinned men; the sound of Spanish voices in the distance. It was very strange.

Constanza pointed, "Just a few houses down, please. Stop here. I'll walk the rest of the way." Tune brought the Cadillac to a stop at the curb. Constanza started to open the door, but Tune put his hand on top of hers and lifted it from the handle. She looked at him.

"I want to thank you for tonight, Constanza. I had a wonderful time."

She smiled. "I think that I talked too much."

He laughed, "It was a celebration. Next time I'll do more of the talking."

"I don't think that there'll be a next time," she said simply.

"Why is that?"

"It is not significant, Tune, it just isn't right, and that makes it impossible."

"Do you like me?"

"You are very nice. You will make someone very happy."

"I'd like to make you very happy, Constanza."

"Do you realize what you're saying?" she asked in confusion.

"Yes . . . yes, I do."

Tune reached around, and put his hand around her shoulder. The softness of the skin on her bare arm inflamed him. Slowly, he led her into his arms. He heard her breathing like a timid animal. He felt and smelled her breath. She was like a fawn, young, fearful. She resisted, but Tune continued to pull her close to him. The scent of perfume on her hair had been maddening to him all evening. He placed his cheek against hers, and slid his lips to meet her lips. Her softness was incredible. He kissed her gently once, still more gently a second time. He felt her heart beating against his. He heard it, and he felt her body fall into place against his chest.

Suddenly, Constanza broke away and opened the door. She was gone before he knew it. He watched her race down the street, past wretched homes, and then into the darkened interior of a house like all the rest. He heard the slam of a screen door. Tune closed his car door and quietly turned the ignition. He didn't turn on the headlights until after he passed her house. But in any event he had made up his mind in those few brief minutes.

It didn't make any difference how difficult it would be, but he had met the only girl he could truly love. He ached for her in his body. His hand still tingled from the brief touch of her skin. He placed a finger to his lips, to mark where he had kissed her.

Tune turned on the headlights and drove through the mean streets on his way to the freeway, and to his exquisite home and beautiful wife in River Oaks.

23

THERE'S no kind of trouble that others can gift you with, that's greater than you can buy for yourself. Devlin could testify to that. It began when she agreed to accompany David Hampton back to California.

Devlin discovered that she had committed herself completely and uncontrollably to a man she knew was unworthy and, in her deepest heart, essentially evil. Devlin surrendered more than her body the night of her River Oaks house-warming. She surrendered her independence and her self-respect.

David Hampton was only thirty-two, but his friends were older Hollywood figures, the heads of studios, bankers and industrialists, political and social leaders in Los Angeles. David Hampton knew and was known by all the pseudo-youth culture, the drug and radical group who were then in vogue in the picture business. Even though that group now controlled the making of motion pictures, David Hampton knew that their days were limited and those who were really in control were the old-money people, the bankers and political figures who were his close and intimate friends.

In Devlin's company, those friends mentioned books that she hadn't heard of, plays she hadn't seen, places she had never been. A few of them spoke foreign languages in which David appeared to be completely fluent. Those moments in which she felt inadequate became more and more painful for her. And strangely, Devlin never for one moment considered going home to Houston.

Devlin had rented an impressive estate in Beverly Hills and spent considerable time in staffing it. She gave elaborate parties for David's friends, parties, he said, that were poorly planned exhibitions of bad taste that his friends endured only in deference to him. His cold angry censure became a mark of her days. Her quick and ready apology on each of these occasions was an automatic and continual response to his criticism.

Devlin didn't know when she decided that they should be married. It evolved naturally, in her mind, as the way she could ensure that David Hampton would be hers. Devlin concluded if they were husband and wife there would be reason to hope that he would settle down.

Devlin understood full well the precarious state of David's financial condition, and for that alone, his marriage to her would be a godsend. But, he was as noncommittal about her proposal as he was about everything else.

He shrugged his shoulders when Devlin suggested it and said, "I suppose, why not, if it makes you happy."

It didn't make her happy, and Devlin was on a collision course with disaster. Nevertheless, she took the prospect of their marriage as a renewal of his interest. The wedding would be held in her home, and Devlin would invite all of his friends. It would be elaborate and Texas. She'd bring in Texas food, an old-fashioned barbecue, Texas music and dancing. She'd dress as a cowgirl. She'd buy herself the Harry Winston fifteen-carat diamond engagement ring she had seen. Visions of the wedding carried Devlin through the days as David continued to be more and more remote.

Whispered to her at lunch by a "friend" was the fact that David was having a serious affair with a new young starlet. Devlin paid no attention to the gossip. She reacted as if there were no reality, except that of the wedding. That night, David and she had dinner at a Beverly Hills restaurant. The two of them sat silent during the meal, David barely eating.

"Can I tell you about the plans for the wedding, David?"

"If you like, Devlin."

"David, you don't seem interested."

"Well, not really, it wasn't my idea, you know."

"The wedding?"

"No, Devlin, getting married."

"David," Devlin said with emotion, "don't I please you any more?"

"Of course you do, darling." He seemed disinterested.

"We haven't been together for a while."

"My God, Devlin, are you one of those women who keep score?" He mimicked, "We haven't fucked in six days, four hours and three minutes. Do you want me to take my cock out and slip it to you now?"

Devlin was silent, angry, and confused. David stood up and beckoned to her, "Come on, let's leave." Devlin followed him outside. The Rolls Corniche that she had given him stood smartly in front, with its personalized license plates, HAM. She got in, and David guided the car up Melrose and above Sunset to Devlin's house. The electric gates opened and he drove in. He parked silently and she went to the door and opened it, then walked slowly up the staircase to her bedroom. From the corner of her eye, Devlin could see David following.

Devlin went into the bathroom, undressed, and stepped outside. On the night table she saw lines of white powder, and David bent forward to inhale the cocaine. Devlin had never seen it before. He heard her and turned around. "Want some, darling? It'll improve your disposition."

"No, David." Devlin lay on the bed, staring at the ceiling. She was disgusted with herself. Still, she couldn't stop the juggernaut of her feelings. She turned around and caressed David's back. He pushed her aside until he had finished the drug, and then lay down. Moment's later, Devlin leaned over him, and began to undress him. With each piece of clothing that she removed, she paused to caress his body. David didn't move.

David lay on the bed, his eyes open, as Devlin continued, trying to enlist his interest.

"Devlin," he murmured, "you're doing it the wrong way. Stand over there like a good girl and play with yourself. I like to watch women masturbate, even you. Although, for Christ's sake, I can't imagine why I bothered to fuck you in the first place. You're a damn boring bitch, Devlin, damn boring, and your taste is abominable."

Devlin couldn't for the life of her remember why out of the clear blue sky she thought of Terry Jordan, but she did. She yearned for someone she could trust, someone who would not take her as a figure of fun, too young to be serious, and too rich to be interesting.

Finding Terry was easier than she thought. Devlin had her Houston office contact several of the cowgirls who worked the rodeos, and in a few hours, Devlin was talking to Terry on the phone.

"Dev, are you still speaking to me?"

"Terry—why not?"

"Well, you're so damn rich, and after all the problems that I gave you with Emilio?"

"Terry, dammit, it was my fault not being in touch with you earlier—to find out how you were, and what you were doing."

Terry rushed to say something. "Dev, I don't want anything from you, nothing at all. I don't presume that just because you and I knew one another then, that I have any call on you now."

Devlin was deeply touched, "Are you feeling okay, Terry?"

There was a moment's pause. "Oh, do you mean am I still on the stuff? No. I gave that up." Then she added brightly, "I still rodeo a little, but not as much as I used to. My bones are too damn brittle."

Devlin heard the forced cheerfulness in her voice. She broke in, "Terry, I don't know if you're working now or anything . . . ."

"Well, I *was*, Devlin, but frankly, I'm between . . ."

"Terry, would you consider coming out here?"

211

"Where's here?"

Devlin forgot that she hadn't identified where she was calling from. "Hell, Terry, I'm in Beverly Hills, with a house that could handle a whole regiment—people to wait on you, and bring you hot and cold anything you want. How about it? I'll arrange for a plane ticket, and I'll meet you at the airport, and we'll have a good time, talking about life at Carmine's. Is the old bastard still breathing?"

"Yeah," Terry laughed, "and still the same. Dev, this is a lifesaver, because I didn't know where I was going to get my rent money. You're not joking now, are you?"

"Cross my heart. As soon as you hang up, I'll make the arrangements."

"Bless you, Devlin," Terry said with a tear in her voice.

The phone went dead before Devlin could tell Terry what her visit would mean to her. Devlin phoned Younger Oil in Houston, and a very efficient secretary, with timetables and "can-do" willingness to find a way, assured Devlin that she would have Terry on a flight to Los Angeles that very night. Devlin put down the phone and smiled. It was the first time she had smiled in a long time.

If Devlin had planned it that way, Terry's arrival could not have been a more perfect counter-irritant to David Hampton. The two of them hated each other on sight, and Terry immediately identified David as someone she completely understood.

"Devlin, you're gonna marry that fella?"

"Terry, we're supposed to."

Terry interrupted, "Bet that he didn't ask you, Dev, you asked him."

Devlin stared at Terry as the two of them sat alongside the swimming pool of her Beverly Hills house. They were alone, except for the nonstop service that was provided by the ever-present butler Clive, who came with the house. The owner, a prominent rock promoter, had insisted that Devlin keep his staff. It was the only way he could ensure that proper care would be taken of his house and grounds. Devlin was certain that the butler had seen much more going on in the life of the rock impressario than she could concoct, but nevertheless, Clive and the others seemed to spend most of their time spying on her, inspecting carpets for cigarette burns, checking the silver, and counting the Japanese carp swimming in the fountain at the main entrance.

Devlin returned to Terry's comment. "Why did you say that? Why did you say I asked *him*?"

"Devlin, because I know men like that. You can't get the time of day out of one of them, and yet they make you sweat. Devlin, I hate to say this, because this brings up old times, but your boyfriend David Hampton would make a perfect pimp."

"What?"

"Hell, yes, Devlin, that's the control pimps have over a girl. They dig

deep into your past, make you feel like you've got to get them to say something nice to you—*anything*. You give them things, buy them things, give them all your money. They never say thanks—no nothing." Terry saw Devlin's expression of acknowledgment.

"A girl can't do enough for a guy like that, and that's the reason that loverboy took a real hate to me when he met me. He knows that I know him for what he is." Then she was silent for a moment and finally completed her thought. "It takes a whore to recognize a pimp."

Devlin took Terry's hand and held it close. God how she had needed someone to say it—say that she was behaving like a fool. If only she could act on this knowledge.

In the brief silence, Clive returned to check on the state of the pool furniture. He bent down to see a spot on the chaise lounge next to Devlin, considered it for a moment, and wet his finger to rub it off. Terry and Devlin saw him put his finger in his mouth to check what it was, then saw him make a disgusted expression, and race to the house.

They laughed uproariously. Any idiot should have been able to identify pigeon shit.

As the days passed, Devlin became more insistent that Terry as her houseguest be included in the dinners and parties to which she and David went. Terry attacked those evenings with spirit, describing her experiences to Devlin. Even though Devlin had not been more than paces away, the party and the people that Terry observed seemed totally different from the people Devlin herself saw.

"The fat one," Terry began as they rested between sets alongside the tennis court, "what does he do, Devlin?"

"You mean from last night? His name is Sumner Gallsworth, and he runs the biggest automobile dealership in Southern California. His wife is named Delia, the tall one with all the jewels."

"What kind of cars?"

"Ford I think, Terry, yep, Fords."

"I'm not going to buy me a Ford, then, ever."

"Why?"

"I don't like him or his wife. And I don't like the one with the mustache and *his* wife, and the one *without* the mustache and his sister."

Devlin laughed. "That's all there were."

"Yeah, last night, but the night before there were twenty—I counted them, used both my fingers and toes, so I'm sure—and I didn't like any of *them* either. They're stuckup and smartass, and they make nasty remarks about you."

Devlin bit her lip. "What kind?"

"You asked me, Devlin, and I've got to level with you. They think you're a hick who got very lucky and hasn't any class, and who has the hots for lovely David, and lovely David is screwing everything in sight."

"Except me," Devlin added.

"Yeah, honey, except you. It goes with the territory, honey. He's a pimp."

Devlin looked over Terry's shoulder and saw Clive examining the net on the court. He looked closely, bent down and examined a place where a string had broken. Quickly, he pulled a pad from his pocket and noted it down.

"What's he doing?" Terry asked.

"Damages, I have to pay any, at the end of the lease."

"What is he staring at?"

"I guess he thinks I made an extra hole in the net."

"Wow, how about that? I figure that's what turned me off my game."

"Sure, Terry."

"Absolutely, Devlin, it will do it every time."

As the two of them walked arm in arm back to the house, Devlin made up her mind: She would call it quits with David. She realized how close she had come to disaster. Only Terry's clear eye had singled out the sickness in her relationship with him. He wanted only one thing from her, and that was her money. David was so expert at the game that he had quickly identified the only way that he could win Devlin—he had intrigued her. Then, after she developed a need for him, he withdrew.

Devlin understood that if David had pursued her as other men had, she would have turned away quickly and expertly. David had read her like a book. He was a pimp.

Devlin glanced out of the corner of her eye at Terry. She wondered whether Terry was still seeing Emilio, and whether she had abandoned drugs. Devlin had been selfish for these two weeks, taking everything that Terry had to give, and giving nothing in return.

Devlin would do something about the situation, and she would do something about David. And she would do something about David's friends. She had suffered a thousand indignities at their hands, been humiliated by their comments to her and about her. She had been excluded from their midst, singled out for disapproval, and they had conspired with David to make her an object of fun.

What an idiot I've been, she thought to herself. He's made me a slave to his lousy moods, his disapproval, and his cock. Where is the person who fought for her life in Big Spring? Am I going to let that son-of-a-bitch whip me?

Devlin and Terry approached the terrace. She smiled at Terry. "I love you very much. I want to talk about you and your future. Why don't we get dressed and go into town for dinner, just by ourselves, and take in a movie. I've made some decisions."

Terry looked over at Devlin. She understood. "Good deal about dinner, but how would you like to drive out to Long Beach instead?"

"What for?"

"Hell, Devlin, where's your patriotism? You've been out of Texas too

214

long. They're having the National Championship of the Cowgirls Rodeo at the Long Beach Convention Center."

Devlin flushed with excitement, "Tonight?"

"Over the weekend. The girls are coming into town tonight, most of them, and if you'd like we can tilt some brew and go someplace where they'll throw some steaks on the fire." Terry looked at Devlin expectantly. "You like them old gals. You know 'em all from before. Only thing different is the number of their broken bones. How about it?"

"Deal," Devlin shouted with pleasure. She would get into her jeans and boots for the first time in over three months. The hell with Beverly Hills, Holmby Hills, and all your other damn California hills. She was Texas, and she could eat 'em all up for breakfast and be hungry at lunch.

Terry ran inside and up the stairs. She looked behind her at the happy face of the young woman she had known in San Antonio. Terry was delighted that she had brought life back to her friend.

Devlin's long legs scooted up the stairs two at a time. From below, Clive stood watching sternly.

"Move your ass, Devlin."

"Moving . . . moving . . . moving."

Devlin passed Terry and swatted her on the backside. Devlin laughed. "Now move yours."

215

24

L. CARTER DIXON III hadn't expected any contact with Devlin Younger after that unpleasant day in the Howard County Courthouse.

But he did hear from Devlin Younger, a week after the party at the Stampede, and wonder of wonders, she offered him a job. Their meeting took place in the hotel rooms that Devlin and her partner had commandeered to handle the affairs of their growing enterprise. As they talked, L. Carter Dixon III sat on the edge of one hotel bed. Secretaries bustled about looking for envelopes, paperclips, and stamps. An accountant, seated on the floor with a pile of ledgers open in front of him, busied himself in a corner of the room. This pandemonium was topped by a chambermaid, running the faucets as she cleaned the bathroom. It was difficult to hear.

Devlin sat astride a wooden beer case, looking more like someone about to rodeo than an oil millionairess.

"L. Carter, what is your *real* name?"

"Miss Younger, that *is* my real name."

"In Texas, no one has a name like that. We call people Buster or Junior, or 'Hey you' or by their initials."

"Miss Younger, I don't know why you asked me here, but it obviously is not just to discuss the name my parents gave me."

"Names are important," Devlin insisted. "Now, you take mine, it properly belongs to a man, but my daddy named me for his daddy. Now I have a brother, who could have been named with my name, but he got a different one, and I think that it influenced his personality. Say, for example, if he'd been called Devlin, and I'd been called John Travis, don't you think things would have been different?"

L. Carter Dixon was dismayed. He had come at her insistence, to discuss something important. He had no need for further unpleasantness from this aggressive young woman.

216

"Tell me," Devlin continued, "you're a Harvard Law School graduate?" He nodded. "And you also got your degree in business?" He nodded. "You also play squash?" He nodded. "Who the dickens plays squash?" she asked. He said nothing.

Devlin continued, "I want you to work for me, to head up the business and legal side of my company. I know you're smart, even if you didn't act that way, but I figure that once bitten, twice shy. You're never going to forget that you were beat once, and it won't happen again. You know the territory here, and you know a lot about oil. I want you to put yourself together a staff of lawyers and geologists, because I want to build my company into a real power."

"You're a gambler, Miss Younger, that's what this business is all about, not lawyers and geologists." He was sincere, and he suddenly found himself liking this pretty, young red-haired woman.

Devlin looked at him with new eyes, and smiled. "When you put down a well, spend a half million dollars to drill it and come up dry, and the joker a hundred yards from you puts down a well and it blows out, then you know that luck has a lot to do with it. I've read myself sick about Spindletop. I could give you a rundown on the drilling reports, the names of the leases, the production of each of the wells—but the one big item is that somebody smelled oil and believed. Lucas, who brought in the field, bought the leases from an oil company that had already drilled a half dozen times, and had come up dry each time. In the Red River uplift near Burkburnett, the drillers made a pact to stop drilling at 1700 feet. The fellow who broke the pact struck it at 1734 feet."

"Miss Younger, you didn't get me here to tell me about the history of the oil business. I'm a student of it myself. All of my classmates at Harvard went into big Wall Street law firms; I came down to Texas because that's where the action is. The oil business is the most exciting one in the world."

"You don't have the name for it."

"God, Miss Younger, will it help to tell you that my first name is Llewelyn?"

Devlin smiled. "Not a lot."

"How would you feel if I call you Carter, and you start work tomorrow at $50,000 a year, and one percent of the profits."

L. Carter Dixon III beamed, "Call me any name you want, Miss Younger, you've got yourself a deal."

"Devlin, that's my name," she said.

"Carter, that's mine," he said.

From the moment Carter Dixon started to work for Younger Oil, he changed as rapidly as the company. Gone were his three-button suits, the button-down Oxford shirts, the silk rep ties, and the brown cordovan shoes. L. Carter Dixon III was a new man. He even had a western twang to go with the custom-made western clothes he got at Cutter Bill's in

217

Houston. Devlin was convinced he would start chewing plug tobacco, but there Carter Dixon stopped.

About a year after he came to work for Devlin, he walked into her office, nervously poised in front of her desk.

"Devlin, something funny is going on with WESTEX."

"What's that?"

"For the past year they've been drilling on the lease they have opposite our Conroy lease, and getting their fair share of the product. Now, what seems to be happening is that they're digging more wells, and operating them around the clock, and my point is that they'll be draining off our oil."

Devlin muttered, "Damn."

"There's a small piece of the law that I've been researching that's called the doctrine of correlative rights."

Devlin smiled, "Forget about L. Carter Dixon III and explain what you mean in words I'll understand."

He reddened. "Well, simply put, Devlin, there's no real law on the subject, but my feeling is that there should be, that somebody can't dig into a joint pool of oil that meets somewhere under the ground and drain all ours out."

"Like sharing a soda with somebody, and he drinks faster than you."

Dixon smiled, "I like the way you put it."

Devlin smiled, "Let's sue the bastards."

He smiled, "I was hoping you'd say that."

"Let's sue them in Howard County, the judge is partial to pretty girls."

"You'll be in court?" he asked.

"You're damn right, and I'll bring along a great big chocolate soda that I'm going to ask the judge to share with me to demonstrate our point."

"How much should I sue them for?"

"Golly, I don't know. How much money do you have in your pocket?"

Curiously, he looked in his billfold, "Let's see, about two hundred dollars."

Devlin laughed, "Okay, let's sue them for two hundred million, and let's get it to court right away. We won't settle unless they come up with at least one hundred ninety-nine million."

The lawsuit made history in Howard County. After Devlin did her chocolate soda demonstration, WESTEX proposed to stop what they were doing and settle for ten million dollars. WESTEX's lawyers, including Dan'l Simon who handled the defense, were chagrined, but not as much as WESTEX's president and the senior partner of Holson and Nichols, Frank Holson. His law firm had been made to look exceedingly stupid twice, by the same young woman.

Carter attended to the many details of production on the Conroy lease, the development of exploratory surveys through the geologists under his control, and the purchase of leases from leasemen all over Texas.

At the beginning, the product from the wells in the Conroy field was held in field tanks and collected by tank trucks that brought the crude oil to the refinery. As production in the field increased, Devlin had to build new field tanks to hold the crude oil waiting for transport to the refinery. The final stage was the building of feeder pipelines from Conroy to a gathering system to transport the oil into a main pipeline to the refinery. Before the gathering system was completed Devlin flew to California with David Hampton.

Peculiar to the custom in the oil business, competitive producers pipe their oil into the same gathering system. At that point, by measuring the field tanks, the pipeline company pays for the oil that it takes from the tanks of individual producers. The tank farm that belonged to Younger Oil consisted of ten huge steel tanks each of which held 250,000 barrels of oil. Oil had accumulated for several months, awaiting the start of the gathering system and the flow into the main pipeline to the refinery.

The night before the first delivery to the gathering system, the connections were hooked up, waiting for the start of the pumps owned by the pipeline company. In the middle of the night, for no known reason, the pumps were tested. A short in the electrical circuit caused the pumps to catch fire, backing the fire into the storage tanks. The workers on duty tried to stop the fire in the pump, but by that time the fire had entered the gathering lines, which mysteriously had ruptured. It provided the necessary oxygen to the flame. In five minutes, the first storage tank was ablaze. In ten more minutes, the entire Younger Oil tank farm was a cauldron of fire, lighting the Permian Basin sky for miles.

L. Carter Dixon III, asleep in his apartment in Houston, was wakened by the supervisor of Younger Oil in Big Spring. He had the direst prediction: The tanks would all go up—almost two and a half million barrels of oil would be lost. All they could do was protect the wells and other property outside the tank farm. After another minute of inquiry, Carter hung up.

Dreading the chore, he proceeded to telephone Devlin in Beverly Hills. He hadn't seen her for six months. Despite her saying that she welcomed his calls about the progress of the company and his weekly reports, he was certain that she paid little or no attention. Frequently, when he called, he got David Hampton on the phone, and was told that Devlin wasn't to be bothered. This didn't prevent him from continuing to try, but as the days progressed, there was every indication that Devlin's interest in affairs at Younger Oil was virtually nonexistent.

It was twelve midnight in Houston, and two hours earlier in California. With a very heavy heart, L. Carter Dixon III began dialing

Devlin's number. He got a busy signal—it was a blessed reprieve. He didn't know how Devlin would react when he gave her the news.

Carter dialed again. David Hampton answered. Devlin, he said, was out. Carter asked him to have her phone urgently. David agreed and hung up. David Hampton didn't bother to note the message. Devlin, he reflected, had gone out without talking to him, without even the hint of permission.

He didn't like that at all.

Terry and Devlin scooted down the hallway of the Ramada Inn in Long Beach. Terry raced to the door of a room at the end of the corridor and banged on it as hard as she could.

"Get that man out of your room," she yelled.

The door opened immediately and Terry was snatched inside by one of the six girls who shared the tiny single. Devlin stood outside in the hallway grinning. The girls were about to pound Terry into the ground in their delight at seeing her. In a moment, Terry popped her head out of the pile.

"Come on in, Devlin, these ladies won't bite."

In all the world there is nothing like the palship of cowgirls. Devlin had understood that from the time she and Terry rode the thousands of dusty miles on weekends in her Eldorado, transporting sometimes as many as seven or eight girls to rodeos in distant places as far away as Wyoming. The girls competed not just for the money, but for the wonderful feeling of belonging to the world of the west, with its riding and roping, and—queen activity of them all—riding rough stock—broncs or bulls. Devlin looked at their lean, hard bodies, still very feminine even though they had stood up to the same shocks and hurts that rodeo cowboys get. Gut-busting hurts.

Devlin knew that the girls mostly worked at other jobs, but their life was rodeo. They were waitresses, secretaries, and teachers who barely kept themselves afloat with the entry fees, expenses for travel and equipment, and the small prizes they competed for. Devlin looked around at the gear on the floor and the beds that had been stripped so that the box-spring could sleep extra people on the floor. Unknown to the Ramada management, one single room now housed six, and maybe another four or five, by the time things got sorted out this weekend.

The girls—Sue, Candy, Gloria, Donna, Linda, and Jan—were as different from each other as could be. Sue and Linda were pretty enough to be models—both of them had posed for ads from time to time. Gloria, pushing forty, was the den mother. She carried the bandages, wrappings, a sewing kit, and occasionally prayed for the girls as protection against bodily harm. Even the cowgirls who might be considered less than beautiful had almost every man who met them pure captive. Cowgirls, Devlin concluded, were something special.

They welcomed Devlin. Most of them hadn't even heard of her good fortune, and when Terry mentioned it in passing, the girls took no big note of it. "No kidding." "Damn, that's fine." "How do you like that?" and then they were discussing more interesting topics, such as the stock contractor who was bringing the animals tomorrow. Was there enough time to check the animals out?

The topic that stopped their conversation was Terry's announcement that Devlin was buying dinner at a nearby steak place. That was a treat for these girls, who lived so close to the bone that luxuries were pretty well unknown. At dinner Devlin's green eyes danced at the girls' antics. Donna lifted her shirt at the restaurant table to show that her entire torso was taped. She acknowledged that a bull had fallen against her. The whole restaurant turned to look.

It was at dinner that Devlin decided on her farewell to Beverly Hills and David Hampton. He had thought her a hick, a pretty but uninteresting Texas country girl. She thought of a way that would be fitting for her farewell. Had they ever had a rodeo in Beverly Hills? Well, they would now. It would be a rousing Texas farewell.

Can six cowgirls, Terry, and Devlin finish off thirty cans of Coors? Absolutely. And two dozen steaks? Sure! Then Devlin made her proposal.

"Girls, the Long Beach rodeo is over on Sunday afternoon. Would you be willing to work at another one Sunday night?"

"Where?" they asked.

"My house," she answered.

"A house?" Jan asked incredulously.

Devlin answered, "On the tennis court, and the grounds around it. There's lots of room."

Terry looked at Devlin and broke into a grin, "You're going home."

Devlin grinned back, "You *know* it."

Terry arched her brows, "All his friends will be there?"

Devlin nodded.

Terry smiled broadly and addressed the girls. "Girls, you'll have a ball tearing up Beverly Hills. The way I figure it, Devlin, in addition to whatever else you have in mind, with something like thirty animals, we can leave about a half ton of shit on Clive's front lawn. How will he like them apples?"

Devlin contemplated the idea with pleasure. "Girls, we'll need more of you, and I'll have to make a deal with the stock contractor for the animals."

Terry added, "Easy to do, he's from Stockton, and he has movable pens and gates, and fences. You'll need a mess of dirt to spread over the court, wouldn't want to hurt the horses or these young ladies, and we'll get the same announcer that works Long Beach, and the band that plays for us here." Terry looked doleful. "You'll have to give the girls something, Devlin. This could come to a big piece of change."

In her mind's eye Devlin could see the guests, those stuffy people

221

who had made life miserable for her over the last months. That, plus the opportunity to say goodbye to David Hampton publicly and with a Texas celebration. She pictured the horrified faces of Clive and the servants. What a picnic!

"Terry, whatever the girls want, and whatever the rest of it costs. Now, tell me, how did you figure out the amount of horseshit we're going to leave behind?"

Terry laughed.

Button Williams, the stock contractor, had heard of a lot of foolishness in his time, and if someone was going to pay for this, and the animals weren't in danger, he didn't give a damn. He listened to what Devlin had to say and nodded. He had only two words to say, "Cost ya." Devlin smiled and said, "Do it."

It would take four semis to bring in the equipment and the animals. The pipe-pens, the stands, the gates, and the fences compacted to one flatbed semi. The animals would need two, and one enormous open semi would carry the dirt needed to cover the tennis court. Devlin arranged to have it delivered on Sunday morning. That was enough time, Button indicated, but his men would have to be paid for Sunday work.

A more difficult task was rounding up the guests—all of David's friends—that she wanted for Sunday night. Her explanation for the short notice and the importance of the event was the simple sentence, "It's in honor of David and me, and our future life."

When Devlin told David of her plans, he accepted the notion of the party, but Devlin neglected to mention the rodeo.

Some people think that Houston is famous for the Astrodome, others think its fame rests on the Oilers, or River Oaks, or the Astros, or the Battle of San Jacinto or the Space Center. Those who know are convinced that it's barbecue. Devlin was doubly certain of that, and more than convinced that a barbecue would be totally unexpected on a Sunday night in Beverly Hills. She made phone calls to the barbecue joints she remembered—for the ribs, the beef, the beans, the chicken, the links, the ham, the jalapeño cornbread, the sauce. Like Button Williams the stock man said, the problem of shipping everything to Beverly Hills was simply a matter of "Cost ya."

On Sunday morning, the caravan began to arrive. Clive heralded the arrival of a big truckful of dirt with six men.

"Madam," he announced on the intercom, "they refuse to go away. They say it's for you, and I can't seem to get through to them that we do not need a truckload of dirt. Madam, have you ever seen a giant truckload of dirt?"

"Clive," Devlin instructed, "just open the gates and tell them to dump it on the tennis court." To implement her command, Devlin pushed the gate control. To the butler's consternation, the truck lumbered up the driveway and headed for the tennis court. Unfortunately for the lawn, there was no road directly to it, but the semi found a way, and by the time Devlin came down a half hour later, the men were busily at work.

Clive stood waiting for Devlin at the foot of the stairs.

"Madam, I'm afraid you can't do what you're doing?"

"What's that, Clive?"

"Putting dirt on the tennis court."

"Oh, Clive," Devlin said as she left him openmouthed, "don't worry about it. There'll be a lot worse before this is all over."

As the afternoon progressed, the semis with the fences, pens, and portable chutes arrived. An additional ten men set about the installation. Clive was joined by the cook, who watched gasping.

"Madam, what *are* you doing?"

"We're going to have a rodeo."

"What?" he screamed. "Here?"

"Hell, Clive," Devlin sighed patiently, "where else? It would be a damn waste of dirt otherwise."

Beverly Hills has laws against virtually everything: Your dog cannot be unleashed. He may not make a nuisance in the parks or the sidewalk. You may not put a "for sale" sign on your lawn, and you may not film a movie without a permit. There are many other regulations which conform to the usual code of laws against traffic violations, breaking and entering, and murder. But there is no law against holding a rodeo. To Devlin's great good luck on this particular Sunday, nobody, particularly the police, noticed what was happening until it was too late, and by that time, *everybody* knew.

Parking attendants; caterers with steam tables, pans, tables, and cloths; bartenders with glasses; waitresses and waiters; and tent people and assistants to put up an outdoor kitchen began to filter in as the afternoon wore on. Clive, nowhere to be seen, was busy telephoning all over the world to try to reach his employer in Marrakesh, or his employer's lawyer in Maui, or his employer's accountant and business manager, who was on a plane to London.

He reappeared, having reached only his employer's insurance man, who told him that it was too late to do anything. Then Clive discovered that almost a hundred people were on the lawn, on the tennis court, and meandering through the house. That was only the beginning. The next thing he knew, two more semis lumbered up the driveway. The sounds from their interiors gave him the frights. When four wranglers appeared from the cabs and began to lead the calves, goats, horses, and bulls into their pens, Clive was in tears.

An hour later, the cowgirls, the wranglers, the announcer, and the band showed up in a bus. By that time, Clive was back in his room, and would not be heard from or seen until the very end.

Spotlights lit up the stands, the arena, and the grounds for the first guests. The food tables and trays were in place. Devlin, in her oldest jeans and boots, munched on a sparerib, which she acknowledged was the finest food she had eaten in six months. She met the first guests with a rib in her left hand, her right hand smeared by sauce, and a mean look in her eye. It was met by the curious look from Seth Black, president of the Los Angeles National Bank, and his wife.

More and more cars appeared and dropped off their occupants, who were thoroughly perplexed. The nonstop flow of drinks, including huge liter bottles of Texas's favorite Big Red, didn't do anything to calm them. Huddled in corners, they spoke among themselves, and waited for some dreadful news, perhaps that they were all in purgatory.

Things improved a little when David Hampton arrived. The guests thought that he at least could make some sense out of this party. Twenty cowgirls threaded through the crowd, introducing themselves. "Dammee . . . you mean you ain't never seen a rodeo?" They helped themselves to ribs and ham, and tried to spread good will and enthusiasm, without success.

David Hampton surveyed the situation and headed straight for Devlin. "What the hell is going on?"

Devlin smiled sweetly and looked at him with what might have passed for affection. "A rodeo, honey . . . just like we have down home." Then she moved away as she saw Terry signal to her.

"Devlin, there's a phone call for you. The man says it's important."

"Who is it, Terry?"

"Someone named Dixon Carter or Carter Dixon or some such thing."

Devlin walked swiftly to the main door and picked up an extension on the hall table.

"Devlin, I've been trying to reach you for days."

"You should have left word, Carter."

"Devlin, I did, with Hampton, twice. Look, I have some bad news."

L. Carter Dixon III proceeded to tell Devlin about the destruction of the tank farm. She quickly asked, "Was anyone hurt?" The answer was "No."

Then she asked the same question that he had asked when he spoke to Big Spring. "Did the WESTEX people have their lines tied into the feed?"

"No, Devlin. They were supposed to, but decided they would wait till after we tested ours."

Devlin sucked in a huge breath of air as she looked out the open door to the mass of humanity on the lawn, stretching out to the ex-tennis court, now the rodeo arena. The phone call had brought her terrible news. Her losses would be high in the millions. She wondered for a moment where T-Bird was, and what he might be doing and thinking. She thought hard about having left the people who counted on her back in Texas, and wondered what the devil she was doing waiting a single minute more. She had planned to make a speech at the conclusion of the rodeo, and say a *not*-fond farewell to these people she detested. She didn't have the heart for it. They needed her back in Texas.

"Carter, it's only money. Don't worry about it. We'll fix it. I'll be home tomorrow."

Devlin proceeded to dial another number, an air charter service out of Van Nuys Airport. As she was making arrangements, Terry entered and stood alongside. When her second call was completed, she told Terry the story of what happened in Big Spring.

"Devlin, that's terrible."

"Terry, I'm going upstairs to pack. The rodeo is over as far as I'm concerned. What's more important is that you've got my undying love. You're my true sister, Terry. You always will be. Will you come back to Houston with me?"

Terry thought a minute, then she hugged Devlin to her. "Dev, don't be upset if I say no. I can stay with the rodeo and the gals, if you lend me a couple of hundred or so, until I find myself."

Devlin nodded agreement. She would leave Terry a check for twenty-five thousand dollars.

"I was going to tell them all something, David and the rest, but dammit, that's dumb kid stuff. I'm just gonna leave, and leave them to themselves."

Terry smiled. "Honey, you go on and pack. I'll figure out something to say."

Devlin walked upstairs to her bedroom and began to throw a few things in a suitcase. She would send for the rest. That, plus the cost of the damage the rodeo had done would be something her office in Houston could work out. Then, something made her walk to the window. She could see the panorama of the lawn arena, the swimming pool, and the hundred or more guests who were clustered in groups all over the lawn. She saw a familiar figure head for the livestock pen. It was Terry.

Devlin followed her with her eyes. Terry headed for the pen with the calves, goats, broncs, and bulls. Without a moment's pause, she opened the gate. With a whoop and a holler and a wave of her cowboy hat, she scooted forty-five huge beasts and twenty little ones out of the pen. Gathering speed as they raced for freedom across the lawn, they scattered everyone out of their way.

Thousand-pound monsters of bucking broncos panicked and shot out of the pen. Goats for the goat-tying, calves for the calf-roping, horses for the barrel-racing, and finally the bulls, huge 1500-pound be-hemoths, crashed out of the pen, over the lawn, delirious in their freedom, chasing every moving thing in sight—the guests.

Stupefied, Devlin stood watching as one brute of a bull chased the largest Ford dealer in Southern California and his wife into the swimming pool. Then, nudged by a second bull, the huge animal fell in too. A tower of water marked its entrance. The Ford dealer's wife screamed madly.

The shouts and the cries cannonaded through Beverly Hills. Terry and the cowgirls sat chuckling on a panel fence, surveying the damage.

Devlin was unable to suppress a smile as she turned away and snapped the valise shut. She went down the back stairs to the garage. She would drive to the airport and leave her car there. As she walked through the kitchen, she saw the cowering figure of Clive huddled under the sink.

"Clive," Devlin said matter-of-factly, "don't wait up for me."

In minutes, Devlin drove out the garage on her way home to Houston.

25

FROM the battledeck of Giroux Frères on Wall Street, Claude Giroux felt the satisfaction of a flag admiral when he viewed the results of his planning and expertise. Surely Admiral Nimitz, in his strategy at Midway, had no more reason to be proud of himself than Claude Giroux did.

Giroux had seen something in John Dowie's eyes that convinced him to put his money on the man, a something that sometimes makes more sense to a banker than business background or previous corporate experience. Giroux had seen well-established, high-salaried, second-tier men in major companies promoted to the head spot, only to fail. He had seen top corporate leaders placed in high-level policy positions in the government, only to turn in hopeless performances. He *had* put his money on John Dowie. He had taken that risk with first his own, then investors' money. Almost a billion dollars had gone into the development and amassing of the giant complex known as HOUCORP. First there had been money to buy the early acquisitions, and then as the news was carefully leaked to a few favorites—friendly brokerage houses, companionable insurance companies, the "institutional investors" who were never named, only whispered in awe—the stock of HOUCORP began to move. Then it had been easy. He was able to appeal to the basic human emotion he had always called upon when things got going—greed.

The printing plant in Bridgeport, Connecticut, that worked exclusively in designing, engraving, and printing the gloriously old-fashioned pieces of paper which were stock certificates, handsomely ornate, colored with the golds and greens that were symbolic of good old nineteenth-century greenbacks, went to work to print hundreds, then thousands, then tens of thousands of pieces of paper.

HOUCORP issued common stock, preferred stock, bonds, convertible debentures, warrants, and other arcane combinations to serve as the currency to acquire other shipping companies, warehouse companies, freight-handling, storage, refineries, petrochemical processing plants—and friends in high places over the next few years. The more HOUCORP issued, the more everything was worth. When things worked, they really worked. The early seed companies turned into veritable cornucopias.

Then, there was the remarkably symbiotic relationship that Claude had with John Dowie. The man was a rascal, Claude was sure of that. More often than not, Dowie found magical solutions to problems that defied logic. As earlier, John Dowie offered to explain them to Claude, but advised him that he might be better off not knowing. There were a half dozen times when Claude was tempted to demand an explanation, except that he was wise enough to be fearful of being told.

Claude stared out the window of his thirtieth-floor corner suite, sipping a cup of camomile tea, and marveled how efficiently things were going, and how thoroughly compatible he was with John Dowie. There was never an argument about what needed to be done, or whether it really needed to be accomplished. Claude simply called the shots, and Dowie accomplished it, with such speed and dispatch that Claude was inclined to add more and more to the scope of HOUCORP. Claude considered frequently that HOUCORP would be a textbook story of how investment banking, thoughtfully and imaginatively conceived, could rule the world.

The most remarkable thing to Claude was that there was not a single moment of labor unrest in the affairs of HOUCORP. One agreement, easily arrived at, was replaced just as easily at the termination of the contract. The increases for the workers were, in Claude's view, not only modest, but in some cases, hardly even noticeable. He had just finished looking at the unpublished first-quarter results from HOUCORP. The saturnine accountants and financial people were showing profits of an extraordinary amount, almost double the first-quarter results of a year earlier.

Another investment banker might have had need to seek help in figuring the value of his own portfolio, but Claude Giroux did not. Figuring dilution in the shares of stock that had newly been issued to acquire a grain-elevator storage company, and accounting for the three stock-splits that he had engineered in order to keep the price of each share below fifty, he knew that Giroux Frères' part of the HOUCORP's pot was worth three hundred and fifty million dollars, plus warrants which, when exercised, would bring his share of this money machine to almost a billion dollars.

Giroux smiled as he stared at the industrious horde on the street below, scurrying back and forth, making deals, worrying about margin requirements, the flow of the market, the questionable management of companies acquired, and the perilous problems of government regulation and interferences. HOUCORP was a textbook example of how to avoid all of these problems. HOUCORP was just a processor, and virtually a monopoly. It could charge whatever the market could bear.

There was one remaining figure in the port who could provide a hint of competition, and that was the crusty bastard, L.C. Younger, the person Claude had first conceived to be the pivot for his ambitions. How lucky he was that Younger had turned him down, and how fortunate he had been to have uncovered John Dowie.

Earlier in the morning he had spoken to John to congratulate him on the first-quarter results.

"Mr. Giroux, I'm pleased you're pleased. We're trying our best to make you proud of what you've accomplished."

"John," Claude laughed, "when are you ever going to take credit yourself? I've never met a man like you before. I tell you, one week here on the street, you'd find a thousand people claiming that each one of them had been responsible for HOUCORP's success. Now, John, fair is fair."

The voice was serious. "Mr. Giroux, I was saving the best for last."

"What's that?"

"Well, you know that I've been staying clear of Black Diamond."

"No matter, John, all in good time."

"Yep, that's the way I felt. It looks to me that we've got the whole port sewed up, except for that one."

"John, it's no matter. From what I understand, they owe a bundle, and their business is way off. They'll be dead on the vine before long."

There was a moment's silence.

"Mr. Giroux, you won't have to wait that long."

Something in Dowie's voice was alarming. Claude knew he shouldn't ask the question, but this time he was impelled. "What do you mean, John?"

"Mr. Giroux, remember I told you some time ago that there was only one man I had a problem about, and that's Younger. Mr. Giroux, I've got a long memory, and I'm only considering that my dear father, may he rest in peace, will be watching to see what happens."

Giroux had heard enough. He had heard more than he wanted to. He swallowed hard, because he understood from the very beginning that with John Dowie he was dealing with nitroglycerine. It was stable and controllable, as long as it was not disturbed.

"John," Claude interrupted, "don't do anything that would interfere with our fine working relationship. You've made me proud of you, almost like a son."

After a moment's pause, John Dowie ended the conversation abruptly. "Mr. Giroux, I appreciate your sentiments. I had only one father, and L.C. Younger killed him."

229

Claude stared at the phone for a moment, then he replaced the receiver. Only now did he reflect on an interview he had less than a week earlier with the agent in charge of the New York office of the FBI.

Regis Tooley had not given him a reason for the appointment, but he learned quickly enough when the man showed up. Tooley started by announcing that the bureau had been involved in a year-long investigation of organized crime in the gulf area, and had come upon solid evidence of Mafia involvement in the activities of HOUCORP.

Did Claude Giroux have any reason to believe that the Mafia had infiltrated this company, using its cover to handle the shipment of illegal goods, drugs, and stolen merchandise, in and out of the country, as well as the laundering of illegal cash. Apart from the government's interest in the Mafia in all of its nefarious activities, the Department of Defense had serious concerns about the prospect of the underworld's control of vital harbor and shipping facilities.

Claude Giroux smiled. He had heard allegations like this before. Everyone in every port was always suspected of being connected with organized crime. Giroux was unimpressed. Labor unions and officials had to deal with this riffraff, and Giroux Frères was very fortunate to have as chief executive someone who knew them for what they were. You can't deal with contagion, if you are a doctor, unless you can identify it and know it first-hand, he explained to the agent. Tooley did not seem satisfied with his explanation.

Claude dismissed it from his mind. Meanwhile he punched up his desktop quotation reader, and there in glowing LED crystals was the current quote on HOUCORP. Up two and a half points. Claude Giroux was very pleased.

John Travis was delighted when the board of directors announced at its meeting that he was to become the new president of Texas National Bank. In truth, he had been acting as chief operating officer for some time, ever since the death of his father-in-law, Melvin Jurdam. Even during Melvin's lifetime, the board of directors had directed much of its attention to John Travis.

The eleven-member board met the day of John Travis's thirty-fourth birthday. The chairman, a garrulous seventy-year-old, Alger Lyles, who was no more a banker than the man in the moon, happily announced the board's decision, made in private before the meeting.

John Travis reacted as he was expected to. He accepted the congratulations of the other board members as they gathered in the tradition-laden conference room. It hadn't changed one whit since Big John Jurdam designed it, as well as everything else in the bank, almost sixty years ago.

The chairman cleared his throat and tapped a pencil on the highly polished walnut table. He looked around the room, so steeped in tradition, and so old-fashioned and worn that it belied Texas National's huge profitability.

"Gentlemen, it's good to know that we're turning the operation of Texas National to a young man who can follow in the footsteps of John and Melvin, and that he's *family*." He looked around at his fellow directors. "True, he's not of the same blood as a Jurdam, but he's married into the family, and if Big John were alive today, he'd be mighty proud of what John Travis has accomplished."

The directors smiled their approval.

"We're bigger than anyone in Houston, and if John Travis's plans go through, we'll have branches in every major Texas city. Our deposits are bigger than ever. Our loan portfolios are like Rembrandt pictures—our profits have never been higher."

John Travis sat in his usual chair at the far end of the table. He would be patient while the old bastard Lyles shot his mouth off. As far as he was concerned, there was nothing he couldn't do better than any member of the board, or all of them together. He had had to lead them into the twentieth century, dammit. It had been like pulling teeth to get them to understand the new needs of business, and how to attract it.

HOUCORP was a perfect example. It started with nothing just a few short years ago, and he had been responsible for bringing in that account. Now HOUCORP was bigger than some of the biggest oil companies, and that was big, and a damn sight more profitable. What's more the bank held a pile of warrants that would make a pot of money when Texas National decided to cash in.

Alger Lyles continued, his eyes twinkling. "I suppose John Travis is asking himself, why the dickens does Texas National need a chairman of the board—that's me—and why isn't he chief executive—that's me, too. Well, it's just this, John Travis. You've got to forgive an old man," he laughed, "that's *me*, too. I love this bank, this building, these walls, these offices. They're all the way they used to be, when I was just a boy. I spent my life here at Texas National, John Travis, and all I want and all the board wants to give me is . . . a little more time."

John Travis smiled. He thought to himself, you old fool, you were useless sixty years ago, and you're useless now.

Instead, he stood up and faced Alger Lyles and the other members of the board. "Mr. Lyles, if you hadn't asked for it, and the board hadn't wanted it, I would have demanded it myself, as president. Age has so much to give, and Mr. Lyles, you're a *young* man." He paused to drink in the approval of the board. "And you can take that as gospel from *another* young man."

The applause was warm and very heartfelt.

That night, another celebration took place in a suite in a downtown Houston hotel. It was a stag party conceived and organized by Troy

Davis, who had been John Travis's friend and confidant from his days at Rice, and best man at his wedding to Harriet Jurdam.

Five of John Travis's closest friends had decided on a stag party for his birthday. That the event coincided with his election to the presidency of Texas National was a bonus. Troy and the other cronies of the guest of honor had gone to a lot of trouble to arrange the party, and John Travis welcomed the prospect of it. The alternative had been too unhappy to contemplate. Harriet planned a small dinner at home for her mother, aunts, and their two young children, Thania and Dolores, the twins.

John Travis made a convenient excuse. He had even forgotten what this one was. His extracurricular life with his other women was so complex that lies came to him in bunches. He was shameless in their use. As far as John Travis was concerned, Harriet got exactly what she bargained for. He never stinted, well maybe a little, in his sex with Harriet. There was always enough left over. Then, in addition, he was twice the banker her daddy was. That was one hell of a bonus.

The party was held in a meeting room which dwarfed the single, round table at which everybody sat. The whiskey flowed, and the steaks were fine, and John Travis was pleased as getout to be out of his tie and jacket and among the men with whom he had had a hell of a lot of good times through the years.

Twelve hours after the meeting in the board room, Troy Davis got up to make a speech and belched. Everybody laughed.

"Hell, fellas, a guy has a right."

"Speech," shouted one of them. "John Travis, make the son-of-a-bitch give a speech."

Troy smiled in anticipation. He held a drink in one hand and a large gaily wrapped box in the other. He belched again to a sprinkling of applause.

"Okay, you jokers, you asked for it." He smiled at John Travis. "Happy birthday to one hell of a guy." There was more applause. "Hell, that's not all I have to say. Look, John Travis, us fellows are mighty proud of what you've done, not in the damn boardroom of the damn bank, but in the damn bedrooms all over Houston. I have the honor to know a man who has fucked more pussy at any given time, in any given place, than the U.S. Marines, and kept coming back for more."

John Travis smiled happily.

"Now, what do you give someone like that, with a pecker that don't stop? Do you just give him your best wishes, and say 'I wish I could do that'? No, you think of ways to honor it." He proceeded to open the box in front of him. It wasn't easy, since he was very drunk. Finally the man next to him ripped off the wrapping paper. Troy reached in and picked out a dark-gray hairy mass in the shape of a curved dagger.

"Do you know what I have here in my hand?" he fairly shouted. "I

232

have here, the horn of a rhinoceros. For those of you dumb bastards who don't know the horn of a rhinoceros from a hole in your ass, let me say that in some parts of the world, a place called China, for example, the Chinese think that it does the trick to keep your pecker up and in good condition by grinding it up and taking it like medicine. Now, I never seen a rhino's pecker, so I don't know if it does *him* any good. Leastways, I don't think that it did this here rhino any good, because I guess this sombitch is dead now, and nobody's pecker works too good when his body is dead."

John Travis was surveying the horn with interest.

"So, it's for you, John Travis, not because we think you need it, just as a sign of affection from a gang of guys who admire the hell out of you."

There was applause, and John Travis leaned over to take the trophy. "This son-of-a-bitch is almost as big as mine."

Among the general laughter, Troy rapped a fork against a glass for attention. "Well, shit, John Travis, we don't want you to think that we would finish this here party on your birthday without a cake, but it won't fit in the damn room. So, B.J.," he said to one of the group, "you go open up next door, and we'll all go in and see John Travis's cake. Then, he can blow out every one of the damn candles."

B.J. went to the double-door entrance to the adjacent room and opened the door.

Troy led John Travis away from the table, and the rest of them followed. As they got inside the room, Troy flicked on the light switch.

John Travis let out a whoop and a shout. "Son-of-a-bitch," he yelled. "Dammee, you did it, you sons-of-bitches."

There on the huge round table were six nude showgirls. Their heads were clustered at the center in a circle. Their legs were spread wide apart and knees bent. Their breasts and nipples were decorated with whipped cream and cherries. A small basket of chocolates was cradled in each of their navels. But the fascinating part, was that each of them had a large lighted candle in her pussy.

John Travis roared with laughter. His buddies looked at each other with delight.

The president of one of Texas's biggest banks playfully blew out each of the candles of all six of the girls as they giggled at his friendly touch.

He grinned at everyone as he removed the candle from the first young lady and tossed it on the floor. He chuckled as he unzipped his fly. This was one hell of a birthday party.

The serious setback in Big Spring, resulting from the destruction of the tank farm, left Devlin with conflicting feelings. She was convinced that it was not an accident, but there was no way to prove it, and even if she could prove it, it might take a lifetime to make it stick against WESTEX.

On the other hand, whoever or whatever caused the accident had done a lot of destruction to her momentum. Younger Oil had drilled in other areas since the Permian Basin discovery, and although there had been some positive results, nothing approached the West Texas field, by a long shot. When the balance of drilling costs to recovery was computed, Devlin discovered that she had been going through a number of highly unprofitable years.

It was true that the Conroy field was still producing, and would for some time to come, but the production curve was slowing down, and Devlin could foresee that unless other discoveries were made, her hopes of growth or even survival would not be realized. The incident at Big Spring made Devlin realize that the establishment would not rest until she had been eliminated from competition. She was too young. She was a woman. And she was a Younger.

Six months ago, Fredrickson, the Younger Oil geologist, came upon an independent oilman who had drilled an abandoned well near the town of Giddings, Texas. There was, the geologist explained, a stripe of geological formation about fifteen miles wide and as much as eight hundred feet thick, which was a stratum of fractured limestone. This stratum, known as Austin Chalk, got its name from the city of Austin, where there was a notable outcropping.

The oilman had hit a fine, paying flow of oil, curiously honey-colored—which indicated a cleaner and more valuable deposit. The independent oilman had made his find when he shocked the old well back into production by pumping hydrochloric acid down the hole. It was the Younger Oil geologist's theory that the acid had vacated some of the crevices in the rock which allowed for the flow of oil.

With this information, Devlin made the decision to buy as many old leases in the Austin Chalk field as she could get her hands on. With the increasing demand and higher prices for petroleum, it looked as if it had interesting prospects.

At first the use of the hydrochloric acid and the drilling of new wells on the old sites were effective, but much to Devlin's disappointment, the flow of this remarkable golden oil was abruptly terminated after not more than six or seven days.

In the meantime, the flow of this peculiar oil from the first well of the independent oilman continued unabated. It was maddeningly frustrating. Fredrickson was certain that the oil on the Younger leases was within the same formation, but that there was just some impediment to its flow. Tank cars of hydrochloric acid followed more and more study into the seismic responses of the old wells and the new ones that Younger Oil had been drilling. The vibrations caused by the explosion of dynamite at various depths provided a readout which gave no indication at all that the young man was correct. None of the telltale jiggles indicated the presence of an oilbearing structure.

Then young Fredrickson came up with a new theory, that there was a shallow reservoir which had provided the early discontinued flow of this honey oil, and below it, separated by natural debris and perhaps even the drilling mud of earlier explorations, was the big source. All it required, he said, was the development of a new technique which would break through that barrier. New drilling wouldn't do it. It was both too expensive and too chancy. Here, he was sure, was a potential source of real production, but in need of a process to open the clogged passages to get to the oil.

Devlin met with L. Carter Dixon III to discuss this new source of trouble.

"Devlin, it's your choice."

"What do you mean, Carter? It's your company too."

"I know that, Devlin, but we've been chasing this rabbit down hole after hole, and they all come up empty."

"Do you trust Fredrickson? He's only twenty-four years old!"

"Sure I trust him. How much older am I?"

"Yeah, but Devlin, it's a big roll of the dice."

"Carter, we're in the richest business there is. I believe in Fredrickson. I think he's smart, and I think he's honest, and I think we ought to go right along with him."

"Are you sure?"

"Sure, I'm sure."

"We'll have to borrow money."

"Carter, what are you trying to tell me, that I shouldn't go ahead?"

"No, Devlin, not a bit. If you look on your desk, you'll find the loan application, just ready for your signature."

Devlin signed it with a flourish. "Come on, I'll buy you some ribs for lunch. I like your style."

Carter followed Devlin as she went out the door. He stared at the remarkably beautiful, ever so tall, ginger-haired young woman who was his boss and who, for all he knew, could go bust any minute, and who didn't appear to give a damn.

26

SEVENTY-ONE MILES from Dallas is the tiny town of Hope, once the site of the famous "Knights of the Road Ranch," on almost five thousand acres of rich farmland. Until fifteen years ago, the ranch was dedicated to the conviction that man is his brother's keeper. In time gone by, the Calder family made the ranch a home for any man willing to work, for board and his keep.

During that period, the buildings—chapel, bunkhouse, and dining room—were kept spotless. The food was excellent, and the men considered themselves part of the Calder family. Some men lived in this hideaway for up to fifty years, finding the life rewarding and healthful. Others, down on their luck, stayed at the Knights of the Road Ranch for just long enough to get themselves together, and gain enough self-confidence to rejoin society. The "family" at the ranch had hardbitten hobos from all over the country who had gotten the word from other members of the hobo fraternity. During the Great Depression, they were former businessmen down on their luck, faced with failure, and unable to find a way out. During the thirties, guests at the Knights of the Road Ranch might have passed for a giant meeting of the boards of directors of a major corporation. During those times, the defrocked captains of industry shucked all their cares away, donned workshirts, heavy-topped shoes, workpants, and labored in the fields, or the barns, planting and gathering the cotton that covered the rich black land.

Fifteen years ago D.D. Goddard, a Dallas millionaire, acquired the Knights of the Road Ranch and, with the same passion that he had shown for making himself enormously rich, set about turning the former waystation for the forlorn and discouraged into the most gigantic and extraordinary playground for men who had great wealth, and knew how to enjoy it. D.D. Goddard built an immense personal game preserve, importing animals from all over the world, for selective

236

hunting by Goddard's friends. In the confines of the Goddard Ranch, the same bunkhouses and mess hall that accommodated the misfits of America for years now housed the playful scions of great fortunes, the net worth of which on any given weekend could probably equal the wealth of many countries around the world.

Apart from importing a white hunter known throughout Africa as the dean of safari organizers, and having given this man carte blanche to import the very best specimens of African wildlife, Goddard had installed his own taxidermy shop to enshrine the kill of his famous guests. Three men who had run such an enterprise in Nairobi, Kenya, operated on the specimens that fell to Goddard's guests after a weekend when thirty friends might bag as many as two hundred separate kills.

In addition to cream- and tangerine-colored reedbucks, the impressive curved-horned ibexes, stately waterbucks and topii, there were hundreds of graceful impalas, the rare hartebeests, giant elands, tiny dik-diks, zebras, barbary sheep, among the seventy-five or more separate breeds that mixed in the compound.

For D.D. Goddard—a forceful man in his early sixties, with a firm chin and piercing eyes—more important than these specimens, was his own hostage to youth, a new wife of only eighteen months. A former Hollywood starlet, her films had never been seen further away from Hollywood than Burbank, but her body and bedroom spirit were terribly endearing to Goddard. Cheryl Cherine Goddard would just as easily and happily have remained in the Goddard mansion in Dallas on those weekends, but her husband was not about to let her out of his sight. One such weekend, almost nine months after Devlin's return from California, she was Cheryl Goddard's personal guest at the Goddard Ranch. Cheryl was willing to come, but only if she could invite someone to talk to. "Daddy" Goddard, as she referred to him, was a perfectly acceptable companion in Dallas, but in the company of a phalanx of his friends, interested only in hunting, drinking, and playing cards, Cheryl was bored to death. D.D. agreed to anything that made Cheryl happy.

When the phone call came to her from Cheryl Goddard, a young woman she had never met, Devlin was surprised at the invitation, but she cheerfully accepted. She had to get away from the serious problems she faced.

Early Friday afternoon, Devlin drove her Eldorado through the front gate. It was a quarter of a mile to the ranch houses, a group of low buildings, brown-shingled, simple and neat. The compound gave no hint that within hours some of the most powerful men in all America would be guests, sleeping on bunks in rooms that held ten of them together, without indoor plumbing, or even hot water to shave.

A former President would be a guest this weekend, plus a current governor, five men worth over half a billion dollars each, and other powerhouses including a prince of a reigning family. No one would

237

shave that weekend. No one would complain about the cold, the hard bunks, the outhouses they were required to use, the lack of telephones or any of the dozens of conveniences that went with wealth and power. Quite the contrary. The men would fawn on Daddy Goddard for another invitation, as they had for the first one.

Devlin had a small private room furnished with a cot and a dresser. A pitcher and bowl sufficed for washing. Cheryl met Devlin at the compound and explained the weekend.

"Now, Devlin, you are not to be worried about those men. You and I will have a fine time together, just the two of us. Do you know Daddy at all?"

"Everybody in Texas knows about D.D., but I've never met him."

"Well, you'll meet him, and I *know* you'll love him to death. Don't get to thinking that this is the way we live in Dallas. Far from it. We have thirty-four rooms and twelve baths. We even have three rooms for the chauffeurs, and a complete garage so that we don't have to send the cars out to be fixed." She giggled, "We could put in a car wash too, in the room we have in the back."

Devlin laughed.

"Lookit, Devlin, you are one real pretty girl. I don't say that to many girls, with all the plastic work you can get nowadays, to fill you out and make all kinds of changes. I always think that the plastic man should be the one you admire. Take a look at my tits, I had a little implant put in to make 'em perkier. D.D. knows all about it. Matter of fact, although I know that he wouldn't like me saying it, he was the one who sent me to the man to have it done. But now I like 'em."

"They sure are perky," Devlin agreed.

"Hmm, yeah, but everything else is mine. My nose, my thighs, and everything. Some of the girls complain all the time about cellulite. I don't have anything like that. Do you? I do touch up my hair, I don't want you to think that this platinum color is natural. Frankly, I'd be mousy brown if it weren't for Antoine. He's my hairdresser. But your hair—that color red. That doesn't come out of any bottle, Devlin. Golly, are *you* the lucky one."

"Thanks, Cheryl."

Cheryl led Devlin across the grass-covered lawn. A high flagpost flew a huge U.S. flag. A second alongside it, equally tall, flew the flag of Texas. A Mexican boy carried Devlin's luggage to the bungalow to which she was assigned. Cheryl left her at the door.

"Look, if you get bored, I've got a portable TV that works by batteries. I mean, books and everything else are okay, but on a quiet weekend, there's nothing better than your favorite program. I bought it because there's no electricity, nor nothing." She whispered, "I have some soft toilet paper you can use. You won't believe the kind that they have in the outhouse."

That night at dinner Devlin sat at one of the three long tables piled high with breads, peppers, butter, and sauces. The men trooped in, looking a little uncomfortable at first in their rough hunting clothes. Men, more at ease in boardrooms and banks, were dressed in jeans and workpants. Devlin met D.D. Goddard, and he and Cheryl introduced her to the other guests.

As Devlin seated herself, she saw the ex-President, the governor, and other familiar and important faces. There was an empty seat on the bench beside her. Moments later the seat was taken by a tall, handsome young man, whom she remembered having met, but had no idea where. He was blond, blue-eyed, and full of smiles.

"Devlin, I'm Jamie Lord. You had me as a guest at your housewarming in Houston. It's been a long time."

Devlin looked at the man at her right. How incredibly handsome he was. Self-confident, warm and welcoming. She felt a glow of satisfaction about the weekend. "You a hunter?"

"Mostly I like the grub here. Wait till you've eaten a handful of steaks this weekend. They'll compare to anything you ever ate anywhere."

"What do you do, then?"

"Mosey around, ride a little, drink a little, and play a little poker."

"Sounds okay, and the price is right."

"Wait till Sunday night. Old D.D. will have some campaign or other that he wants everyone to contribute to . . . like arming the K.K.K. and setting fire to every Mexican and black in America. This weekend will cost you."

"I don't think I'll contribute. How are the poker games?"

"Not as good as the food." He turned as four Mexican servants, loaded with trays, headed in the direction of the tables. Devlin thought she saw another familiar face at the other table, but as the generous bowl of chili was put at her place, and a steak the size of Oklahoma, and refried beans, and, and . . . Devlin looked at the food, then at her companion. "Last one in is a rotten egg."

Jamie laughed, "Wait till they bring the main course, and they usually have five desserts."

After dinner the men moved into the large gameroom, where four separate card tables had been set up. The conversation at Devlin's table had been loose and friendly. The former President was expansive, full of anecdotes and stories about secret CIA exploits, and congressional sex habits. He also was all eyes on Devlin, a fact that was obvious to everyone, especially Jamie Lord. As they broke away, he took Devlin aside, "It's a shame the President's not in the White House."

"Why is that?"

"I think you'd give the First Lady a run for her money."

Devlin reddened. "You noticed."

"Oh, yes." Then he spied a place at the poker table and left to take a

239

seat. The other places were being filled, and Devlin realized that the men would consider it a heinous crime if she joined them. She turned and faced a man who was standing behind her. It was pudding-faced, tall, impressive Frank Holson who stood smiling at her.

"Miss Younger, this is a strange place to find you."

"Why is that, Mr. Holson?"

"I thought you'd be working—the industrious and dedicated wildcatter. Finally, you've taken time out to enjoy yourself. Do you ever really let go?"

"I really don't know, Mr. Holson."

"Please call me Frank."

Devlin remembered all too well their last unpleasant exchange. She had put Frank Holson in his place. Now, he seemed to have completely forgotten that first unpleasantness.

Behind them the room had settled down to a pleasant hum. The sounds of poker chips, cards being dealt, the clinking of glasses, were part of the pleasant background of men at play. Devlin hungered to get her hands on some cards. She would make them dance and sing. It would cause a few eyebrows to raise. But now she was faced with a man she couldn't avoid. Frank Holson's eyes burned with desire.

"Frank, I take it you'd still like to fuck me."

He laughed, "My God, you're my kind of woman. I like that in you Devlin. You certainly *know* it."

"And things would go a lot better for me?"

"Yes indeed, Devlin, a lot better."

"Like that fire in Big Spring that destroyed my tank farm . . ."

"Devlin, if you want to go it on your own, I can help you. Of course my advice to sell is still the same. As for the fire, it was a tragedy, but accidents *do* happen."

"Frank, between you and me, it wasn't any accident. Whether it was from the top or the bottom, someone at WESTEX decided to put the torch to almost three million barrels of my oil."

Frank Holson feigned sadness. "They play a little rough here in Texas."

Devlin laughed, "Frank, you said just what I was thinking."

Relieved, he smiled. "We could excuse ourselves, and no one would know." He looked around furtively.

Devlin put her hand on his, "Frank, you go first and wait in your room. If I don't show up in an hour or so, start without me."

Devlin turned on her heel and walked to the first poker table and watched hungrily as she saw some easy money going into the winning hands of men she wished *she* were playing with. The ex-President saw her and smiled. "Do you play poker, little lady?"

Devlin smiled, "Yes, Mr. President, some, now and then." The President addressed the man sitting next to him, "Ben, why don't you

240

get up and give the lady your chair. Even if she's not a whiz at the game, she'll be a damn sight more entertaining than you are." As the man got up, Devlin seated herself in time for the deal.

"Seven card stud," the dealer declared.

The President whispered, "You need jacks or better to open. Any questions, just ask me. It's a cut-throat game, but I'll be your friend." Devlin felt the President's hand on her thigh, and picked up her cards. Out of the corner of her eye she saw Frank Holson and Jamie Lord. They were talking earnestly. Devlin wondered what they were saying.

The bet came around to her and it was time to play poker. She glanced at the beaming faces around her and wondered how much they would be good for, until they got tired of losing.

The dealer surveyed the cards and looked at Devlin's ace of hearts showing. "Your bet, young lady."

Devlin smiled and put her chips in the pot.

The President beamed and Devlin felt his hand tighten on her thigh. She wondered if she could use the same out with the President as she did with Frank Holson. She guessed not, but on the other hand, she didn't have to go to bed with *him* either. She hoped it wouldn't be necessary to prove her patriotism that way.

Tune had located, rented and furnished an attractive apartment on Memorial Drive long before he was positive that it would be useful to him. The manager had no difficulty in discreetly adjusting to the fact that even though he recognized the former star quarterback at SMU, the man who signed the lease, for all intents and purposes, was not Tune Richards.

Less than two weeks after his dinner with Constanza, Tune searched out the apartment. True, she had said that she didn't want to see him again, but as carefully as Tune had planned his campaign, first to solve the case of Jesus Hernandez, and then to hold that private victory dinner, he planned to have Constanza for himself.

As far as Constanza was concerned, the evening she spent with the handsome Anglo disturbed and angered her. Her disturbance stemmed from her attraction to Tune. Her anger was with herself. She had carefully plotted out her life and committed herself to the old ways taught by her grandmother. She had promised herself to serve her people. The ambitions that she happily discussed with Tune, to become a council member, and perhaps even more, were her secrets. She had never confessed them to a soul, but that night she admitted them to an Anglo, and someone she had met only one time before.

Tune was wise enough to forego the usual techniques that he might have used to attract one of the young women he knew in the past. He didn't telephone; he didn't write; he sent no flowers—but only for two weeks. During that time, with a diligence that amazed him, he unearthed

241

the location of the storefront office where Constanza worked. He determined her hours. He discovered who her father worked for, his salary, the names of her mother, her sisters and brothers, *and* he rented that apartment.

None of this information was particularly useful to him, but it kept him in contact with her. It made him feel closer to Constanza, with whom he had become obsessed.

Two weeks to the day after their dinner together, Tune waited in his parked car a half block away from the storefront office, knowing that Constanza would pass his way. A full hour later Tune spied her tall, graceful movements as she headed in his direction. Moments before she came even with his car, Tune got out and stood in her path. When she saw him, she reacted as if she were frightened to death.

"Constanza, I was waiting for you."

She looked confused. From houses alongside, she saw curious faces look in her direction.

"Please, don't do this, Tune. Please leave me alone."

The sound of Constanza saying his name was intoxicating.

"Constanza, please let me drive you somewhere. I just want to talk to you." The attention in the street to the two of them was becoming more noticeable; Constanza noted it with displeasure. "Go away," she commanded.

"Just to talk, please."

She wavered, and finally she entered the open car door. Tune quickly closed it behind her. Moments later, he was inside and started the car. He had at least trapped this timorous bird, for a moment or two.

Tune swiftly moved the car through the city streets, and onto the freeway. It was dusk, and the traffic had slowed. For all that time, Constanza sat in the corner, next to the door, too angry to say anything.

"You're *not* taking me home," she muttered.

"Please, Constanza, give me some time." She said nothing. Tune stared straight ahead at the road, fearful of even looking at her. "Constanza, believe me, please. I'm in love with you. I know that you're Mexican and I'm Anglo, and that we come from different traditions, but I haven't stopped thinking about you from the very first. Every day I dream of what it would be like to be close to you again. I'll be patient. I won't press you, or force you into anything that you don't want to do. I just want to see you occasionally, and have us get to know each other better. Maybe in time, you'll feel the same way about me that I feel for you."

There was quiet in the car. All Tune could hear was his own heart beating, and the sound of Constanza's breathing.

"I know that you like me a little. I saw that in your eyes the time we were together. It's not so strange or impossible to think that two people like ourselves could fall in love."

Constanza shouted, "Please take me home."

Tune was rocked for a moment, and then, in response to her demand, he exited the freeway. It was dark as he drove onto the downramp, preparing to cross back to the return side. Something prevented him from doing just that. Instead, he pulled into a side street, under the darkness of overhanging trees.

From the deepest region of his soul, near to a cry for help, he murmured, "Constanza, I love you. I really love you." He bent to grasp her, expecting the worst. For a moment Constanza resisted, and then, to his complete surprise, she met his lips with a fire that astounded them both. From the first contact, the young Mexican girl was released from every inner restraint that had bound her sexually. She kissed him as hungrily as he did her.

Her body pressed against him in an insistent way that had more force than Tune could have imagined. Her small breasts through her thin dress forced themselves against his chest. Her fingers caressed and played with the hair on his neck, touched his ear, brushed his eyes. Never for a moment did she let go.

Many minutes later, she broke away. The two of them were breathless. Tune had never been more excited in his life, more conscious of his need for anyone. He looked at Constanza, and tiny tears were forming in the corner of her eyes. She had broken all the taboos of her past, and awakened all the longings of a lifetime.

Tune started the car and quietly drove to a motel not far distant. He parked the car and headed for the office. Moments later, he returned with a key and drove to a remote corner. Only then did he stop and help her out.

Quietly, shyly, her eyes still wet with tears, Constanza walked inside with him, and Tune shut the door. The outside light gave enough illumination to show each of them to the other in silhouette. Constanza moved into Tune's waiting arms, and he pressed himself into her body. She responded with a pressure born of intense passion.

Slowly he led her to the bed, and as she stood passively against it, Tune began to undress her, savoring each moment, feeling the electricity of a woman he had been waiting for all his life, praying that his love for her and his instincts would make it right.

Constanza stood naked in front of him, slim, youthful, and virginal. Tune removed his own clothes, and pressed himself against her. She shied away for a moment as she felt his hardness against her stomach, and then bound herself to him in a grip of iron.

Moments later, Tune and she lay on the bed, closer than two people thought they might be, holding each other, fearful of making any move that could mar the perfection of a pair of humans hungry for something indefinable in the other.

Slowly, Tune began to caress her luxuriant body. With infinite

243

patience, he spent ever so long making her ready to accept him. Her tiny cries of pain and pleasure, mixed with an emotion he could feel, but not understand, met, when he first entered her.

At that moment, Tune sighed. He was where he had always wanted to be, with someone he had never known existed until such a short time before. He felt the gentle touch of her hands on his back, caressing every part of his body as he lay quietly inside her.

It would be many minutes before Tune ventured to move, and when he did, his mounting passion was met equally by the woman in his arms.

Saturday at the Knights of the Road Ranch, Devlin pored through the books in the library. They were as spare as a virgin at an orgy, so Devlin settled in for an afternoon's read of *Guns and Ammo,* not her favorite magazine. When the honking horns of the pickups announced the return from the hunt, she emerged to see the victorious billionaires with all their trophies. Cheryl informed her that the leading hunter with the biggest kill of the day was Jamie Lord. Later that night, after dinner, he guided her to the side of the room.

"They won't let you play poker again, Devlin."

"Why is that?"

"It's illegal."

She laughed. "They're big boys."

"Devlin, look, in Texas what you did to them last night is armed robbery without a gun. Now you've got to understand that no self-respecting man is going to allow himself to submit to that twice in a row. Texas needs a law to protect *us* from poker players like you. Where did you learn your evil ways?"

"Jamie, is it evil to kill unsuspecting animals? You did it your own way. I did it mine."

"What's with you, Devlin? Last night, if Frank Holson is to be believed, you set out to humiliate him, and now, out of the blue, I'm trying to be decent and friendly, and you start taking pot shots at me. Let me ask you, are you just down on men?"

"Mr. Lord, you seem to have a pretty high opinion of what my opinion is worth. You sought out my company this evening, and as for Frank Holson, the less said about him, the better. I suspect that he can survive the next hundred years or so without my good opinion of him."

Devlin turned and joined Cheryl, who was nursing her own concoction of gin, crème de cocoa, and sweet cream on top.

"Devlin," Cheryl whispered, "he likes you, he really does. I can tell."

"Hmm . . ."

"You know who he is, don't you? His daddy is Tarquin Lord, and he owns everything, and I hear from D.D. that Jamie is going to get everything that his daddy has, and more."

"What could be more than that, Cheryl?"

"Just the entire United States of America. D.D. says that Tarquin has a timetable, and has the money put aside to make Jamie Lord President of the United States in twelve years. He'd be some catch, I'm telling you."

Devlin sniffed, "Could I get Alaska as a wedding present?"

Cheryl was surprised but reacted seriously, "I don't know if that's legal. I'll ask D.D. after the poker game. He knows *everything*."

On Sunday, the men at the ranch were nostalgic about the events of the last two days. In the course of the weekend, they had collected at least one specimen which Goddard's taxidermy shop would mount and send on to the proud hunter, plus a score of anecdotes about the hard life at the ranch. For each of them, there would be a collection of "war stories" of the weekend that would impress their friends for weeks to come.

Devlin found it difficult not to like them. Despite their money and power, they behaved like happy little boys who had discovered a new set of things to play with—the miracle of man the hunter. For hours, each of them had been transported into a Disneyland that, except for Devlin and Cheryl, was exclusively men's and dedicated to man's primitive instincts. They had found themselves free of the inhibiting influences of the world of industry and commerce and were back to basics.

Of course the basics were supplemented by a hidden staff of close to forty-five people who handled the game, the service in the mess hall, the cooking, the cleaning, and the gassing up of the cars, and then quietly disappeared to a place out of sight so as not to disturb the sense of wilderness.

Sunday afternoon Devlin completed her goodbyes to Cheryl and D.D. Goddard and a number of the men she had met during the weekend. Missing from view were Frank Holson and Jamie Lord. No great loss. The ex-President cornered her and offered to give her a refresher course in American history and government, or some such nonsense that would bring Devlin within his satyr's grasp. She managed to extricate herself, and make for her Eldorado. Servants had packed it with her belongings, and she started happily toward the main gate for the long drive back to Houston.

It was a beautiful, sunlit afternoon when Devlin exited the Goddard Ranch and joined the blacktop road on her way to the main highway. Not more than a quarter of a mile from the exit of the ranch, she saw a huge Cadillac crashed into the bottom of a ravine, and smoking.

Devlin slammed on her brakes and raced down the incline to the wreck. Her attention was diverted by someone sitting on the grass playing solitaire. It was Jamie Lord. He looked up and smiled.

"I was hoping it was you."

"Are you hurt?"

"Nah," he said with obvious relish. "I pushed it off the road, and lit a little fire inside."

Devlin was incredulous. "My God, you *are* insane."

"Look, Devlin, you spent the whole damn weekend with an ex-President and paid me no mind at all. I think that I'm in love with you, and plan to marry you after a decent courtship. Surely a week-old Cadillac is a cheap price to get you to stop. Now you've got to take me where you're going."

Devlin was struck by the craziness of the moment. He had destroyed his car just to get her to stop.

"What if it hadn't been me? What if it had been someone else?"

Jamie stood up and surveyed her. He looked into her extraordinary green eyes. "Devlin, but it *was* you. Why worry about what might have been?"

Devlin burst into laughter. "How many miles did you have on the car?"

"Devlin, it's not the miles—it's the ashtrays. They're full."

27

IF "The eyes of Texas are upon you, all the livelong day," then the Lords of Texas are with you day *and* night. Tarquin Lord, head of the distinguished Dallas family, was as much a part of Texas royalty as Sam Houston. His crown prince was James T. Lord, known to his friends and family as Jamie.

There was a Lord in the first colony in Texas established by Moses Austin in 1821, and his son Stephen F. Austin took command on his death. In Columbus-on-the-Colorado and Washington-on-the-Brazos, the first sites were settled late in the year. Austin's first grant was for three hundred families. This group was known as the "Old Three Hundred" and they went down in Texas history as did the settlers in Jamestown and Plymouth.

There were descendants of the original Lords noted as soldiers and patriots in every important event that took place in Texas from the battle of Velasco, which was the first engagement in the controversy between Texas and Mexico; the battle of Gonzales, the first conflict for independence; the battle of the Alamo; the battle of San Jacinto which decided the rebellion; statehood; the Civil War; and the explosive growth of Texas from the late nineteenth century until the present.

In the one hundred and fifty years during which there was a Lord family member in every important event of Texas history, the Lords produced governors, senators, bankers, statesmen, and a huge empire in land. Some of it was consecrated to ranching. Other portions to oil. Substantial tracts went to building major parts of a half-dozen Texas cities.

At this time, Tarquin Lord was the third generation head of Lord Construction, which had a worldwide network of engineers and construction workers. Lord Construction built airfields, dams, great military and civilian complexes around the world, power stations, and atomic plants. Tarquin Lord commanded legions like a conquering Caesar, causing monuments to his godlike presence to be built in his vision around the world.

Only one monument remained for Tarquin Lord to build. From the top of his aerie on the Lord Building in Dallas, he was in the process of engineering the strategy by which his son, James, would become President of the United States. Tarquin Lord had allocated one hundred million dollars to that project, and he was so intent upon it that he would gladly put up more.

The Sunday afternoon after the weekend at the Goddard Ranch, Jamie Lord was Devlin's passenger on the long ride back to Houston. He listened to her intently as she told him the story of the Conroy field, the story of her friendship with T-Bird Johnson, her father's history in the port of Houston, the colorful story of the first Devlin Younger, and her current gamble to find oil in the Austin Chalk deposits. No one could have been more attentive or more interested. So it seemed to Devlin.

Jamie Lord hardly spoke about himself. He chose only to listen to her. Each thrust of Devlin's to learn more about him was blunted, "Devlin, come on now, you're being shy. I know all about me, but I don't know anything about you."

It was dark by the time Devlin drove into the grounds of Fairlawn. She had scarcely been conscious during the drive of what Jamie Lord's presence foretold. She was taking him to her home, and he clearly had no interest in any alternative. Devlin reflected that this very attractive man was not about to be sent away with a sandwich and coffee.

She had spent hours trying to read Jamie Lord. He seemed like two different people. The first was the one she saw the first night at the Goddard Ranch, arrogant and a thorough-going snob. The second was the one she discovered on the drive, a warm, interested, and genuinely attractive man.

That Jamie Lord was possibly the handsomest man Devlin had met, was a given. That he came from one of the most important families in Texas was a fact. That she now found Jamie Lord an inevitable sexual partner was becoming more and more obvious to the two of them.

Fairlawn at night was refreshingly beautiful after the stark landscape of the ranch. The gently manicured lawns and the blossoming trees were lit by lamps which cast a spell of moonlight over the palatial establishment. Jamie properly admired the house and allowed Devlin's butler to remove his baggage. Devlin instructed the servant to bring it upstairs. Jamie followed as Devlin led him up the wide central staircase, down the hall and into her bedroom suite.

"I thought you'd be more comfortable sleeping in my bedroom, Jamie."

He laughed, "Do I have a choice?"

"I hadn't thought you were giving me any, but there *are* other bedrooms. You can have any one you want."

"Devlin, I have the urge to make love to you in every bedroom in the house, but it may be too much of a challenge unless you tell me just how many you have."

"Let me see, are you good for 15?"

"In one night?"

She laughed, "You can stay longer."

Jamie closed the door of the bedroom with his foot, and moved to Devlin as she stood in front of the bed. He smiled as he proceeded to undress her. "You know 'The Eyes of Texas.' "

"Naturally."

"Do you know the Lords of Texas?"

"Hmm, maybe." Devlin's shirt was unbuttoned. Her breasts were freed. Her nipples stood hard in anticipation. She waited patiently as Jamie continued in an expert way. He unbuckled her belt. "The Lords of Texas are upon you, all the livelong day," he sang.

Devlin caught her breath, and suddenly looked into Jamie Lord's eyes. There was an expression that resembled that of a greedy little boy, who had carefully prepared the way for a much wanted present. He had been good, oh so good. He had tidied up his room, completed his homework. There was no way that he could escape gaining his prize.

On the other hand, Devlin wondered how much of the real Jamie Lord she had seen on the drive, and how clever he had been in carefully grooming her for this moment. As handsome and rich as he was, Jamie Lord could have virtually any woman he wanted. But since her experience in California with David Hampton, Devlin was not willing to give herself to that kind of man.

"Devlin, let me show you what the Lord family is all about."

Devlin sighed to herself. That was not what *she* was all about, anymore.

Jamie Lord was an accomplished lover, in the same way that he was an accomplished hunter, athlete, yachtsman, and tennis player. He was a natural at anything to do with his body, except that Devlin had the deep and abiding feeling that he kept score. Devlin wanted desperately to feel at peace and treasure the intimate moments after sex, and for Jamie Lord there was never any afterward, until late in the morning when Devlin, spent, turned on her side and went to sleep.

When Devlin awoke at ten the next morning she looked at the empty bed alongside her. Devlin knew Jamie must be about the house. She paid no attention until she went into her bath, showered and began to get herself ready for breakfast.

In the library, Jamie Lord sat at Devlin's desk, which was full of

Younger Oil correspondence. As he talked, his eyes skimmed over her private papers. His feet were resting on the desk as he leaned back in the chair. He was in the middle of a very long telephone conversation with Tarquin Lord.

"I think that she's ideal, dad, really ideal."

"I'll have her checked out, Jamie, I don't want anything to come up in the future that could embarrass us."

"Dad, there's some stuff that's colorful as hell."

"What's that?"

"Well, her daddy is a crusty old bastard, made it on his own, and get this, *his* daddy was strung up by the neck."

"What for?"

"For murder, not one, but a couple or so."

"What else?"

"She's got this nice-sized oil company, started it on her own, but Frank Holson says that she'll undoubtedly be selling out very soon."

"That's good."

"Yep, I told you what she looks like, she'll photograph like crazy, and she speaks up, lots of gumption and all that."

There was a chuckle at the Dallas end. "Jamie, I'm very pleased. I think the research boys were right, figuring what kind of wife you'd need. I think that our family is too old and too rich to appeal to the blue collar workers, and somebody like what's-her-name, Devlin, is the right kind of mix. Her grandfather hanged." He laughed. "My God, that should be good for a couple of hundred thousand votes. We'll leak it to the opposition when the time comes and let *them* bring it out, like Nixons Checkers business. Great stuff. One thing, Jamie, she's got to get out of business. Women don't trust a woman who's doing big business while they're changing diapers and washing dishes. Men won't abide them. Seems to me that you'd have the best of it, seeing that she made it, and then quit for love of her man."

Jamie changed the position of his feet. He thought that he heard someone in the hall. "I understand what you're saying, dad, everything in good time."

"Jamie, there's the matter of children. Do you think that you could get her to the doctor to see whether she's fertile or not?"

The door opened in the study, and Devlin stood at the entrance with a cup of coffee in her hand. She smiled. Jamie put his hand over the mouthpiece, "Just a minute more, Devlin," he whispered to her. "I want to tell you what a terrific night I had last night, I really do." She waited as he removed his hand to conclude the conversation.

"I'll be back in Dallas sometime soon. Everything has to wait. I'm involved in something very important, that's right, yes, someone I fell in love with, and am planning to marry." Devlin was shocked at the seriousness of his words as he hung up the phone, stood up and walked to embrace her.

"Who was that?" she asked.

"Just my father, Devlin, come on, let's have something to eat. Christ, I'm hungry. Love will do that to a man." Jamie Lord put his arm around Devlin's waist and hugged her tightly to him.

•

Tune had hoped and prayed for Constanza. Then when his fantasy merged with the reality of the night they spent together, his imagined prospects took a gigantic leap forward. In his mind's eye, he imagined a series of explanations he would give to Sue Lingen for his frequent absences. Ruefully, he recognized that she wouldn't care one way or the other. He knew about *her* secret life. How he knew!

Over the next weeks, the two of them met as often as Constanza's schedule would allow. Curiously, although she responded to Tune as passionately as he had ever known anyone, there were always obligations that seemed to prevent them from meeting, or if a rendezvous were made, Tune was under no illusions that it would be kept. Too frequently she telephoned him at the last minute to explain that some matter had come up that needed her attention.

Tune scarcely paid attention to her explanations. He would have been prepared to defend what he imagined to be his rights, had the difficulty been represented by Constanza's problems with her parents. She was still living at home, and it had been accepted between them that they would return to the same motel in the early evening, make love, and then Tune would take her back home.

It was routine for him to stop his car a half block away from her house, and let her off. Those moments were the most difficult for the two of them. The evil of what Constanza was doing presented itself to her dramatically at that moment. She was within the sound of hearing of her parents and neighbors. The arrival of the familiar Cadillac in the neighborhood made her fearful.

Each of those moments set Tune and Constanza back. Every next time, then, was a new occasion to reaffirm their attachment.

The messages that Tune did not hear, were the ones that had to do with the cases that Constanza was working on, the people in the community who depended upon her, and what life was like for her and the unfortunate Mexicans she helped. Then, an event took place in Houston which had the entire Mexican community in arms. A Mexican, Ernesto Diaz, had been arrested by the Houston police, and a day later had been found floating in the channel, handcuffed and beaten. Constanza was in the forefront of the protest.

251

That night, Tune insisted that Constanza keep an appointment with him that she had just cancelled, and when he picked her up on the street corner that they always met on, he drove in silence to the apartment he had rented months earlier, and had never once spoken about.

Not a word was exchanged between them as Tune drove into the underground parking garage, and escorted her to the elevator. The clean and protected building was a strong contrast to the community in which Constanza lived and worked. Silently, Tune opened the door with his key, and flicked on the light. He stood aside as Constanza walked in slowly, and gazed at the luxurious living quarters. Without any explanation, she knew what he was saying.

"Tune, I'm not like other women. I do things for myself."

"Connie, I have plenty of money, and it would give me pleasure to see you in your own place."

"My name is Constanza, not Connie."

"It's the same thing."

"No, it isn't. It's like everything else about me, Tune, it's Mexican. No one calls a Mexican girl a nickname like Connie—it's a way for you to avoid the things that are all about me. I'm Mexican, and I'm proud of it. It's just like the business of this apartment."

"What do you mean?"

"You want me in an Anglo neighborhood, because it makes you feel uncomfortable to come to a Mexican neighborhood. The sounds and smells bother you, Tune."

"You're wrong, Constanza."

"I'm not wrong, it's like my politics."

"Those riots about Diaz aren't politics, Constanza. It's a goddamn mess."

"Tune, don't tell me what it is. In your heart you know what it was—the police picked him up for questioning because he's Mexican. All of us are suspicious."

"And he resisted arrest."

"So they say, against five cops of your Houston police department?"

"What difference whether it was one or five?"

"Just that they beat him, Tune. He was handcuffed when they found him in the water. He didn't jump in."

"They were looking for someone who committed a holdup. It was a natural mistake."

"A mistake that they wouldn't make with an Anglo."

"And you go along with the riots?"

"Yes, I go along with the riots."

"The cop cars burned, and destroying property."

"All of that, Tune; my people are angry."

"They have no right to destroy things like that. There are courts, they protect all people."

"They didn't protect Ernesto Diaz, Tune, same way that you and your dear L.C. Younger didn't protect Hernandez on his job."

"We made it up to him."

"Show me the court that is going to bring Diaz back to life."

"Constanza."

"Yes . . ."

"Are you sure it isn't because you're running for the city council, and maybe you want that congressional seat in the future."

She slapped Tune's face, hard. It was totally unexpected. "I never want to see you again. You are a real bastard. You made me do things that I thought I never would, Tune. You made me love an Anglo, a married man. You made me leave the things that I hold precious, my honor, my family, my purity, and you place no value on my honesty. Never try and see me again."

Constanza wordlessly left Tune standing where he was. She didn't look back, but walked out, resolute and determined. She managed to fight back her tears until after she closed the door behind her.

Tune sat on the sofa in the living room for hours thinking about what he had done. He finally lay back and fell asleep, not even caring to go into the bedroom. He had really messed up the one thing he truly cared for in his life.

Unshaven, and in the same clothes that he had worn the night before, Tune Richards kept an appointment that morning that he had made the previous day. At nine-thirty, Tune sat outside the door of John Travis Younger's office in the Texas National Bank. In the huge central hall, the twenty-foot portrait of Big John Jurdam looked down benignly on the depositors and those who came to do business in the bank. Tune Richards felt uncomfortable. The eyes of John Jurdam seemed to be everywhere, and the man he was going to see, John Travis, was now the president of Texas National. Melvin Jurdam's son-in-law had more than lived up to his arrogant claims.

Tune sat opposite John Travis's secretary. He tapped his toe nervously. He realized how unkempt he looked. The woman stared at him. Even the slight sound he made as he nervously fingered a copy of the *Wall Street Journal* appeared to disturb her. Finally, the buzzer on her telephone sounded. She picked up the handset and returned it without a word. She moved back her chair, rolling it quietly on the plastic mat and motioned to Tune to follow her.

It had been years since the fateful Thanksgiving Day dinner at the house on Montrose. That was the last time that Tune had seen John Travis. Tune had kept up with his progress. Photos of John Travis frequently appeared in the business section of the Houston papers, and in magazines that featured the goings and comings of Houston society. But, seeing him now, fleshier than Tune remembered, softer in his features, looking older than his years, made Tune realize the passage of time. As Tune reached across the desk to shake John Travis's hand, he saw a curious look in his eyes.

"It's been a long time," Tune muttered.

The banker looked at him strangely, "What are you doing here, Tune?"

"Well, John Travis, I don't know how to begin, but maybe you know that Black Diamond has been having a lot of problems."

"I know," John Travis replied, "HOUCORP is one of our customers, but I still don't understand what you're doing here."

"It's just that we have a very substantial need of money, John Travis, and we've been turned down by our own bank, and a couple of others. You're pretty much the last person I can look to. I thought about going to Devlin, but the two of us didn't part in that friendly a way, and I thought that between men, after all, L.C. *is* your father." Tune's voice trailed off.

"Where have you been?" John Travis asked.

"What do you mean?"

"You don't have any idea what happened?"

"What are you talking about?" Tune asked angrily.

John Travis turned over a newspaper he had on his desk. It showed a front-page photo of the dock area massively in flames. Tune grabbed the paper. The story told of a huge explosion, the result of a chemical fire at Black Diamond. The immense heat and the speed of the conflagration had virtually destroyed the Black Diamond wharfs, storage facilities, portside equipment, and the vessels that were tied up. Ten firemen were injured, and the flames were still not under control at the time the paper went to press.

Tune stared at John Travis in wild disbelief. "What about L.C.?"

John Travis sniffed, "It says that he went down to the docks. He had a stroke. They say he's paralyzed. That's what the radio said this morning. Tune, where the hell have you been? Don't tell me that you've got yourself a little gal you're playing house with. Looks that way to me."

Tune read the story in disbelief. "The story says that the fire came from the chemicals we were unloading yesterday. There were no such chemicals yesterday anywhere near Black Diamond, none at all."

John Travis tapped his pencil on his desk. "Well, be that as it may, that's the way it is now."

28

IT was three in the morning when Devlin was awakened by the ringing of the telephone by her bed. She slowly emerged from slumber and reached out her hand to pick up the receiver. The voice at the other end seemed dim and faraway until its insistence caused her to waken. Finally, Devlin identified the caller as an interne at Ben Taub Hospital.

With the carefully practiced technique used to inform the next of kin, he first established preliminaries. Was she Devlin Younger, the daughter of L.C. Younger? In desperation, Devlin demanded to hear the news. Without waiting for a full description of L.C.'s condition, Devlin hung up and switched on all the lights. She hastily pulled on her clothes and made her way downstairs and out to her car.

L.C. was in stable condition in the intensive care unit. Two nurses hovered over his bed as he was fed oxygen. Devlin stared at the ashen-faced, unmoving figure in the bed. Here was L.C., the man who had been the key influence in Devlin's life, a man jammed with vitality and fire, a man who Devlin suspected could travel twenty leagues in one step, a vegetable, invaded by the impersonal monitoring and life-support systems of the hospital.

Here was a captain, a pirate, a lover, a symbol of fierce independence, reduced to a helpless state of pale skin, angular bones, intruding pipes, conduits, and hoses, over which he had no say at all.

Devlin sat alongside the bed, looking for a sign of life, anticipating the flicker of an eyelid, a sign of the angry, unpredictable giant of her childhood.

For a moment, Devlin felt sorry for herself. This minute was *her* loss. Where had the protection gone from her life? Where was the only person in the world she knew would defend her, no matter what. He had been capable of creating sparks out of their clashing wills, but he had been there nonetheless as her last defense, her knight.

Devlin decided that she would be her father's protector. By the power of her prayer and dedication, somehow, L.C. would recover.

Devlin fantasized as she looked at the helpless creature lying in bed. This state was only temporary. Soon he would be well. How great his anger would be, to think that he had been helpless in some stranger's hands. Devlin, in her reverie, heard his voice, complaining against this unfamiliar surrounding, a hateful and malevolent confinement for what had been the freest of men.

Devlin decided that when L.C. could be moved, and that must be soon, she would take him home, not to Fairlawn, but to the house on Montrose. When L.C. awoke from his sleep, and she knew he would, he would be in his own surroundings, his home and bastion. Until that time, Devlin would remain with him in the house on Montrose. She would perform the required vigil, the watchful waiting, provide the ministering and love. Now, in fact, he was her child and she would not desert *him*!

Devlin stood up as the doctor entered the room. "I'm Mr. Younger's daughter. Tell me when he'll be able to go home, what I must do to make him comfortable."

"Miss Younger, I don't advise it. He would be better off in the hospital, where he can get anything he needs. The situation with a stroke is that other complications are bound to develop, and we can deal with them here."

"Doctor, my father is going to recover, and he'll do it in his own home. I'll care for him, and he'll have anything he needs."

"Miss Younger, please listen . . ."

"Doctor, listen to *me*. I know my father."

The house on Montrose seemed to have grown smaller when Devlin first arrived to organize it for her father's return. The neighborhood, which she had not seen for over eight years, had turned into a variegated bazaar, with Casbah-like shops catering to a bohemian array of local residents, and a continuing gaggle of tourists. From the downstairs window of L.C.'s study, Devlin watched the strange parade, so different from her memory.

Walking the neighborhood, Devlin trod the familiar turf, but it was all remote—the abandoned Southern Pacific railroad tracks on Graus-tark, the food market on Richmond where the faces now seemed inhospitable. A sign said that checks were cashed. They were open twenty-four hours a day. Walking along Montrose itself, boutiques abounded. She passed extravagantly dressed homosexual couples, Mex-ican children, tradespeople selling tawdry goods. On the corner of Montrose and Alabama, where one of the most elegant intersections in all Houston had once been, the only remaining landmark was the Younger house.

Devlin stood staring at the places of her childhood, tucked her hands into the belt loops of her jeans and bit her lip. She had expected it would be different coming home.

Devlin quickly took charge of Alma and Manuel, who had momentarily panicked when they learned about her father. They were reassured when they learned that Devlin was returning. Without saying a word, Alma made up Devlin's old room. Devlin quietly and unobtrusively returned to life in the house, living in the room she had known as a child.

Her first meeting with Tune in the hospital had been tense. Devlin saw a man she had not remembered. He appeared tentative and withdrawn, and said very little. Somehow, Devlin thought he was expecting something from her. It never came. Devlin made no personal inquiries about his life, and Tune appeared a total stranger to her. He was still as handsome as ever, but the nine years that had passed since that Thanksgiving Day were like eons.

Pressures at Black Diamond forced Tune to talk to her the day that L.C. was moved back into the house on Montrose. Devlin sat in her father's chair in his souvenir-lined study. Ship models, photos of the port, and yellowed clippings lined the wall. She leaned back in his swivel chair, feeling very comfortable to be sitting where he had sat. Tune sat opposite, uncomfortable and unhappy.

"Tune, why don't you spill it? I know you've been waiting this long."

"I went to see John Travis, the day that L.C. . . . ."

"What for?" she demanded. "What did you want to see him about?"

"Devlin, you don't understand how bad things are. He was the last person I could go to. L.C. didn't know it, but we needed money so bad—there was no one else."

Devlin stared at him. Where was the heroic figure she once knew, the man who every other boy in Houston idolized on the playing field, in the Marines?"

"Why didn't you come to me?"

"I didn't know how you'd feel about me, whether you'd do anything to help after what we'd been together."

"Oh, hell, Tune, we were lovers, big deal—but the situation must be different now, the insurance will cover it. Rebuilding will be tough with today's prices, but L.C. will be up and well again, you'll see, and I'll help, I promise I will."

Tune appeared embarrassed and speechless. "It won't be that easy."

"Tune, it never is, but let's make a start. Do you have the report on the damage, and the most recent financials on Black Diamond?"

"Devlin," he blurted, "it *wasn't* insured."

"Dammit," she shouted, "you must be joking."

"No," he muttered, "there was a whole string of violations. The insurance company found them over a year ago, and they wouldn't renew the insurance until we fixed them. It would have cost about a half million dollars, and L.C. didn't have the money, so the insurance lapsed."

"My God, Tune, and Black Diamond owes money too?"

"Yes," he said handing over the documents, "take a look."

Devlin scanned the top page, "You would have been forced into bankruptcy without the fire, and now, it's for sure." She raised her head and stared at Tune with her green eyes cold and demanding. "How in hell did you let things go this way?"

"It was L.C."

"You're not an infant, Tune, you knew what was happening."

"I guess I should have . . . but hell, Devlin . . . you know L.C." Devlin sat expressionless. "There's an offer from HOUCORP . . . they're willing to take over the land and assume the obligations . . . pay off the creditors, and that's the end of that. It would leave L.C. with nothing."

"No deal, Tune."

"Do you want to go into bankruptcy?"

"No, Tune, of course not. I'll pay off the creditors, and maybe L.C. will want to start over again when he gets well. At least that way he'll have the chance. I'll help. I promised I would."

"Devlin, you and I know that L.C. isn't going to start all over again. He's too old, even if he gets well, and that's not likely. The reason we got into the fix we did was because he wouldn't change his ways."

Devlin stared at him coldly, "Don't tell me that. If you had anything to contribute, it might have been different. How have you been spending your time, Tune Richards—married to a rich girl who screws everyone in town, and you're involved with some Mexican gal who you can't even take into polite society. *You* don't have any worries. Sue Lingen can afford the luxury of having a hero on the payroll, even if Black Diamond can't."

Tune got up, wordlessly. There was nothing he could say. She had nailed it down pretty damn well. Devlin sat staring at the wall as she heard Tune's heels on the hardwood floor, followed by the sound of the front door opening and closing behind him. God, she hated him for being so weak. Why hadn't he said something to stop her? Why had he let her get away with talking to him that way?

She walked out of L.C.'s study, and looked up the wide staircase, and felt the warm sunlight on her face coming through the colored glass of the skylight. She looked up, and saw the image of a Black Diamond tug, *Colfax I*, in the stained glass ceiling. Slowly, Devlin walked up the stairs to her room. Down the hall on the main landing, she saw one of the nurses who attended to L.C. She called to her. "How is he?" The nurse shrugged. "He's the same, Miss Younger, he's always the same."

For several weeks, Devlin was content to spend most of her time at the house on Montrose. It was almost impossible for any of the people at

Younger Oil to reach her on the phone, and clearly impossible for them to get an answer from her to their increasing daily problems.

Finally one afternoon, L. Carter Dixon III arrived unannounced. Alma came upstairs to L.C.'s room, where Devlin was sitting, doing nothing more than watch her father's motionless form.

"Señorita, there is a man downstairs. He works for you—a Mister Carter."

Devlin was annoyed at being disturbed. She reluctantly left L.C.'s room, and walked downstairs. Carter was waiting for her in the hallway. She greeted him perfunctorily and led him into L.C.'s study, and resumed her place at L.C.'s desk.

"Is it something important?"

He smiled grimly. "Devlin, are we friends?"

"Sure—of course we're friends."

"Well, I tell you what. Let's just both of us be friends forever, because I want to let you know that I'm quitting."

"What are you talking about?" she demanded angrily.

"Devlin, at least I got your attention. Do you know how you've been over the last weeks?"

"Carter, you know, it's my father. You know how he is. I'm the only one he can count on."

"To do what, Devlin?"

"To care for him, Carter. Haven't you any feelings?"

"I'll tell you what I don't have, Devlin, and that's any understanding of why you're in mourning."

"You son-of-a-bitch," she spit.

He smiled. "I see that I still have your attention."

He continued, "Devlin, you are doing nothing more for your father than a hired nurse could do. I know you love him, and that's fine. I know you care, and that's good. But I think that you're making a big mistake turning this place into a mausoleum, with you the chief mourner. I know what the doctors say, and I know how you feel. You may be right, but dammit, Devlin, you've got to live, and you've got to show the spark that put you where you are."

Devlin looked at him curiously.

"If you don't, you're as good as dead too, Devlin. They're closing in, and we are badly extended. You haven't paid any attention to business in a long time. Things won't wait till you see whether your prayers for L.C. work or not, and even if they do work, Devlin, what of *your* life? Are you supposed to quit living at the age of twenty-eight and care for your father for the rest of it?"

Devlin glared at him and drummed her fingers on the desk. Scarcely raising her voice, Devlin muttered, "What do you want of me?"

"Devlin, I want for you the same things you want for yourself. Excuse me, wanted, up till this thing with L.C. Your needs haven't changed. Younger Oil's needs haven't changed. I want you to pick yourself up and start living, and start working. I want you to get your things and come on down to the office and let me lay out the problems we have. We need you just as much as L.C. does, and you have just as much an obligation to the living as you do to him."

Devlin stood up. There was a smile on her face. "I knew that I was right to pick you out of the dung heap they call WESTEX." Her grin was larger still. "Carter, have I ever told you how much I like and admire you?"

Carter Dixon blushed.

"Dammit, you're shy, Carter. How am I gonna fix you up with my pretty sister if you blush when you get complimented?"

It was Devlin's standard joke, when she herself felt uncomfortable at someone's warm words. "Carter, what are we waiting for? You've got gas in your car, don't you? Let's git."

Carter talked animatedly on the trip downtown. Devlin listened, interested and involved. She asked questions and made comments.

"Our position in the Giddings wells is something you ought to consider."

"What choice do we have?"

"Devlin, we have close to seven million dollars invested in the field, and our people say that Fredrickson, our genius geologist, is spending money like it was just invented. He wants to try one more technique to try and frac a couple of old wells."

"Has anybody ever done it successfully?" Devlin asked.

"On a test basis, in special situations. Never on a big scale. He's convinced there's oil down there—a huge field, if we can only find the way to uncork it."

"What's involved, Carter?"

"About another three or four million, maybe more."

"Do we have it?"

"Not in cash, but we can borrow more against Conroy. That's no problem."

Devlin reflected, "We may need to borrow more, Carter. I've got to pay off some of my daddy's debts . . . better make it one trip to the bank. I'll give you some numbers to work with as soon as I get the word from Black Diamond's accountants. It'll be a big number, Carter, so make a nice polite request—no bad language—and wear a tie, a sincere one, when you go."

He laughed, but was very worried. He hoped she knew what she was doing. It was okay to gamble in oil; that's what the business was all about. It had worked in the Conroy field, but Devlin was pyramiding her bets in a crazy way, and now with the need for money to pay off Black Diamond debts, things were going to be very tight.

Later in the afternoon, following Devlin's meeting with people on her staff, a meeting in which her very presence made the bleak picture begin to show hope, she stood in front of the big window in her office, high above the city. Carter was gathering the reports and charts that had been spread out on her desk. He heard her clap her hands and call to him.

"Come take a look, Carter."

"At what, Devlin?"

"Look at the way downtown is being crowded out."

"Sure, I see. Maybe we ought to go into real estate and forget about oil."

"Hell, Carter, you ought to know that we are already in real estate."

"What and where?"

"Black Diamond—all of the area is close to one hundred acres, alongside and behind the ship channel. Now listen, Carter, this is a crazy idea, but what would you think if we turned the whole Black Diamond area into a new downtown development . . . business buildings, a sports complex, convention center, hotels—plenty of room for building condominiums—a whole darn city, close enough to what already is, but cheap enough in land price so that we can afford to build the most beautiful and the best. We'd have the most luxurious restaurants, a shopping palace . . . from around the world . . . like the port of New York . . . they have their Trade Center, those two big ugly buildings. We'd have a romantic view of the port—ships, tugs going and coming, going to far away places."

L. Carter Dixon III stared out the same window. All he saw was a gray ship channel in the distance, dirty low buildings, old access roads to warehouses, and in the middle, the huge darkened spot where Black Diamond used to be.

"Devlin, we're in the damn oil business."

"Carter, you're being antsy." Devlin could scarcely contain her excitement. "Carter, this is a touch of genius, use what we have—like the Austin Chalk fields—just do a little retouching, a little frac-ing, and there she goes, oil, buildings, hotels. I know what I'll call the whole complex. Skycastle . . . yep, that's it. It's going to be the biggest thing in Houston. Hell, Carter, Houston may make me a saint."

"Yeah? Joan of Arc had a vision too, Devlin, and they burned her at the stake."

"But she had fun, Carter. Be adventurous."

"Devlin, we are exposed, but big, and do you have any idea what this project of yours is going to cost?"

"No, Carter, and that's the beauty of it. Nobody else will care either. They'll just love the idea, and we'll have the money."

"Devlin, let me tell you that not everybody has the same romance in her spirit that you do, and not everybody has your . . . imagination, shall I call it?"

"Yes, Carter, and not everybody has five hundred acres of the most beautiful land on which to build Skycastle, overlooking the rest of the city. Look, Carter, unless you build *away* from what's been built, you can't *see* it. All of downtown will be part of the view."

"Yes, Devlin, I see," he said halfheartedly. "You know the history of the Shamrock Hotel and wildcatter Glenn McCarthy?"

"Uh-huh," she said, unimpressed.

"He should have stayed in oil, Devlin, the hotel nearly ruined him, and here you're about to do the same."

"Not the same, Carter. Not one hotel, three, and a sports complex."

"Isn't the Astrodome enough, Devlin?"

"Of course not, Carter, this is Houston. Spell it H-O-U-S-T-O-N. Nothing's too good for Houston."

Devlin felt euphoric as she drove back to the house on Montrose that evening. She had buried one of her problems, the Austin Chalk exploration, with another problem, Black Diamond, and had buried them both with an even bigger problem—Skycastle. Still, she felt incredibly light and unencumbered.

At dusk, she stared at the opposite corners on Montrose and Alabama and the gas stations that had been so ugly that morning. Now, they looked like modern art. She walked into the kitchen where Alma was preparing dinner. As she had years ago, Devlin went to the cupboard and dragged out a warm bottle of Coca-Cola. She unzipped the cap, and took a swig. "Alma, what's for dinner?" The Mexican woman smiled at her happiness. It had been a long time since she had felt it in the house. Things had changed. "Meat loaf," she replied. "Love meat loaf, Alma, how about some tortillas with them, and chili, and some ice cream for dessert?" Devlin patted her trim stomach. "Think I'll get fat?" The Mexican woman laughed, "No, not you señorita."

Devlin walked through the swinging door, sipping from the bottle as she did, and walked up the stairs to the main landing. Quietly, she approached L.C.'s door, and carefully opened it. In the dim light she saw the nurse reading by the bedside lamp. L.C. was lying perfectly still, his eyes closed, an intravenous needle sticking into his vein.

"Is he okay?" The nurse nodded.

Devlin left the room, and walked down the hallway to her own. She lay down on her bed, her boots resting on the bottom bedboard.

Devlin placed the Coke bottle on the night table and saw framed pictures on the wall that she had seen for a lifetime, but had not even recognized as there. They were drawings she had done as a child.

She remembeed clearly when she had made them. They had pleased L.C. so. She had crayoned them by the light of her bedlamp, when she should have been asleep. She remembered how L.C. had come into her room each night to put her to sleep, telling her fairytales of his own invention.

The prince always wore boots and carried a six-gun, and the princess always had ginger-colored hair and green eyes. L.C. had said the princess in his stories was the most beautiful princess in the world. The stories had delighted her. They had quieted her fears of the dark with the knowledge that her father was always there for her. The handsome prince was hers, to protect and defend her.

Devlin remembered the magic land of her father's creation, peopled with gloriously colored animals and waterbirds, like in the Buffalo Bayou of the past, subjects who loved the princess dearly, and the happiest of happy-ever-afters. She had filled up page after page of drawings of the land and people in his stories.

The prince and princess lived in this magic land, in a palace so beautiful, so extraordinary, that father had named it "Skycastle." Devlin smiled at the memory.

L.C. would be very pleased at what she was about to do.

29

THE NEXT WEEKS were full of delight for Devlin. Skycastle would be her very own creation. It would rise like a phoenix out of the ashes of Black Diamond. In her mind, she pictured how the achievement of this dream would somehow make everything right for L.C., and like a sleeping prince, he would awaken on the day that Skycastle became a reality.

In the meantime, the prospect of what Devlin had envisioned in her fantasy was overwhelming. Before she made a public announcement of her plans, Devlin was certain that she would first need designs of this city within a city.

Devlin envisioned soaring steeples climbing high into the clouds, spires that lifted your eyes, light, airy, gossamer buildings, built off the ground, seeming to float in air.

She realized that what she wanted was so unusual that no western designer could capture her concept. Finally, Devlin decided upon a Japanese artist and sculptor whose work she had seen in a Houston's Museum of Fine Arts. Unfortunately, he was not an architect, but in Devlin's innocence she could not foresee the problems this would create.

A Los Angeles firm of architects was more than willing to do preliminary site inspection, make a survey, and provide initial plans. They were offended to learn that Devlin only wanted their technical functions. The Japanese artist would do the conceptual work. The senior partner of the Los Angeles firm who came to Houston was mollified when Devlin offered him twice his usual fee for the task. He returned to California content in the knowledge that Devlin Younger was rich, but would be much poorer before long. She was an amateur, and whatever happened to her Towers of Babel, with a California architect and a Japanese artist and sculptor who spoke no English, would be her own fault. He would pocket the money from the headstrong and very beautiful young Texas woman.

264

Devlin decided that Skycastle's hotels would be something beyond conventional commercial efforts. She first thought that one of the major hotel chains might be interested in managing the three structures she planned on building, but they turned her down when they learned of her stringent design demands. Devlin envisioned an international flavor for Skycastle's hotels. Claridge's in London is without peer in its country. The Ritz in Paris is the ultimate in France. In Rome, it's the Hassler. She quickly dispatched Carter to meet with the heads of each of those hotels. Each would respectively manage and be responsible for Skycastle Claridge's, the Skycastle Ritz, and the Hassler Skycastle. When they demanded a free hand in ordering special beds, furnishings, linens, silver, and training hundreds of people in advance of employment, Devlin agreed. Further insanity, but by God, Skycastle would have hotels of such incredible luxury that people who were used to the very best in Europe could only find it at Skycastle.

Devlin envisioned a spacious open area, seemingly out in the air but actually enclosed by Plexiglas, that would become the Casbah of Skycastle. The most elegant purveyors of laces, linens, candles, toys, bibelots, foodstuffs, game, cheeses, herbs, spices, and precious handmade goods from all over the world, would be sold in open-air stalls. Beautiful Texas girls, in brief attire, would accompany visitors on their shopping and bring them to each of the stalls, speaking their languages.

The sports complex would be both an indoor and outdoor amphitheater for football, baseball, and soccer. Rodeo would be featured daily. Steer-roping, bull-riding, and trick-riding would be continuous daily activities. Houston was the West and Skycastle would be the best of the West. A movie complex, both for seeing films and for making them, would be part of Skycastle. Some of her friends in Hollywood would have the right connections to start a huge moviemaking industry right in the midst of the hundreds of thousands of visitors. She remembered the very successful Universal Pictures tour. Skycastle would have one as well.

Major electronic companies would be invited to install innovative labor- and energy-saving devices for the twenty new buildings that would be part of the first wave of construction. She would make the city of Houston build new roadways, improve existing land, condemn unsightly access roads to Skycastle, and build a beautiful, tree-lined esplanade from other parts of the city to Skycastle.

Then Devlin smiled to herself. On the seventh day she would rest.

Curiously enough, the Japanese artist and the California architectural firm, though they could find no common language, with their joint efforts did create a most beautiful and remarkable design for a city complex. True to Devlin's vision, the entire city of Skycastle appeared to be resting above ground, as if a fairyland were magically suspended in space. Below the jutting spires and the globes, spheres and soaring shapes, was a huge dark labyrinth, enclosed in black basalt, in which all of the complex machinery, the power sources for the entire city were to be housed. It would be like an enclosed inferno, allowing the beauty and grace of Skycastle to be unencumbered by the mundane problems of heat, light, air conditioning or other pedestrian matters.

Less than six months after Devlin conceived the enterprise, newspapers throughout Texas, the nation, and the world, displayed front-page architectural drawings of the miracle that would be Skycastle.

Network television, international journalists, and the curious from all over the world were properly impressed. For the first euphoric day, Devlin thought that she had pulled the sword Excalibur from the enchanted rock. She had done all that she had to do. The rest would be forthcoming in a parade of people from all over the world who would want to make her vision a reality. Unfortunately, she hadn't recognized the reluctance on the part of most people to accept change, novelty, and particularly to accept a twenty-eight-year-old woman's concept of a bold new project.

When Devlin arrived at the world headquarters of IBM, it was the first of several appointments that she had fixed for this first trip to New York. Two hundred and fifty thousand dollars worth of art and slides plus a recorded musical accompaniment, plus documentation of all her facts and figures came along with her. A group of men from the architectural firm, statisticians, and technicians accompanied her. The dark-suited and serious key executives of IBM were all in attendance. They may have been curious to learn the details of this fairyland. Or their curiosity may have come from their desire to see Devlin Younger, its creator.

Devlin thought seriously about how to dress for this first meeting. She was certain that the executives would not appreciate a western cowgirl outfit, the jeans, workshirt, and boots that she favored. In their place, Devlin wore a handsome Yves St. Laurent suit in navy blue, with a white-and-blue polka-dot silk shirt, and a red kerchief. It took her a while to accustom herself to the way she looked in the mirror. She smiled to herself. She was prepared to make certain small sacrifices for Skycastle.

After the hour-long presentation in the IBM private theater, there was no doubt in her mind that the executives were impressed. The bewildering freshness and audacity of Skycastle were infectious. "Miss Younger," the chairman said with a smile, "you are to be congratulated. It makes my head swim to see what your plans are. My only question is why no one ever thought of approaching an enterprise with as much imagination as you seem to have."

Devlin smiled. "No one else you deal with is twenty-eight years old and a woman." The chairman laughed. "That's part of the problem, Miss Younger. You understand that we are a conservative company, and if we were to decide to occupy the first building in Skycastle, it would mean that we would have to make immediate plans for such a move. It would probably mean the relocation of three or four thousand employees, the transfer of their families, the movement of functions from other parts of the country to Houston, and the reassignment of responsibilities, not to mention the necessary computer equipment which would have to be built to specifications."

Devlin nodded in stupefaction. How had she been so dumb? It was a damn snowball. IBM had to know that Skycastle was certainly going to be built, and could be occupied by a definite date.

"Miss Younger, when do you plan construction to begin?"

"We'll begin excavating in sixty days," she said, making the decision as she spoke. The architect looked at her dumbfounded. She had no tenants, no financing, and she had just committed herself to digging the biggest hole in the history of America since the Grand Canyon.

Devlin laughed at their consternation. "I just made the decision now. My architects think that I may be a little rash."

The chairman nodded, "Miss Younger, I hope you're not. I appreciate that this means a substantial commitment, but that would only be the very tip of the iceberg. I don't think it's any secret—you don't have the financing to do the building as yet. I think I can speak for my board of directors, we would have considerable interest in being with you in Skycastle, but only if we could be assured that Skycastle will really come to pass."

The chairman stood up, as did the rest of his group. He came over to Devlin, shook her hand, and walked out of the screening room, leaving Devlin with more problems than she had before. If he had said "no," and others were to say the same thing, her problems would be over. Skycastle would never be built, and the embarrassment of the announcement and the expenditure of several million dollars on the plans would be the limit of her danger. Now, if others were to act as IBM did, she would be walking an incredible tightrope. "We'll do it if you prove it." The only way to prove it, would be to do it.

The IBM people thought she was pretty, and the Yves St. Laurent suit looked like a dream, but she could have worn dungarees if only she could convince them that it would happen. She had to get the money, and it would be a mountain of money. Five hundred million dollars would be needed, and that would only be the beginning. That would be stage one.

The chief architect came over to her after the IBM people had left, "Miss Younger, do you know what you're doing? You really don't *have* to excavate, it will cost a fortune."

"I gave my word. If I took it back, it would cost me even more." Devlin walked out of the room and in the direction of the chauffeured Cadillacs that had driven the contingent to Purchase, New York. She

267

would be departing with a quarter of a million dollars worth of a traveling circus that told how wonderful Skycastle would be. But nobody would believe her.

Devlin was silent on the road back to Manhattan's Regency Hotel where she had set up headquarters. Sitting next to her was Charles Thornhill, the managing partner of the California architectural firm.

"Miss Younger, it would be a tragedy if something were to prevent Skycastle from coming into being. It is a magnificent concept."

"Don't worry, Charlie, I'll get the money, if I have to play poker day and night for a year."

"Miss Younger, I appreciate your sense of humor, we're talking about hundreds of millions of dollars."

Devlin laughed, "You've never seen me play poker. Never mind, Mr. Thornhill . . . we're gonna dig the hole. I've got to show everybody that this isn't a joke, and I'm going to get the money. Get yourself a pick and shovel. We may need willing hands."

Charles Thornhill wasn't used to dealing this way. His old-line firm was distinguished by its conservatism, stability, and reliability. For a moment he considered that it might not be appropriate for the firm's image to be involved in a project that was probably doomed to failure. He could see the cavernous excavation lying open and empty for years to come, filling slowly with refuse and water. He recoiled at the thought of a project widely trumpeted, only to be consigned to the ignominy of defeat. No, Charles Thornhill would not like to be associated with such a failure.

He reflected on this as the limousine took them both down the parkway into Manhattan. How could he bow out gracefully, particularly now that Thornhill Associates had pocketed huge fees in the preparation of the plans. Even today's appearance had been charged for outrageously.

He had seen the computer readout on the billings to Devlin Younger for the work already done. Miss Younger, as pretty as she was, did not appear to be smart enough to come in out of the rain. It was very, very profitable to be in business with Devlin Younger, but Thornhill considered that the time was very soon coming for him to abandon ship. What a shame.

In a week, Devlin had been to see the real estate investment heads of Prudential, Metropolitan Life, and Connecticut General insurance companies. The story was exactly the same from each of them. "Surely, Miss Younger, you understand that we must be conscious of our obligations to our customers, the people who purchase insurance from us. They look to us to be conservative in our investments, so that in the event of a claim, we will have sufficient assets to cover our obligations." They continued, "We must, Miss Younger, be extremely cautious about where we place our funds. If only we could be assured that by giving you the money, Skycastle would actually be built. We would need to know that the money was being properly administered and, if there were cost overruns, that your company would have the resources to complete building. Then, in addition, we would need to know that you had at least forty percent of Grade A occupants signed by the beginning of construction."

Devlin shook her head, "You know of course that I can get the occupants if I can assure them that it's going to be built." They nodded. Devlin continued, "In the last week, ten major corporations have indicated their interest in taking big parts of it."

"Miss Younger, interest by major corporations costs them nothing. To hand you a half billion dollars would be an indication of more than our good faith."

"What you're saying is that you'll give me the money if I don't need it."

They smiled, "Miss Younger, you're young, and quite attractive."

"And a woman," Devlin added pointedly.

"It seems to us," they concluded, "that you would be very well advised to turn this project over to a company that has the means to carry out this deal. We would be pleased to suggest the Lord Construction Company in Dallas—your own state. We know them, and we respect Tarquin Lord. Now, coincidentally, we've spoken to Mr. Lord about this project, and I might add that he has an interest in this, provided that we are interested. Of course if he were, then we definitely would be."

Devlin restrained her anger.

When she returned to the Regency Hotel, there were phone messages from L. Carter Dixon III. Devlin phoned him and told him to order the excavation. The bids were all in the same neighborhood, around four million dollars.

"Devlin, you're going to have the world's largest swimming pool if this doesn't work."

"I know, Carter, but it's going to work."

"But are you sure?"

"Sure I'm *not* sure. This is the worst fix I've ever been in. There are a couple of thousand men, in dark suits and big damn offices, waiting for me to fall on my face. They'll jump on my bones, cart them away, and smile and say, she was too damn smart for her own good, thought she knew the damn score. Well, that isn't too swift for me, Carter. I'm one gal who is as proud as my daddy, and they never got him down."

"Devlin, we need more money for Giddings . . . the first frac-ing didn't work, and Fredrickson, our genius geologist, thinks that we may have the answer with some new kind of infusion . . . only thing is that it will cost us more."

"Can we borrow more?" she asked resignedly.

"Devlin, I guess so, but they'll want you to pledge everything you own

. . . all of your personal possessions—Fairlawn and such."

"What do you mean by 'and such'?"

"I mean everything."

"My douche bag?"

Carter was embarrassed, "Well . . ."

"Tell them that they have to leave that out, Carter. Oh hell, throw that in too, if I go belly up, what the hell fun would anything be."

"About Giddings?"

"Give him the money, Carter, there's oil out there, somewhere."

"Only God knows exactly where, Devlin, not meaning to be sacrilegious or anything. But I think that He's got an exclusive consulting agreement with another company."

Devlin laughed, "Borrow the money, Carter. Start the digging. Hock the typewriters and any damn thing you have to, just hold out a deck of cards. I may need it to make a living if this stuff doesn't hold."

"What about T-Bird?"

"I'm going to stop by Big Spring and see him, Carter, and see whether he'll lend us a hand for old times."

"Devlin, there's been a couple of phone calls from Jamie Lord in the last couple of hours. Says it's crucial you call him the minute you're back in town. He's in Houston."

"I wonder how Dallas is surviving without him."

"Devlin, what about bringing a partner in like Lord Construction?"

"You always thought me a lady, Carter, yes?"

"Well, kind of."

"A little?" she asked.

"Ah, yes, at least a little."

"Well, Carter, you hang up, and I'll tell you what I think of that idea into a dead phone. I'd like you to keep the rest of your illusions." L. Carter Dixon III took Devlin seriously and rang off.

Big Spring Airport took small jets, and Devlin's Lear made the trip from LaGuardia in New York in less than three hours. Devlin reflected on the luxury of travel on the private wings of a million-dollar plaything, ready to roll the very minute she was on board, free of the problems of check-in, security, check-out, and handcrafted perfectly to her taste. She might not have that luxury much longer.

It had been a long while since she had seen T-Bird, and she hungered for the contact. The time years ago on Conroy had been the best in her life, on the way to making it. It hadn't been so much fun afterwards, trying to live through the expectations of what she thought success was all about. It was nice to have everything she wanted. Every whim could be satisfied with a check, but that wasn't as much fun as she thought it would be.

Now, it was like the old times, when every move was tinged with the prospect of failure. It was the doing of it that was the most fun. And yet,

270

when Devlin thought that perhaps she might have to start all over again if her hopes were too big for reality, she shuddered at the thought of failure. She was running her biggest risk right now.

Before, there had been the certain knowledge that no matter what happened, there was always L.C. to fall back on. There was always that quiet cushion to her life, her father. Now, there was none, and she was playing fast and loose with everything. She had a responsibility to care for him. Would L.C. have approved? She knew that he had always been prepared to risk big. To hell with the problems, he would say, "Work it out."

Coming down for a landing at Big Spring, she expected to see T-Bird waiting for her as she disembarked. When she phoned to tell him of her plans, the phone was answered by a woman. She asked to speak to T-Bird. The voice said that he wasn't available, but she would give him the message. Devlin gave the woman the information. Would she tell T-Bird that she would appreciate his meeting her at the airport? The woman said yes in a strange way. Devlin didn't know whether that meant that T-Bird would be there, or that she would tell him. It was curious.

The Lear jet rolled to a stop. The door opened and the stairs lowered. Devlin stepped outside. It was late afternoon in early spring, weather not unlike the way it had been on the fateful eve of Lady Luck No. 1. At the bottom of the steps, a young woman in a simple cloth coat stood shivering in the chill. Devlin was wearing her handsome mink. Her St. Laurent suit and Charles Jourdan shoes, part of her New York uniform, made her an anomaly in the middle of West Texas. The young woman made directly for her. Devlin thought her face was familiar.

"Miss Younger, glad that you could get to come."

Devlin held out her hand and looked for T-Bird.

"He can't come, Miss Younger, he's been in bed for almost ten weeks now, and he can't make the effort."

"What's the matter?"

"He had a heart attack. You know it wasn't the first, and while he was recouping from this one, he had another. Wouldn't think of staying at the hospital, so I'm caring for him at home."

Devlin looked puzzled at the young woman.

"You forgot me, Miss Younger. No reason you shouldn't. Remember when T-Bird was working at the Denny's next to the Holiday Inn?" Devlin nodded. "Well, when he was bussing tables, I was a waitress. He took a shine to me, and after you and he hit it big in oil, he asked me to marry him."

"You're T-Bird's wife?"

"Yes," she said shyly, "Sally Truslow Johnson is my name, just Sally to you, Miss Younger."

"Devlin, please. I'm so happy that T-Bird has someone to care for him."

The young woman pointed to an old Buick that was parked nearby.

271

"That there is my car. You don't mind coming into town in that one, do you? It's a little dirty in the back, from taking the dogs to the vet, but it'll get us there. I was going to put you into the Holiday Inn. It's still the best place in town, but T-Bird said that you wouldn't hear of staying any place but with us. It won't be as comfortable as the hotel, but you'll be close. Our house is pretty small."

As Devlin got into the car, she brushed away the newspapers and wrappers on the front seat. She wondered what had happened to T-Bird. He was an equal partner with her, and regularly huge checks had gone out to him in Big Spring. Devlin hadn't kept count, but she knew that he had received millions of dollars in income over the last six years.

Sally read her thoughts, "T-Bird didn't keep it. I mean the money. He just gave it away, Devlin. Not that he did wrong, you understand, but it just went through his fingers as fast as it came in . . . those big checks and all."

The Buick started and Devlin sat in deep sadness. "I understand," she said simply. Sally stared straight ahead. "Not that I minded, you understand. I never married T-Bird for his money, but he gave it to a lot of undeserving folks. Some of it went to prison funds to help some of the folks in jail all over the country when they got out. You know that he was in Huntsville for a time." Devlin nodded. "But the most of it went to straight-out crooked oilmen who were in need. He never gave a damn about signing a paper, or asking for the money back. If they was in a spot, T-Bird would whip out his checkbook and write a check for whatever they needed, and maybe a little more to have some fun with."

The Buick was traveling down the snow-edged road into the town. "We had a bigger and nicer house, but we had to move. Miss Younger, how come there wasn't no money for the last couple of months?"

"We've been reinvesting it in some new fields, Sally, and I've put everything that I own into a new project. Maybe I shouldn't have."

"Don't be sad, Miss Younger, we all fall on hard times every so often. It don't mean nothing at all. If T-Bird lives, then everything will be all right. I really love that man, Miss Younger."

"I do too, Sally, I can't wait to see him."

"Miss Younger, tell him all the good news you can. He really needs cheering. You understand."

Devlin nodded.

30

THE OFFICES of Lord Construction in Dallas were unlike anything else in Texas. Tarquin Lord, the mythical king whose reputation for power was only exceeded by his lust for glory, ruled his legions of worldwide engineers and artisans from a penthouse suite on the roof of the Lord Building in downtown Dallas.

The moment Devlin emerged from the elevator on the thirty-fifth floor, she was immersed in the Lord atmosphere, quiet, calm, serene. A very upper-class British secretary stood at the elevator as Devlin got off. She introduced herself, and asked Devlin to follow her. As Devlin walked down the corridor, she was struck by the quiet of the place. A deep beige carpet on the floors, beige felt on the walls, and recessed spotlights overhead seemed to continue endlessly.

She saw quietly dressed, discreet-looking secretaries sitting outside beige private offices. The occasional gentle burr of a telephone indicated activity. The softspoken tap of a keyboard and the quiet movement of papers was testament to the fact that business was being conducted in an untroubled manner.

Along the hallway, Devlin passed a continuous display of modern art, light, simple, and unobtrusive. Its colors were muted, as was everything else she observed. Devlin was wearing her own brand of clothes. She wore a whisper-thin pair of suede pants, custom-made boots, a turquoise silk shirt that was more open than not, and her Bulgari bracelet of rubies, diamonds, and sapphires. Devlin's custom clothes, ginger-colored hair, and her long-legged frame made her feel like a circus poster in this restrained atmosphere.

Devlin had decided to look pretty, and to make a good impression, but it seemed that she emerged from another planet. Lord Construction Company might very well have been a museum or a Christian Science reading room. She looked very much out of place.

A pair of majestic double doors opened for her, and the secretary motioned her toward an antechamber next to Tarquin Lord's office. Two other young women, as attractive as the first, with the same beige silk shirtwaist dresses were at their secretarial desks. Instantly, the center door to Tarquin Lord's office opened, and Devlin walked inside. Jamie Lord, seated in front of his father's desk, stood up to greet her with a wide smile.

"Devlin, I know how busy you are, but dad and I are very glad that you could manage to break away."

Devlin smiled, and shook Jamie's hand, and then addressed the tall, silver-haired, distinguished-looking man behind the desk. Tarquin Lord looked regal. He had cloudy, gray eyes, and a noble head. His cold, dry hand reached forward to grasp Devlin's. She looked in his eyes and saw absolutely nothing. A lifetime of communicating blank stares to mask his intentions had evolved, forcing others to think what they would. Tarquin Lord thought what he chose, and no one was the wiser.

The spacious office was a masterpiece of understated elegance. A green marble pedestal held an absolutely plain stainless-steel top. The only tool of his trade in view was a silver-gray phone, recessed in the desk. It contained an array of buttons that appeared to be capable of contacting anyone and commanding anything anywhere.

On the walls were a Rembrandt and a Titian, handsomely lit. A section of the office was given to a sunken sitting room area, and at the head of the U-shaped couches was a Chinese throne chair. Devlin smiled to herself. Tarquin Lord had absolutely no identity crisis. He was by his own admission a reigning monarch. Devlin searched for the princely scepters, and fully expected members of a royal guard to appear and sound the trumpets.

"I've told my father all about you, Devlin. You've got a big fan in him already."

"Jamie, I'm happy about that. Mr. Lord, I've never seen such beautiful offices. I fully expected to see the Mormon Tabernacle Choir appear in a doorway. But that's the only disappointment I feel."

Tarquin Lord did not consider the remark amusing. He ignored it and emerged from behind his desk. He looked out the window. "I don't suppose you know Dallas the way we Lords do, Miss Younger."

"I must say that I know it as much as I want to, Mr. Lord. Houston is a bit like taking a shower with your clothes on, but it's what I'm used to. The only thing about Houston that makes me believe in God is that He must have invented air conditioning to make it heaven on earth."

Jamie smiled embarrassedly. His father was still unmoved.

"Mr. Lord, I have heard your name mentioned for the last ten days when I was in New York. You must have a set of burning ears, because every time I sat down to talk Skycastle, all they wanted to talk about was Tarquin Lord."

"I'm very pleased that I have a good reputation, Miss Younger. It

274

comes from generations of making a contribution to our city, our state, and our nation."

Jamie must have sensed Devlin's impatience with his father's pronouncements. "Something to drink, Devlin?" She nodded. By a secret signal the English secretary opened the door an instant later and looked expectantly at them.

"Miss Younger would like some refreshment. Jamie, would you like anything?"

"Yes, dad. Coffee, please. Devlin?"

"Warm Coca-Cola."

The secretary turned. It was a mark of her professionalism that she showed no reaction to the bizarre request. That rankled Devlin. She hoped it would have.

"Miss Younger, about Skycastle, our people have noted with considerable interest the concept you developed. We ourselves have been working for several years on a comparable approach to a city within a city in the Southwest, not adding to the downtown congestion, but simply by building another downtown."

"Where would you put it?" Devlin asked.

"It would work many places, and I suspect that Houston is as good a place as any to start."

"Houston will be the biggest city in the world before long, Mr. Lord."

"That may be as may be, Miss Younger, but when it does become that, if indeed it does, I certainly will go out of my way to avoid it."

"Hmmm . . ." was all that Devlin said. As Tarquin Lord spoke, she became more and more conscious that he had no accent at all. Devlin wouldn't have noticed a Texas accent. It would appear natural to her. She spoke that way, and everyone else in Texas did too. On the other hand, she had had ten days of exposure to New York, and heard a conglomeration of sounds and regional accents, mostly East Coast, that grated on her ear. Whatever historical background the Lord family had since the Pleistocene Period, somehow Tarquin Lord had been totally sanitized. Just like his desk top, his offices, and as Devlin looked at the handsome face of Jamie Lord, so perhaps even his son.

"Devlin, I talked to Dad at considerable length. We got all the reports in from New York. Everybody seems to agree that Skycastle has a big chance to succeed, but I think that you need some help."

Tarquin Lord was astounded at the breech his son made in his careful presentation that would have followed a logical and thoughtful pattern. Jamie had blundered in failing to maintain his distance. "Miss Younger, what my son says is true. Lord Construction has the experience and the financial capability to bring this project to completion. I've seen some of your plans, and although they are imaginative and daring, they will have to undergo some modifications to make them cost effective. After all, we can't be building a whole city just for the sake of the residents. There has to be an incentive for the builder."

275

"I don't think that I'd be inclined to change anything, Mr. Lord."

He looked at Devlin cooly and shrugged. At that moment the secretary entered with coffee in an antique porcelain service. Devlin's Coke was in a crystal goblet. Devlin was hoping it would still be in the bottle, so she could shock the pants off the two of them by swigging from it. Alas, she didn't have the opportunity.

"What sort of deal did you have in mind, Mr. Lord?"

"I thought that you would contribute the land, Miss Younger, and we would stand behind the construction. We would both be partners, in the ratio of the value of the land to the building. You've had expenses along the way, you're in the middle of excavation, and we would take that over. You would be reimbursed for the plans you've paid for. What I'm proposing is that Lord Construction would take the worry off your hands."

"How would you figure the value of the land, Mr. Lord?"

"Well, it clearly is depressed land not of any more value than comparable warehouse space alongside the ship channel. We would have it appraised by some outside party, just to be fair."

"I see," Devlin said meaningfully.

Tarquin Lord began to wax more effusive. He had the feeling that Devlin had softened up considerably. "Of course, you would benefit from the city we'd be constructing on the land, but it would be the construction that would make it all possible."

"Mr. Lord, who would have the say about what went, and what didn't?"

"Simply the builders, Miss Younger—Lord Construction. IBM and the others would be looking to us to ensure that our stamp of quality went on the project. Apart from that, as you discovered, it almost certainly is doomed to failure. After all, a modest percent of something is better than one hundred percent of nothing."

For the first time, Tarquin Lord smiled. He was happy in the presentation he made. He was convinced that it had been straightforward and convincing. Perhaps it was tough in its terms, but after all she was only a young woman who had been very lucky in oil. From what he heard, he understood that her finances were stretched paper-thin, and if he understood anything about human nature, after a bit of reflection she would grab it. He was certain that she wouldn't say yes at this juncture. Let her think about it, he said to himself. Do not press, he thought. How many times had he told men in his employ, and particularly his son Jamie, that high pressure is counterproductive. Simple, gentle application of reality is all that is necessary. The passage of time brings things your way. The Lord family can wait. Things always come around. He sat and waited as the very attractive young woman sipped her Coca-Cola. The drink itself was repugnant to him. At room temperature it was a desecration.

Devlin smiled at Tarquin Lord and put down her drink. "Mr. Lord, in the spirit of fair play you have proposed that everything that I have done, everything that I have risked, all the work that has preceded this minute is worth practically nothing—the value of second-rate land. Your share of Skycastle will be paid for by one or more insurance companies, whom you have charmed to death over the years. Then in addition, I know that you plan to change the design, and Skycastle will be just another Lord money machine." Devlin stared into his gray eyes, boring into them with all her might. "In looser language, Mr. Lord, you plan to rape me, and have me pay for the privilege."

Devlin stood up and smiled. Her green eyes were dancing with pleasure. She guessed that she had really done it this time, blown Skycastle out of the water. It had been an extraordinary gesture, but one she didn't regret. Tarquin Lord looked stunned. Jamie Lord was beet red with embarrassment. Devlin started for the door, which opened at her foot pressure. Jamie Lord followed her, imploring her to wait.

"Devlin, for God's sake, nobody talks to Dad that way."

Devlin was striding down the beige carpeted corridor. Secretaries were suddenly paying attention. "Jamie, who the hell does he think he is?"

"Devlin . . . the deal could be improved. I'll admit that. I'm sure Dad didn't mean it to be his last offer. Stick around, let's talk this over. Hell, don't you know that it doesn't make a damn bit of difference who owns what?"

Devlin was approaching the elevator and pressed the button. "What do you mean by *that*?"

"Devlin, you can figure it out. I'm the only son and heir to the Lord name and money, and all that Dad wants is for me to be happy."

"And be President."

"Yeah, well, that's in the cards, he had the money set aside to do it. It'll happen—faster even than old Joe Kennedy bought it for Jack—but then, you and I can have the whole damn thing."

"You and I?"

"Yes, you and I are going to get married, you know that."

The elevator arrived and the doors opened. An elderly couple who entered first thought they heard the ginger-haired beauty tell the handsome blond man to "go fuck himself." Or did they hear wrong?

Devlin was preoccupied in her thoughts on the flight to Houston. She had gone off like a misplaced rocket in her meeting with Tarquin Lord. She disliked the man intensely. His superior ways and snobbish attitude had gotten to her. On the other hand, why had she dealt with him the way she did? Why had she burned her bridges behind her?

Tarquin Lord had outlined a deal that on the face of it was a legal theft. He had looked down his purebred nose, from the background of generations of privilege, and had *told* her what to do. He had wiped her off the earth as someone of no consequence. No matter what the cost, and it may just have cost her the ability to make Skycastle come to pass, Devlin couldn't accept that. It hadn't only been luck that made Conroy come true. It wouldn't only be luck if she made Skycastle a reality.

She fired herself with anger. Jamie Lord, the forty-fourth President of the United States. Devlin Lord, the First Lady of the United States. What a laugh. Except that Tarquin Lord would probably have his way. Every TV station, billboard, matchbook cover across America would have Jamie Lord's picture on it. What Jamie Lord couldn't do the advertising boys could. Jamie was pretty enough for a postage stamp. Devlin grimaced. She would have to satisfy herself without the White House. Meager pickings.

Men! What made them think that their offer of marriage was the only thing that every woman was waiting to hear? What did they think they had that every woman wanted? Someone to watch over them? Someone to tell them what to do? Someone to crowd them off the map? Tune had thought his offer was good as fact. Jamie Lord figured that it was always understood. All he had to do was to say he was ready. Well, dammit, she wasn't.

Sex? There were good times and there were bad times. She had had it with the athletes, and she had had it with the tender, loving men who had digested books on women's sexual rights, and were intent on following the dotted line to take women to the promised land. It was like going to the AAA for a routemap on how to get from Broken Elbow to Fractured Fibula.

Men could follow the route, but there was nothing natural or exciting about it. There was nothing in the way of self-discovery.

For the time being, she could take it or leave it, and as far as she was concerned, save it up for some national holiday, when the banks were closed, and businesses were shut down. Right now she needed money, and she needed inspiration. Her holes in the ground were eating her up alive.

When the Lear jet taxied to the ramp and let down the stairs, Devlin saw L. Carter Dixon III waiting. He looked troubled. Only two hours had gone by since she last spoke to him from Dallas. What could have gone wrong now? On the drive from the airport, he told Devlin.

"It's not a good day," he stated solemnly.

"You can say that again."

"I mean *really* not a good day."

"Carter, don't fool around. What happened? Is my father okay?"

"Yep, Devlin, but Younger Oil isn't."

"Giddings?"

"Well, Giddings, and the borrowings. The sum total of what has happened, Devlin, is that someone has bought all of our bank borrowings *from* the bank, and we don't owe the bank anymore, we owe another party."

"Why would anyone do that?"

"Well, banks get nervous from time to time, and when someone comes in and offers to take their place, pay back all their money, what happens then is the bank bends down on the floor and kisses their shoes."

Without really asking, Devlin knew the answer, but still she inquired. "Don't tell me, let me guess."

Carter sighed with discomfort. "WESTEX Petroleum, and they sent over a demand notice three hours ago. We've got to pay back the money we borrowed or they foreclose.

"Let's kill those bastards."

"Devlin, I like your spirit, but that's not going to prevent them from foreclosing on everything you own."

"You mean Younger Oil . . ."

"Devlin, I don't know if you saw those men at the ramp going into your Lear when you got out, but they went in to take an inventory of everything you've got there—the whiskey in the bar, the potato chips, the magazines in the rack, all the equipment . . . ."

"No," Devlin squealed.

"And when you get to River Oaks, Devlin, you'll find an army of accountants climbing through every single thing you own, your jewelry, furs, paintings, furniture, garden equipment, all your clothes, shoes, dresses, boots—every damn thing."

"What do they want, Carter?"

"I'll tell you what they *don't* want, Devlin, they don't want you to pay the money back that you owe the bank, and the reason is they want to own the Conroy field, and they want to own our leases in Giddings, and they want most of all, Devlin, just to break your pretty back, and rub your pretty face in the mud."

"Frank Holson?"

"Sure, Devlin, that genius lawyer masterminded the whole thing, that's for sure, but the WESTEX folks never forgot those sessions in Big Spring, when you wiped up the floor with them. Devlin, this is not only business, real hardball business, but what makes it rough to deal with, is that it's worse—it's personal. Frank Holson has waited to get even, and he's doing it now."

Devlin was frightened. Here was the result of all her carefree wildcatting ways come home to roost. She had bet it all this time, but now the man with the heavy money was calling the pot. For the first time in Carter's memory, she looked at him with fear in her eyes. "Carter, what are we going to do?"

"Devlin, I don't know, but I took a chance when this happened, and I called a man you know. I asked him if he would like to help."

"Who is that?"

"You remember in Big Spring the man from Houston who was with Holson and Nichols . . . to try the case?"

"Dan'l Simon? But he's *with* Holson and Nichols."

279

"He was, Devlin, up till six months ago. He left them. He was fed up with their methods. He was a very political fellow in the sixties and seventies, but that doesn't make any difference about his being a lawyer. In my opinion, he's the best lawyer in Texas."

"He wasn't so smart in Big Spring."

"Devlin, nobody was, except you, *and* you were lucky. Now you're not so lucky, and it could be *his* turn."

"Carter, things are tough, but surely we can find someone else to represent us."

"Devlin, forgive my French, but there's a big fucking conspiracy against you. You're too young, too pretty, and . . ."

"Too female."

"Yeah, our regular attorneys would only go through the motions. They're starting to look fish-eyed at you because they're not sure that you can pay their fees. There's no time to go looking for someone at this time."

"Carter, but he's only one man."

"Devlin, you were only one girl in Big Spring."

"One *woman*, Carter. Right now, I'm a girl, and unless that genius of yours, Dan'l Simon, comes up with a solution, then the answer is that I'll be removed from the telephone book."

"Look, he's waiting for us back at our office. You'll have to fight your way through the dark-suited men checking into our books."

Devlin was disgusted, "Will they let you go to the bathroom by yourself?"

"Yeah, Devlin, I can, but I don't think that they trust you."

"Yeah, okay, partner, let's see what that smartass lawyer of yours has to say . . . Dan'l Simon? Is he Jewish?"

"Uh-huh, you're not prejudiced, are you?"

"Only against poverty—mine."

L. Carter Dixon's car pulled into Rusk Street, and headed down into the parking arena under the building. Things were going too fast in her life. The blessed cool and darkness of the basement garage became an attractive place to hide. Devlin was tempted to stay in the car. She was on the verge of saying that she had gone one step too far. Let them take everything away, but suddenly she was struck by another idea. "Dan'l Simon," she said, "do you know he's the first Jew I ever met?"

"That's funny," Carter replied, "he said you'd probably say that."

Devlin thought that Carter had been overstating when he said that a plague of accountants had made Younger Oil their home. On Devlin's arrival, she saw the receptionist in tears. A dark-suited man was rummaging through her desk, tabulating the office supplies.

"Susan," Devlin murmured, "be a good sport, we'll get out of this, and everything will be the same."

Susan wept openly. Walking through the corridors and past the offices, the men and women who should have been working were openly

280

dispossessed. Seated at their desks, with huge ledgers and pocket calculators and yellow accounting paper, were the black-suited men she expected. They didn't even acknowledge her presence. Devlin's secretary was standing at her desk, replaced by a young man.

"Miss Younger, your visitor is inside."

Devlin swept into her office and saw the tall dark-haired man she had met, and twice disliked, sprawled on a couch. His collar was open. His jacket was off, along with his shoes. Surrounding him were files almost three feet high.

"Mr. Simon, welcome to Younger Oil."

Dan'l looked at Devlin and smiled, "You don't look like any corpse I've ever seen before. Call me Dan'l, you're entitled to. It goes with the fee."

"We may not be able to pay you, or so it seems."

"Then you can certainly call me Dan'l. Deadbeats have no manners."

Devlin laughed. "Carter, ask someone for some drinks, unless that's been locked up too." She sat down opposite Dan'l in an easy chair that had a superb view of the Houston skyline. She had loved to sit just where she was now, staring out the windows in the late afternoon, happy in her achievements, thrilled with the fun of a game that she had thought herself expert at.

"First . . . if they try to prevent you from getting at the liquor closet," Dan'l intoned, "tell them that we'll have their asses in jail for assault. If they try to interfere with the normal course of business, throw them the hell out. If they won't go, give them warning, then shoot them."

Devlin was aghast. "What are you saying?"

"Just bringing a little levity to the situation, Devlin. I've got to tell you that they are within their rights to go through every piece of paper, every drawer and wardrobe, every closet and cabinet in search of assets."

"My house too?"

"Devlin, particularly your house. You won't get out of this office without their taking a physical inventory of what you brought in—that bracelet, say." He stared at the Bulgari monster, Devlin's red, white, and blue signature bracelet.

"What should I do?" she asked him. "Swallow it?"

"Maybe we can have you mail it to yourself in Brazil."

Devlin was angry. "Look, Mr. Simon . . ."

"Dan'l . . ." he insisted.

"Whatever, Carter says you're a whiz. Okay, prove it, but also, why are you now on our side when you were a gun for hire at Holson and Nichols?"

"Good question, last things first. Frank Holson and his group were too cute by half for me. Once, twice, three times I turned my head at what was going on. The fourth time was a killer, and I turned in my badge, my partnership, and my key to sainthood in Houston. Carter the Third, whom I admire, told me that I could help a lady in distress. He also may have told you that once I was in love with you. Don't worry, it was only for three minutes in Big Spring, when I first saw you in your workpants, muddy boots and eating a doughnut. I tend to fall in love fast, and in your case, Miss Younger . . ."

"Devlin," she insisted.

"Out again, just as fast. It happened when you did that magic number of spudding in your well and seducing that judge in the most outrageous display of *chutzpah* that I have ever witnessed."

Devlin squinted at the unfamiliar word. Dan'l ignored her reaction. "As for genius, I don't qualify, but I have a few ideas. A legal secretary will be coming in here in a few minutes, I called my recent one from Holson. What I intend to do is to throw so many lawsuits at WESTEX Petroleum, its shareholders, the bank and its officers, Holson and Nichols, and their brothers-in-law, that they will have a wonderful time meeting themselves in court."

"What, for example?"

"Devlin, everything but alienation of affection and the Mann Act. Doesn't make a damn bit of difference what I sue them for. We don't have a case, except for the confusion, and the hope that the judge in some court where we sue them will order a stay of this foreclosure, long enough to give you enough time to get the money to do whatever it is you're doing with it."

"Where do I get the money?" she asked.

"Well, if these lawsuits don't work, and I don't get you the time, you won't have to worry about getting the money."

"But if they do work, how much time will I have?"

"Devlin, until I run out of ideas and legal paper, or until your enemies become my enemies and they decide to shoot me on Fannin Street."

Dan'l Simon looked at Devlin suspiciously. "Now I have news for you, Miss Younger. The judge I have in mind to file with is partial to redheads and girls with chocolate sodas, who flirt outrageously."

Devlin looked at Dan'l, "When?"

"Tonight, right after my secretary types the papers."

"You and me?" Devlin asked.

"Yep, lady! Big Spring or bust! Your car or mine?"

"Mine," she answered, "and *I* drive."

"Okay," Dan'l smiled, "and *I* get to play the radio."

L. Carter Dixon III reentered Devlin's office carrying two bottles of Coca-Cola. Devlin looked at him. "Carter, I can only drink one."

Dan'l Simon grabbed at one. He jerked his hand back as if stung. "It's cold, Carter, I only drink them warm."

Devlin paused and stared before she added, "That's the way I drink them, too."

31

BEFORE Devlin left Houston that night, a half-dozen messages remained for her to answer. She knew what they were about. When she finally returned the call from her house, her butler at Fairlawn was in a state of panic. Ten men had descended on him hours ago. They were accompanied by a deputy sheriff who had a court order. What was he to do?

"Franklin, you did the right thing," Devlin assured him.

"But, Miss Younger, they're into everything. Everything in the kitchen was taken out and counted, in the living room, all your closets, the silver, the pool house, everything. They even went into cook's room." Franklin continued to wail in pain. "Miss Younger, I think that I have a right to know what this is all about. Cook and I have been talking. We have never been in a house before where *our* privacy has been violated." He said tartly, "Miss Younger, please consider this my two weeks' notice."

If it weren't so funny, Devlin would have been more upset. Her own sense of violation was deep. They had invaded *her* house. She knew that it was Frank Holson at work. She could hear his smarmy instructions, Just get in there. Doesn't make a damn what you're looking for. Just mess it up. Go through her nighties and her bedclothes. Check out her perfume and her shampoo. Get *in* there. Make her feel it.

This was just the icing on the cake for WESTEX Petroleum. The loans were already called. They would have exactly what they wanted to snap up Conroy and the Austin Chalk leases.

Devlin drove to the apartment house where she was supposed to pick up Dan'l Simon. She walked into the lobby and gave her name to the doorman.

"Please just tell Mr. Simon to come down. Tell him that I'm waiting."

The doorman walked to the intercom. He stared at Devlin and looked at her closely from head to toe. He listened and then hung up.

"Mr. Simon says you can go up. Apartment 7B."

The doorman looked at her suspiciously as she got in the elevator. She found the apartment. The door was ajar. From inside she heard strange loud sounds and then a shout, "Stuff it. Dammit. Don't let him get away with it."

Devlin walked in to see Dan'l Simon hunched practically inside an enormous color TV set. A suitcase was sitting on the floor. She stared incredulously at the screen; he was watching a basketball game.

"Mr. Simon," she said icily. "We have more important things to do."

Dan'l turned and looked at her with condescending pity. "It's the Houston Rockets, Devlin. It's the playoffs and we're behind by six. What's more important than that?"

To answer his own question, he resignedly walked to the set, and steeled himself to flick it off, but not before he saw Calvin Murphy drive San Antonio crazy with a floor-length dribble in between five defenders and wind up with the most beautiful back-door layup that one ever could see.

Dan'l smiled and picked up his suitcase. "Devlin," he said provocatively, "what kept you?"

Devlin gritted her teeth.

An hour out of Houston, Devlin found Dan'l readjusting the radio, switching from the tape she was playing, sliding all over the dial until he found a news program. Devlin was driving along the near empty road at over a hundred. She was annoyed at the sounds coming out of the radio. "What are you looking for?"

"It's our Rockets, Devlin. I'm ashamed of you."

Fifteen minutes later Dan'l got the score. Houston won. He was overjoyed, and he sat back gloating. "See, that was worth waiting for."

It was four in the morning when the Eldorado died. It coasted to the side of the road, and sat quiet, sullen and immovable. The loving animal had been Devlin's transportation for ten years, chasing leases all over Texas, carrying cowgirls all over the west. The Eldorado she had almost lost, but reclaimed after Conroy, just quit.

"It won't run," Dan'l stated accusingly.

Devlin seethed. He was criticizing her.

"Maybe it needs gas," he commented.

"Maybe you need to shut up," Devlin bit.

"Do you know anything about cars?" he inquired as he surveyed the lonely road they were on. Hardly any traffic had passed them for hours.

"I know *everything* about cars," she said defiantly.

"Well," he challenged, "tell me what's wrong with this baby."

"This *baby* is suffering from its company. It has taken an instant dislike to the task it has been asked to perform—namely the transport of an unpleasant and difficult person for a long distance."

"Hmmm, well, each to his own. Devlin, we clearly have a choice. We

284

can wait here in the car and freeze to death. I have known people who like to drive with the top down in the middle of summer, but never one who likes to drive that way under arctic conditions."

Devlin pressed a button on the dashboard. Nothing happened. "The top won't go up," she announced.

"Devlin, about a quarter of a mile behind us is a motel. I remember these things, because creature comforts mean a lot to me. I propose that we leave this beast here. Unfortunately it won't go anyway."

"You hate my car," she spit.

"No, Devlin, I haven't made up my mind about your car. I'll admit that it has not gotten off to a good start with me, but if it reconsiders tomorrow morning and welcomes me with the sound of the motor running, I'm perfectly willing to forgive and forget."

Devlin got out of the car and joined Dan'l, and the two of them trudged in the direction of the motel. It was more than fifteen minutes later when they arrived at the completely shuttered and darkened establishment. Dan'l rang the night bell without pity. Finally, a young man in a bathrobe appeared in the office and switched on the light.

He yelled through the glass door. "Go away. We're filled up." Devlin smiled at Dan'l in satisfaction.

Dan'l yelled back in. "We're escaped convicts." The young clerk tried to turn away, but Dan'l's incessant yelling, which he obviously couldn't understand, plus his placement of a hundred-dollar bill clearly and distinctly on the glass, caused the clerk to open the door, grab the money and allow him inside. Moments later, Dan'l reappeared. "Come on, Devlin, we're sharing a room."

"What?"

"Yeah," he muttered, "and keep your hands to yourself."

He led her into a doorway, fit the key and flipped on the light. The room held two queen-sized beds. He tested the mattress and felt the bed covering. "Not bad." Then he turned to Devlin, "Your turn in the bathroom, but I've got to warn you, I sleep in the nude, so when I come out of the bathroom, you better be prepared for the sight of the most bare-assed lawyer you ever hired, or just close your eyes."

Devlin bit her lower lip. "I sleep in the nude myself, and I don't want you leering at me when I get in bed."

He surveyed the place. "Lookit, we can put up your blanket between the beds, like they did with Clark Gable and Claudette Colbert."

"*My* blanket. There's only one on my bed."

"Well, I'm not going to waste *my* blanket to cater to my modesty, Devlin, so I'll just have to brave the exposure."

"*Your* modesty?"

"You keep repeating what I say, Devlin, is that for emphasis?"

In fifteen minutes the two of them were asleep.

Dan'l awoke at six, and when he looked out the window, he saw

Devlin sitting in the driver's seat of her Eldorado, the motor running. She beeped her horn. He dressed quickly and walked outside. Devlin stared at him, her green eyes bright, looking as if she had just come back from a three-week vacation at Acapulco. "Get in," she commanded, "I spoke to it, and it promises to be nice, if you'll be."

Dan'l smiled, "Tell it thank you, and tell it I'll try."

Tune was awake early. The apartment on Memorial Drive was now his home. Without much ceremony, he had announced to Sue Lingen just a week earlier that he was leaving her, and that he wanted a divorce. He had thought she would take it as easily as she had taken her three previous marriages and divorces. Tune was completely wrong.

"How dare you do this to me?" she demanded.

"Sue Lingen, I'm not doing a damn thing to you. We haven't had a marriage since the first day. I know what you've been doing all over town, and I didn't say a word about it. That was my fault. I should have come down on you. I should have done lots of things . . . ."

Somehow Sue Lingen summoned up tears. "But those didn't mean a thing, not a thing. Now you are leaving me, and you have no right, and for a Mexican. You shamed me, Tune Richards, and I was planning to have your baby."

Tune recoiled, "You *what?*"

"Yes, I was planning it, I was going to break the news to you that I wanted to get pregnant, and now you're leaving me for another woman." She simpered in an orgy of self-pity.

"You're out of your mind."

"I knew you'd say that. You never *did* appreciate me, Tune Richards. Go and do any damn thing you want to, I don't care, but I'm warning you that you won't get off cheap. My lawyers tell me that we can skin you alive, and that's just what I'm going to do."

Tune laughed, "You're not going to get a hell of a lot. I'm practically busted. Black Diamond is a shambles, and you've got all the money in the world. What do I have that you could possibly want?"

She sobbed outrageously, "A baby, I want you to make a handsome boy baby for me. Everyone has one now, and then you can go, and do *anything* you want to."

Tune turned his back on Sue Lingen and walked out the door. He had packed earlier and loaded his car. He felt better than he had in years, freer and more in control of his life. He left Sue Lingen's beautiful River Oaks home that he had shared. It was all hers now, but his life was all his.

On this first day of freedom for Tune, it was just seven-thirty, and he had exercised, shaved, and showered. He did his daily calisthenics with more vigor than he remembered since he had been in the Marine Corps. He took a long look at his body. He was in good, but not great shape. He

286

would do something about that, but for real. Tomorrow he would start running, and then begin to work out. He'd play a little touch with the guys at the "Y," and start lifting weights. He wanted to get into real shape. After all, he was thirty-five years old, and he was planning to marry a much younger woman.

Seated at the breakfast table, he read the front-page news, scanned the page-two story about Devlin and Younger Oil. He shook his head. He hoped she would fight her way out of this one. Today he would phone her and wish her luck. How badly he had behaved with her, and with every other woman. He thought about L.C. Younger, and how he had enslaved himself to him. He had cheerfully walked into captivity time after time. First it had been L.C., and then as a symbol of his slave status, he was prepared to perform L.C.'s task for him, keeping Devlin in line by marrying her. Yes, that's what it was. He and Devlin, Hansel and Gretel, while L.C. Younger kept them both as children.

He had fallen into the same trap with Sue Lingen. Fallen? Hell no. He had leaped into it. Here was his very last chance in life to make it on his own. He wasn't even sure that he would be able to afford the apartment he occupied on Memorial Drive. Well, all in good time. It would be a shame to leave comfort behind, but that was captivity. The hell with that. Whatever came, came. Then there was the matter of finding a job. What kind of work do you give a thirty-five-year-old who played quarterback and was a Marine Corps hero with a leg full of shrapnel? He had some ideas. Maybe coaching in high school. His time at Black Diamond had prepared him for nothing. What a joke that had been. He had only learned to duck and weave to L.C.'s punches and bullshit with the guys. What else do you do if you're the perfect son-in-law?

He poured some cold cereal in a bowl, splashed in some milk and added sugar. God, how great cornflakes tasted without a butler and a maid and Sue Lingen hanging over his head. He turned to the sports section and began to read one of the stories when he was interrupted by the sound of the buzzer from the lobby. He went over to the wall phone and listened for a moment. Then he beamed, "Please tell her to come right up."

It was Constanza. He had telephoned her last night from his apartment. She was in the middle of a family crisis, she said, with her little sisters and her mother. Yes, she said, she would listen to what he had to say, even though she had said that she would never speak to him again.

He told her what he had done, and was going to do. He told her that he wanted to marry her, and that it didn't make any difference to him where they lived or what her family was like. He wanted to come and call on her, the same way any Mexican man would do, meet her parents, and in time ask for their approval. He knew, he said, that it would be difficult for them to give, but maybe if he showed them how much he loved their daughter, they might understand.

As for Constanza, he said, all he wanted was for her to know that she was the only woman in the world for him, and would always be. He prepared to hang up after he said that he hoped someday she would forgive him, not only for what he had said, but for what he was. He was having a hard time forgiving himself.

As the noise from Constanza's side of the phone grew louder, and the screaming of the family argument drowned out his words, all Tune heard was Constanza saying "Goodbye."

The front door buzzer sounded, and Tune rushed to the door to open it. He stood quiet, silent, and hesitant in front of the beautiful dark creature he had chosen to love.

Constanza stood before him, serious, determined, and still uncertain. "Tune," she said in her lowest voice, "can I come in?"

Tune was too full of emotion to say anything. He simply nodded.

Constanza looked at his eyes. "Tune, I mean for good. I was praying for your call."

Constanza rushed into his arms, and Tune held her with all his might.

On the other three occasions when Claude Giroux came to Houston, he had chosen to stay at the Warwick Hotel because it had a certain Old World charm. As each trip showed him extravagant changes in Houston's skyline, with building after building, industry after industry exploding before his eyes, he was pleased that he had established a beachhead against the new developments and new hotels. The Warwick was his home in Houston.

It was eight-thirty when John Dowie arrived at his suite. Very little had changed in the man he had first met seven years earlier, when he had forced himself upon Claude. Dowie didn't look much older. He did, however, look well dressed and sleek. Claude would never have guessed that Dowie could have taken so well to power.

His tall frame was clothed in a perfectly tailored suit. His shirt had to be custom-made, Claude could tell. Even though everything about Dowie's choices were in dreadful taste, there was no doubt that he was showing all the signs of affluence—the twenty-thousand-dollar gold and diamond watch, the diamond pinky ring, and a bodyguard.

That was what disturbed Claude the most, when John Dowie entered his suite that morning. There was no way that he could insist on the man's removal. He began, but Dowie wouldn't hear of it.

"Mr. Giroux, when you break a few heads, you'll find that you have enemies all over. It pays to be safe."

Claude surveyed the swarthy man. A handgun was clearly outlined inside his suit. Claude felt a chill, but said nothing further.

288

"I see you ordered breakfast," Dowie remarked. "Don't bother to get anything for him," pointing to his bodyguard and laughing, "he only eats nails."

Claude led Dowie to the table and motioned him to a chair. Dowie lifted the glass of orange juice to his lips and sipped. "Is it fresh?" he inquired.

"I think so."

Dowie lifted the bell cover from the scrambled eggs, helped himself, buttered his toast and began eating. Notwithstanding a full mouth, he started to talk. "What's the panic about, Mr. Giroux?"

"John, we have to talk seriously."

"Shoot."

Claude cleared his throat. He had to be extremely careful how he handled this. "Now John, you've had a completely free hand in running HOUCORP. You agree with that, don't you?"

Dowie nodded.

Claude repeated his comment. "A free hand. You had it right?"

"Yeah, I said yeah."

"Well, you know that I've been visited by the FBI, who made certain allegations against HOUCORP which, to say the least, are disturbing."

"Yeah?"

"They say that HOUCORP is serving as a giant front for the illegal passage of drugs, stolen goods, and the laundering of underworld funds."

Dowie smiled.

"John, I never asked you about certain men whom you employ in HOUCORP in very key roles. I have a file of names here, and photos. Let me read them to you."

Dowie brushed the paper aside. "Forget about that, Mr. Giroux."

"John, they all have links with organized crime. They have prison records."

"Mr. Giroux, like I said to you one other time, you can't make an omelet without breaking eggs."

Claude sipped his coffee. "Are they bringing in drugs, John? The FBI says that they are. Please tell me, John. I need to know."

"Mr. Giroux, what you don't know won't hurt you, I told you that before."

"But you *offered* to tell me before, and then I chose not to, because of business pressures."

"Well, now, it's not convenient to discuss these kinds of things. Look, Mr. Giroux, you and your *frères* have made a bundle. No reason a couple of other people can't help themselves too. It doesn't hurt you any. Hasn't driven the stock down. Now let's forget it."

Giroux was upset and worried. "John, tell me about the fire at Black Diamond. You said you were going to do it. Did you?"

"Mr. Giroux," Dowie's face beamed a wide smile, "would *I* do a thing like that?"

"Younger may die."

"That's tough, Mr. Giroux. We all die sometime. Maybe it's his turn now."

Dowie was losing patience. "Look, Mr. Giroux, I don't know what's eating you, but I've got a business to run." He turned to face his bodyguard who stood up and headed for the door. The man opened it, and stepped outside in the hall, looking left and right.

"Okay," the man said.

"So long, Mr. Giroux. It'll all blow over. It always does." He walked out the door and closed it behind him. Giroux walked slowly back to the breakfast table. Shaking nervously, he tried to lift his cup of coffee. It fell, spilling the liquid all over the table. He picked up a napkin to clean it up, then looked up as he heard a sound.

Three grim-faced men walked into the sitting room from the bedroom next door. Giroux faced them.

"Did you get everything?" he asked hopefully.

The agent in charge of the Houston office of the FBI shook his head. "Look, Mr. Giroux, we have a videotape of the conversation, but it's not very useful. He didn't say a thing."

Giroux was sweating. "He said that he hadn't told me anything that he was doing. You heard that, and you have *that* on tape, don't you?"

"Whatever he said, we have."

The second agent added, "His bodyguard is Dominick Porta, convicted murderer and a member of the New Orleans family."

"My God," was all that Giroux could say.

The agent in charge nodded, "Mr. Giroux, you'll have to come with us down to the office of the bureau. We want to speak to Washington on a clear phone. They want me to tell you that the attorney general is bringing all this to a federal grand jury. We have enough to go on, and I'm afraid that they're going to bring down an indictment on quite a few people."

Giroux shook violently. "Me?" he fairly shouted.

The agent in charge of the Houston office nodded, "Yes."

It was just 2 P.M. when Dan'l Simon and Devlin reached the Howard County Courthouse in Big Spring. The Eldorado had behaved admirably, and Dan'l Simon had too. Somehow the night the two of them spent together had made a difference. It hadn't been sexual, because nothing happened, except peeking, to which they both pleaded guilty. Then they laughed.

But, they were in a predicament, and grudgingly at first, each of them recognized that they needed one another to survive. For Devlin, it was perhaps the death of Younger Oil. For Dan'l Simon, it was the death of the promise that he had shown as the best of the bright young men to come to Houston, full of the excitement of the place, and certain that at Holson and Nichols he was on the verge of a brilliant future. It wasn't worth a damn, he realized, because he lost his self-respect. He told that to Devlin on the morning drive. He said it in many ways as they stuffed themselves with a hurried breakfast, as they stopped for a fast burger for lunch.

"Devlin, it's funny, that it's come down to this, a court appearance for the two of us, on the same side of the aisle, right where the whole thing started for you."

For Devlin, the cleansing air of the West Texas countryside and the gentle edge of her companion's conversation were pleasant diversions from the dread reality of things. She found listening to Dan'l Simon agreeable. He really wasn't a smartass, and he listened to her. He really listened.

"You know if it all ends today, I really will care, Dan'l. I said I wouldn't, but I do. You have no idea what a dumbbell I've been. The money, sure it slipped through my fingers, but it wasn't as if I had a good time with it. I was running as fast as I could to keep up with what I was supposed to be, what a young Houston millionaire should be. I made mistakes with men, didn't appreciate the right ones, and was dumb about the wrong ones. Right now, I'm in this pot just because I want to show my father how smart I am."

Dan'l looked at Devlin's profile. She stared at the road ahead, expertly maneuvering the Eldorado. "Nothing out of the ordinary about that."

"Yes, there is, Dan'l. My father is in a coma and may not ever come out of it. What use is there to prove to him that I'm better than my brother, and the one he should have counted on? Skycastle is a joke. It's a little girl's fantasy that she got on her daddy's knee when she was four years old."

Dan'l swallowed hard. "None of us is much older than that, inside. Take me and basketball, the world's biggest jock, the oldest kid in the playground."

Devlin turned to him and smiled. "Thanks."

He added, "Skycastle is no joke, Devlin. It could happen. It's a wonderful concept."

"Hmm," was all she said. "What kind of medal do they give for last place?"

Big Spring was so familiar to Devlin. And so were the good times. She parked the Eldorado in front of the barber shop. The barber turned to look at her curiously, then returned to his customer. Then Devlin and Dan'l walked up the steps of the Howard County Courthouse and through the corridor to a familiar door. The sign on the door indicated that Judge Nathaniel Cameron was sitting.

As they entered, a pair of lawyers were arguing a point in front of the judge. Dan'l motioned to Devlin to be seated. The two of them moved to the front row, waiting patiently for the lawyers to finish. Devlin thought she saw Judge Cameron acknowledge her presence, but she wasn't sure. Finally, after almost a half hour, the two lawyers shook hands and walked out arm in arm.

Judge Cameron paused and looked at them both. They were alone in the courtroom. Dan'l stood up, and as he walked to the bench he smiled.

"Your honor, do you remember me?"

Judge Cameron looked at Dan'l and squinted. "Do you have an appointment? Are you on the court calendar?"

"Judge Cameron, you remember Miss Younger?"

The judge looked at Devlin and squinted. Then he broke into a broad grin. "Glory, how are you, Devlin? Haven't seen you in a long time. I thought it was you, but my eyes aren't too good. You don't see too many pretty girls in my court."

"No you don't, your honor," she smiled.

"Judge, Miss Younger is in a lot of trouble."

"It seems to me, young man . . ."

"Simon, Dan'l Simon."

"It seems to me counselor that you were the one who gave her all the trouble."

Dan'l smiled. "Now we're friends." He looked at Devlin. She nodded her head violently to indicate assent.

Judge Cameron sat down. "Tell me all about it."

And Dan'l did, for over one solid hour, citing chapter, verse, and points in law that hadn't been resurrected since Hammurabi established them ten thousand years ago. Devlin watched with awe as her attorney explained why WESTEX Petroleum should not be allowed to foreclose on Younger Oil. The paper had already been prepared by Dan'l, and Judge Cameron signed it with a flourish.

Devlin considered that the action merited a kiss, and Judge Cameron was more than happy to get one. "Devlin, come on by the house later, my wife took a great shine to you." Then he chuckled, "I guess you can say I did too."

Devlin let out a whoop and a holler as the judge walked out of the court, and grabbed Dan'l around the neck and hugged him madly. After so much time that others might have criticized as being unseemly, Dan'l said, "Devlin, let's get a Coke. You remember that joint across the street where we had that charming meal. How about it?"

Devlin nodded and tucked her arm in his. "Yeah, I'd love a warm Coke." Then she smiled. "I guess you would too."

When they had ingested the sweet warm liquid from the first Coke and then another, and devoured a burger apiece, Devlin leaned back. "Where did you get that crazy idea you gave the judge?"

"Not crazy." Dan'l smiled. "Look, if anyone can go round buying up your mortgages from banks that lend you the money without asking your permission, all of Big Spring could wake up one day and find that Moscow had bought up all the mortgages in town, and the whole city could consider itself a part of Soviet, heathen, communist Russia."

Devlin laughed deliciously.

Dan'l continued, "Remember, I didn't say it would happen, just that if WESTEX wasn't stopped, it might give others ideas, and the judge didn't cotton to the idea of going to sleep under the Texas flag and waking up under the hammer and sickle."

Devlin's face was aglow. She was sure that this crazy decision wouldn't hold, but it was something. She had seen it happen. Dan'l got up to find a pay phone to call Houston and tell Carter about the injunction Judge Cameron had just signed. He sighed, "It might be good for another twenty minutes before Armageddon."

After Dan'l left the table, a familiar face passed by. The man turned and stared at her, and grinned. It was Amos Stuckey, the tiny pouter-pigeon president of Big Spring National Bank. He walked in and came over to Devlin.

"Miss Younger, what are you doing in town?"

"Hi, Mr. Stuckey, just some business with Judge Cameron."

"You know, Miss Younger, I sure have to hand it to you."

"What do you mean?"

"What are you going to call it this time?"

"What do you mean?"

"Do you mean you haven't heard? Golly, it's all over Midland and Odessa. You really hit it big in Giddings, Miss Younger. The well came in yesterday. That frac-ing did the trick. Honey-colored oil. Well, the rich get richer. I'm darn glad that it happened to a nice lady like you. You're not going to forget us folks in Big Spring are you? Lady Luck is right."

32

IT took Devlin almost ten minutes to stop crying. Amos Stuckey was convinced that he had said something to offend her terribly. All he could think of was to apologize profusely, and as quickly as possible he made his retreat from the luncheonette before he did any more harm.

He was mystified, but he hoped that Devlin Younger would forgive him for *whatever* it was he said.

By the time Dan'l returned from the pay phone, Devlin had managed to pull herself together. Still, the moist remnants of tears were in evidence. He slid into the booth opposite her.

"I spoke to Carter and I waited while he got the bank attorneys on the other line. They were really jolted. Like I said, Devlin, it will only buy us a little time."

Dan'l took her hands in his. "It's too damn much, isn't it?"

"Yep," Devlin said, "but not the way you mean it."

"I know, Devlin. Carter broke the news to me about Giddings. That's it, isn't it?"

Devlin nodded.

"It's all wrong, Devlin. You're looking at life upside down."

"What do you mean?"

"Look, Devlin. It had to happen to somebody. There's nothing wrong with good things happening to you."

"I'm so damn lucky."

"Yep," Dan'l agreed, "but you're not an axe murderer."

"What do you mean by that?"

"Well, hell, Devlin, you've got nothing to be ashamed about."

"No," she nodded, trying to smile through the tears that were beginning again.

Dan'l continued, "You don't kick dogs, don't run down little old ladies."

294

"No," she began to smile, but just a little. "What are you trying to say?"

"Near as I can make out, Devlin, you're a decent human being. You're a little nuts, but prettier than any crazy person that I ever met. I don't know where you get your guts, but I'm convinced that we make our own luck, and nobody who likes you begrudges you any of it. You're honest. You're decent, and it seems that you won't have to go to the poorhouse after all."

Dan'l still had Devlin's hands enveloped in his. "Come on lawyer, mine. I want you to meet one of the world's noblemen, my partner, T-Bird Johnson."

Devlin was herself again. Dan'l scooped up the bill, left a generous tip on the table and the two of them walked out the door onto Main Street.

Dan'l stopped, "By the way, Devlin, Carter says that you're just getting out of the fix you're in by a hair, and Younger Oil will prosper once again. He asks you to drop Skycastle. He suggests that you turn it into an alligator farm or something."

Devlin paused. "What do you think?"

"I don't know *all* about you, Devlin, but for some peculiar reason, I think it's something you've got to do."

"Dan'l," she said with sudden fear, "I can lose—lose everything."

"I suppose, but there's only one Devlin Younger. Hell, Devlin, you're an original. Do it your way."

Devlin smiled. They came to the Eldorado. Dan'l looked at her. "Get in. It's my turn to drive. Your turn to play the radio."

"I knew that you'd win, Devlin." T-Bird addressed Dan'l and Sally as the four of them sat on the old-fashioned sofa in the living room of T-Bird's house in Big Spring. It was a lopsided house, dating back to the turn of the century, made of red sandstone, with a Victorian-gingerbread roof and decoration. "Let me tell you, I knew that Devlin had the goods from the very beginning. Course, she wouldn't 'a done it without me, but for a woman, she ain't too dumb."

Devlin was dismayed to see how T-Bird had changed. The frail wisp of a man had lost the spark in his eyes that had first fueled Devlin's imagination.

Sally glowed as she listened to the conversation. Devlin could see that she adored the man who was easily twenty years older than she was, and in such frail health that she couldn't be certain how long he would live.

"T-Bird says he taught you all you know about poker, Devlin."

She laughed and watched T-Bird redden. "Not everything, just the finer points."

"T-Bird is being too modest. I couldn't count kings over jacks until T-Bird showed me."

T-Bird decided to change the conversation. He looked at Dan'l.

"You're a lawyer, huh?"

"Yep, for Younger Oil, at least in this dustup with WESTEX. Later on, we'll see."

"That means you're working for me."

Dan'l smiled. "Sure thing."

"Well, then, I want you to draw up a will. I'll say it fair and square in front of everybody. I want to leave enough for Sally for her life. This is her house, and her folks before her, and she made me welcome in her life. She was my first real woman, and I want her to have enough for as long as she lives. I want her to marry again, and she better, 'cause even though I know that I'm the love of her life, there just might be some fella who'll show up and sweep her off her feet. I don't want her and him to worry about where their next dollar is coming from."

Sally sat silent. Devlin was embarrassed, but she knew that it was right to let T-Bird continue. It was important to him.

"Then, I want to leave a big percent for those folks coming out of Huntsville—to get them started in life. Making furniture and license plates in jail ain't no preliminary for going back to the straight life." He looked at Devlin. "Devlin—you'll be happy to know that I'm off my plan to get everybody in prison to take huge doses of vitamin C every day. They say that it may cause cancer in rats. Course, most rats I've seen wouldn't know vitamin C from A, B, or Q. And one other thing, lawyer, I want to save ten thousand dollars and give it to the city of Big Spring for a party. Devlin and me had a wingding blowout at the Stampede when we hit Lady Luck No. 1, and what with inflation, I figure that it'll double that much for the next one."

Devlin stood up and moved alongside T-Bird on the sofa. She took his hand. "T-Bird, what with inflation, in fifty years when you kick off, you'd better leave one hundred thousand."

T-Bird grinned. "Okay—that's a deal. You got that, Mr. Lawyer?"

Dan'l smiled, "You bet. It's as good as done."

Calvin Larabee, president of WESTEX Petroleum, was not a man to fool with. He was a Texan who took things very seriously. The problem was that someone *had* fooled with him good and proper, and as far as Calvin was concerned, that person was Devlin Younger.

WESTEX had come to bat four times against that young woman and he had come away bloody each time. It was Devlin Younger who had done the damage, he was sure, but the person he felt was responsible for allowing it to happen was his lawyer, Frank Holson.

Five minutes after Larabee heard the news that an injunction had been served against WESTEX to prevent it from foreclosing on Younger Oil, he was on the telephone to Houston.

"Miss. I don't give a damn where Mr. Holson is, or what he's doing. You get him on the telephone."

"But Mr. Larabee, Mr. Holson is in conference. The light is on over his door, and when that's on, I just can't disturb him."

"What's your name, little lady?" Larabee demanded.

"Gloria Martin, Mr. Larabee."

"You know who I am, don't you, little lady?"

"Of course, Mr. Larabee. You're a client, but Mr. Holson has a great many clients, and each one has the same rights. It's only fair. Besides, you wouldn't want me to lose my job."

"Little lady, I'm a simple man. I'll tell you one more time that you better put me through to your boss, or I will come on down to Houston and personally bite off your left titty, and when I'm through doing that, I'm gonna pull out whatever color hair you have on your head, by the handful."

There was a click and a moment later Frank Holson was on the line.

"Calvin," he beamed, "good to talk to you. I was just going to put in a call to you. It's a damn shame about the Big Spring situation, but I've got a few of our bright boys working, and I'll tell you one thing," he said conspiratorily, "I'm going to get into it *myself*."

"Frank, one of your bright boys who used to work for you—Dan'l Simon, jammed it up your ass good and proper. How does it feel to sit down, Frank?"

"Look, Calvin, you're upset, but there's still time. We can vacate that injunction in no time. Hell, it's a goddamn joke."

Calvin was enjoying the conversation in a perverse kind of way. It was clear that Frank Holson didn't have all the news.

"Did you hear about Giddings, Frank?"

Holson was wary, "No . . . I don't think so. What about it?"

"Frank, that little gal did it again. She hit it big, Frank. The oil is golden color. She's got leases that don't stop, and her damn geologist, some kid, figured out what was holding it in the ground. Do you know what it was, Frank? I'll tell you what was holding it down; driller's mud, Frank, damn driller's mud that had caked up and hardened . . . and that no-good kid geologist figured that out for that no-good redheaded gal you've been trying to screw now for years."

Gloria Martin flew into Frank Holson's office like a woman possessed. She flagged and signaled her boss with semaphore hand-waving that looked like a distress signal from the deck of the *Titanic*. Holson was listening to Larabee scorch the phone with his blistering indictment. He was becoming annoyed by the antics of his secretary.

In frustration, the young woman wrote on the pad on Holson's desk. "Tarquin Lord is on the phone. He is *furious*."

Frank Holson was now in deep trouble with two of his clients. Larabee continued as Holson tried to get off the phone to deal with his other problem.

"Calvin, this is nothing that can't be dealt with. Why don't I get together with some of my bright boys and give this a think? I'm sure we can come up with something."

"Frank," Calvin concluded, "you go pull your pudding by yourself. Not only is WESTEX no longer your client, but you and your foolishness are gonna be the talk of the Gusher Club in Houston for a lot of time to come. We fellas in oil stick together."

Larabee hung up. Reluctantly, Frank Holson punched up the other line.

"Tarquin, good of you to call. I was just about to ring you."

"Mr. Holson," came the cold, chill aristocratic voice of Tarquin Lord, "you are a liar. Furthermore, you are stupid and incompetent. You have been advising me on this Skycastle transaction. Your phone calls to the major insurance companies have made them very enthusiastic about this transaction, but it appears that events in the past few hours have made it very conjectural for Lord Construction. Mr. Holson, I cannot and will not allow this project to escape me."

Frank cleared his throat. "Tarquin, there is no way that this little lady can get it underway. She has the biggest damn hole in the ground that you ever saw. I might add that I've closed off every door in Houston. I shut her off from the insurance companies. All you have to do is wait. I don't suggest that you need to, but if you wanted, I could dream up another piece of real estate for you, Mr. Lord. I can get HOUCORP—they're clients of mine—to part with some land for a joint venture."

"You idiot," Lord shouted, "where are your Washington connections? That whole gang is going straight to jail. Holson, Miss Younger has a head start. I hesitate to threaten, but Mr. Holson, you get your act together, and, I'm telling you now, I want Skycastle."

Frank Holson brightened. Things might not be so bad after all. He could get a lot more of the Tarquin Lord business if he delivered. And he would. The hell with WESTEX Petroleum and Larabee's friends.

"Tarquin," he smiled into the phone, "it's as good as done. I'll make a few more calls and nail it down."

Frank Holson returned the phone to its cradle. His rumpled shirt was damp with moisture. Gloria Martin, who had stood alongside her boss during the conversation, was herself troubled. She considered that it might be very well if she looked around for another job. Working at Holson and Nichols paid well, but she could not be sure when Mr. Holson would be struck dead with a heart attack caused by very angry clients.

She sincerely hoped that Mr. Holson would be able to work things out. Even so, at lunch, she would ask around to see if there were some other openings—places where it wasn't always life or death.

Not for a minute did Devlin seriously consider Carter's suggestion to abandon Skycastle. She knew that she had escaped disaster only by the

narrowest margin. How close she had come scared her. The Giddings'
find had reestablished the flagging fortunes of Younger Oil, but if she
persisted with Skycastle, all might still be lost.

She and Dan'l drove all night on their return to Houston. Devlin was
anxious to get back to the house on Montrose, and to resolve this
still-hanging problem. The drive from Big Spring was without incident,
except that Devlin, for the first time in her ten years of ownership of her
beloved red Eldorado, let someone else drive.

"I like the way you drive," she grudgingly admitted in the wee hours
of the morning.

"Yeah? Well, I don't have the same style that you do, Devlin, but I'm
workmanlike and practical."

Devlin looked at the speedometer, which hung exactly at one
hundred twenty, as if it were nailed.

"You know how fast you're going?" she inquired.

"Oh sure, Devlin, always."

"I'm in a hurry to get back, Dan'l, but you're out of a job. It doesn't
have to be, you know."

"Devlin . . . I thought over your very kind offer, and it's not that I
mind working for a woman . . . but I think maybe the best thing for me
to do is go back to California. Tell you true, I love Houston, but I've got
a damn good offer from a Los Angeles firm, big in politics, lots of room
to grow."

Devlin mused. "What about me?"

"I've been thinking a lot about you, Devlin. I don't know how you're
gonna do it, but you'll bring off Skycastle, and I love you for it. You're a
gambler and you want things your way. You're young and you're
beautiful, and you may own all of Houston by the time you hit
twenty-nine. I'm really not into money. Sure I like it, but I think that I
was dumb to think only about it when I joined Holson and Nichols. Hell,
Devlin, I'm still a big kid. I like to do good things, like a damn Boy Scout,
and I like basketball."

"I like it too."

"Well, how about *that*," he grinned, "now you have everything going
for you."

Devlin thought long and hard before she spoke again. She looked at
the man at her left, who was different from every other man she had
known. He alone had not wanted to possess her, to have her conform to
some preordained mold. Dan'l had said it, she was an original. But,
dammit, so was he.

"Is there anything that could change your mind?"

"Devlin," he muttered ruefully, "only one thing could do it, and that's
if I touched your fine skin, and held you very close. You're special,
Devlin. I was right the first time I saw you, but I don't want to be owned
by anybody, even Devlin Younger."

The Eldorado speeded up. The needle was climbing. Devlin looked at it, and then at Dan'l. "What's your hurry?"

"Devlin, tonight's the last game of the NBA semifinals—Houston and Kansas City. I've got to get in shape."

It was ten in the morning when Devlin pulled into the driveway of the house on Montrose. She bounded up the stairs into the kitchen where Alma and Manuel were busily working. They turned when they heard her walk in.

"Señorita, I'm glad that you're back."

"Is there something wrong, Alma?"

"It's your father, señorita. I think he has changed. The nurse says that he is the same . . . always the same. But my eyes tell me something different."

Devlin had to know. She raced through the hall and up the stairs to L.C.'s room. Quietly she opened the door. In the shade-drawn room, L.C. looked gray, forlorn, and pitiful, lying perfectly still in the sea of white linen.

The nurse, seated in the corner, stood up. "Miss Younger, there's no change."

Devlin scanned her father's face. The lined, rugged visage was unmoving. But Alma was right. Devlin could tell that his condition had worsened.

"Nurse, could you leave? I want to talk to my father."

"Miss Younger, he's in a coma. He can't communicate at all. Besides, doctor asked one of us to be on duty at all times. Doctor said it was according to your *own* request."

"Nurse," Devlin said angrily, "just leave us alone."

The woman in the starched white uniform walked to the door. She was angry. She would reconsider whether she actually wanted to stay in a house like this, where a nurse was taken for nothing.

Devlin moved close to her father's bed. She pulled a chair to her and sat down. Sitting inches away from L.C., she saw the lines in his worn face. The once proud man was silent and unmoving.

"L.C.," Devlin began, "I want to come to peace with you. I really do. I blamed you all my life for your wanting to keep me a little girl . . . daddy's little girl . . . not letting me do the things that I wanted, working with you at Black Diamond. Daddy, it doesn't make any difference any more."

Devlin stopped. There was no sign, not even a perceptible breath. Not a flicker of movement.

"Daddy, I had to grab it for myself . . . just like you did. I had to risk it all, because I wasn't sure that I had the right to win . . . to be grown up. Up till now, I would have been just as happy to lose everything that I won in Lady Luck, because I didn't think that I deserved the good things that happened to me. But, L.C. I think so now."

300

"I met a man who I think I could love. You'd hate him. He's against everything that you stood for, except he's strong and determined, the way you were. But, I'm gonna try and grab him for myself, before he gets away, 'cause I know I can make him happy, and daddy, that would make *me* happy."

The light in the room had begun to fade, almost imperceptibly. Thought it was near midday, darkness had begun to descend on L.C.'s room.

"Do you know what I blame you most for, L.C.? You never gave Vonnie a chance. She was frightened and unsure. You could have helped her, and that would have made you a happier man. You blamed me for her death, but it was you, daddy, who made her need someone else."

"L.C.," Devlin continued, holding her father's hand in hers, "I don't know how I'm gonna do it, but I'm going to make Skycastle come true. When it's built, it's gonna have a big damn bronze replica, lifesize, of the *Colfax I*, right smack in the middle of the main plaza. I don't care how much it's gonna cost. A big damn tugboat in bronze, and there are gonna be two people standing on the rail, looking out on the channel, looking out over Buffalo Bayou. You'd better believe it, L.C., you and Vonnie are gonna be up there big as life, for as long as Skycastle lives, and that's gonna be as long as there is a Houston."

Devlin was unable to say another word. She bent over her father's face and gave him the softest kisses she could, on his cheek, his forehead, and the gentle fold of his eyelids.

She turned to go, but something told Devlin to look back. She stared at L.C.'s impassive face. In the corner of his eyes, Devlin was sure there were tears.

Devlin touched his lips with her finger, and then turned away to hide her own tears. Slowly she walked downstairs to L.C.'s study, to secure something she needed, changed her clothes quickly, and then strode purposefully out the kitchen door to drive to her appointment.

In the big old-fashioned boardroom of Texas National Bank, the eleven members of the board of directors had been listening to a ninety-minute presentation. Alger Lyles, chairman of the board, and the other ten members sat quietly while Devlin talked nonstop about Skycastle, and why Texas National should move its ancient offices there, and occupy the biggest building, and furthermore and most important-ly, provide the financing for the entire project.

Devlin was dressed in her custom-made suede jeans and whisper-soft vest, over a low-cut turquoise silk blouse. Her ginger-colored hair outlined the happy glow of her face, with its sea-green eyes.

On her wrist was her signature diamond, sapphire and ruby bracelet. It sparkled as she moved her hands, her body, and her face in an animated story of the wonder of Skycastle.

301

The stony-faced men, including John Travis, stared at her at first, and then warmed to the fantasy she pictured for them. Then, these same stony-faced men grew excited as she outlined the huge profits that would be forthcoming from their partnership with her.

Only John Travis sat without any noticeable sign of interest.

"Gentlemen," Devlin concluded, "I saw that painting of John Jurdam downstairs in the lobby. He was a man."

They nodded.

"Not a change has been made in Texas National from the day he built it. Do you suppose John Jurdam, if he were alive today, wanted this to be the only home of Texas National? Do you suppose he said to himself, 'I just want this bank of mine to be a measly-size bank—not as big as the other banks.' Hell, no, gentlemen. He was Houston, clear through. He built it when he did, to be the biggest and the best. If John Jurdam were alive today, he'd say, 'Texas National is the best. Let 'er rip. If we have to put a building on Mars in the twenty-first century, just to keep ahead, that's what we're gonna do.' "

Chairman Lyles smiled. "Damn, Miss Younger. Why didn't I think of that?" He continued, "About the main building, it would have to have a central hall big enough for that painting of John Jurdam. That goes without saying."

Devlin grinned, "And enough room for a portrait of the present chairman of the board, *almost* the same size."

Alger Lyles beamed.

For the first time, John Travis spoke, "Miss Younger, I have the sense of the board of directors that we do have an interest in this project. We like the idea of our own new building to match our growth, and the investment for fifty percent of the profits is not without interest either."

Devlin grinned, "John Travis, you old son-of-a-bitch. I knew you'd come through."

He reddened. "But let me speak for the board once again. We believe that we would be entitled to have the entire project named Texas National Plaza."

The board members nodded.

"John Travis, I like your style, but it's no deal. Skycastle means a lot to me. It should mean a lot to you. It's gonna be dedicated to yours and my daddy and mother."

Devlin reached under the table. She pulled an object out of a leather bag and put it on the table. It was a .32-caliber repeating rifle with a shortened stock.

"John Travis, you never saw this before. I found it in L.C.'s big old safe. It's the gun your granddaddy used to kill a man in Galveston in 1900. Don't ask me how L.C. ever found it, but he has all the facts, including the Wanted posters from Texas, Louisiana, and Florida for a murderer named Devlin Younger."

They stared at her.

"That's not *me*. That's our granddaddy, John Travis. I want all the men in this room, nice, safe, conservative citizens, to think about where they came from—from men and women in the history of Texas who fought it out—good or bad."

Devlin smiled, flirting outrageously with men who realized that somewhere in their own history there had been such forebears.

Lyles broke in, "Miss Younger. You have a point, but John Travis is a practical man. Texas National Plaza, known all over the world, would be a very useful thing."

Devlin mused for a moment. They waited. Finally, she smiled, "Mr. Lyles, why don't we settle it like Texans, one hand of poker. How about it?"

Lyles eyes lit. "Devlin Younger, I like the way you think." He turned to John Travis. "Ask one of the secretaries to bring in a deck." Then he turned to Devlin. "Poker is my favorite game, young lady. All right with you if we cut for deal? Dealer calls the game."

Devlin smiled, "Funny, Mr. Lyles . . . poker is my favorite game too."

It was eight o'clock when all the details were settled. Devlin freed herself from the happy hands of the board of directors who had congratulated themselves for almost two hours, consuming almost a case of Jack Daniels.

An hour earlier, a reporter for the *Houston Journal* got hold of the rumor, and after he phoned John Travis for confirmation, he called Frank Holson for a reaction.

Frank Holson's heart almost stopped beating when he heard the news. He finally gave a quote to the *Journal* before he hung up in cold fury. "Tell them that Frank Holson says, what's good for Houston is good for the whole damn world."

It was eight-thirty when Devlin arrived at Dan'l Simon's apartment. She handed the doorman a twenty-dollar bill to prevent him from announcing her. Besides, he knew who the beautiful redhead was. He had seen her pictures in all the papers.

"Go right on up, Miss Younger. I won't bother to disturb Mr. Simon."

When Devlin arrived at the door to Dan'l's apartment, she heard loud sounds from inside. She pressed the button and waited.

From inside she heard a loud voice, "Come in. The door is open."

Devlin walked in. The story was the same. Dan'l sat not more than a foot away from the TV screen. The Rockets were doing their number against Kansas City.

"Dan'l," Devlin murmured, "I don't want you to turn handsprings or anything, but I won."

Dan'l turned away from the screen, looked at her happy face and

303

grabbed her to him. The two of them tumbled on the floor. She felt overwhelming love from someone who adored her for what she was. She knew that he could accept her as a woman, as a winner, or anything that she turned into—just as long as she was always Devlin.

Dan'l held her close, wrapped in his arms, flooding her with kisses.

The TV set was going crazy. Moses Malone was hitting points, blocking shots.

Devlin couldn't stop talking as Dan'l began to undress her. She moved her body to help him unbutton her shirt.

"So, he cut to a ten of hearts, and I cut to a jack of diamonds. I thought I'd pick a fast game—get the agony over. 'Hurricane,' you know what that is, two-card poker, deuces wild, best high or best low beats."

"Now I dealt," Devlin lifted up her hips to allow Dan'l to pull down her jeans, "and it was just plain luck, I guess, with maybe a little peek while I mixed the deck, and Lyles, that sly old tiger, they were *his* cards. He had two kings. It was only right that he have a little fun for a while, but then I turned my cards over, and I had an ace deuce. That, my friend, is unbeatable."

Devlin's jeans were off. She never wore panties, but she did help with her shirt, slipping out of it magically. The TV set was still screaming.

She peeked at the screen, and then looked at Dan'l as he began to undress.

"Don't you want to know the score?" she asked.

Dan'l was naked against Devlin's body. He took her in his arms with love, with tenderness, and the sense that both of them were finally and miraculously together.

"The answer is 'no' Devlin," he whispered, "I just lost interest in the Rockets."

Devlin held her lips away from his for a moment. "Are you in love? Don't answer that, Dan'l. For the first time I am, enough for the two of us."